"Set in a metal city at the center of the mountain ringed Heartland, *The Cityborn* is sprawling space opera centering on Alania, born to the City's privileged caste, and Danyl, a lowborn scavenger. . . . This is one suspenseful sci-fi thriller not to be missed."   —Unbound Worlds

"Willett wraps his capable new adult science fiction adventure around the fate of a mysterious many-tiered city and its inhabitants. . . . [*The Cityborn*'s] spunky protagonists and colorful world will entertain SF adventure fans."   —*Publishers Weekly*

"Willett brings J.G. Ballard's *High-Rise* into the distant space age in this dystopian tale of class, power and freedom that will entertain devotees and non-genre fans alike. The worldbuilding in this book is impressive, creating an atmosphere that is both fascinating and oppressive, and characters who are magnificently complex."
   —*RT Reviews*

"Filled with dramatic scenery and character detail. Sci-fi and fantasy fans should find this story full and entertaining."   —Darque Reviews

"The author was constantly surprising me, which doesn't happen often, twisting the usual sci-fi conventions into more than just a shoot 'em up space opera. Edward Willett has created people, personalities with belief systems and misguided judgments who make mistakes in trying to do what they believe is right."   —Boomtron

"Willett's books in this series have a wonderful, driving pace, which, when coupled with multiple well-rounded characters and fascinating stories, make wonderful, captivating books that deserve to be read over and over."
   —Book Chick

**DAW BOOKS PROUDLY PRESENTS
THE SCIENCE FICTION NOVELS
OF EDWARD WILLETT**

THE CITYBORN

WORLDSHAPER

THE HELIX WAR

MARSEGURO *(Book One)*
TERRA INSEGURA *(Book Two)*

LOST IN TRANSLATION

THE
CITYBORN

EDWARD WILLETT

DAW BOOKS, INC.
DONALD A. WOLLHEIM, FOUNDER
375 Hudson Street, New York, NY 10014

ELIZABETH R. WOLLHEIM
SHEILA E. GILBERT
PUBLISHERS
www.dawbooks.com

ACKNOWLEDGMENTS

I ALWAYS SEEM to be thanking the same people in my acknowledgements, but then, it's always the same people who help make my books happen.

First and foremost, my thanks to Sheila E. Gilbert, my Hugo Award-winning editor, for a) believing this was a story worth telling and b) helping me to tell it better than I told it in my first attempt. She has an uncanny knack for identifying both what works and what doesn't in a book, and all of us fortunate enough to work with her admire her for her dedication, warmth, and ability.

More broadly, thanks to everyone at DAW Books for all their hard work and mad publishing skillz. I still have to pinch myself sometimes to be sure I'm not dreaming that I'm being published by the same house whose yellow-spined paperbacks, once upon a time, were a guarantee to me of a story worth reading. I couldn't be happier to be part of the aptly named DAW family.

Thanks to my agent, Ethan Ellenberg, for all of his excellent suggestions and support.

And, as always, thanks to my amazing wife, Margaret Anne Hodges, P.Eng., and astonishing daughter, Alice, for putting up with a husband and father who lives a bit more inside his own head sometimes than he does in the real world.

Finally, a shout-out to Shadowpaw, the Siberian cat (also a part of the DAW family—Betsy Wollheim picked him out for us and owns his Uncle Roscoe!) for not making a habit of lying on my lap when I'm trying to work. Not much, anyway.

Edward Willett
Regina, Saskatchewan

PROLOGUE

THE BLACK-CLAD FIGURE crept through the unlit corridor on Second Tier, silent and slippery as the sludge oozing from the corroded pipe running the ceiling's length. The gunk from the pipe had *very* conveniently covered the lenses of the surveillance cameras at each end of the hallway, and this corridor was so unimportant in the grand scheme of the City that it would be days—possibly weeks or months—before anyone would even notice, much less come to clean them.

At least, the corridor *had* been unimportant, Yvelle Forister thought. Now it was potentially the most important corridor in the whole reeking edifice that those who had set her on this path hoped to bring figuratively, if not literally, crashing down. Because three-quarters of the way along its length, a maintenance hatch opened into a no-longer-used elevator shaft that rose all the way to Twelfth Tier.

Through her night-vision visor, the corridor glowed deep green, the blinking light of the obscured security camera at the far end flashing brightly every few seconds. Yvelle didn't like the thought of that thing looking at her, grease-covered or not, so she hurried to the hatch and knelt beside it.

The tool she pulled from her belt was as illegal as her night-vision equipment, if not *quite* as illegal as the beamer holstered at her hip. The worker who had "lost" it had done so knowing it would cost him his job, but like Yvelle herself, he no doubt had good reason to help the shadowy anti-City forces who called themselves the Free Citizens.

Her own reason had returned to her two months ago, from the notorious prison on Tenth Tier, as ashes in a small plastic urn. The cheap aluminum plaque embedded in its side bore a name, once as precious to her as her own: THOMAS DEVILLE.

Yvelle's hand tightened on the maintenance tool. Then she leaned forward and touched its tip to the first of the hatch's access points. There was a sharp click, and a light on the tool's handle flashed green. Eight clicks and eight green flashes later, she pushed at the bottom of the hatch. It sank into the wall a centimeter, then popped out, and she dug her fingers under the edge and swung it upward.

The inside of the hatch had three metal ladder rungs built into it at thirty-centimeter intervals, a small segment of a ladder that she knew continued above and below the opening. She turned around and backed through the meter-wide portal, feeling with her feet for the rungs below the hatch. Once firmly on the ladder, she pulled the maintenance hatch closed. It clicked as it locked back into place.

The square shaft, three meters on a side, glowed green, lit by the luminescent tubes called "eternals" because they were supposed to last forever. Like most things in the City, though, several of them were out of order, belying their nickname. Still, with the night-vision goggles, they provided more than enough illumination for Yvelle to see the intimidating climb ahead of her.

They also showed her the old elevator doors, presumably sealed, on the opposite side of the shaft, and the rails on which an elevator car would ascend and descend. Those gleamed suspiciously brightly, which meant this "abandoned" shaft maybe wasn't as abandoned as she'd

been told. She just hoped whatever surreptitious purpose to which it was being put did not involve a car moving through it tonight, or she'd be a smear on the wall
before she got anywhere near her destination. *Presumably* the shaft was being secretly used by the Free, not
the Officers, and since her mission was theirs . . .

She took a deep breath and started climbing.

The City's First through Seventh Tiers were each fifteen meters in height. Eighth and Ninth were each
twenty meters tall, as was Tenth, where Thomas had died
in prison. Eleventh and Twelfth, home to the Officers,
were a lofty twenty-five meters. And the crown of the
City, Thirteenth, dwelling place of the Captain . . .

Thirteenth was a mystery.

Fifteen meters of infrastructure in two levels separated the Tiers: pipes, conduits, service corridors. That
meant well over three hundred meters to climb. Yvelle
had to be at the top within twenty-five minutes.

The shaft gave no hint of what lay beyond its closed
doors on each Tier, but she could picture it well enough.
At the very bottom of the City, below even First and
Second Tiers, were the Bowels: four levels, some sixty
meters tall, full of mysterious machines. Some func-
tioned to provide power and water and other services to
the rest of City, some were *supposed* to but had long
since malfunctioned, and some served no purpose anyone could decipher. Only squatters lived in the Bowels,
in dark corners and for dark purposes. Occasionally the
Provosts would attempt to evict them. Sometimes they
managed to arrest half a dozen people. Sometimes they
came back empty-handed. Sometimes they didn't come
back at all.

First and Second Tiers were crazy quilts of temporary
structures made of any materials the denizens could ob-
tain, dividing and subdividing what had once been a neat
grid of orderly structures. Many of the original metal
walls had been cut down, the pieces used elsewhere. The

only remnants of the original neat, logical layout were the old street signs embedded in the corroded metal floors. Condensation from the ceilings dripped like rain into the dank, fetid streets, the ventilation systems overwhelmed by the sheer number of people crammed into spaces never intended to house so many. Fog, smoke from cooking fires, and strange vapors from the overworked and failing recycling plants—and the equally overworked but thriving illegal drug labs—drifted through the air, sometimes so thickly you couldn't see your hand in front of your face and every breath burned. Like the ventilation, lighting was poor and erratic. Only the lucky or ruthless had reliable sources of power.

In those dark, dangerous, deceiving streets, people went missing all the time. Sometimes they'd been robbed and murdered.

Sometimes they'd been secretly arrested.

Like Thomas.

Despite the mask he'd worn, the Provosts had identified him at a protest held after an overhead pipe had ruptured and sprayed a market courtyard with an acidic sludge that had killed twenty-three people and disfigured a hundred more. They'd seized him in the middle of the night, dragging him and Yvelle out of bed. He'd been imprisoned; she had not. Instead, they had torn up her precious Reproductive Right card before her eyes and explained with cold contempt that since her husband had been identified as a Level-Two Security Threat, her right of reproduction had been terminated—as would be the now-unauthorized child she carried.

She remembered the horror of that conversation and the brutal drug-induced miscarriage that had followed. She remembered the doctor explaining to her, his face impassive, his eyes focused not on her but on a spot over her right shoulder, that the drugs had also sterilized her.

Two weeks later she had been contacted by the Free: an "accidental" encounter with a woman who gave her name as Bertel, who claimed to have been a friend of Thomas's. Bertel ran a First-Tier bar—"a nicer place than most," she'd said—and she'd invited Yvelle to come have a drink and a friendly talk. One conversation had led to another, always in Bertel's Bar, a small place in which Yvelle never saw another guest. Bertel had confided her hatred of the Officers, and Yvelle had responded in kind, grateful to have someone she could safely talk to.

Maybe all that sympathy and support had only been bait to get her to bite the Free's hook, but when Thomas's ashes had been returned, Bertel had somehow known it, and she had been at Yvelle's door within an hour. *Do you want to make them pay for what they've done?* she'd asked, and Yvelle had replied, *Hell, yes.* They'd gone to Bertel's Bar. Bertel had produced a highly illegal commset, and Yvelle had found herself talking to someone named Prime. His voice had been digitally distorted and his image blacked out, and he had claimed to be the Commander of the Free. He had told her what the mission entailed, what she might have to do to make it succeed, and then gravely asked if she had the courage to carry out such a task. Yvelle had gripped the silver locket she now wore beneath her snug-fitting black top—a locket containing a hologram of Thomas as he had looked the day he asked her to marry him and two grams of the ashes that were all that remained of him—and sworn that she did.

Two weeks later, Bertel had given her detailed instructions. Following them, she'd found the maintenance tool in a back alley on Second Tier, right where the "negligent" worker had "dropped" it two minutes before. She had retrieved the night-vision goggles and beamer from a box buried in a rubbish heap on First Tier that hadn't been disturbed in a decade. And tonight, at the appointed time, she had come to the sludge-slicked corridor and this ladder.

She continued climbing. She'd passed two more sealed doors, so she had to be past Third and Fourth and ascending toward Fifth. In all three, she knew, conditions were better than in First and Second. Though still over-crowded, the streets were wider and cleaner, the structures less haphazard in location and construction. There were proper factories and residential blocks for those fortunate enough to have jobs in them.

Sixth and Seventh were middle-class respectable, Seventh more so than Sixth. The managers of the factories lived there, and, unlike on the levels occupied by their workers, they didn't have to shove furniture in front of their doors every night in case some bloodlust-gripped flash-user made a midnight call.

Yvelle had never been there, but she'd heard that on Eighth there were green spaces. A lucky few even had balconies and windows through the ancient metal skin of the City, providing views out over the rolling Heartland to the distant snowy peaks of the impassable Iron Ring. Accountants and lawyers and engineers and doctors lived there, and lived well . . . though not as well as those on Ninth, home of the wealthy. Yvelle could only dream of what that must be like.

She could only dream of what Tenth must be like as well, but those dreams were nightmares, the nightmares that had haunted her night after night when she'd still held out some hope Thomas would return to her alive — nightmares that had only grown worse when that hope was so brutally and finally crushed. All the time he'd been held there she'd had no contact with him, no way to comfort him. No visitors were allowed on Tenth, at least not for a Level-Two Security Threat snatched from the lowest Tiers.

Eleventh and Twelfth Tiers, home of the Officers, the City's hereditary ruling class? They were unimaginable to Yvelle, yet it was to Twelfth that she was ascending. Or almost: her goal was another access hatch, this one in the service corridors beneath the Twelfth-Tier deck. From there, she would make her way to the hospital, her ultimate destination ... provided a second Free operative known to Yvelle only as The Officer had done *his* job. If he hadn't, this mission would come to a bloody end in—breathing hard, she looked up the ladder—about five minutes.

She reached the access hatch. She glanced over her shoulder; there were the expected elevator doors. She looked up and found herself staring at the underside of an elevator car, perhaps thirty meters above her head. *Stay where you are*, she thought fervently as she drew her stolen maintenance tool from her belt once more and applied it to the hatch. Eight flashes, and she was able to swing the hatch out into the darkness beyond.

The corridor into which she emerged wasn't much different from the one where she'd entered the shaft. They were both part of the City's under-street infrastructure. Robots and maintenance workers and Provosts (and on the wealthiest Tiers, servants, or so she'd heard) used them to move around more freely than the hoi polloi above, who were putatively forbidden to enter them. The biggest difference between this corridor and the one she'd started in was that this one was clean. It ran unimpeded in both directions. There had to be security cameras and possibly motion detectors in here, keeping a watchful eye, since up above her Officers and their families slept snug in their palatial quarters, but Yvelle had been assured no security systems would pose a threat to her this night. She hadn't been told how such a feat had been accomplished, but she had no choice but to accept the claim. If it turned out to be a lie, she'd know soon enough.

Yvelle consulted the map in her head and set off at a jog down the corridor to her right. It intersected another after twenty meters or so, and she turned right again, then left, then right one more time, finally stopping at a closed door with a lockplate to its right. She inserted the tip of the maintenance tool into the key port as she'd been instructed, and the door swung silently open, revealing a flight of metal stairs. She climbed those to another door with another lockplate. Another touch of the tool, and it, too, opened, sliding aside rather than swinging upward, to reveal a dark street. City lighting on all Tiers was synced with that of the natural world, and it was now 2630: half an hour past midnight. Across the street she could see a decorative light post, but the crystal globe that hung from it was dark, as her instructions had promised it would be.

She stepped through the door. The floor felt odd; she looked down and saw that rather than being made of bare, pitted metal like those on First and Second Tiers, it was paved with white, overlapping, brick-shaped tiles. She raised her eyes and looked both ways. There was little to see: tall buildings with stone or brick facades surrounded by high walls; dark windows. She filled her lungs with the freshest air she had ever breathed, scented with something sweet and spicy and delightful, then consulted her mental map again and hurried a few meters to the right. As she'd been promised, she found a dark gap between two stone-covered buildings, barely wide enough to admit her. She slid through it into an ornamental garden, trellised blossoms overhanging white gravel paths, the air heady with the scent she had first detected upon emerging into the street, and then hurried down a longer and wider passage with closed, locked doors on either side. She finally emerged into a far larger garden space, this one filled with shrubs, surrounding a building of white stone, so brilliantly lit that her night-vision visor shut down completely, letting her see it with her own eyes.

Stone pillars supported a portico from which hung ferns and trailing vines, ablaze with red and yellow flowers. Along the front of the portico, green-glowing letters spelled out TWELFTH TIER HOSPITAL. Through the glass doors below she saw movement—people in white coats, a few robots—but *her* intended entrance lay on the far side of the building. She closed her eyes, consulted the memorized map, and backed up ten paces to yet another maintenance hatch, this one in the surface of the street. It, too, opened at the touch of her stolen tool, and she climbed down a short ladder into another utility corridor. Presumably it connected at some point with the ones she'd been in when she'd first entered the Tier, but for whatever reason, it had been deemed safer for her to approach the hospital at street level. She pulled the overhead hatch closed, then headed along the corridor in the direction of the hospital.

Her tool unlocked a doorway into the hospital's sublevel in an out-of-the-way corner behind an air-filtering unit. Unlike the corridors, the hospital basement was brightly lit, but Yvelle had been assured that all surveillance cameras would be disabled here as well: The Officer's work again. He was burning through all his access privileges tonight. But then, after tonight, as she understood it, he wouldn't be an Officer any longer.

That was probably just as well. Once the Provosts figured out who was behind the various outages and overrides, as they surely would, he'd be a dead Officer if they found him.

Yvelle hurried past laundry facilities and a darkened kitchen to a particular stairwell in a particular corner. Up the stairs to the fourth floor. A quick peek through the door: dark—another "lighting failure"—but bright enough to her enhanced vision, which had adjusted again to the dimmer illumination. A dash along a deserted hallway. She used the maintenance tool to unlock a room. She slipped inside.

Seven bassinets, a baby in each, long pale-green cocoons in her night vision.

Yvelle's breath came in short gasps now. Her heart thudded in her chest. She went to the first bassinet. It had a name written on a card tucked into a plastic sleeve: Danyl.

The babies had *names*. She hadn't considered the fact they might have *names*. The realization hit her like a blow to the stomach . . .

. . . no, a blow to the womb, the womb violated by the City, the womb scarred and burned and ruined by the chemicals that had slain her unborn child.

"Danyl," she whispered. She pulled a new device from her belt, a short metal tube. She pressed it to the sleeping baby's hand. He stirred but didn't wake. She pressed a button. A light flashed green.

She took a deep breath, then lifted Danyl from the bassinet and slipped him into the harness on her chest. He whimpered a little but his eyes never opened, and after a moment he slept soundly once more.

The unfamiliar weight made Yvelle feel strangely unbalanced as she moved to the next bassinet. A girl. Astril. She pressed the metal tube to the child's hand. It flashed red, and she heaved a sigh of relief.

The next child: another boy. Karril. Red.

The fourth child: a girl. Stellina. Red.

The fifth child: a girl. Mari.

Green.

Yvelle whimpered. She looked at the sleeping child, at the downy hair on her head, her perfect, tiny hands curled into loose fists, her long eyelashes, her beautiful mouth, slightly open. Yvelle reached out a trembling hand. *Forgive me*, she whispered to God, or the universe, or Thomas, or no one at all . . . and then she covered the sleeping girl's nose and mouth and pressed down hard.

Mari struggled feebly, but she had no strength, none at all, and in a surprisingly short time she stopped struggling and turned blue, and then she was dead.

Yvelle pulled back her hand. It shook. She clenched it into a fist, whispered, "There, there," to the child sleeping between her breasts, though he hadn't stirred, and moved on to the sixth bassinet. Another boy, Kevi. She reached out with the small metal cylinder. *Please let it flash red*, she whispered to whomever she had asked for forgiveness, and He or She or It must have heard her, because flash red the cylinder did, when she touched it to the boy's hand.

The final bassinet. She moved to it, looked down into it. *Alania*, said the card at the foot of the bassinet, a girl's name . . .

. . . but the bassinet was empty.

Yvelle stared at it. She had no orders covering this eventuality. She'd been told there would be seven babies; that she should take the first one for whom the strange little device flashed green; that any for whom it flashed red could be left undisturbed; that if it flashed green for any besides the first baby she took, that baby had to be eliminated.

But if a baby were missing . . . ?

Yvelle looked around wildly. *She must be ill*, she thought. *They took her somewhere else . . .*

Could she find . . . ?

Even as she thought that, the lights flashed back on in the hallway outside. She had already waited too long. She had to move *now*.

She ran to the door, looked both ways down the deserted hallway, and dashed to the still-darkened stairwell. She clattered back down to the basement, holding on to the railing, her balance still thrown off by the weight of little Danyl on her chest.

Through the basement, back into the utility corridor, up the ladder, down the wide alley, through the garden, back down the narrow alley, running as fast as she could now, expecting at any moment to hear a hue and cry, alarms, shouts, to see Provosts or robots bursting into the streets to search for her . . . but all remained quiet.

Down into the service tunnel. Back to the maintenance hatch . . . and there she pulled up short, heart racing, because someone was waiting for her: a man, dark-skinned, dressed in black. Someone was *supposed* to be waiting for her, but was this really . . . ?

"Good work," he said, unsmiling.

"You're The Officer?" she said, though obviously he was, or she'd already be under arrest.

"Not after tonight. I think we've done it."

"But *what* have we done?" *What have I done?* The baby boy on her chest stirred and whimpered, and she put a hand on his back to calm him.

"What needed to be done," The Officer said. He reached out and touched the baby's cheek. "What's his name?"

"Danyl." Yvelle looked down at the boy's downy head, yearning and loss mingling in her heart. "*I* could take him," she whispered, before she'd even realized she was going to. "I'd be a good mother to him . . ."

"You know where you're going," The Officer said. "It's no place to raise a child."

"And where you're going is? The Middens?"

"There's a place prepared. I will raise him and protect him, give him what he needs to survive, teach him what he needs to know, so that when the time comes, he will be prepared to do what he must do . . . just as we have."

"But what does he need to know? What will he be prepared to do?" *Why have I done what I have done this night?* That was the real question, but she left it unspoken, knowing no answer would be forthcoming.

"He will know what he needs to know when it is important that he knows it," The Officer said. "As you know all you need to know. You have done an immeasurable service to the Free Citizens. And you have avenged your husband. Someday you'll be honored for it."

"When?" Her throat closed on the word. The thought of being honored for what she had just done repelled her.

"Twenty years will tell the tale."

"Twenty years?" Yvelle stared at him. "I'll be in my forties."

"And I in my sixties. But the time will be upon us before you know it."

An alarm echoed through the streets, an angry ringing attenuated by distance.

"Time to go," The Officer said. "Give me the child."

Reluctantly, Yvelle slipped out of the harness and handed Danyl over to The Officer. The boy whimpered a little, but he quieted again as The Officer settled the harness in place. Yvelle turned and touched her maintenance tool to the lockplate by the door. The door slid open, and she hurried down the stairs beyond to the service tunnels and along them to the hatch into the old elevator shaft, The Officer a few steps behind. She squeezed through the hatch and began her descent. The Officer climbed onto the ladder above her, and a tool the twin of the one Yvelle carried flashed eight times as he sealed the hatch behind them.

Together they descended into the depths of the City . . . but neither of them would stop in the Second Tier, or the First, or even the Bowels. Their destinations were far, far lower than that.

Twenty years, Yvelle thought. *Will I even remember Thomas in twenty years?*

The lump of the silver locket hung between her breasts so that she felt it anew against her skin with each beat of her heart. *Yes*, she thought fiercely. *I will. As I will remember what I have done to avenge him.*

She could still feel the little girl's warm lips and nose beneath her tightening hand. She knew she always would.

Twenty years.

The ladder led down, down, down into endless darkness.

ONE

PANTING HARD, ALANIA Beruthi peeked through the barely open door of the servants' staircase and watched the humanoid robot that was supposed to be keeping an eye on her stride past with its peculiar too-careful gait. A moment later she heard a series of thumps. She let out her held breath in a rush and promptly burst into giggles, echoed by Sandi Praterus and Lissa Smilkoni, her best friends, who were crowded onto the off-limits landing with her. Both the same height, both skinny, Sandi pale-skinned, Lissa dark-skinned, they looked like matching chess pieces from opposite sides of the board.

"How did you do that?" Lissa whispered breathlessly.

"Disabled some sensors," Alania said, trying not to sound proud of herself but failing miserably. "Pulled some wires. Lieutenant Beruthi told me I should learn as much as I could about robots since it's the family business. So I did." She rubbed the backs of her knuckles. She'd scraped them badly on the sharp edge of the watchbot's skull hatch when it had moved unexpectedly and she'd jerked her hand back. But she'd washed away the blood, and the skin was already closed; she'd always healed quickly.

"But it fell down the stairs!" Sandi said, sounding slightly shocked. "Won't it be damaged?"

"No, it's tough," Alania said with more certainty than she felt. If the watchbot *were* damaged, whatever punishment she was already guaranteeing herself with today's escapade would be ten times more severe. "But it won't be able to get up with its sensors disabled. It will just lie there until we get back and I fix them."

"You're terrible," Sandi said, but now she sounded less shocked and more impressed.

Alania grinned at her. "Thank you!" she said cheerfully. "So now the coast is clear. Ready to go?"

Strictly speaking, they weren't supposed to go anywhere. Which was the whole point of this exercise. They were *supposed* to stay right there in Quarters Beruthi and have a tea party or something. They weren't even allowed to go out into the safe, pristine white streets of Twelfth Tier, although at least Lissa and Sandi weren't completely *forbidden* from doing so, like Alania was.

They definitely weren't supposed to go to another Tier altogether, but that was precisely what Alania had in mind.

Had there been an actual human in Quarters Beruthi to chaperone them, escape would have been far more difficult. But the only human employed in the house of Lieutenant Beruthi was Sala, Alania's private servant, and she was away on one of her four-times-a-year visits with her parents. They lived in Agricultural Compound 27, a hundred kilometers east of the City—a farm that was, oddly enough, owned by Sandi's mother, Lieutenant Commander Varia Praterus—and Sala would be there for another two days.

Alania had sneaked out even on Sala once or twice, using the stairs they were on now to get into the service tunnels beneath the streets and then climbing up into a public building, but before now she'd always limited her adventures to Twelfth Tier. Since she was under constant surveillance whenever she was in the streets, like everyone else, she was perfectly safe, and her guardian's reprimands had been mild, the loss of vid privileges and lack of dessert for a week well worth the break from the mun-

dane. She'd broached the idea of a *real* adventure today
with Lissa and Sandi at her twelfth birthday party a week
before, a dreary affair to which all Officers' daughters
within two years of her age had, by custom, been invited.
As usual, Lissa and Sandi had sat with her at the head
table, and that had given them time to scheme. Alania had
invited them over today with her guardian's permission,
knowing that Sala would be away and babysitting would
be a robot-only affair. Now the watchbot was disabled and
they were free, as she had never been before in all her
twelve years, and she knew a secret she didn't think her
guardian knew she knew: he had a private elevator.

A noise had awakened her one night, and she'd
peeked through her door just in time to see him enter
the utility room a few meters down the hall from her . . .
and not come out again. Since the room where the cleaning robot switched attachments and stored itself for
charging was only about three meters on a side, that was,
to say the least, peculiar. After twenty minutes, she'd
gathered enough courage to go and knock in case the
Lieutenant had had a heart attack or something, but
there'd been no answer. Then she'd tried the door. Although it was normally locked, it had opened to reveal a
utility room that looked the same as always, with no sign
of the Lieutenant.

Puzzled, she'd gone back to bed. In the morning, the
Lieutenant was back, and the door was locked.

Not that that had stopped her investigating. She'd
simply waited by the room one morning until the cleaning 'bot came out, then grabbed the door so it couldn't
close and lock. A quick examination of the walls had revealed the room's secret: a standard elevator control pad
behind a sliding panel. It needed a key, of course, but
Alania happened to know where the Lieutenant kept a
copy of his. She probably wasn't supposed to know that
either, but you couldn't spend the bulk of your life con-
fined to a house, however spacious, without exploring

every nook and cranny, and Sala didn't watch her nearly as closely as the watchbot did. The Lieutenant didn't even keep the spare key locked up; it was in an open drawer in his desk, and he was equally careless about locking his office door.

The key, a golden rod about ten centimeters long and a centimeter in diameter, was already in Alania's pocket. It would open the utility room door and let them use the elevator. And from there ...

"It might let us go to any floor we want," she said. "So which one?"

"Not Eleventh," Lissa said. "I go there all the time."

"We can't go to Tenth," Sandi said. "That's the jail."

"Ninth is still too ritzy," Alania said. "Let's head to Eighth—no, Seventh!"

"Five Tiers down?" Lissa said excitedly. "I've never been lower than Ninth."

"I've never been lower than Eleventh," Sandi admitted.

"And I've never left Twelfth," Alania said. "So it'll be new for all of us!"

"Won't it be dangerous?" Sandi asked, though she sounded a little ashamed for doing so.

"We're not talking First or Second," Alania said. "Although if you really want an adventure, we could try the Bowels ..."

Sandi blanched. "Captain, no!"

Alania laughed at her. "Not serious," she said, although deep inside she wondered very much what the Bowels looked like. Or First and Second, or Third, or Fourth. Sometimes even the Middens sounded intriguing. Anywhere but Twelfth.

Her friends had not only been allowed to travel to other Tiers—high-level ones, at least—they'd even been allowed to leave the City. Their parents had Estates in the farmlands of the Homeland and Retreats in more scenic locations, and they visited them often, as well as the Resorts that catered to Officers and their families.

Lieutenant Beruthi also had an Estate not far from the City and a Retreat way up in the northern foothills of the Iron Ring, but he'd made it clear Alania wasn't allowed to go to either, though he'd never told her why.

He'll kill me after today, she thought, but even that thought held little dread. He couldn't *literally* kill her. The usual loss of privileges, even for an extended time, would be worth it, and what other punishments could he come up with? Lock her in her room, she supposed, but that wouldn't be noticeably different from her regular life.

"Seventh it is, then," she said. "Ready?"

"Ready," Lissa said.

"I guess," Sandi said.

"Follow me." Alania opened the stairwell's door wide and stepped boldly into the upstairs hall, although she couldn't help glancing to the right, the direction the watchbot had gone. It hadn't climbed back up the stairs, which it surely would have if it had somehow recovered. Emboldened, she strode to the utility room door, produced the Lieutenant's spare key with a flourish, pushed the golden cylinder into the round opening in the lock-plate, and opened the door when the end of the cylinder flashed green. Retrieving the key, she held the door open for her friends. "After you!"

They crowded in. Alania let the door close behind them. Lights came on automatically, an antiseptic white illumination from glowtubes in the ceiling. It made Sandi look even paler than usual.

At least, she *thought* it was the lighting.

"Is this really an elevator?" Lissa said. "We're going to feel like awful idiots if—"

Alania touched the panel hiding the elevator controls, and it sank into the wall and slid aside. Lissa's voice trailed off to a slightly breathless, "Oh!"

"Seventh Tier, here we come," Alania said, but her own heart raced a little as she pushed the key into the control port and a touchscreen lit up. She blinked at it. It only showed three numerals: twelve, where they were, five, and, astonishingly, one.

"It only goes to Fifth and First?" Sandi said.

"The Lieutenant's robot factory is on Fifth," Alania said slowly.

"But why does it go to First?" Lissa said. "*Nobody* goes to First."

"I don't know," Alania admitted.

"Please don't press that one!" Sandi said.

"I won't," Alania said. But just for a moment, she was sorely tempted.

"Even Fifth . . ." Lissa was usually braver than Sandi, or at least she pretended to be, but she didn't sound it now. "That's . . ."

"Seven Tiers down," Alania said. "Talk about an adventure!" Refusing to give in to her own sudden fluttering attack of internal butterflies, she pressed five.

The room sank so suddenly and quickly that she gulped as her stomach, butterflies and all, tried to jump out of her throat. She looked at her friends, their eyes wide and white in the stark lighting, and grinned at them. "Having fun?"

"Uh-huh," Sandi said, but she sounded uncertain.

Alania felt more than a little uncertain, too, now that they'd actually done what she'd been planning for weeks, but she tried to push the feeling aside. Lieutenant Beruthi had no right to keep her locked up in his Quarters, not when her friends were allowed to travel. She wasn't a little girl anymore; she was twelve years old, and however angry he might be after today, he'd have to admit that much, at least.

The descent was shorter than she would have thought, the elevator clearly a fast one. It stopped after only half a minute or so, as abruptly as it had begun to sink, and Alania staggered a little as her weight momentarily seemed to double. Sandi grabbed Lissa's hand. Lissa let her.

The door opened, revealing an utterly ordinary corridor paneled in the City's default white plastic wall covering. The three girls stepped out. The door closed behind them, and they heard the car ascend. "Will it come back?" Lissa said anxiously, Sandi still hanging on to her.

"Once I put in the key," Alania said, hoping she was telling the truth.

She looked left. The corridor stretched unimpeded about twenty meters before ending in a closed door.

She looked right. Different direction, same view.

"Some adventure," Lissa said. "Sandi, let go, you're hurting me."

"Sorry," Sandi said, and she released Lissa's hand. Lissa rubbed it.

"We're inside the factory," Alania said. *I hope.* "We have to get out if we're going to see the Tier." She looked left and right again, shrugged, and turned right. "One way looks as good as the other."

"What if the door's locked?" Sandi said.

For an answer, Alania held up her key. But the door wasn't locked, and when they passed through it, they found themselves in long, narrow room with a door to their left, another to their right, and a glass wall across from them. Alania went to it and looked down.

"Wow," said Lissa, which is what Alania would have said if she weren't so busy staring at the mesmerizing scene: Beruthi's primary robot manufactory, she supposed. The space below them, easily twice the size of Quarters Beruthi itself, was filled with robots in the process of building other robots. But every one of them was frozen in place, unfinished robots waiting on motionless conveyors for other robots to continue assembling them. The factory was manufacturing nothing at the moment. It might have stopped a minute ago or ten years ago; there was no way to tell.

"That's . . . weird," Sandi said.

"Maybe it's break time," Alania said, because she felt

like she ought to say something, and "wow" and "weird" were already taken. Although she felt silly the moment she said it, because why would robots need to take a break? She looked at the two doors out of the otherwise empty room and decided to go left, since they'd gone right the last time.

It proved to be an auspicious choice; the door led to a flight of stairs that took them down to the level of the factory floor. A featureless door to their right presumably led onto that floor. A light above the door burned red.

But a few meters farther, at the end of the corridor, was a second door, and above it was the single word Alania most wanted to see: EXIT.

"At last," she said, and she pushed at the panic bar. The door swung open, and she hurried out into Fifth Tier proper.

She found herself in a narrow alley between the factory and an apparently identical building, both clad in the same City-standard plastic sheets as the corridor they'd first entered, although these were dark gray rather than white. The floor was bare metal—no sign of the white tiles of Twelfth—but what shocked Alania the most was that it was dirty: blackened and smudged and greasy-looking. She raised her head and sniffed, and her nose wrinkled. "What's—"

"—that smell?" Sandi finished for her.

It was sour and kind of salty: definitely organic.

"People," Lissa said. "Dirty people." Her nose was wrinkled too, giving her heart-shaped face a look of comical disgust. "My brother plays grifterball when we go to Ice Canyon Resort. It smells like the arena locker rooms."

"Maybe we've gone far enough?" Sandi said meekly.

"We haven't seen anything yet," Alania retorted firmly—at least, as firmly as she could with her heart racing. To their left, the alley ended in a wall, in the middle of which a single narrow window glared blankly down at them, nothing visible beyond its dirty panes. She turned right again and headed resolutely to the other end of the alley.

It opened into a square courtyard. To their right was the blank front of the robot factory, broken only by two large doors, one marked DELIVERIES, one that simply said STAND CLEAR WHEN LIGHT IS FLASHING. The Beruthi name did not appear; there was nothing at all to reveal who the building belonged to.

To their left was a very similar factory, though the exits were smaller and completely unlabeled. There was no way to tell what it manufactured.

Two-story windowed structures surrounded the rest of the courtyard. The only path leaving it was a broad thoroughfare that ran in the direction of the Core, its familiar curved, silvery wall rising about two hundred meters from where they now stood. Though the courtyard itself was empty, beyond the buildings surrounding it, the thoroughfare thronged with people crossing the street or moving along it. It was no wonder the whole Tier smelled of them. The air was far warmer than on Twelfth and far more humid, which probably accounted for the streaks of rust on the—

Alania's aimless thoughts suddenly stilled as she realized there were also people in the square now, people who had just emerged from one of the windowed buildings, and that those people were looking at them . . . and coming their way.

Not just people, but young men. There were six of them, shabbily dressed in shades of gray and black, and they moved en masse.

"Alania?" Sandi whispered.

"A gang of some kind," Alania said, "Maybe we should—"

"What?" said a voice behind them, and all three of them yipped and spun to see another young man behind them. A boy, really, Alania thought, taking in his smooth face and piercing gray eyes. He was maybe four or five years older than they were, but that didn't make her feel any better, because there was something in that face that terrified her—something hard and predatory, something she had never seen before.

Not that she'd seen a lot of boys before, since no boy had ever been invited to one of her birthday parties, obviously. She'd met some of the other girls' brothers, though, including Lissa's grifterball-playing one, at the occasional function the Lieutenant had hosted, and none of them had had the . . . *edge* this boy did.

The boy stepped forward. "Welcome to Fifth Tier," he said. His eyes flicked past them, and Alania glanced back to see that the other boys had stopped and were staring at them, arms folded, faces impassive. "Don't worry about them," the boy in front of them said. "They're mine."

"Your what?" Alania whispered.

"Followers. Henchmen. Soldiers. Take your pick." The boy leaned against the factory wall and looked all three of them up and down with an appraising glance that made Alania uncomfortable, though she didn't know why. "How old?"

"Twelve," Sandi said, while Alania was still trying to decide if it was a good idea to answer that question or not.

"Twelve," the boy said. "Perfect."

"For what?" Lissa asked, saving Alania the trouble. She was having difficulty forming any words, to tell the truth. Breathing was a lot harder than it should have been, too.

The boy ignored the question. "Came slumming, did you? Looking for adventure?"

"My guardian is—" Alania began, finding her voice at last, but the boy cut her off.

"Not here," he said. "Not here, and there's no surveillance either. We own this courtyard. Nobody will know what happened to you." He straightened and looked past her at the rest of his gang. "You want adventure? You're about to get more than you—ungh!"

His eyes rolled up in his head, and he crumpled to the ground, twitching, a puddle of urine forming beneath him. Alania gaped at him, then jerked her head up to see the watchbot she'd thought she'd disabled in Quarters Beruthi standing just outside the door through which they'd exited the factory, its right hand raised, palm out. "Please step aside, ladies," its mechanical voice said, and then it strode past her as she, Lissa, and Sandi pressed themselves against the wall. Alania saw the rest of the gang turning to run, but of course that was useless against a robot. Four flashes of light, and they'd all joined their leader, stunned on the metal ground. The watchbot's head rotated a full 180 degrees; its sensors were clearly no longer disabled. If anyone else was watching from the surrounding windows, they wisely chose to remain hidden.

The watchbot strode in its strangely smooth manner back to Alania and her friends. "And now, miss," it said, "we will return to Quarters Beruthi."

A small part of Alania wanted to say, "You can't make me," which might have been technically true—the watchbot could not stun her as it had the unfortunate Fifth Tier boy, nor could it manhandle her and haul her to the elevator. But it was a distinction without a difference, since the watchbot *could* call for Provosts. And in any event, after what she had just witnessed, she wanted nothing so much as to return to the security of the home she no longer saw as quite the prison she had thought it.

They rode the elevator up in silence. The watchbot had nothing to say, Lissa and Sandi were subdued, and Alania's mind kept circling around one thing: what would Lieutenant Beruthi say . . . and do?

She didn't have to wait long to find out. A tall, thin, deeply tanned man with short black hair and a stylus-thin mustache awaited them at the door of the utility closet. "Sandi, Lissa," Lieutenant Beruthi said, "I think you should go home."

"Will you ... tell our parents?" Sandi asked in a small voice.

"Tell them what?" the Lieutenant said evenly. Lissa and Sandi's eyes widened, they glanced at each other, and then they dashed away like the tiny street-cleaning bots that kept Twelfth Tier sparkling and which Fifth Tier had so obviously lacked. The Lieutenant watched them disappear around the corner of the upstairs hallway, heading for the same stairs the watchbot had tumbled down earlier, and then turned back to Alania.

She met his gaze defiantly. "I'm *not* sorry," she said. "You've kept me a prisoner my whole life. I'm glad I escaped, even if it *was* scary."

The Lieutenant just looked at her, his dark eyes steady, his thin brown face unreadable. "What did you learn?" he asked.

She blinked. "What?"

"From your adventure on Fifth Tier," he said. "What did you learn?"

She stared at him. That was the last question she'd expected. "Well," she said slowly. "I guess ... that the lower Tiers really are very different from Twelfth Tier. That the people on them aren't like the Officers and their families. That there are people who will do bad things to other people ... even people from Officers' families."

The Lieutenant nodded. "Good lessons all," he said. "The City contains some fifty thousand people. Far more live in the lower Tiers than the upper. Life is indeed very different there: more diverse, more crowded, more difficult. The people who live there must struggle to survive, and it is very difficult to move beyond the niche into which you are born. And you were only on Fifth; the lower Tiers are even more difficult and dangerous for their denizens, and below us all lie the Middens. Even there, in the most difficult and dangerous place of all, people live . . . though at least they are not subject in the same way to the City's laws."

Alania stared at him. "What?"

He almost smiled—had she really seen that or imagined it? Imagined it, surely. "And your final understanding, that there are people who will do bad things to other people, even members of Officers' families, is the most valuable lesson of all, for it applies as much to Twelfth Tier as to the Middens and everything in between."

Alania felt lost, but there was one question she wanted answered above all else, so she asked it. "How will you punish me?"

"In the most severe fashion possible," the Lieutenant said. "I am going to ensure that you learn those same three lessons over and over again."

Alania opened her mouth to say, "What?" again, then closed it.

"Tomorrow you begin a new school regimen," the Lieutenant said. "You will learn, in as much detail as is permissible for you to learn, everything there is to know about the City and its operation. It will serve you well when you are grown."

"When I'm . . . ?"

"Give me back my spare key," the Lieutenant said. "You have had your adventure. I will not allow it again." Alania drew the golden rod from her pocket and held it out. The Lieutenant slipped it into his own pocket. "Now," he said briskly, "I believe you will find food waiting for you below." And then he turned and walked away, leaving Alania staring after him.

She descended to the main floor and sat in the relatively small kitchen, rather than the cavernous dining room, for a meal which, to her surprise, consisted of some of her favorite foods: mashed redroots, candied vatham, even a hollowed-out frozen bluemelon. She felt like she was being rewarded more than punished, but that made no sense.

No less sense than the robot she had been so certain she had disabled suddenly appearing in the alley on Fifth Tier to rescue them. She scooped up a spoonful of melon, then stopped it halfway to her mouth, suddenly realizing the truth.

I will not allow it again, *he said. Again. That means he* did *allow it this time.*

I didn't disable the watchbot at all, she thought. *It probably plugged those wires back in itself the second I was out of sight. Lieutenant Beruthi programmed it to let us go. He made sure I knew about the elevator and the spare key. He* wanted *me to get out of Twelfth Tier.*

But why?

She had no answer.

She wouldn't have one, it turned out, for many years.

TWO

THE TRASHSLIDE STRUCK without warning.

They didn't always. Sometimes there was a preliminary tremor, a sign you should look for something more stable to stand on, if you could find anything suitable; "stable" and "The Middens" were words that didn't have much to do with each other. Until today, Danyl had only ever been in the Middens in the company of his guardian, Erl, but he'd learned that much. Erl seemed to have a sixth sense for how the trash would move, and half a dozen times he had hurried them to some safer spot just before a sinkhole had opened or a slide had come roaring down one of the valleys that provided more-or-less reliable paths through the mounds of trash.

But today Danyl was on his own, having rebelliously sneaked out to follow Erl to the forbidden Last Chance Market, just to get a glimpse of it, and though Erl was in sight, he wasn't listening for trashslides; he was engaged in intense, secretive conversation with someone wearing a black synthileather coat and dark glasses. Hearing the rumble above him as the trash began to move, Danyl scrambled up and dashed through the scraggly stand of tangleweed he'd been hiding behind, hoping to reach the Last Chance Market's platform, secure on its massive iron beams anchored to the Canyon wall. But the slide caught him before he'd covered a quarter of the distance, sucking him down from behind.

He did as Erl had taught him, rolling up into a tight ball to protect his most vulnerable organs, eyes squeezed shut behind his goggles, but he felt an agonizing burning pain as something slashed his left leg open and another as something stabbed him in the side while he tumbled helplessly in the welter of plastic and paper and wood and metal and nameless gunk.

Then everything was still and dark. Danyl couldn't tell how deeply he was buried, couldn't see any light even when he dared to open his eyes, couldn't move, could hardly *breathe*, the pressure was so great . . . and he knew he was bleeding.

He pushed as hard as he could against the confining trash, but it didn't budge, and the cold realization crashed in on him that he could die here, suffocate or bleed to death; that no one would ever find him; that no one even knew he was here. He'd just turned twelve years old, and he was going to die . . .

He'd never really thought of that as a possibility before. He could *die*.

He tried to scream for help, but he didn't have the air or the space. He could only remain there, curled tight in the darkness, trapped, helpless.

Then the trash moved around him. The pressure eased. The light turned from black to gray, and he glimpsed sky through cracks in the rubbish. And then the trash was suddenly swept aside, and the blue sky appeared, and a lined brown face looked down at him, wisps of gray hair peeking out beneath a synthileather cap.

Erl!

"Help," Danyl said weakly, but of course Erl was already reaching down to him. There was someone else with him, the man in the dark coat and glasses, and that was weird, Danyl thought, though the thought was rather fuzzy. Erl had always said that no one from the Last Chance Market would ever step off the platform and into the Middens, and yet . . .

He drifted into unconsciousness, half woke in a daze as he was hauled out of the hole and pain stabbed his leg and side, drifted off again, had a transient moment of awareness of being slung over Erl's shoulders and carried through the Middens, and then another of Erl lugging him down the tunnel leading to their hidden home in the Canyon wall. Erl laid him on the dining table— *We'll have to disinfect it*, Danyl thought fitfully—and fetched the old docbot he'd scavenged years before. A sphere about twenty centimeters in diameter skittered across the reddish stone floor on three spindly metal legs. A glowing blue scanner orb extended on a flexible stalk and turned to Erl. "Please select a function," the docbot said in a light female voice.

"First aid," Erl said.

"Please identify the injured person."

"Danyl."

The docbot's orb turned toward Danyl. "Please remove the patient's clothing to permit diagnosis and treatment."

Erl hurriedly and roughly stripped Danyl to allow the docbot to get at his wounds. The pain brought Danyl more fully awake, and he tried to help as best he could, gasping as he saw how much blood covered his pants and shirt, then going pale when he saw the hole in his side. He shouldn't be able to see inside himself like that ...

But shouldn't there be even more blood? he thought. Because it looked to him like the wounds were already starting to close, and even though his ordinary scrapes and cuts had always healed quickly, that couldn't be right, not so soon ...

Something hissed against his arm, and the world faded out again.

He woke in his own bed down the hall from the living/dining room, clean and naked and bandaged beneath the blankets. He stared up at the familiar stone ceiling for a moment, blinking, trying to make sense of the scattered jumble of disconnected memories since the rumble of the slide had startled him.

"How do you feel?" Erl said from his right, and he turned his head to see his guardian sitting there, finger marking his place in the old water-stained book he was reading, another bit of salvage from the Middens.

"Okay," Danyl said. Surprisingly, it was true. He didn't hurt, and the dazed, foggy feeling was gone. He sat up. "How long have I been asleep?"

"A day," Erl said. "The docbot thought you needed that long, so it put you under."

Danyl touched the bandage on his side, expecting to feel a twinge, but he felt nothing. In fact, it felt as if there were no wound there at all, but it had only been a day, how could . . .

Erl reached out and touched his arm. "Don't play with the bandages," he said.

"I don't feel anything," Danyl said.

"The docbot has some powerful analgesics."

"Anal . . . what?"

"Pain medicine," Erl said. He put his book down on Danyl's cracked plastic bedside table. "Hungry?"

Danyl hadn't thought about it until then, but now that he *did* . . . "Starving!"

Erl laughed. "I thought you would be. I've got a treat in the kitchen. Fresh vegetables and a couple of real steaks, not vat-grown."

Danyl's mouth suddenly flooded with saliva. He'd only had real meat once, when he was nine, and he'd been craving it ever since. "How . . . ?"

"That's what I was bargaining for at the Last Chance Market," Erl said. "You know, the place you had absolutely no business being."

Danyl felt a little ashamed, but only a little. "I'm twelve years old," he said stoutly. "I'm not a kid anymore. I want out of the Middens someday, and you said the only way out was through the Last Chance Market, so I —"

"Disobeyed me and almost got yourself killed," Erl finished. "Was that the responsible action of someone who is 'not a kid anymore'?"

Danyl opened his mouth, couldn't think of anything to say, and closed it again.

"Exactly." But then Erl's stern expression softened into a near-smile. "All the same," he said, "I can't fault your stealth. I had no idea you'd followed me until I heard you yell." The smiled faded. "Good thing I *did hear* you. Otherwise you would have just vanished without a trace, and I would never have known what had happened to you." He looked positively grim at the thought, and his hand snaked out and gripped Danyl's arm again, this time hard enough to hurt. "*Promise me.* Promise me you'll never do anything that stupid again."

"You'll *never* let me go out there on my own," Danyl said, a little frightened by Erl's intensity, which made him sound more petulant than he'd intended.

Erl squeezed his arm a moment longer, then relaxed his grip and drew back his hand. "Yes, I will. But you need more training. And someday you *will* get into the City, I promise you. But you need more training before that, too." Erl got up. "Get dressed and come down the hall. You're right, you're not a kid anymore, and there's something I want to show you before you eat."

Erl went out, and Danyl swung his legs over the side of the bed. Despite what Erl had said, he touched the bandage on his side, then the one on his leg. He felt nothing. He hesitated, then peeled back the edge of the adhesive holding the round patch of synthiskin on his flank.

Underneath it, his real skin was as smooth and unbroken as its artificial covering, only a shiny pink mark showing where he'd been impaled. He stared, then hastily pushed the synthiskin back into place. He didn't disturb the leg bandage, but he was certain he'd find the same thing under it.

He hadn't imagined being injured. He hadn't dreamed

it. The pain and blood had been real. But somehow, the wounds had healed . . . in a day.

If it's really been only a day, he thought. *Maybe I've been out a lot longer and Erl didn't want to worry me.*

That was easy enough to check. His scavenged watch lay on his bedside table. It confirmed what Erl had first said; it had been a little more than twenty-seven hours since the trashslide had rumbled down on his head.

Weird, he thought. *Maybe the docbot sealed the hole in my skin, but I'm still healing underneath?* For a second he thought he'd figured it out, but then he frowned. *But if the skin is sealed up, why do I need a bandage?*

There was no way to ask the ancient docbot, whose AI could not respond to those sorts of questions, and he wasn't sure Erl would know—he certainly wasn't a doctor. But Danyl still intended to ask him . . .

. . . except it went out of his head when, dressed but still barefoot on the cool stone floor, he followed the mouth-watering scent of cooking meat down the hallway to the living/dining room, and Erl opened a door across from the hallway that he'd never seen open before.

Erl had always said he kept the door locked because the room on the other side had collapsed and was filled with rubble, but nothing could have been further from the truth. In fact, it was the largest room in their carved-from-the-Canyon-wall hideaway. In the middle stood a circular dais maybe half a meter high. Hanging from the ceiling was a helmet that would completely cover Danyl's head if he put it on.

"What is it?" he asked in wonder.

"A reality simulator," Erl said.

Danyl blinked at him. "A what?"

Erl frowned. "Did the trashslide make you deaf?"

Danyl shook his head. "No, it's just . . . how did it get here?"

"How does anything get here?" Erl said. "I salvaged it. Before you were born. Same hoard I found the docbot in. I kept it because I thought the parts might be useful, but when I found you . . . I decided to see if I could get it working. Took some serious trading at the Market, but eventually I got the equipment I needed to fix it."

"But . . . what's it for?"

Erl sighed. "For you, of course. I told you—one day you will go into the City, and when you do, you'll need to know a lot more. And long before that, you're going to be running around the Middens on your own, and for that"—he gave Danyl a frown—"you *also* need to know a lot more. As you proved yesterday."

"But . . . what will it teach me?"

Erl pointed at the machine. "For one thing, with this, you can explore every Tier of the City—well, every Tier that's not restricted. Of course many of the Tiers have changed a lot from the way they looked originally . . . but still, it will give you a feel for what to expect when it's finally time for you to go inside."

"Wow," Danyl said, because it seemed like he should say something.

"That *will* be useful someday, but of more immediate use will be weapons and self-defense training. It can help with that too."

Danyl's face split into a grin. "You're going to teach me how to *fight*?"

"Yes," Erl said. "You were lucky yesterday in more ways than one: lucky because I heard you yell and rescued you from the trash, but even luckier that you didn't run into the Rustbloods. You'd be their slave right now if you had."

Danyl swallowed. He'd seen the Rustblood compound from a distance; the desiccated corpse that hung on a chain beside the gate as decoration and warning had been enough to give him the chills. "But I've never even seen a Rustblood."

"That's because I know how to stay clear of them," Erl said. "Something else you need to learn." He looked up at the helmet and the bank of equipment from which it hung, bolted to the ceiling of the stone chamber. "I intended to start this part of your training when you turned thirteen, but your little escapade yesterday has convinced me it can't wait any longer." He turned back to Danyl. "So. Eat. You need another week of convalescence before you can do any serious training, but—"

"But I've already healed!"

Erl frowned at him. "You lifted the bandage?"

Uh-oh, Danyl thought. "Um, it's just . . . It doesn't hurt, and I thought . . ."

"Appearances can be deceiving," Erl said. "The docbot sealed your skin, but you're still damaged underneath."

"That's what I thought, but it doesn't even—"

"I'm not a doctor," Erl snapped. "I just know the docbot said to leave the bandage on. So *leave the bandage on.* Got it?"

"Got it," Danyl said meekly.

"As I was about to say before you interrupted me," Erl said, "you can't start any physical training yet, but you can start your virtual tour of the City, and I'll fill you in on what I know about each Tier."

A thought struck Danyl. "Can we take a virtual tour of the Thirteenth Tier? Say hi to a virtual Captain?"

Erl went strangely silent for a moment. "No," he said. "No, you can't see the Thirteenth Tier. Not yet."

"Not *yet*?" Danyl pounced on that. "Then I can *someday*?"

"Anything is possible," Erl said shortly. "Now, eat. Your body needs fuel to heal, and even without that, you're growing like a tangleweed. Steaks tonight. Synthetics again tomorrow, but extra-large helpings for a bit."

Maybe getting buried in a trashslide isn't so bad after all, Danyl thought as he took his first succulent bite of steak a few minutes later. *If it means eating like this, I'll have to try to get buried at least once a month.*

He stared at the door to the training room as he ate,

anxious to get started on learning everything it could teach him.

I will get into the City someday, he thought fiercely. *Someday.*

Anything that brought that day closer, he was all for.

He took another bite of steak and bit down fiercely.

THREE

THE CITY'S CURRENT First Officer, Staydmore Kranz, stood on the black-tiled floor of the Twelfth-Tier hangar and waited for Falkin Kranz, the young man who would be the City's *last* First Officer, to emerge from the just-landed aircar. Beyond the hangar's giant open hatch, the First Officer could see the distant ice-covered peaks of the western Iron Ring. The aircar carrying Falkin had come from Resort Kranz in the shadow of those peaks, a place the First Officer had loved when he was a boy but now only thought of when he was receiving his regular reports on the progress of the youth he was about to meet.

Perhaps Falkin had loved the Resort, too, though his life there had been far different from that of young Staydmore. Staydmore Kranz had grown up with four identical brothers, all of them clones of the previous First Officer, as he had been a clone of the one before him, and he of the one before him, all the way back to the original First Officer Kranz almost five hundred years ago. But Falkin Kranz, Staydmore's only clone, had grown up alone.

Like Staydmore, Falkin Kranz had been kept ignorant of his inheritance as he'd matured. He'd been well edu-cated by the elderly couple who ran the Estate, though he'd been shown little affection. He believed himself to be an orphan.

He was, by all accounts, weak in both mind and body,

weaknesses that had also been present to greater or lesser degrees in Staydmore Kranz's "brothers." It was why Staydmore had sailed through the battery of tests they had all been required to take and his brothers had not, why he was now First Officer and they were . . . not.

Their regrettable but necessary elimination would have horrified the young Staydmore Kranz, who had been fond of his brothers, dimwitted and/or clumsy though they had been. But fortunately, by the time it had been carried out, he had no longer been Staydmore Kranz in any significant sense. He was, in mind as well as body, his ancestor, First Officer Thomas Kranz; the nanobots he had been injected with at birth had been fully activated when he'd turned twenty, rewriting his mind and personality.

With that sea change had come the heavy burden he now carried: the burden of being the only person in the City or Heartland who knew the truth about how humans had come here . . . and how humanity's place in this world teetered on a knife's edge of catastrophic collapse.

A new man, literally, Staydmore Kranz had worked side by side with his predecessor for many years, absorbing all the minute details of the day-to-day management of the City. When the previous First Officer had turned eighty, the nanobots had shut down his body as programmed, and the full authority of the position had passed to Staydmore Kranz.

Three days ago, Falkin Kranz's nanobots had been fully activated, beginning the process of rewriting his mind as they had rewritten Staydmore's, imprinting upon it the mind of their original. Staydmore Kranz would live another twenty-eight years, barring catastrophe, but it was past time to begin working with his successor, especially since Falkin would be the last First Officer Kranz of the line.

Science Officer Prentis claimed there had been a

terminal failure in the ancient and poorly understood cloning equipment, something that they did not have the knowledge or technology to rectify, but Kranz suspected that was Prentis being diplomatic. She probably thought it safer to risk lying to the First Officer than to baldly state the truth, though he himself had already guessed it: that only one clone had been successfully created, and that one was badly flawed because there were only so many times you could copy anything before it became garbled. With Falkin, First Officer Thomas Kranz's grand scheme of protecting the City forever had stumbled to its inevitable end.

Still, Kranz hoped that the nanobots that had rewritten Falkin's mind might also be able to strengthen his body. It was not important that Falkin live to the programmed limit of eighty years, but it *was* important that he live long enough to assist in the great project Kranz had launched to save the City. It was a new take on Thomas Kranz's original vision, one which would rejuvenate the ancient City's faltering infrastructure and keep at bay for another half a millennium the dreadful fate all the First Officers had been striving so hard to avoid. Kranz needed someone he could trust completely to help him oversee the project, and the only person he absolutely knew he could trust was himself—which, in all important respects, Falkin Kranz should now be.

Everything depends on the Cityborn, Kranz thought, staring at the aircar. He could see movement through the darkened canopy. *The Cityborn can save us, but there are so many things that could go wrong. With Falkin at my side, the transition will be so much easier to manage.*

There was another reason he was relieved to have Falkin here at last. Sixteen years ago, Ensign Erlkin Orillia had almost derailed the Cityborn Project and ensured the City's eventual collapse. He'd kidnapped one of the candidate babies and murdered another. Only by fortuitous happenstance had he failed to destroy all Kranz's plans. Orillia had flown off with the kidnapped child from this very hangar, landed in the Iron Ring, and then vanished. No doubt the two had long since perished. But Kranz knew there were other malcontents in the City, and no matter how tight a lid he tried to keep on things—and the Provosts kept a very tight lid indeed—it was not entirely outside the realm of possibility that someone might manage to assassinate the First Officer before the Cityborn Project came to fruition. Having a spare First Officer Kranz on hand would provide some insurance against such a catastrophe.

The aircar door opened. A Provost stepped out first, hand on the hilt of his slugthrower, and looked around the hangar. When he saw Kranz, he snapped to attention and saluted. Kranz impatiently sketched a salute back. The Provost stepped to one side, and Falkin emerged at last.

He was thin to the point of gauntness, pale, and even from his vantage point twenty meters away, Kranz could see that he was shaking. Kranz could barely recognize his own features in the youth's emaciated, stubbled face, though the ice-blue eyes flicking nervously from side to side were certainly the same. The boy's dark brown hair stuck up in all directions. Kranz frowned. He'd been warned that Falkin had not taken the reprogramming well. A day or so of unconsciousness was normal—Kranz had been out for some thirty hours himself—but Falkin had been unconscious for three days and all but catatonic for another five. He'd hardly spoken since.

Well, Kranz thought, *I'll soon whip him into shape. Who better to get through to him than an older version of himself?*

Science Officer Prentis, who had overseen the nanobot reprogramming, came out next. She saw the First Officer and started toward him, saying, "Bring him," to the Provost. Then, to Kranz, "First Officer, I'm pleased to—"

A sharp bang echoed through the hangar. Kranz jerked his eyes from the approaching Prentis to the aircar. The

Provost, clutching his stomach, blood welling over his fingers, dropped to his knees and then to his side on the black tiles. Falkin dropped the man's slugthrower and leaped back into the aircar, the door closing behind him.

Kranz started to run toward the vehicle, but it was far too late. It lifted, spun, and roared out of the hangar, the backwash of its rotors tumbling Kranz across the hangar floor. Groaning, he sat up just in time to see the aircar, still accelerating, drop its nose toward the ground and vanish from sight.

A moment later the hangar vibrated with a thunderous explosion. By the time Kranz had staggered to his feet and run to the lip of the hangar, Prentis at his side, the black smoke from the wreckage had already climbed as high as Twelfth Tier.

Danyl stood in the Last Chance Market, trying not to look as nervous as he felt as he faced the trader he'd contacted surreptitiously two weeks before via a mail drop he wasn't supposed to know about. Four years had passed since the trashslide. He didn't think this was the same trader he'd seen Erl talking to the day he'd almost died, but it was hard to be certain, not only because so much time had passed but also because the trader's face was hidden behind a stained red handkerchief and dark goggles. None of the traders in the Last Chance Market showed their faces if they could help it. Danyl wouldn't even have been certain it *was* a man if the trader hadn't said, "Well?" in a gruff bass voice.

"I want to know what it would cost me to get into the City," Danyl said.

The man cocked his head to one side. "You want a City Pass?"

At least he didn't laugh in my face, Danyl thought. "Yeah."

The trader shrugged. "It's not impossible. Takes a hell of a salvage score, though."

"I know that," Danyl said impatiently. "But what, exactly?"

"That's valuable information, that is," the man said. He crossed his arms. "TANSTAAFL, kid. There ain't no such thing as a free lunch. What've you got to trade?"

Danyl had expected that. He reached into his pocket and pulled out something that gleamed even in the gloom of early morning, made all the gloomier by the shadow of the looming City. "Jewelry," he said. "Found it in an old box eight feet down. Looks like diamonds."

"Synthetics," the man said. "Diamonds have more fire. But good enough." He took the necklace and tucked it into one of his deep pockets. "So. I've heard of only two scavengers who scored something worth a City Pass. First was a woman who found an old-style data crystal from Officer country. Don't know what was on it, though I have my suspicions."

"You didn't make the deal?" Danyl asked.

The man snorted. "Wish. No, she traded with Char. Char got her a City Pass, all right, and they both went in. Char dropped out of sight soon after; no one I've talked to knows what happened to her. Maybe she got rich and she's up on Eighth or Ninth. On the other hand, maybe she's rotting in Tenth." He shrugged as if he didn't care either way. "Know what happened to the woman, though." He jerked a thumb over his shoulder at the black underside of the City. "She came back out again. In pieces."

Danyl ignored that, fiercely focused on what *really* mattered. "But she got in."

"She got in."

Danyl glanced around. They still had the platform to themselves. That didn't mean they weren't being observed—the Rustbloods certainly kept a watch, although the Market was a safe space by long-standing tradition. Nobody in the Middens could afford to spook the traders by starting anything anywhere close to it. If the traders stopped coming down, life would get even nastier, and probably shorter, than it already was.

Danyl looked back at the trader. "And the other person?"

"Guy who used to run the Rustbloods was sifting through some wastepaper, found a document that shouldn't have been there, covered with some very interesting figures showing that the finances of a Fifth-Tier Bank were not *exactly*—or even *close to*—what was being reported to regulators. Guy got out, handed the paper over to the Bank in exchange for a nice nest egg—keeping a copy tucked away somewhere it'll get passed on if anything happens to him, of course. He runs a respectable cleaning business on Fifth Tier now." The trader grinned. "Can always get a loan, I hear."

Danyl frowned. "Neither of those is helpful. How can I *look* for something like that?"

The trader laughed. "Kid, that's the point. You *can't* look for that kind of score. You can only luck into it. But I'll tell you this—you've got a good eye for salvage. Wouldn't expect anything else from someone Erl's raised. If anyone can find something that'll net him a City Pass, it's you."

"Are those the only two City Passes anyone has ever scored or just the only two you know about?"

"Now, how can I answer that?" the trader said. "Of *course* I can only tell you about the ones I know about."

Danyl grimaced. "Sorry. But there *could* be others?"

"There could be," the trader said. "But I doubt there are. You gotta understand, kid, it's not easy even for one of *us* to get a City Pass. You can't just buy one from the first Provost you see. You have to make a deal with some people it's not always safe to deal with. They take a big cut, so whatever you're trading has to be worth a *lot*. Besides, nobody knows exactly what something like that is worth until they try to sell it. And sometimes just *try-*

ing to sell gets you dead or hauled off to Tenth Tier." He shrugged. "Keep looking." He gave a rough chuckle. "You're young. Maybe by the time you're Erl's age . . ."

That felt like a punch to the gut, and Danyl's hands clenched. He would have loved to have shown the trader just how far along he'd come in his combat training in the simulator. But he controlled himself for the same reason the Rustbloods did near the Market—he and Erl couldn't afford to risk losing access to the Last Chance Market, and that was what would happen if he stepped out of line.

"Don't think I got a fair trade for the necklace," he growled. That much he could say.

The trader laughed. "I told you, kid, the stones are synthetic. I'll be lucky to get twenty creds for it. You got exactly what you paid for."

Danyl forced his hands to relax and took a deep breath. "What a waste of time." He turned to go—then looked up, startled, as something roared out of the City from somewhere very high up. Just an aircar—four or five of them launched from or landed in the higher Tiers every day—but they didn't normally dive like—

The aircar vanished from his sight beyond the Canyon Rim. The explosion a moment later echoed from the bottom of the City and Canyon's far wall like a clap of thunder. A tower of black smoke poured up above the Rim.

"What the *hell*?" The trader dashed for the ladder stretching from the Market to the Rim. Danyl couldn't follow—not up there. He stayed where he was, staring at the smoke, wondering what damage the aircar had done to the warehouses clustered outside the City Gate. Or had it hit the giant, mysterious, white Cubes scattered haphazardly around the City on both sides of the Canyon? Would that be enough to force one open? He doubted it; no one in the entire history of the City had ever managed to make so much as a mark on their shining surfaces, much less pry, cut, or blast one open.

There was no sign of the aircar's passenger compartment, which should have separated at the first sign of trouble and descended safely. A shame, because if there was one thing Danyl was *sure* must be worth a City Pass, it was rescuing some upper-Tier VIP from an ejected aircar passenger pod that just happened to land in the Middens.

He pulled his synthileather hood up over his head, snugged his goggles over his eyes, and headed for the ladder he could take from the Market back down into the trash. Turning to get on it brought the City into view once more. As he descended rung by rung, he stared up at the massive metal tower, wreathed in fumes and vapors from hundreds of exhaust vents and pipes as well as in the black smoke from the burning wreckage of the aircar.

I'll get in there. Someday I'll get in there.

He reached the rubbish, turned his back on the City, and headed for home.

As Alania, wearing a fuzzy pink robe over a damp swimsuit, crossed the entrance hall of Quarters Beruthi on her way back to her room after a morning swim, she heard voices coming from the Lieutenant's reception office, the first door on the right.

She hesitated with her hand on the banister of the stairs leading to the second floor. Both voices belonged to men. One was the Lieutenant. The other ...

... the other, she was almost certain, belonged to First Officer Kranz, and that was what gave her pause.

As First Officer, Kranz ruled the City—in the Captain's name, of course, but since there had officially been only one Captain in the centuries-long history of the City, it was widely thought she was not just a figurehead but an *embalmed* figurehead.

As Alania had learned from the rigorous course of study Lieutenant Beruthi had imposed on her since her adventure to Fifth Tier with Sandi and Lissa four years before, there had been many First Officers in the almost five hundred years since the First Citizens awoke and set about making lives in the Homeland, but *all* of them had been Kranzes. To be sure, all Officer positions were hereditary, and though there were occasional shufflings in the ranks (when, for example, an Officer died without issue), the line of Kranzes had not only remained unbroken, it had remained male. The First Officer was always a man.

Staydmore Kranz, now sixty-two years of age, had been First Officer for some thirty years. His own son had just turned twenty—or so Alania had heard; she'd never met him. She saw Kranz himself once a year at Lieutenant Beruthi's midwinter ball, as de rigueur a social requirement for him as the tiresome birthday parties involving all the other girls near her age was for her.

She recognized his voice, but she'd never heard it like this: tight with emotion, raised to a strangled shout. At first she though he was angry, but then she realized that wasn't quite right. He wasn't an*gry*, he was an*guished*. Or perhaps both.

She hesitated on the stairs. The Lieutenant didn't know she was there. Sala was upstairs, cleaning her room, and she knew Alania was swimming but not for how long. Since Sala was on duty and the Lieutenant was home, the watchbot was inactive. Alania was in the relatively unique position of being able to act freely.

The proper thing to do was certainly to demurely climb the stairs and shut her ears to the First Officer's pain. But for Alania, any chance at rebellion was worth taking, so instead she slipped off her pool shoes, figuring bare feet would be quieter, and hurried soundlessly across the marble floor of the main hall to the closed door of the office.

She put her ear against it.

". . . too soon," Beruthi was saying, voice intense. "Sir, you know it's too soon. She's only sixteen. Her brain development . . ."

Sixteen? They're talking about me! Alania realized with a shock. *But . . . why?*

"Don't talk to me about brain development!" Kranz raged. "Falkin's brain is *never* going to develop, is it? And he was the last."

Puzzled and *intensely* curious, Alania pressed her ear to the door harder.

"Sir," Beruthi said, "I understand your problem and the magnitude of your loss. But it's a physical impossibility."

"You understand nothing. The magnitude of my loss is greater than you can possibly imagine."

"Sir," Beruthi said, and he sounded hurt, "you know that's not true. I have been by your side from the beginning of this endeavor. I know what you are trying to accomplish, and I have done everything I can to help you achieve your goals, as my ancestors always helped your ancestors. I *do* understand. This tragedy is shocking and adds risk to your efforts, I admit, but it hardly presages disaster. It has removed a fail-safe—one that would be nice to have, I admit, but is hardly crucial. You just have to wait and keep yourself safe for four more years, sir. Just four more years."

Kranz muttered something Alania didn't catch, but she was pretty sure it was obscene. "The little fool," he said then. His voice dropped so she had to strain to hear just a few words here and there. ". . . Thomas . . . the nanobots shouldn't have . . . Prentis says . . . the Captain . . ."

"Alania!" came a sharp whispered rebuke. Alania straightened and spun to see Sala staring at her from the bottom of the stairs; she had been so focused on the half-heard conversation that she'd neglected to keep watch, and now her heart pounded in her chest. "What are you doing?" her maidservant whisper-shouted. "If the Lieutenant catches you . . . !"

Alania shot a regretful look at the closed door, then hurried across the room to Sala. "It's First Officer Kranz," she said in a low voice, pushing her feet back into her pool shoes. "I heard him talking to the Lieutenant—he sounded upset. I just wanted to know what was going on."

"No excuse for eavesdropping," Sala said primly. "Up to your room."

"You won't tell the Lieutenant?" Alania asked, starting up the steps.

"Of course not," Sala said, following her, and Alania grinned. Sala might be her servant, but she thought of her more like a big sister most of the time—sometimes more like the mother she'd never known. "No harm done. And anyway, I can tell you why Kranz is here."

"Why?" Alania asked, glancing back at her.

Sala made a shooing motion to keep her moving, and Alania climbed the last few steps and then turned to look at her servant again. "Why?"

Sala glanced down the stairs, then leaned in close. "His son died," she said in a low voice. "Aircar crash earlier this morning. Terrible thing." She straightened. "Now get into your room, get out of that wet swimsuit, and get dressed. Lunch is in half an hour."

Alania didn't move. "Did someone kill him?" she asked, fascinated. "Was it an assassination?"

Sala snorted. "You read too many adventure stories. Of course it wasn't an assassination. It was a tragic accident, that's all." She strode past Alania to the door of her room, opened it, and motioned her inside. Alania sighed and obeyed, but as she passed Sala, the servant said thoughtfully, "Might mean things are going to change when Kranz dies, though. As far as I know there's never been a First Officer without an heir."

"No, there hasn't," Alania said. "And his wife died a long time ago, didn't she?"

Sala nodded. "Giving birth to his son, I heard. Never saw her; never knew anybody who did. They say she never came into the City at all—lived and died on the Kranz Estate. She'd be too old now, anyway." She shrugged. "Well, won't matter to me, whoever's in charge. Nothing will change. Nothing ever does. Now get dressed, and don't be late for lunch."

"Will the Lieutenant be joining me?" Alania asked hopefully, thinking she might be able to ask a question or two without revealing she'd been listening at the door.

"Not he," Sala said. "He's leaving for his Retreat as soon as he can get away. He'll be gone for a month."

The door closed.

As she changed, Alania thought back over what she'd heard. It made no sense. Kranz had sounded upset—furious, even—but not sad, not like a man grieving the loss of his son. He'd seemed more worried about something else entirely, something his son was supposed to play an important role in ... important, but apparently not vital.

She's only sixteen, Beruthi had said. *Her brain development ...*

Me, presumably. But what could I and my brain development—or lack of it—have to do with the loss of Kranz's son and some enormous problem facing the First Officer?

And what would change in four years, except that she'd be twenty?

The same age as Kranz's son, who had just died. That thought was a little shiver-making.

She shook her head and reached for her brush to swipe the tangles from her wet hair. *Nothing ever changes in the City*, Sala had said, and it certainly seemed like nothing ever changed in Alania's life. It was hard to imagine what difference four more years would make.

I guess I'll find out.

FOUR

FOUR YEARS LATER, not quite eight years after their nearly disastrous "adventure" to Fifth Tier, Alania sat with Lissa and Sandi at a table at the front of the Quarters Beruthi dining room, supposedly celebrating her twentieth birthday while really suffering the torments of the damned with a fake smile plastered on her face.

The Amazing Belgrani's Hour of Magic and Mystery was finally — finally! — drawing to a close. The titular magician climbed a spindly plaster column. Teetering on tiptoe, he spun three times, then vanished with a sound like tinkling wind chimes in a puff of purple smoke. A collective gasp followed by applause dispersed the smoke into the general haze of the candlelit and overly warm room.

Alania applauded far more out of relief than appreciation. She looked down at her plate. Half of her honey-berry sorbet, a palate cleanser served after the initial overly complicated salad, remained uneaten. It no longer looked the least bit appetizing, having puddled into muddy-gold syrup in the glassy pink bottom of her silver-trimmed bowl.

She turned to speak to Sala, hovering as always just over her left shoulder. "The main course now, please."

"Yes, ma'am." Sala, far more deferential in public than she ever was in private, curtsied, removed Alania's bowl, turned, and vanished into the kitchen, moving

upstream against the outflowing tide of robots coming to
clear away the sorbet dishes. Each wheeled, multiarmed
machine rolled out of her way so she never had to side-
step at all. Alania watched her go and wished she could
go with her, and then maybe sneak out a side door into
the street . . .

Of course, if she did, she would immediately be
fetched by the same watchbot she had pretend-disabled
all those years ago, which had saved her and Lissa and
Sandi from the gang on Fifth Tier. A terrifying experience at the time, and she didn't *really* want a repeat of
it . . . and yet, on a day like today, she kind of did.

But of course it was impossible for her to sneak off
anywhere, since she was putatively the guest of honor
and the center of attention for this whole odious, tedious
affair.

Stagehands in black began removing the magician's
props and setting up for the next bit of "entertainment,"
the Seventh-Tier Acrobats' Association (whose act was
enjoyable enough but whom Alania had seen so many
times at other girls' birthday parties that she almost
thought she could fill in for an injured acrobat should the
need arise). Alania stared gloomily down from the head
table's dais at the elaborately coiffed heads of twenty-
three young women more or less her own age. Clad in
long formal gowns of red and green and silver and gold,
they chatted and gossiped animatedly amongst themselves, because that was what one did at these affairs;
that was the *real* entertainment, after all.

Overhead, projected stars twinkled among scudding,
holographic clouds, designed to give the room the appearance of a walled outdoor patio at night. Alania
looked up at them and wished they *were* real and that
she could fly away into them. When she was a little girl,
these obligatory parties had at least included games.
Now they were tediously adult affairs.

Some of the other young women were fortunate only

children, which meant they would inherit their fathers' or mothers' ranks and take over their families' Quarters, Estates, and for the wealthiest, like her own guardian, Retreats. They were the only ones who could truly hope to enjoy themselves at parties like this. Others had older siblings and could only remain on Eleventh or Twelfth if they married into other Officer families. For those girls, marriage prospects were everything, and they understandably resented being stuck at a party where there were no young men. If they *failed* to marry into other Officer families, they would be shipped off to their families' Estates to help manage farms or mines that supplied the City: a social fate worse than death.

Alania, on the other hand, was in the very strange position of being the *ward* of Lieutenant Beruthi, not his daughter. He had never so much as hinted that she would inherit his business, Quarters, Estate, or Retreat. She had no idea what her future held ... except for that overheard snatch of conversation between Beruthi and First Officer Kranz in the entrance hall all those years ago. She'd half convinced herself she'd misunderstood and that they couldn't really have been talking about her ... but what if they had?

The four years were up. Would something happen?

Captain, I hope so, she thought, staring at the sea of simpering socialites. Otherwise, what would become of her? It appeared she couldn't inherit, and yet she could not marry into an Officer family either—her status as a ward rather than daughter ensured that no Officers would allow their precious sons to waste time on her. The only boys she'd ever seen had been at the Lieutenant's midwinter balls, and they'd studiously ignored her. She saw no possibility that she would be shipped off to Beruthi's Estate, since she'd never been formally allowed to leave Twelfth Tier. And anyway, as she understood it, the Estate was even more automated than the household, without any living people there at all unless the Lieutenant was in residence and had invited guests. Perhaps that was to be expected of the Officer whose family made almost all the City's robots.

Which left ... what?

She thought back again to that long-ago escape with Lissa and Sandi and the strange conversation she'd had with the Lieutenant afterward. He'd been as good as his word. She'd learned so much since then, things she knew, from talking to her two friends, that other girls were not learning. She knew the structure of the City inside and out from detailed plans she'd been made to memorize; its history—or what there was of it, since it had simply begun, without explanation of what had come before, with the awakening of the First Citizens; the organization, recruitment methods, training, and weaponry of the Provosts; the hierarchy of the Officers, and who was responsible for what. She knew it all, but she didn't know *why* she knew it. It was all useless trivia. She couldn't change any of it. She had no say in how the City was run. She didn't even have anyone she could talk to about what she knew. Lissa and Sandi, much as she loved them, simply stared at her, uncomprehending, while the Lieutenant ...

... well, if she'd hoped that that moment of communication after the watchbot had rescued the three of them on Fifth Tier was a sign of a greater rapport to come—and she had—it had proved a fool's hope. He'd remained as distant and cold as ever.

She still didn't understand exactly what had happened that day. Certainly no similar opportunity to escape the Tier—or even the Quarters—had ever presented itself again. While she had indeed disabled the watchbot's sensors when she'd disconnected the wires inside its metal skull, it had repaired them itself the moment she was out of sight; she'd learned that, too, when her education had suddenly accelerated. She knew now that the watchbot's tumble down the stairs had been nothing but stage dressing for the theater of her supposed escape. She even suspected the Lieutenant had *hired* the young gangsters on Fifth to threaten them; they had been so suspiciously close at hand and the courtyard otherwise so utterly deserted ...

Alania shook her head. One of the hazards of spending so much time in her own mind was a tendency to overthink.

In any event, the restrictions on her movement were as tight as ever. Whereas all the girls in the dining room were also forced to hold formal parties like this one for their birthdays, afterward they traveled to their families' Estates in the country for more celebrations with their closest friends, young men included. Or they received gifts like water-breathing lessons in Lake Glass or balloon trips to the Green Plateau.

She held her formal party and then returned alone to her room to bury herself in books or music or video plays. *She* had never been water-breathing or ballooning. The closest she had come to leaving the City was standing on a balcony cut into the City's curving side and staring down at the mysterious white Cubes, five meters on a side, which lay in massive geometric piles to the east and west of the City. She had looked past them at the checkerboard of fields and plantations and workers' villages in the Heartland and finally at the distant, glittering glimmer of the ice-capped Iron Ring, wondering if she would ever be allowed to travel those open spaces herself.

For twenty years, she had been caged like a pet animal. A pampered pet, she had to admit—Quarters Beruthi was hardly Tenth-Tier Prison—but however lavish it might be, a cage was still a cage. The holographic stars overhead were the only stars she had ever seen.

Lissa and Sandi, seated together on her right, had been engrossed in whispered conversation since the Amazing Belgrani had finished his act. Now they glanced her way. Then they gave each other what Alania instantly recognized as a Significant Look.

Oh, no. They're going to try to make me feel better.

Sure enough, Lissa, closest to her, leaned in. "Millicred for your thoughts. You look like you're a thousand kilometers away."

Alania didn't *want* to feel better. She wanted to brood—having practiced brooding her whole life, she was very, very good at it—but she didn't want to hurt her friends' feelings, either, so she did her best to imitate the smile on Lissa's round brown face. "Just thinking. Sorry."

"You can't blame her for looking like she's at a funeral," Sandi put in. With her golden hair and snow-white complexion, made up to the hilt like every other young woman in the room, she looked more like a porcelain doll than a real person. "After all, a funeral would be more fun. Why our mothers put us through this . . ."

Her voice trailed off as Lissa lasered her with a look. "Sorry," she mumbled.

Alania sighed. "It's hardly news to me that I don't have a mother, Sandi," she said. "Or a father. I *have* noticed their absence from time to time over the past twenty years." She managed to dredge up another smile to take the sting out of her words. "I'm living proof that these horrible traditions exist independently of parents. Maybe they're Captain's Orders."

"May she live forever," Lissa and Sandi said in unison. Although in private they used the Captain's name in vain often enough, as Alania well knew, in public they were circumspect and careful to provide the properly-brought-up girl's automatic response to any reference to the Captain. Considering the Captain had supposedly ruled the City for some five centuries, Alania wondered why She needed benedictions from the beneficiaries of her beneficence.

Her unspoken alliteration pleased her enough to turn

her smile genuine. She took her amusement where she could find it.

"There," Lissa said triumphantly. "You *can* enjoy yourself."

"If you could do whatever you wanted for your birthday instead of hosting these stupid parties, what would it be?" Sandi asked.

"I'd go horseback riding," Lissa said instantly. "I only got to go that once, last summer out at our Retreat, and it was *incandescent*."

"Incandescent" was the current word of choice for something wonderful. Alania thought it a silly choice, but no one had asked her.

"I'd go paragliding off the Silver Cliffs," Sandi said dreamily. "What about you, Alania?"

"Me?" Her mouth quirked. "I don't know. Maybe a quick trip to Fifth?"

"Urgh," Sandi said. "No."

"*Definitely* no," Lissa added.

Alania laughed and felt better for it. "Well, since we're all stuck here instead, I guess we'll just have to make the best of it." Plates and platters were entering the room, borne by robots. Sala, in the vanguard, carried a silver tray covered with an opalescent dome, reminiscent of the dome atop Thirteenth Tier, beneath which the Captain supposedly lived. "I programmed our Master Chef to make my favorite: candied vatham with mashed sweebers and red gravy."

"Incandescent!" Sandi and Lissa said together, and Alania laughed again.

But the laugh died on her lips as a deep gong sounded, announcing a new arrival and interrupting the spangle-clad Seventh Tier Acrobats in the act of rushing into the room. The one in front pulled up short, and the others piled into her, knocking her to her hands and knees. She scrambled to her bare feet just as the dining room's main door slid silently open, its gold-trimmed black lacquer disappearing inside the matching walls.

Two men stood in the foyer beyond, both in the crisp white dress uniforms of Officers. Alania had been expecting Lieutenant Beruthi—more with resignation than the excitement she had felt when she was little and hadn't yet realized her childish affection for him was sadly misplaced. But the second man ...!

The second man was First Officer Kranz.

Conversation around the tables died when the gong sounded. Everyone turned to look as the two men entered. Now, with a collective intake of breath, all the girls rose to their feet, the movement starting in those nearest the door and rippling through the ranks. The acrobats backed out of the room in even greater disarray than that in which they had entered.

The ripple reached Sandi and Lissa, who jumped up. Alania stood last, much more slowly, the overheard words of the Lieutenant suddenly echoing in her mind: *You just have to wait and keep yourself safe for four more years, sir. Just four more years.*

Kranz, an easy smile on his face, flicked his left hand. "Please, ladies, be seated, be seated." Though he was not a large man, his deep, resonant voice effortlessly filled the big room. "Go on with your festivities."

The girls exchanged glances, then sat rather hesitantly. A few excited whispers broke out, and jewels glittered as tiara-bound heads tilted toward each other, but most of the guests watched wide-eyed as Kranz and Beruthi picked their way through the tables toward the dais, the robots deferentially rolling out of their way. Alania remained standing, watching them, and stepped back from the table to face them as they came up onto the dais to her right. Sala and Lissa quickly removed themselves to the far-left end of the table, hands folded and heads bowed.

"Guardian. First Officer," Alania heard herself say,

years of drilling in protocol and politeness somehow carrying her through her astonishment. "So kind of you to come."

"Happy birthday, Alania," Beruthi said. He didn't offer a hug or even a handshake; he never had, that she could remember.

"Thank you, sir."

"Yes, happy birthday," Kranz said. He was several centimeters shorter than Beruthi and much slimmer, and had an ordinary face framed by steel-gray hair, only a hint of brown remaining in it. He smiled, but it was a mere flexing of muscles; his ice-blue eyes did not warm. He held out his hand as he spoke, and Alania took it hesitantly. His palm was smooth and dry, his grip firm.

"Thank you, sir," she said, because she didn't have anything else to say.

Just four more years . . .

"I'm sorry to take you away from your dinner," Kranz went on as a robot lifted the dome covering the platter it had just set on the table in front of Alania. A savory-sweet smell rose from the pink mound of vatham, surrounded by scarlet mounds of mashed roots. "It looks delicious." He glanced toward the door through which the performers had retreated. "And the entertainment. The Seventh-Tier Acrobats are excellent."

"Lieutenant Beruthi hired them," Alania said.

"I know," Kranz said. "I recommended them to him." He turned back to Alania. "Unfortunately, however, I have another meeting this evening and can only stay a few moments, and I'd very much like to have a word with you, if I may?"

He made it sound like a request, but Alania knew it was nothing of the sort. "Of course, sir." She glanced at her guardian.

"The music room, Alania," he said. "I will fulfill your duties as host until you return."

Alania had a sudden incongruous image of Beruthi

attempting to make small talk with Sandi and Lissa, and despite her bewilderment, her mouth twitched with amusement. She turned to Kranz. "If you'll follow me, sir?" Fierce curiosity had replaced her initial alarm, and she had to admit that she enjoyed leading the First Officer—the *First Officer*!—past her wide-eyed guests, especially the ones she couldn't stand, like Bacrivia Jonquille, who looked like she'd just bitten into a puckerberry.

The music room contained a glittering white concert knabe, which Alania was spectacularly mediocre at playing; the instrument's three keyboards—plus foot pedals!—had defeated her. There were also enough string, brass, woodwind, and synth instruments to outfit an orchestra. None of them, so far as Alania knew, had ever been taken from the ceiling-high glass cabinets for dusting, much less playing. Apparently one of the previous Lieutenant Beruthis (or his or her spouse or offspring) had been musically inclined; the current one had no interest.

A rather spindly gold-colored couch and a matching chair huddled beside a low glass-topped table in the center of the black-and-white checkerboard-tiled floor. "Please have a seat," Kranz said, indicating the couch, and Alania settled herself primly on the very edge of the cushions. To her relief, Kranz remained standing; she'd been afraid he'd sit beside her and found the idea rather horrifying. He looked down at her, hands behind his back. "I won't keep you long. I know how anxious you must be to return to your party."

I doubt it, thought Alania. "I am entirely at your service, First Officer," she said demurely.

His gaze never wavered; she found it uncomfortable. "I remember when you were born," he said after a moment.

This, Alania thought, *is beyond weird*. He remembered when she was born? *Why?*

"You're too kind," she murmured, because she had to say *something*.

Kranz's mouth twitched. It wasn't much, but it was

closer to a real smile than the one he'd pasted onto his face back in the dining room. "And you've been very well brought up. Because I know perfectly well that what you really want to know is what in the Captain's Name I'm talking about."

Alania *had* been well brought up. It was one thing for her friends to take the Captain's name in vain in private, but to hear the First Officer do it so casually startled her despite herself. Something must have showed on her face, because Kranz's almost-smile broadened by perhaps a millimeter. "Pardon my language. I'm not used to the company of young ladies." He shrugged. "But that's about to change."

Alania took a giant mental step away from bemused and toward alarmed. "Sir?"

Kranz shook his head, the almost-smile melting into an irritated frown. "I'm not making inappropriate advances, Alania. I'm here to tell you that your circumstances are about to change for the better."

Alania said nothing. Eventually he *had* to tell her what he was talking about.

She hoped.

He looked toward the door. "Have you been happy as the ward of Lieutenant Beruthi?"

Alania blinked. "He . . . has taken very good care of me," she said carefully.

"He has done his duty well," Kranz said. He looked down at her again. "But you are twenty now. It is time for your new life to begin."

Here it comes, Alania thought, heart suddenly pounding. "Sir?"

"You're going to have a new guardian, Alania." Kranz spread his hands. "Me."

Alania stared at him. He might as well have said she was going to sprout wings and fly over the Iron Ring and out of the Homeland forever. Ward of the First Officer? Leave Quarters Beruthi, the only home she'd ever known? Yes, five minutes ago she'd been dreaming of just that, but she'd had in mind a trip into the country, or maybe shopping on Eighth or Ninth, not moving into Quarters Kranz. The idea was . . . ludicrous.

No, not ludicrous. *Terrifying.* Quarters Kranz, twice the size of Quarters Beruthi, was a fortress guarded by Provosts. She already felt like a prisoner in Quarters Beruthi. How much worse would it be there? She only had two friends. Would Lissa and Sandi even be able to visit her? And what about Sala?

She wanted to ask, but . . . this was the First Officer. You didn't question him that way. It would be impudent, improper, and very likely imprudent. If the whispered stories were true, some people who questioned Kranz's decisions had simply . . . vanished.

And looking at the unsmiling man in front of her, with blue eyes as cold and hard as cobalt steel, it was very difficult to discount those rumors.

"Sir, I . . . I don't know what to say," she murmured at last. "Why me? Who . . ." Her voice trailed off. *Who am I?* was another question she'd learned long ago would not be answered beyond the barest of facts: her parents were dead, and Beruthi had taken her in. How her parents had died, no one would tell her. Nor would they tell her why Beruthi, of all people, had become her guardian. Sala either did not know or would not say. Lissa and Sandi didn't have a clue. At parties, she'd overheard other girls speculating about it, some of them in ways that made her coldly furious and hotly embarrassed at the same time, but none of them *knew.*

Sometimes Alania thought her parents must have died bravely defending the Captain from assassins. Sometimes she thought instead that her parents must have been criminals and that her imprisonment was punishment for her poor choice of ancestors.

Sometimes she even toyed with the idea that her parents still lived somewhere, perhaps in exile far from the

City, and she was a hostage to their continued good behavior. It would explain why she was never allowed to travel into the countryside.

For a time when she was quite little, she'd believed that Beruthi felt guilty concerning her parents' deaths and had taken her in because he was a man of deep compassion. However, considering he'd shown no inkling of compassion, deep *or* shallow, in all the years since, she hadn't thought *that* in a very long time.

In any event, none of *those* explanations explained *this*. But she felt certain of one thing: this had something to do with that overheard conversation when she was sixteen and quite probably with her adventure to Fifth Tier, the one Beruthi had clearly arranged, and the subsequent change in her education.

"I can't tell you why," Kranz said. "Not yet. I promise I *will* as soon as I can, but for reasons of City security . . . not yet." His gaze sharpened still further, as if he were looking at a fascinating specimen through a microscope. "I have long been observing you, Alania Beruthi. You are important and special. Unique, in fact."

Unique? Me? How?

He stared at her intently a moment longer, then cleared his throat and glanced at his watch, breaking his intense focus on her, as though afraid he had betrayed more than he had intended . . . which he hadn't, since nothing he'd said made the slightest bit of sense to Alania. "Duty calls," he said. He lifted his eyes to her again. "Go back and enjoy your birthday party and final evening here, Alania. I will send an escort for you tomorrow—it will have to be rather early, I'm afraid—to bring you to Quarters Kranz. Everything from your rooms will be packed and moved for you; don't worry about that." He held out his right hand. She took it and let him help her to her feet.

She tried to pull free, but his grip tightened. "Just one more thing," he said. "A . . . precaution." He reached into his pocket with his free hand and pulled out a short metal tube, open at one end. "Hold out your hand."

Alania recognized the device. Every six months, a doctor came to examine her. She poked and prodded Alania from head to toe and then bundled her into the full-body docbot (kept in a room near the swimming pool) for an even more detailed examination. Alania was put to sleep for an hour during these exams, so she never knew exactly what was done to her. When she woke, the doctor helped her out of the docbot, then performed one final test: this one. Neither Beruthi nor the doctor would tell her what it was for, but at least she knew it wouldn't hurt. She held still as Kranz turned her hand over, then placed the open end of tube against her palm. He pressed a small switch on the tube's side. The light on the closed end of the tube flashed green, as it always did.

"Good." The tube vanished into Kranz's pocket. "Well then, I'll leave you to your celebrations, Alania. Once again, congratulations. I'll welcome you to your new home tomorrow." He strode to the door and out.

The moment he was gone, Alania's knees buckled, and she collapsed back onto the couch, feeling as if her whole world had not only been turned upside down but dropped on its head. She didn't want to return to the party, but she knew her guardian—her *former* guardian—must be tiring of Sandi and Lissa, whom she was even more certain must be tiring of *him*. Still, she had to sit another three or four minutes before she could gather wits and strength enough to rise.

Tomorrow I'm leaving this house forever, she thought as she walked to the music room door.

Twenty minutes ago, that would have seemed a dream come true.

Now it felt more like the start of a nightmare.

Kranz was not a frivolous man, but he was willing to admit—to himself, if no one else—that he *was* somewhat vain about his position as de facto ruler of the City. And so, though it was not strictly necessary, he exited Quarters Beruthi as he had entered: right through the middle of Alania's birthday celebration, although this time without endangering the acrobats, who would not resume their act until Alania returned. Along the way he rescued Lieutenant Beruthi from the attentions of Alania's two young friends. He pasted one of his bright-but-utterly-fake smiles onto his face and waved to the rest of the girls as he passed them. Unusually, despite the enormous, pressing sense of urgency and approaching calamity that darkened every hour of his days, he felt the smile turn genuine as he and the Lieutenant made their way to the main entrance. "You've done good work, looking after her all these years," he said to Beruthi.

"Thank you, sir," said the Lieutenant.

"I'm sorry to have to take her away. I'm sure you've grown very fond of her."

Beruthi opened one side of the double front door. "No, sir. I have been very careful not to."

Kranz stepped through the door onto a broad portico overlooking a small garden-courtyard, one of many scattered through Twelfth Tier. Other Officer's Quarters bordered the other three sides. Six Provosts stood at attention on the broad stairs leading up to Beruthi's front door, three to a side: Kranz's bodyguards. He turned to Beruthi. "Very wise, Lieutenant Commander."

Beruthi froze in the act of closing the door, then turned toward Kranz somewhat jerkily, as though he were one of his robots with a motor-function fault. "Sir?"

"You heard me," Kranz said. He held out his hand. Beruthi took it, and he shook it firmly. "Congratulations on your promotion. Considering everything the Beruthi clan has done for the City, the First Officers, and of course, the Captain ... it's long overdue." He released the new Lieutenant Commander's hand and looked up at the house's imposing greenstone façade. "Although considering how Beruthi Robotics has prospered in its long service to the City, I don't believe there'll be any need to find you quarters more befitting your rank."

"No, sir," Beruthi said. "But the honor to the Beruthi name . . . I'm very appreciative."

You should be, Kranz thought. Promotions were few and far between; the last one had raised Sub-Lieutenant Praterus, father of Alania's friend Sandi, to the rank of Lieutenant fifteen years ago, after Lieutenant Sparrow had carelessly drowned while water-breathing before fathering an heir or even freezing sperm. Since Beruthi had never married, remained childless, had likewise failed to bank his genetic material, and was already in his fifties, Kranz thought it likely the promotion and the Beruthi name would end with this generation. He didn't understand why Beruthi had chosen that course of action. Perhaps it was due to a misguided desire for revenge—he knew the current Beruthi had hated his own father. Whatever the reason, it was of no real concern to Kranz or the City; if the Beruthi line failed, there were many others eager to take over his rank, Beruthi Robotics, and especially his luxurious Quarters, Estate, and Retreat. Science Officer Prentis came to mind . . .

"No need to accompany me further; I'll make my own way from here," Kranz said. He nodded to the Provost Captain who commanded his bodyguards and started down the steps, the Provosts falling in behind him and to either side.

The unnatural lightening of his mood faded as he crossed the garden-courtyard. One of the few green indicators on the Captain's status panel had slipped to yellow just that morning, something to do with liver function; a week before, a yellow indicator had turned red as she entered the last stages of heart failure. The medical machinery had been pushed to the limit, and so had her ancient, frail body, which was aswarm with nanobots. As for her mind ... well, that had been overwritten so many times it barely connected with reality anymore.

The City had been declining for decades, but the rate of decline had increased during Kranz's lifetime, as the Captain slowly failed. Living in a world of delusion, the Captain did not give the orders that would have sent out the maintenance robots to fix failing systems; she believed all systems were operating normally. The cursed Builders had insured that *only* the Captain could give those orders, and despite everything else he had accomplished, First Officer Thomas Kranz, Kranz's original, had not been able to change that.

Of course, there were *some* things humans could fix on their own, but there were many more they couldn't, because they didn't have access to the necessary details of the City's construction, which were locked within databases only the Captain could access. All repairs were jury-rigged at best, and some attempts at repair only made things worse. From the smoothly functioning, integrated machine it had been at its founding, the City had deteriorated to little more than an extremely large and ugly building housing far more people than it had been designed to hold.

Kranz's hands clenched at his sides. Four years ago, he had almost despaired. The suicide of his clone, Falkin, meant that he would be the last First Officer Kranz. He had wanted to advance to the endgame of the Cityborn Project then, afraid that something would happen to him and that all the knowledge—the dark, secret knowledge—that had been passed through the Kranz line since its beginning would be lost. Without that knowledge, the City would fail finally and utterly, and everyone in and around it would eventually die.

But as Beruthi had reminded him then, there had been no way to hurry things along. Alania had not been ready, her brain not yet developed enough. And so, for the four years since Falkin's death, the fate of the City had dragged on Kranz ever more heavily. The fear that he might die by accident or assassination despite every precaution or that the Captain would die too soon filled his days with dread and his nights with nightmares

Kranz shook his head, furious all over again at the raid twenty years ago that had forced him to put all his eggs in one Alania-sized basket. Seven candidate children had been produced. Genetics dictated a fifty-fifty chance any particular child would be suitable. Sure enough, of the seven, only three had been. Of those three, one boy, Danyl, had been stolen away by Erlkin Orillia. The second, a girl, had been murdered. No doubt Alania would have been murdered as well if she had not been fortuitously ill that evening and held in a different part of the hospital. The unsuitable children had been left unharmed by the kidnapper, though of course Kranz himself had ordered their elimination, just a few months later, once he was certain they were of no use to the project.

As for the kidnapped boy . . .

Nobody knew why Orillia had stolen Danyl, but there was no doubt he was behind the kidnapping and the murder. He had made no effort to conceal his meddling with the environmental and security controls, to cause convenient blackouts to cover his entrance into the hospital, and he had left an equally clear trail afterward. Not fifteen minutes after the boy was taken, Orillia's personal aircar had launched from the same hangar from which Falkin had flown to his death sixteen years later. Orillia had also disabled the City's air traffic control systems, so his flight had not been tracked. It had taken the Provosts a week to locate the aircar, abandoned in the foothills of the eastern reaches of the Iron Ring. Any trail that might have led from it had vanished beneath fresh snow, the first freezing onslaught of a particularly vicious winter.

Neither Orillia nor the boy had been seen since. Whatever his plans, it seemed clear that the Ensign and the baby must have perished in the Iron Ring, as had many other people foolishly seeking freedom there from the rule of the Captain. Neither the vegetation nor the wildlife could be safely eaten—the wildlife couldn't safely eat humans, either, but that didn't stop it from trying—so all food had to be stolen from the farmlands. Such thefts were always discovered sooner or later, and the Provosts inevitably arrested the thieves shortly after that, if they even bothered taking them alive, which they usually didn't. Some bandits had survived for a year or two, but never longer.

Kranz had spent several fruitless days hoping Orillia *would* be found so he could thoroughly, painfully, *fatally* interrogate him. The man had almost destroyed everything.

But not quite, because Alania had escaped. Beruthi, who knew more about the true scope of Kranz's plans than anyone else—the Beruthis had been loyal supporters of the Kranzes since the beginning—had raised her as his ward. Carefully watched her whole life, carefully educated, she was the only one who could save the City.

Tomorrow she would be safely ensconced in Quarters Kranz, though not for long. Within a week, she would fulfill her destiny, and the City would be reborn.

Today, though . . .

He sighed. Today he still had mounds of reports to get through and dozens of decisions to make. Not to mention an execution to attend on Tenth. As Kranz and his bodyguards exited the courtyard, he glanced over his shoulder at Quarters Beruthi, sheltering Alania, the Cityborn, behind its tall stone-covered walls, as it had for twenty years. *This had better work. It's our last chance.*

It will work, he reassured himself, facing forward again. *She'll be in my Quarters tomorrow, and she won't be out of my sight again after that. When the time comes, she'll be ready.*

And so will I.

FIVE

ON THE DAY after his twentieth birthday, Danyl woke early to the insistent beeping of his watch. He groaned but rolled out of bed at once; within two hours, he *had* to be in position.

His feet hit icy rock, and he gasped a little. He could have had a rug by his bedside, of course, but he preferred the shock of the cold stone against the soles of his bare feet. He could have made the room warmer, too, but the isotope-powered space heater Erl claimed to have found and repaired long before Danyl was born stood cold in the corner. Danyl had found that rising naked in a chilly underground chamber was another excellent method of bringing oneself to alertness.

Shivering, he grabbed his underwear, pants, and shirt from where he'd dropped them on the floor the night before, pulled them on, tugged socks onto his feet, and padded out of his chamber and down the hallway to the bathroom. He didn't shower; he'd definitely need a shower after the day's adventure, and why shower twice? Bladder relieved, he washed his hands and went in search of breakfast.

Erl was in the kitchen, through an archway to his right as he entered the living/dining room. No matter how early Danyl rose, Erl woke first and had breakfast waiting. Danyl paused in the archway, breathing in the comforting smells of fresh bread and crisping vatham.

Erl stood by the cookbox, which looked as new now as it did in Danyl's earliest memories. Erl claimed he'd scavenged it and the meat-growing vat next to it just a month or two before he'd scavenged Danyl, bringing the squalling infant he'd found abandoned in the Middens into his hideaway to raise as a son, but Danyl had never seen anything in such pristine shape in the Middens since.

Or another infant, he reminded himself. *Yet here I am. Just because something is highly improbable doesn't mean it is impossible.* He liked to remind himself of that every single day, since all his hopes for the future rested on it being true.

He took the plate Erl proffered him, then sat at the table in the main room to eat his breakfast. The bread dripped with sweet oil, obtained through trade at the Last Chance Market like all their foodstuffs other than the vatmeat, and he savored his first mouthful in silence before asking, "What do you expect today?"

"Not certain," Erl said. "But I have high hopes. Some Officer died without an heir, and someone else is taking over her Quarters on Twelfth Tier and throwing out everything she doesn't want. Could be anything from bed sheets to 'tronics. I'm hoping for 'tronics, of course." He lifted the lid of the pot he was heating on the cookbox, sniffed the pot's contents, then replaced the lid. "Best thing: it's a Direct Drop."

Danyl's fork stopped in midair. "A Direct Drop? From *Twelfth*?" Direct Drops, Drops that simply fell out of the bottom of the City without being sorted by the desultory recycling crews who worked on the First Tier, were rare. They occurred only when those crews— mostly made up of drunks and addicts who didn't work very hard or very well, which was why so much salvage made it to the Middens at all—were unable to keep up with the trash generated by the many Tiers above them. But a Direct Drop from Eleventh or Twelfth—Officer

Country—was unheard of. Any Direct Drop might contain treasures. But one from Officer Country . . . ?

This could be the day.

Trying to hide his excitement, Danyl gave a thoughtful nod. "I'll keep my eyes open," he said, then resumed eating.

"You always do," Erl said.

Danyl didn't ask how Erl knew what would be Dropped that morning or where it was coming from; he knew Erl wouldn't tell him. "Mystical means of divination" was the closest he'd ever gotten to an answer, but Erl wasn't mystical about anything *else*. Danyl suspected Erl had some sort of contact very high up in the City, possibly through the trader who had helped rescue him from the trashslide when he was twelve, though he couldn't imagine how a Last Chance Market trader could have high-level City contacts, either.

He shoveled in the rest of his breakfast, uneasily aware of the passing time. "Better be going," he said, wiping his mouth with a ragged-but-clean napkin and getting to his feet.

Erl took the kaffpot off the cookbox and poured its steaming blue-black contents into a silvery tube. He twisted it closed, then handed it to Danyl. "Be careful."

"Always," Danyl said. Tube of kaff in hand, he opened the steel door, revealing a tunnel with smooth walls of reddish stone. That smoothness and precision, here and in the rest of their dwelling, was testament to the undeniable fact that excavation bots from the City had carved out their hidden refuge sometime in the distant past. Why, Danyl didn't have a clue, and Erl claimed he didn't either. Danyl wondered if it had something to with the Cubes, many of which were scattered on the other side of the fenced and fortified Canyon Rim above them. Since no one knew what the Cubes were, why they had been placed there, or what, if anything, their impenetrable shells might hide, the notion was only idle speculation.

Just before he reached what looked like a dead end, Danyl stepped into a side chamber. It smelled of decaying food and mold and general rot, but he hardly noticed; it was the smell of the Middens, nothing more. He pulled on a hooded coverall made of tough synthileather, painted and stained to a muddy brown color, overlaid with green and yellow smears. Around his waist, he buckled a tool belt from which hung pliers, a hammer, a good-sized crowbar, and his particular pride and joy: an actual sword, a Provost's ceremonial blade that had somehow been lost in the Middens, which Erl had given him on his fourteenth birthday. Thanks to the virtual reality teaching machine, he even knew how to use it.

He pushed his socked feet into dark green waterproof boots, hung a pair of shiny black gloves and the tube of kaff from his belt, tugged the hood of the coat into place, and snugged the attached goggles over his eyes. Then he went out into the corridor, reached into an alcove in the wall, and pulled the metal handle inside. Silently, the stone blocking the end of the corridor swung inward, letting in a flood of mist-softened light. Danyl stepped through, then turned around and pushed at a protrusion in the cliff. It sank in a couple of centimeters. The stone door swung back into place, and the entrance vanished.

Danyl turned. He stood in a one-room shack, furnished solely with two rude rag-covered cots on either side of a circular stone depression in the floor, blackened by fire. A few old pots and even older clothes hung from hooks on the walls, which were made of different-sized planks of wood chinked with scraps of metal and plastic. Orange plastic roofed the shed, held up by a central metal pole rising from the middle of the fireplace. A ragged smoke hole was cut in the plastic just to one side of the pole.

Not for the first time, Danyl thanked the Captain that Erl had been the one to find his infant self mysteriously abandoned in the Middens. This hovel hid their real living quarters in the comfort of the tunnels, but had Danyl been scavenged by one of the gangs, he really would be living in a place like this . . . or far worse.

More likely, he would already be dead.

The thought of the gangs propelled him out the door. He needed to reach the Drop Zone unseen and get tucked out of sight before the Drop. If the Rustbloods got there first . . .

He didn't like to think about that. He'd seen the remains of Rustbloods, losers in some internal power struggle, staked out as punishment in the Middens in the primary Drop Zones. If they didn't starve or die of thirst first, they died when tons of garbage fell on them from the City's Bowels.

Danyl didn't want to die. He *especially* didn't want to die buried in garbage. He'd escaped that fate twice: once as a baby, once when the trashslide caught him when he was twelve. He intended to keep right on escaping it.

No one lived directly under the City, in what was known as (rather unimaginatively) the Undercity. The residents of the Middens stayed out here, where sunlight could still reach during at least part of the day and where the rubbish was years or decades old. Half a kilometer deep, the Middens grew every day, not just from City trash but from rubbish from all over the Heartland, which automated disposal trucks dumped into massive chutes near the main gate.

Every few years, a trashalanche—a massive, roaring catastrophe that dwarfed the ordinary trashslides— thundered down the middle of the Canyon. To avoid that and other hazards, the wisest and longest-lived of the Middens' various squatters clung to the Canyon walls. One of those walls, the east one, rose fifty sheer meters directly behind the hovel, barren of vegetation, a mass of smooth red rock offering no purchase to anyone who might think to climb out of the Canyon into the Heartland above. Not that succeeding at such a climb would do the climber any good—armed bots patrolled a fenced no-man's-land on the Rim and would shoot to kill anyone who so much as raised his head up above ground level.

Danyl ignored the Canyon wall. He had to make a different climb: dangerous, but at least not impossible.

The Middens sloped sharply up to his right. Overgrown with sickly green weeds and with noxious streams trickling through the valleys between the mounds, it might almost have been mistaken for a natural—if highly unpleasant—landscape. But dig into it, Danyl knew, and you would find no honest soil, nothing but moldy paper and cloth, rotting wood and rusting steel. Dig too deep or in the wrong place, and you might never dig again, should you puncture one of the bubbles of gas trapped beneath the surface. You'd die of incineration should the gas ignite, asphyxiation if it didn't; neither choice appealed to Danyl. Smart travelers through the Middens— if that wasn't a contradiction in terms—stuck to the well-marked paths.

But the well-marked paths were also well-watched by the Rustbloods and the handful of solo scavengers, and so Danyl ignored the one that wended its way past the base of the rickety stairs leading down from the hovel's door. Instead he cut across it and over two ridges, their surfaces quaking like gel beneath his feet, to follow his own path. It was as safe as the others—or nearly so—but secret, picked out with markings only he could recognize: a twisted bit of aluminum, a blue wire stuck into a piece of packing foam, a doll's head. It wound up the mountain of trash between tottering piles that hid it from any watchers along the Canyon walls.

Looking up to the first marker, an upside-down jug of red plastic, he took note of the City for the first time that morning.

From down here you couldn't see much of it, but Danyl didn't need to; he had studied it in detail in the teaching machine. He knew it was shaped like a giant, elongated egg, pointy end up, bottom end flattened and truncated; that it had thirteen Tiers, plus the Bowels at its base; that the Captain lived alone in luxury under the pearly dome at the very top and had supposedly done so for centuries, though how that was possible Danyl didn't know; that the Officers lived in the two Tiers below that, and the rest of the populace lived in the Tiers below those. But Danyl had never seen the inside of a City Tier except in simulations, where they were devoid of people and looked as they had on the Day of Awakening, which had very little to do with the way they looked now. All he had ever personally seen of the City was what he could see from here. The Bowels, the four-story black underbelly of the City, hung in his sky like a permanent thundercloud of metal, supported by four impossibly massive jointed legs on enormous feet, sunk so far in the stone the legs seemed more to grow out of the Canyon walls than to rest upon them. They held the City in its permanent crouch above the Canyon, some two hundred and fifty meters wide at this point.

Danyl kept climbing, and ten minutes later, he passed into the City's shadow. There he paused, breathing hard, and took a welcome swig of hot, bitter kaff while he studied the Bowels.

That metal overcast was far from featureless. At the very center of the Bowels gaped an enormous opening, stretching right up through the Bowels to the underside of First Tier, as though there had once been some vast mechanism there that had been dismantled. Everywhere else, yellow, red, and pale-green lights glowed and flashed and rotated amidst a bewildering maze of pipes and chutes, exhaust vents and antennae. Things clanked and swung, groaned and twirled. Black, oily ooze slicked large areas, like pus from some vast, infected wound. Sometimes streams of boiling green liquid poured from the pipes, sizzling when they hit the trash. Sometimes steam erupted in vast howling clouds, hot enough to scald the skin from a man should he be unlucky enough to be caught in it. At fairly regular intervals, one of fifty-six huge hatches opened, a chute extruded like a vast tongue of bronze metal, and the City excreted another mass of trash, sending it thundering down into the Middens in a cloud of choking dust and stink.

Shortly afterward, the scavengers always arrived.

In the City above, social rank determined the Tier on which you lived: Captain, then Officers, the higher ranks on Twelfth, the lower ranks on Eleventh; factory owners and celebrities; small business people and skilled artisans; workers and shopkeepers. Each tier was a little larger, a little more crowded, and a little more common than the one above.

Down at the very bottom, just above the Bowels—or sometimes within them—lived the most menial of workers: the cleaners and swabbers and garbage-sorters, and a few starving artists.

And then, down here in the Middens . . . down here lived those who had fallen so far from respectable society that they had plunged out of the City altogether.

Thieves, murderers, escaped convicts; addicts, abused children and their abusers; those chased from the City and those who had fled, the City as willing to be rid of them as they were to be rid of it. Sometimes the City even provided safe passage down into the Middens via the Last Chance Market . . . but a path up again was only possible for those with City Passes. Once you moved into the Middens, you no longer had the right to even enter the City, much less live in it.

These human dregs were even more unwelcome in the Heartland than in the City, hunted down and arrested (or shot) if they dared to try to flee out into the illusory peace of the farm country. So they fetched up with the rest of the City's trash in this place of final resort, where only the strong-arm tactics of the gangs—

Rustbloods on this side of the City, Greenskulls on the other—held total anarchy at bay.

Erl had never said how he had ended up down here. As for himself, Danyl liked to think he was the illegitimate offspring of some powerful Officer who would swoop down and take him to his true home on Twelfth Tier someday. But knew in his heart that he was most likely nothing but the unwanted—and for some reason unaborted and unstrangled—by-blow of a meaningless liaison between Rustbloods, born in the Middens and likely to die there.

But not today, he told himself as he resumed his scramble up a shaking slope of paper, precariously welded together by damp and mold. *Not on the first day of my twenty-first year. And maybe . . . just maybe . . . not ever.*

Because Danyl had a plan. He wanted up and out, into the City. Even the Bowels had to be better than here, and he would work his way out of them and up the Tiers as far as he could, given half a chance.

Thanks to Erl's mysteriously obtained teaching machine, he knew the layout of the City in detail. He understood City technology. He knew how to fight barehanded or with any weapon that came to hand. He even knew how to shoot, though he'd never held a real weapon. He could take care of himself in the City, but to get there, he needed a City Pass. With that, he could walk right in through the main entrance. A Pass wouldn't guarantee him a job or a place to sleep or food to eat, but then, neither did the Middens.

He didn't need a handout. He just needed an opportunity.

And maybe, just maybe, he'd find something in today's Drop that would give it to him.

At the top of the paper mountain, he lay flat and slowly raised his head to examine the west wall of the Canyon, two hundred meters away. The Rustbloods kept a lookout there sometimes . . . but today no one moved atop their platform of scrap lumber and rusty iron. Danyl seized his moment and snaked over the top of the mound on his belly, then rolled down the other side in a cloud of stinking dust, splashing into a stagnant pool at the bottom. He ignored the damp and the smell, scrambled up, and squeezed between the rusting hulks of two old-fashioned groundcars. He found himself in the dim shade of the most secret of his paths: a narrow, winding almost-tunnel always threatening to collapse but never quite doing so—at least, not yet. Thick yellow-green tangleweed leaves shaded the path for more than a hundred meters. When he emerged at its end, he'd be safely past Rustblood territory and on the verge of the no-man's-land of the Undercity . . . and not far from the small, seldom-opened hatch through which Erl predicted today's very special Drop would arrive.

A Direct Drop from Officer Country! Danyl let the excitement he'd squelched in Erl's presence ratchet up again as he squeezed between walls of compacted paper, crawled under rusting girders, and eased past corroded, goo-oozing barrels. The trader he'd talked to four years ago had made it clear that if he were ever going to escape the Middens, he needed a big score. Someone up above needed to make a mistake and discard something valuable—valuable enough that Danyl could barter it at the Last Chance Market for a Pass.

The trader had known of only two examples, but in the four years since Danyl had spoken to him, there had been a third: one of the Rustbloods had unearthed a locked box containing . . . something. No one knew what, but she'd knifed two of her gangmates to keep it and get it to the Market, and she'd gotten her City Pass.

Of course, two weeks later, she'd shown up in a Drop as a naked, bloody corpse, presumably having been robbed, raped, and murdered by one of the equally vicious lower-Tier City gangs, but that wouldn't happen to Danyl. Just let him into the City, and he would make a new life for himself, and then he'd come back and free Erl from this hellhole, too.

It could happen. It *would* happen. And maybe, just maybe, it would happen today.

He reached the end of the almost-tunnel and, crouching in the shade of its mouth, peered out into what Erl had said would be today's Drop Zone. It was within a few dozen meters of a familiar landmark: the Hazardous Waste Holding Tank, filled with the most dangerous of the many nasty liquids discharged from the City, originating from the factories and Captain knew where else. As Danyl knew from his studies, it had originally contained a multitude of special tanks, each designed to hold a particular type of hazardous waste. When a tank filled, it was supposed to be hauled away for safe disposal elsewhere. But the interior tanks had long since vanished, the roof that had covered them had been stripped away, and even the baffles meant to separate the tanks had corroded and failed. Now there was only a single hellish lake, a witch's brew that gave off noxious, corrosive vapors and bubbled and seethed as though boiling—and into which new waste was still pumped on a regular basis. The only time he'd ever seen anything leave that tank was in a steaming, deadly gush of fluid as an overflow valve triggered automatically. The liquid had eaten through four stories of trash before vanishing into the depths of the Middens. If the main tank walls ever failed, Danyl thought the resulting flood would burn its way to the Canyon floor and probably cause a massive collapse of the trash pile on which he now stood. Whether anyone in the Middens would survive such a calamity, he didn't know—but he doubted it.

One more reason to get *out*.

Nothing moved—nothing he could *see*, at least, in the uncertain light beneath the vast metal sky. The gangs didn't have access to Erl's mysterious knowledge of Drops, so Danyl almost always had a few minutes to himself before and, most crucially, after a Drop, especially a Drop from a little-used hatch like this one. But only a few, and how few depended on how close he was to one of the gangs' compounds.

Today he was very close indeed. Even if the Rustbloods didn't know this particular Drop was about to take place, it wouldn't take them long to react once it began.

Which should be any moment. Danyl gathered his legs under him and waited.

For a minute ... two ... an eerie silence hung over the Middens. And then ...

High overhead, a light that had been burning green suddenly turned red and started to flash. A klaxon sounded, a harsh blatting sound, and Danyl knew Rustblood watchers would be scrambling onto their platforms to pinpoint the site of the impending Drop.

The klaxon sounded for thirty seconds. Then, with a spine-chilling screech, a rusty-red hatch irised open, and Danyl's heart suddenly beat faster.

'Tronics? Maybe. Weapons, datadots, jewelry ... *anything* could end up falling into the Middens in a Direct Drop from Twelfth.

My City Pass, Danyl thought.

The hatch was fully dilated. The Drop Ramp emerged, suspended on cables, red lights flashing from its lower end. And then ...

With a thunderous, scraping tumult, the Drop began.

This Drop was better organized than most; everything seemed to be encased in giant plastic bags the color of moldy bread. There was no way to tell what was in any of them, and Danyl felt a jolt of dismay. Digging through those would take time, time he almost certainly didn't have, not when the Rustbloods had to be gearing up even as he—

Then something slid from the chute that wasn't encased in plastic: a giant bundle of cloth. Curtains, bedding, carpet, or all three—he couldn't tell. The cloth caught the air and slowed as it fell, billowing like a parachute.

And from the middle of that falling mass of cloth, Danyl heard the last thing he'd ever expected to hear, the one thing that could make him forget about 'tronics or jewelry or all the other possible riches this fresh Drop from high atop the City might contain.

He heard a girl's scream.

SIX

ALANIA SLEPT POORLY the night after Kranz's unexpected appearance at her birthday party. She was rather surprised she slept at all, but her body's need for rest eventually overcame even the churning resistance of her troubled mind, which kept turning the events of the day over and over and over . . . to no avail, of course. The deed was done. She was the ward of First Officer Kranz now, and clearly that had always been the plan, the subject of that strange overheard conversation four years before, after Kranz's son died in the aircar crash.

Unsatisfactory as she had found her life in Quarters Beruthi, the more she thought of abandoning the only home she had ever known for the company of the First Officer, the more the prospect terrified her. When she did sleep, her dreams were of the trapped-in-a-dark-room-with-a-noisily-breathing-monster-and-unable-to-find-the-way-out variety, from which she kept waking with a pounding heart and sweating body, only to fall back asleep and experience it all over again.

Sala came into her room in the morning far earlier than usual. She turned on the lamp in the corner by the door, put down the silver breakfast tray she carried, then opened the shutters, letting in the wan glow of imitation predawn twilight. Alania sat up and blinked blearily at the clock. 0600. She *never* got up that early.

Sala turned back from the windows. "I'm afraid it's time to rise, miss. I've brought your breakfast."

She'd done just that every morning Alania could remember—but *this* morning, without warning, she suddenly dropped into a chair against the dark-paneled wall and buried her head in her hands, sobbing.

Alania was up out of bed in a moment and kneeling beside her. "Sal, what's wrong?"

"You're leaving, miss," Sala choked out. "And so am I."

For a moment Alania's heart leaped with hope. "You're coming with me?"

But Sala looked up at her, face chalk-white, eyes red with weeping, and shook her head mutely.

"Oh, Sala." Alania's heart suddenly jolted. *Beruthi's fired her!* "But there's no cause for that! He could give you other duties—" But of course Beruthi's robots did all other duties, and she knew it. Barefoot in her thin pink nightgown, she suddenly felt very cold. She wrapped her arms around herself. "You've always . . . You said you needed this job, for your family . . ."

"It's all right, miss. I'll be fine. Please don't worry about me. It's just . . . I'll miss you." Sala's sobs suddenly stopped. A red spot flamed on each white cheek. "But before I go . . . before you go . . ." She stood up so suddenly Alania took a step back.

"What?"

Sala didn't say anything, just extended her arms. Confused, Alania accepted the proffered hug. Sala's lips brushed her right ear. "Look in the corbels," she barely breathed. Then she stepped back again. "Thank you, miss." She turned away and busied herself with the breakfast tray.

Look in the . . . ? Alania knew what corbels were: the carved, ornamental brackets that pretended to support each end of the gold-painted ceiling beams. In fact, as she knew from the detailed lessons in the City's construction that she'd begun at Beruthi's insistence after the aborted trip to Fifth Tier, the beams were steel with a thin overlay of expensive wood from the forests of the Iron Ring. There were twelve of them in her room, running lengthwise. She looked up at them. They were identical . . .

. . . except for the one in the center, at the end of the beam that ran directly over her bed. In that one, almost invisible in the dark furrow between two ridges of wood, there was a small black circle. She'd stared up at it many times and always thought it was nothing more than a flaw in the wood. After all, what else could it be?

I have long been observing you, Kranz had told her.

Her heart skipped a beat.

Oh, no, she thought. *No. Lieutenant Beruthi would never have . . . Kranz wouldn't . . .*

Long been observing you. And Sala didn't want to say anything out loud.

A small round hole . . .

The truth hit her like a bucket of ice water to the face. *There's a camera in my room. Someone has been watching me. When I'm sleeping. When I'm eating.*

When I change clothes.

When I come out of the bath.

My whole life.

She wanted to scream. She wanted to throw up. But if she reacted at all, Sala would get into trouble. Maybe *permanent* trouble. If the rumors about Kranz were true, maybe even *fatal* trouble.

Alania stood. She didn't look at the incriminating corbel again. But she didn't unfold her arms from her chest, either. "I'm going to get dressed," she said. "It's going to be a long day."

"Yes, miss," Sala said, still not looking at Alania. "I'm to tell you your escort will arrive at 0730. And not to worry about your things. I'll pack them up and have them sent after you."

Alania nodded. She went over to her dresser and carefully but casually kept her back to the suspicious corbel, trying not to hunch her shoulders—though the urge was strong—as she slipped off her nightgown and pulled on her most modest, ordinary clothes: tough, dark-blue duracloth pants, soft, black, calf-high leather boots, and a red long-sleeved pseudosilk blouse. She brushed her long brown hair and tied it up in a sensible ponytail. Only then did she turn around and make her way over to the waiting breakfast.

She forced herself to eat, though she still felt ill. Whatever happened to her today, she wanted the energy to face it.

Once she'd finished breakfast, she went to the door, intending to take a last walk around Quarters Beruthi before her escort arrived.

It wouldn't open.

She turned back to Sala, who was putting the breakfast dishes back on the tray. "Why is the door locked?" Alania asked. Despite her best efforts, her voice rose in both pitch and volume.

Sala didn't look at her and most definitely did not look at that suspicious corbel. "I don't know, miss."

Except you do, don't you? Alania looked at her servant—until today, she would also have called her her friend and confidante—with narrowed eyes. For the first time, it occurred to her to wonder if the arrival of Kranz had been as big a surprise to Sala as it had been to her. Sala, who had obviously known about the hidden camera *and had never told her*.

Rage suddenly swept through her like a wall of red flame racing across a slick of oil. She wanted to attack Sala, scream at her, demand to know why she was being spied on, how Sala could have known about it but never told her . . . but she forced her fury down under the surface. She couldn't do that to Sala. How *could* Sala have told her? She had a family, friends, people who might be in danger. First Officer Kranz had to be behind the surveillance, and no one crossed him with impunity. If she revealed that Sala had finally told her at the last possible moment, innocent people might suffer.

I'm *innocent*, she thought angrily. I'm *suffering. Why shouldn't others? I've been in prison my whole life, watched and guarded and manipulated. But why?*

She had no answer, and however much she wanted to, she couldn't demand answers of Sala and still live with herself once her anger finally faded.

Sala turned with the breakfast tray. "Excuse me, miss," she said, and Alania moved aside to let her reach the door.

For her, it opened. Alania glimpsed a bulky man in a white uniform on the other side. He closed the door firmly again in Sala's wake. When Alania tried it a moment later, it once more refused to budge.

Alania prowled her room for the next three-quarters of an hour like the caged bloodweasel from the Iron Ring she had once seen displayed in the drawing room of a great house during a Winter Festival dance. In the end, she dragged a chair directly under the camera, hopefully out of its field of view—*though who knows how many others are hidden elsewhere*, she thought bitterly—folded her hands in her lap, and waited.

At precisely 0730 hours, as promised, the door opened, and her escort entered to take her to Quarters Kranz.

There were two Provosts. Rather than wearing their usual dark-blue duty uniforms, they were resplendent in white dress uniforms with red piping on their trousers and caps and gilded, glittering body armor. *Kranz wants to convince me they're honor guards, not prison guards*, Alania thought sourly. They each wore a slugthrower on one hip and a sword on the other, and their eyes were invisible behind the mirrored visors of their golden helmets.

"Come with us," said the one who was slightly shorter,

though both were tall enough to tower over Alania even after she clambered to her feet.

She looked past them at the open door. It might as well have been a million kilometers away. There was nowhere to run, and she had no doubt one of them would simply pick her up and sling her over his shoulder if she resisted in any way.

She'd been humiliated enough. She stood straight, brushed her red blouse smooth with hands that only trembled a little, and nodded.

The taller of the Provosts stepped to one side and motioned her through the door. Head high, she left her room at Quarters Beruthi for the last time.

The hall was empty. She led the Provosts—she refused to let *them* lead *her*—past the discreet door to the servants' stairs where she and Sandi and Lissa had hidden from the watchbot she'd thought she'd disabled all those years ago. She descended the red-carpeted treads of the stairs down which the watchbot had tumbled, trailing her fingers along the gleaming brass of the banister. In the marble-floored entrance hall, she glanced one last time into the dining room where her birthday party had been the evening before. The decorations had vanished as though they had never existed; no stars twinkled on the high vaulted ceiling.

But at the far end of the room, behind the table where Alania had been sitting when First Officer Kranz had so unexpectedly inserted himself in her life, she saw Sala watching her. Their eyes met. Alania gave her a long, cold stare, then deliberately looked away and walked on toward the foyer and the tall double doors of the main entrance.

One of the Provosts increased his pace and moved past her to open them for her. "Thank you," she said, the first words she had said to them, and stepped out onto the portico.

Imitation sunlight poured through illumination panels

far above, making the just-watered greenery sparkle in the garden-courtyard Quarters Beruthi fronted. The air breezing in through the man-high ventilation pipes hidden among the bushes smelled moist and fresh. In the world outside, it must have been a beautiful autumn morning.

But Alania had never visited the world outside the City. Now it seemed likely she never would.

Together, she and her taciturn escorts walked through the park, out through its ornate iron gate, and into the street. Two black-clad servants hurrying by gave the Provosts and Alania a wide berth. The Provosts turned in the opposite direction from the servants. Alania didn't look back to see if they were staring after her; she was sure that they were.

They passed the homes of many of the girls who had been at her party. Quarters Smilkoni: that was Lissa's house. It had windows overlooking the street, but though Alania looked up, she didn't see anyone watching from them.

Quarters Eltha. Quarters Praterus, Sandi's house. Quarters Jonquille, home of the odious Bacrivia. No one looked out of those windows, either.

They emerged into the Grand Circle. There were no illumination panels here. Instead, a holographic sky mimicked the pale blue of early morning. At the center of the Circle rose the vast round pillar of the Core, whose multiple elevators took travelers down into the lower Tiers, brought up goods from the City's factories and artisans, and carried away the trash of the elite. The roads that ran between the various Quarters and other buildings of the Tier radiated out from the Grand Circle like spokes from a wheel. Around the Grand Circle were expensive shops and fancy restaurants, all still closed this early in the day.

One of the big freight elevators stood open, revealing a cavernous interior stuffed with giant green plastic bags and a mass of old cloth. There were also a few bits of furniture—ratty old chairs and a lone sofa—which made Alania think the rubbish must have come from someone's Quarters. From the looks of it, it should have been discarded long ago, but people often hung onto things they didn't need.

Like hope, Alania thought.

Two workers lugged a mattress toward the open elevator as Alana and her escorts approached. The Provosts ignored them. Focused on guiding Alania around the edge of the Grand Circle to the tall gate that led to Quarters Kranz, they also ignored the flash of green light and the soft two-tone chime signaling the arrival of one of the smaller personnel lifts.

Then the lift's door opened, light flashed, and the head of the Provost next to Alania exploded into gray-red mist. His body crumpled to the ground. Alania stared down at the steam rising from the massive hole in the back of his half-melted helmet, too shocked to even process what she was seeing. A black scorch mark on the wall beyond him showed where a second beamer, fired an instant after the other, had missed her second escort, who had flung himself to safety around the corner of one of the radiating streets.

A siren began whooping, a frantic sound. The workers who had been loading the freight elevator ran for cover. Four men burst out of the newly arrived personnel lift. They wore black from head to foot. Masks and goggles hid their faces. Three of them spread out, kneeling, beamer rifles raised, covering the roads on this side of the Core. The fourth ran straight for Alania. She backed up, terrified, tripped over the body of the dead Provost, and stumbled, her back slamming hard against the brick wall of the shop where she had bought her birthday dress.

"Come with—" the black-clad man began, his voice distorted by an electronic filter, but he didn't finish the sentence. Holes stitched themselves across his chest, and blood spattered Alania's pseudosilk blouse, a darker shade of scarlet against the red. He collapsed at her feet.

Four new Provosts burst out of the street into which her surviving escort had ducked. Slugthrowers spat flame. Brick shattered by Alania's head, a fragment scoring her cheek. The pain broke her shocked immobility, and she ran for the only cover she could see: the freight elevator stuffed with rubbish. She dashed into it, then turned and punched the red button on the wall. The door slammed shut with startling force, and the elevator began to descend rapidly, far more rapidly than the genteel Officers-only Core lift she had ridden to parties on Eleventh Tier, faster even than the secret elevator in Quarters Beruthi she and her friends had ridden to Fifth.

Something in the Core squawked as if in outrage, the elevator car vibrating with the noise. It rocked, throwing Alania from her feet into the pile of bedding. She stayed there, breathing hard, trying to process what had just happened, wondering what would happen next.

Where would the elevator stop? Whichever Tier it ended up on, all she'd have to do was report to the nearest Provost post. They'd . . .

They'd what?

Take her back to Quarters Kranz, that's what.

It suddenly dawned on her that when that door opened, she would be, for the very first time in her life, free to decide for herself what she should do next.

You can't run from the Provosts. They're everywhere.

Maybe so. But maybe she could *evade* them for a little bit, see something of the rest of the City before she was locked up again, spied on, imprisoned. The worst that could happen was that she'd be taken back to Kranz.

Or was it?

The attack on the Provosts couldn't have been a coincidence. Those black-clad attackers had wanted *her*, wanted her alive, and wanted her badly enough to kill to get her. But why? To hold her for ransom? Or something worse?

The elevator jerked to a stop. Alania's heart, which had calmed a little, started pounding again. She held her breath, listening.

For several minutes, nothing happened. Then, without warning, the lights went out, plunging her into sudden darkness. She bit back a scream. Horrendous clanging and banging sounded outside the car. Something struck it a mighty blow that rang it like a bell. Then she felt it rotate. It traveled sideways. It stopped. It sank again. Metal shrieked on metal.

Finally, the door opened—and an instant later, the whole car tilted sharply.

This time Alania *did* scream as she, the cloth, the plastic bags, and everything else in the car began to slide, slowly at first, then faster and faster.

She kept screaming as she slid through the doors, onto a giant bronze-colored chute. Above her, a vast ceiling of filthy black metal oozing oil, lit by a rotating red strobe, slid by and shrank away.

And then, still screaming, she plummeted into empty air.

SEVEN

DANYL CAUGHT A GLIMPSE of the screaming girl as she
fell: red blouse, black pants, black boots, long brown hair.
Then she vanished, plunging into the piled refuse as
though she had leaped into a deep pool of water. He
fought his way through the rubbish toward her. *She's
probably dead. A bit of broken wood, a steel beam, a lump
of concrete . . .*

But that didn't stop him from trying to find her. Forget
'tronics or any of the other things that might have fallen
in a Direct Drop from Twelfth Tier. A human being had
to be valuable to *someone*, alive *or* dead. More valuable
than anything else in the Middens.

City Pass-valuable.

Living human beings didn't just drop out of the City
into the Middens, though corpses sometimes did. The
only other *living* human he'd ever heard of being found
in the Middens was himself.

The Rustbloods would arrive within minutes. But he
was here *now*.

Panting with exertion, he reached the site of the Drop.
He could see where the girl had plunged into the Middens along with a lot of old sheets and curtains. Flinging
himself full-length on the rubbish and pushing his goggles up onto his synthileather hood, he peered into the
hole.

To his astonishment, relief, and excitement, he saw two

wide eyes staring up at him—eyes the same pale blue color as his own. He could see at once what had happened. The mass of cloth with which she had fallen had formed a protective cocoon around her, while the garbage bags—mostly filled with paper, it looked like, and bits of carpet and other soft materials—had cushioned her landing. He thought he could get her out if he had enough time.

He had rope. He sat up, pulled off his pack, opened it, pulled out the rope, tied one end around his waist, and threw the other end down into the hole. "Take hold!" he shouted, and two pale hands gripped the rope. Then he turned, slung the rope over his shoulder, and began inching his way back down the fresh mound of trash, pulling with all his might. For a moment he stalled, unable to make any headway, but then the rope slackened—the girl had had enough wits to help by trying to climb out on her own. A moment later, he heard her gasp, "I'm out!"

He undid the rope, letting it fall, then turned and scrambled back up the slope to where she lay. Blood from a cut on her scalp and another on her cheek coated one side of her face. Beneath the blood, she looked as pale as the paper fluttering all around them, but otherwise she seemed unharmed.

"We've got to get out of here," Danyl said. "Can you run?"

"I . . . I don't even know where I am."

"The Middens. *Can you run?*"

She twisted her head to look up at the looming black bulk of the City's underside. "The Middens? I'm outside the City?"

"You're under it. And there's no time . . . What's your name?"

"Alania," the girl said. "Alania Beruthi."

"Alania, my name is Danyl. Listen to me. We'll figure out where you came from and how to get you back there just as soon as we can, but if we don't get moving *right now*, we stand a very good chance of being captured by some very not-nice people who will do things to us that we don't want done. Do you understand?"

The way she blinked at him, he doubted she did, but at least she struggled to her feet. He leaped up to join her and reached for her hand. She snatched it away. "I'm not allowed—"

He lunged and grabbed it, squeezing it tight to keep her from pulling away again. "I assure you my intentions are honorable," he snapped. "I intend to honorably see to it that we both survive the next few minutes. Now hold tight, and let's get out of—"

A red dot appeared on Alania's face, right between her eyes. Danyl froze.

The Rustbloods had found them.

He dropped Alania's hand. "Raise your arms," he told her, *sotto voce*. "And don't do *anything* else." Then he raised his own hands above his head and very slowly turned to look down the slope.

Four men and two women stood there, their clothing motley and stained. Each wore a rust-colored armband, a rust-colored headband, and makeshift goggles jury-rigged from scavenged glass, far cruder than the Erl-scavenged ones Danyl currently had shoved up on his head. At the center of the group stood a man a foot taller than Danyl and massing twice as much: Cark, the leader of the Rustbloods. His left ear was nothing but a mangled lump of tissue, and an angry red scar slashed down his cheek from it almost to his throat. He held a slug-throwing rifle of antique design at the ready. The red dot on Alania's forehead came from its aiming laser.

Danyl recognized all the other Rustbloods, too. The young women, Sara and Lora, were identical twins. Danyl had heard they were lovers, too. That might have been just a nasty rumor, but their sadism and viciousness were nasty facts. The second-largest man was Burl, Cark's second-in-command, bald and bearded. The other two men were Jisk and Rori. This was the very core of the Rustbloods. Clearly Cark had realized a Drop in this unexpected location had the potential to be very valuable indeed and had come with his most trusted associates.

Only Cark had a firearm; the others wore long knives at their belts and carried spears fashioned from bits of wood and scrap steel. Faced with those weapons alone, Danyl might have been tempted to try to outrun the gang. But Cark's rifle made that impossible.

Danyl had no idea how the Rustblood leader had come by the weapon—firearms were tightly controlled in the City above and certainly didn't find their way into the refuse stream by accident—but its provenance hardly mattered. What mattered was that Cark's rifle made him the most powerful man in the Middens, the Tyrant of Trash. Danyl used to wonder if the thing even had any ammo. Then he'd stumbled over a bloated Greenskull corpse with a massive hole in its head, staked in the rubbish at the border between Rustblood and Greenskull territories, and he knew the weapon had held at least one round.

"Hello, Danyl," said Cark, without lowering the rifle. "What have you got there?"

"Who are these people?" Alania whispered from behind him.

Danyl ignored her. "She's nobody, Cark. Let us walk away, and you can have everything in the Drop."

Cark laughed, a nasty chuckle echoed by the other Rustbloods. "She's not a nobody, Danyl. She's a woman. And she's mine."

"I am *not*!" To Danyl's horror, the girl suddenly pushed him to one side so she could stand beside him. She glared at Cark. "They'll be coming for me. Leave now, or you'll be sorry."

Danyl stared at her, startled by a level of spark he never would have expected to see in a pampered Twelfth-Tier girl. Both her wounds had already stopped bleeding, but the blood drying on her face made her look fierce and fiery.

It didn't change the fact she'd get them both killed if she wasn't careful.

Cark frowned. "Who'll be coming for you?"

"Provosts."

Danyl hurriedly interposed himself between the girl and the gang leader again. "She's bluffing, Cark. She fell out with the garbage, probably from First Tier. No way are Provosts going to—"

"Shut up, Danyl," Cark said. The rifle twitched, and red light flashed across Danyl's eyes. "Or I'll shut you up permanently." He returned his gaze, and his aim, to the girl. "What's your name?"

She shoved Danyl aside *again*. "Alania Beruthi."

Cark blinked and lowered the rifle a fraction. "Beruthi? As in Lieutenant Beruthi, the robot manufacturer?"

"That's right," Alania snapped. "I'm his ward. Now will you let me go, or will you wait for the Provosts to come make an example of you?"

Cark's lips pulled back from his teeth into a savage grin. Danyl knew exactly what he was thinking, because he was thinking it, too.

Alania was the ward of an Officer.

Ransom!

He didn't take the threat of Provosts suddenly descending on the Middens seriously, and he knew Cark didn't either. The Middens were huge and navigable only by those who lived there; even old paths and hideouts Danyl knew well had been known to disappear overnight as the unstable Middens shifted position like a restless sleeper. Provosts who raided the Middens rarely found who or what they were looking for, and they sometimes vanished in the attempt. Cark might have the only firearm Danyl knew about, but spears, bows, and booby traps worked just as effectively.

When valuable objects were inadvertently dropped into the Middens—like the firestone necklace Cark had found tucked away in a hidden pocket of a bloodstained jacket a year ago—the preferred method of retrieving them was to offer a reward. A knife fight with the leader of the no-longer-extant Bluesmoke gang had secured the necklace for Cark (and given him his facial scar). Then he'd let the traders at the Last Chance Market know he had it, and what he wanted before he would give it back.

Money served little purpose in the Middens, but food supplies and tools and technology were invaluable, and both had been forthcoming. The impressiveness of the Rustblood fortress had increased substantially after that. It now boasted airtight walls of cinderblock and proper windows that could be sealed against the noxious vapors that occasionally swept over the Middens when the wind blew from directly under the City.

If this had been an ordinary Drop and Danyl had been jumped by the Rustbloods, he would have surrendered without a fight and slipped away to scavenge elsewhere.

But this was no ordinary Drop, and Alania, if she really was the ward of an Officer, was the biggest score in the history of the Middens scavengers.

All that flashed through his mind in an instant.

"Grab the girl," Cark said, lowering his rifle. "Kill Danyl."

"No!" Alania cried.

He is *short of ammo, or he'd do it himself,* Danyl thought. *That means we've got a chance.* The slope of the mound on which he and Alania stood was unstable, making the Rustbloods' ascent a struggle. He glanced over his shoulder. Just past the mass of cloth and garbage bags from the Drop, the mound sloped steeply toward a pool of oily liquid, black lumps floating on its iridescent surface.

At the top of the slope teetered a flat piece of standard

white-plastic City wallboard. Without another glance at the Rustbloods, Danyl grabbed Alania by the shoulders and threw her backward and himself forward onto the cracked plastic sheet. Their momentum sent it and them tobogganing down the rubbish heap toward that noxious black pool. Danyl quickly snugged his goggles back into place.

"Get them!" he heard Cark roar, but the Rustbloods still hadn't fought through the loose rubbish to the top of the mound when the particleboard hit the black pool. Foul liquid—raw sewage, from the smell—sprayed Danyl and Alania. The girl gasped and choked.

"Now we run!" Danyl shouted, grabbing her hand and trying to pull her to her feet. Infuriatingly, she resisted.

"There they are!" a voice shouted, and he looked up to see Burl glaring down at him. "Sara, Lora, that way." The Rustblood second-in-command pointed right, and the twins angled in that direction. "Jisk, Rori, the other way. Head them off." Burl hefted his short spear, a nasty-looking weapon with a jagged steel blade bound to a shaft of black wood, and started directly down the slope.

"Come *on*," Danyl said, and Alania, staring up at the goggled Rustblood thug, at last understood the danger and scrambled to her feet.

They could run neither left nor right. That left only one direction, and Danyl began to scramble up the slope in the direction of the City. It was far higher than the one they'd just slid down, and he knew perfectly well what awaited them when they reached the top of it, where greenish vapor drifted.

"Where are we going?" Alania asked breathlessly.

"Hell," Danyl said, and kept climbing.

EIGHT

ALANIA FELT LIKE she'd fallen into hell even before Danyl announced that was where they were going. The plunge into the garbage; the terrifying moment when she'd been trapped, blood pouring down her face; Danyl pulling her out; the sudden appearance of the vicious ragamuffin warriors; the orders to seize her and kill Danyl; the plunge down the hill into the noxious pool of . . . had that been what it smelled like? No part of that had *not* seemed hellish.

She touched the cut on her head and found it already closed, as she'd expected, as was the cut on her cheek from the flying splinter of brick up on Twelfth. She'd always healed very quickly. She just hoped the cuts had closed before any of that black liquid had gotten into them . . . although she'd never been prone to infection, either. She'd never had so much as a cold.

She and Danyl were toiling up another tottering slope of paper and cloth and bits of wood and chunks of foam and round slimy objects that could have been anything, toward a strangely well-defined ridge over which drifted smoke or vapor of a most unpleasant green. She still didn't know who she was fleeing, or who she was fleeing *with*.

And yet . . .

There had been a shock of recognition when she had first looked up at the face staring down at her in the hole in the trash, as Danyl had pushed his goggles up and reached down for her. Those eyes, a pale, icy blue, were identical to the ones that stared back at her from the mirror every morning. She'd never seen eyes that color on anyone else, though the First Officer's cold gaze came close. Danyl had pulled her from the nasty embrace of the trash, and after that . . . well, the expression "lesser of two evils" seemed to have been crafted specially to suit this circumstance.

"What do they want me for?" she panted out now. She glanced over her shoulder. The big man with the nasty-looking short spear was fifteen meters behind them, cursing monotonously and not making much headway; his mass seemed to be working against him in the soft, shifting footing. To her left, the two other men were now angling in their direction; to her right, the two women were doing the same. Of Cark, the man with the rifle, there was no sign. He seemed to be the leader; maybe he felt himself too important to go scrambling through garbage personally. Or perhaps he was busy imagining what he would do with her once he got his hands on her. She was pretty certain that the Twelfth-Tier focus on young ladies maintaining their virtue until they were properly married—fictitious though that virtue might be in some of her friends' cases—held no sway at all down here in . . .

Could this really be the Middens? She supposed it had to be.

You wanted out of the City, she thought. *Careful what you wish for.*

"Ransom," Danyl said. He wasn't breathing nearly as hard as she was. Only slightly taller than she, he looked older, his tanned face lean and stubbled. "You're a ward of an Officer. You're worth . . ." He bit off whatever he was going to say. "Save your breath," he growled instead. "You're not going to want to be gulping too much air where we're headed."

She looked up at that sharp ridge, very near now. "Hell?"

"Close enough."

Then, suddenly, they were at the top, and Alania realized the strangely sharp edge of the ridge was in fact a wall, one onto which Danyl scrambled, then turned to help her. She clambered onto it on her hands and knees. It was about a meter and a half thick, solid concrete, and on the other side . . .

Red-lit, smoking, seething, and bubbling, it would certainly do as a simulacrum of hell until the real thing came along. The vapor rising from the foul surface below stung her eyes and brought on a coughing fit. She jerked her head back and turned the other way, trying to clear her lungs of the stinking fumes, clapping one hand over her mouth and nose in a futile effort to filter them out.

"Hazardous Waste Holding Tank," Danyl said.

He's right, Alania thought with a sudden shock. *I've seen it in the teaching machine. But . . .*

"But it's not supposed to look like this," she gasped out. "It should be covered, and—"

Danyl stared at her, one hand over his own nose and mouth. "How would you know?" he said, the words muffled.

"I've studied the City in detail."

"Well, this is the way it is now. Come on." He set off to their right, where the tank met a wall of metal descending from the City's underbelly. Alania scrambled to her feet and followed, her hand still pressed to her lips and nostrils, though it seemed not to make much difference—every breath burned. The big man with the spear shouted something, and she saw the two women change their angle of approach so they would intercept Danyl and Alania at the top of the wall.

But just before the twins reached the wall, and just as the big man, grunting, hauled himself onto it behind Danyl and Alania, Danyl suddenly stopped and took his hand away from his face. "Ladder," he choked out.

"Follow me." He turned, knelt, lowered himself over the wall, and vanished.

Into hell? Alania thought, but unless she wanted to throw herself at the mercy of Cark and his followers—all of whom seemed unlikely to *have* any—she had little choice. She knelt and felt a hand on her ankle, guiding her foot to the first rung of the ladder below. She eased herself over the edge and descended.

The ladder didn't go far—only three meters or so—but the choking vapor thickened as she descended. Eyes streaming, coughing, she stepped off the rungs. Danyl, standing to her right, turned without a word and hurried along a ledge whose end she couldn't see in the uncertain light. The City hung over their heads like a night sky made of metal, and the handful of red lights hanging from the inside of the wall lit the swirling green vapor but did not penetrate it.

Danyl must have hoped to get past the women—Sara and Lora, Cark had called them—but he and Alania had stumbled barely twenty meters before the duo dropped onto the ledge in front of them, landing with cat-like grace. They were the same height and size, and though their goggles hid their eyes, their faces had the same structure. *Twins?* The only other twins she knew were the Letaria sisters, Lilli and Lotti. Three years younger than she was, they were the most annoying people she'd ever met.

These twins didn't look annoying. They looked deadly. Without a word, they advanced toward Danyl, knives as long as short swords at the ready.

Danyl drew his own blade, and *it* was a real sword: a Provost's dress sword, in fact, identical to the ones on the hips of the Provosts who had escorted her from her room that morning. It gleamed in the dim light. "Let us pass," he said. "I don't want to hurt you."

"Don't worry," said the first twin. "You won't." And then she charged, low and hard.

Alania gasped and took a step back, but Danyl, moving faster than she'd ever seen anyone move, twisted out of the way of the woman's thrust and drove the hilt of his weapon down onto the back of her skull. She crumpled.

Her sister, already in motion, tried to strike while Danyl was preoccupied, but he'd clearly anticipated her attack. Her blade whistled over his head as he ducked under the stroke and drove his shoulder into her. She stumbled, tripped over her unconscious sister, and fell off the ledge. She shrieked as she splashed into the glistening pool and thrashed, a mindless scream of agony, but her struggles and screams lasted only an instant. Her clothing dissolved, her skin melted, and she sank from sight, curdled eyes staring sightlessly up from the sockets of her exposed skull as she disappeared.

Alania turned her head, gorge rising, but a roar sounded from behind them, and she twisted back that way to see the big man with the spear jumping off the ladder and running toward them. Danyl grabbed her hand, and they jumped over the remaining twin and hurried on.

Lungs on fire, eyes watering, she collided with Danyl's back a minute later as he stumbled to a halt at the end of the ledge, where the tank joined the wall of metal. She saw a closed hatch, a lockplate beside it, and for a moment dared to hope that Danyl had a key to open it and let her back into the City. She'd find the elevators, ride back up to Twelfth Tier, turn herself over to Kranz, settle gladly into her new life as ward of the First Officer ...

But Danyl didn't open the hatch. Instead, he turned to another ladder and scrambled up it. Alania climbed up after him only to find her guide standing frozen in place atop the tank wall, staring back across the liquid-filled valley they had crossed earlier toward the mound into which she had plunged. She followed his gaze.

Cark stood at the top of the mound, rifle aimed. Alania glanced at Danyl and saw a red dot over his heart.

"Nice try," Cark said. "But not good enough. I didn't want to waste ammo on you, but now I'm thinking I will." His scarred face split into a predatory grin. "And just because you've pissed me off, after I've killed you—and *properly* initiated the girl into the Rustbloods—I think I'll even waste another bullet on that old man you shack up with in that miserable hovel of yours. After all, he won't want to hang on after his fuckboy is gone, will he?"

Alania heard a noise behind her and looked down to see the big man who had pursued them staring up at her from the ladder. "Fun's over, little girl," he snarled, and seized her ankle.

Alania reacted without thinking, half turning and driving her free leg back as hard as she could. Her foot connected with the man's nose, and as blood splattered, he released her ankle to rear back, roaring in pain. Alania turned the rest of the way and stamped down on his fingers on the ladder's top rung. He let go and overbalanced. His hand shot out in a desperate grab for the ladder, but he was already falling backward. She saw his eyes, wide and white and suddenly terrified, above his bloody nose, and then, with a hoarse cry, he vanished into the dimness.

She turned away in horror, realizing what she'd done, and heard him splash into the liquid far below. If anything, his scream was even more high-pitched than the woman's, but just as short-lived. Alania's knees gave way, and she dropped to the top of the concrete wall, leaned forward, and vomited into the trash.

"You'll pay for that, you fancy little bitch!" Cark bellowed. "Right after I—" Suddenly, he turned to look behind him at something Alania couldn't see on the other side of the mound. He stiffened. "Wait—" he began, but he got no further before the top of his head blew off, just like the head of the Provost who had been escorting Alania on Twelfth Tier. He fell backward and out of sight.

A moment later, a new face appeared over the ridge of trash: an old face, brown-skinned, framed by gray hair peeking out from beneath a black cap.

"Don't just stand there, boy!" the new arrival shouted. "Let's get out of here!"

"Erl!" Danyl cried, and the joy in his voice suddenly made him sound so youthful that Alania wondered if she'd misjudged his age and he was actually younger than she. He leaned down to Alania, still on her hands and knees, and held out his hand. "Come on!"

She heard shouts from down in the tank: the surviving Rustbloods hurrying toward them along the ledge. Swiping the back of her arm across her vomit-fouled mouth, she grabbed Danyl's hand, let him pull her to her feet, and then jumped with him onto the slope of rubbish. They stagger-stumbled down it.

Erl, whoever *he* was, stayed put. Like Cark, he had a weapon: not an ancient slugthrower, but a modern beamer rifle, like the ones the black-clad attackers on Twelfth Tier had been carrying. He kept it aimed over Alania's and Danyl's heads. It flashed once just as Alania and Danyl splashed through the oily sewage they'd tobogganed into before, and someone cried out, though in anger rather than pain; the shot must have missed. The foul black liquid around Alania's ankles seemed homey and clean after what she'd seen in the Hazardous Waste Holding Tank. They scrambled out of the pool and up the slope toward Erl. When they reached him, he snapped to Danyl, "Grab Cark's rifle. We're going to need it."

Alania glanced at Cark's body, saw what was left of his head, and her stomach rebelled again. She leaned over, hands on her knees, and threw up the final sour contents of her stomach. Then Danyl, now with Cark's rifle slung over his back, grabbed her hand once more.

Mouth bitter with bile, eyes streaming, throat raw as

sandpaper, stinking like a sewer, Alania Beruthi staggered with Danyl and Erl through the teetering, slimy piles of the Middens and promised herself that if she ever made it back to Twelfth Tier, she would never leave it again.

NINE

DANYL HOPED LIKE HELL Alania was as valuable as he thought she was, because she'd already almost gotten him killed four times by his count, and he'd only known her for twenty minutes. Now, covered in oily sewage, face covered with drying blood from the already-closed cut on her forehead, with a little vomit on her blouse for good measure, she didn't seem like someone anyone would *want* to claim. But if she was telling the truth about being Lieutenant Beruthi's ward . . .

Time enough to worry about that when they got to safety, which for the first time he thought they might have a realistic chance of. The Rustbloods, thanks to Erl's unexpected arrival with a weapon Danyl had never even had an *inkling* existed, had been decapitated. Almost literally in Cark's case, of course, but with Burl and at least one of the twins gone as well, no one was likely to come after them. Not right away, at least. And probably not any time soon, either. The Rustbloods were going to be busy fighting each other as wannabe Cark-replacements jockeyed for position.

Erl slowed soon enough. He was in his sixties, after all—although to tell the truth, he wasn't panting much harder than Danyl and not nearly as hard as Alania when at last the pace eased. As soon as he had the breath to speak, Danyl demanded an answer to the first question on his mind: "Where the *hell* did you get a beamer rifle?"

"I'm a man of mystery," Erl said. "You should know that by now." He glanced over his shoulder, and Danyl followed his gaze. Nothing moved among the mounds of rubbish along their trail. "I don't think we're being followed, though I'm not sure why. Cark is dead, but Burl would—"

Danyl realized Erl hadn't seen what Alania had done. "Burl is dead, too," he said.

"What?" Erl looked surprised. "How?"

"I kicked him into the hazardous waste pool," Alania said. She was trudging along, head down, and she didn't look up as she spoke. Her voice sounded flat and strained. *If not in shock, next thing to it*, Danyl thought.

Erl barked a harsh laugh. "That would do it. Still, the Rustbloods will regroup and come after us eventually. And the Greenskulls might have been watching. With Cark dead, they might try a raid on this side of the Middens."

"At least we're armed." Danyl hefted Cark's rifle, still sticky with the dead gang leader's blood. "With this and that beamer rifle . . ."

"We could hold them off for maybe half an hour," Erl said. "And then they'd overrun us." He glanced at the girl again. "You're Alania Beruthi."

Danyl stared at him. "How do you know that?"

Alania reacted more slowly, as if she had to surface from deep underwater. She looked up and blinked. "You know who I am?"

"I do. And you are *not* supposed to be down here." There was a strange undercurrent to his words, and Danyl knew Erl well enough to recognize it: anger. But why?

"No," she said. "I'm supposed to be in Quarters Kranz."

Danyl stumbled a little as he jerked his head around to look at her. "Kranz? As in *First Officer* Kranz?"

Alania nodded. "As of today, he's my guardian. Provosts came to get me this morning from Quarters Beruthi. We were passing the Core when ... someone ... attacked. With beamers just like that one." She nodded at Erl's surprising weapon. "They killed one of the Provosts. They tried to get me to go with them, but some more Provosts arrived unexpectedly. There was more shooting, and ... I panicked. There was a bunch of rubbish being loaded into a freight elevator. I ran into it, the door closed behind me ..."

"And you got dumped into our laps." Erl shook his head, lips pressed thin.

Danyl frowned at him. *What is he angry about?* "You *knew* that drop was happening."

"Yes, but I didn't know *she'd* be in the middle of it. I didn't even know she *existed* until today."

And there it is. That's what he's really angry about. But why? Why does he think he should have known Alania existed? And if he just found out she exists, how does he know her name?

"Can you take me home?" Alania asked plaintively. Danyl, looking back at her again, found himself staring once more into eyes the same ice-blue color as his own. That startling similarity made him uncomfortable. He turned away and focused on the path.

"No," Erl said. "The last place I want you to go is 'home' to First Officer Kranz. And it should be the last place you want to go, too."

"I don't understand." Alania sounded as if she were about to cry, and Danyl felt a strange sense of panic, like he should do something, *anything*, to stop that from happening. *How odd*, he thought; but then, his experience with girls had been limited to trying not to be killed by Sara and Lora, which was unlikely to be representative of normal male/female relationships. If it were, the human race would surely have died out by now.

"No, you don't," Erl agreed. "And I'm sorry, but I can't explain it to you. You'll just have to trust me."

Danyl felt a surge of irritation, some of it aimed at

Erl, who had clearly kept even more secrets from Danyl than he'd thought—that impossible beamer rifle of his was proof enough of that—and some of it aimed at Alania. The whole situation frustrated him. She was the most valuable bit of salvage that had appeared in the Middens in his lifetime. She should have been his ticket to a City Pass. But it turned out she was *too* valuable. Ward of the First Officer? If what she said was true, the Provosts *would* come to the Middens for her, with overwhelming force. If they found him and Erl with Alania, they were as good as dead.

Is that why Erl won't help her get home? Because if she goes home and talks about us . . . ?

He frowned. No, that was too simplistic. Erl might not have known she'd existed until that morning, but the fact he had shown up so fortuitously to rescue her had to mean he had somehow found out she was going to be in that Drop. Not only that, he'd produced a beamer rifle out of nowhere in order to rescue her. Alania said it looked the same as the beamers used by the men who had tried to snatch her from the Provosts on Twelfth Tier.

There's something else going on.

"Home sweet home," Erl said as they reached the rickety staircase that led up to the hovel they supposedly shared.

Danyl glanced at Alania again to see what she made of it, but she was staring blankly at nothing much in particular, her face white. Who could blame her? She'd been in the Middens for . . . what? Three-quarters of an hour? And already she'd fallen three stories and been buried in garbage, threatened with rape, covered in sewage, held at gunpoint, and chased by armed thugs. She'd seen two nasty deaths and caused another. Moved by the same strange impulse that had made him want to stop her from crying, he put out a hand and touched her shoulder.

"There's clean water and clean clothes and hot food waiting inside," he said gently. "Just a little farther."

She nodded, biting her lip, and let him lead her to the staircase.

He climbed up first with Alania close behind and Erl, scanning their trail with his beamer rifle at the ready, bringing up the rear. Danyl opened the hovel's unlocked door and ushered Alania in. Erl crowded in after her. "Still nobody in sight," he said.

Danyl nodded and moved to the back of the hut.

Alania, meanwhile, was staring around in obvious horror. "You live *here*?"

"No," Danyl said. He put his hand on the biometric scan plate hidden behind one of the boards of the wall, and the camouflaged inside door swung open. "It's our front porch." He stepped through the door into the smooth reddish stone corridor beyond, then turned and held out his hand to Alania, who was staring open-mouthed down the long tunnel. "Please come in."

She took his hand again, and he led her forward. Behind them, Erl closed and secured the door.

They paused at the side room for Danyl to strip out of his scavenging coverall, leaving him feeling much cleaner. "I'll go ahead," Erl said. "There's food cooking." He went on down the corridor while Alania hung back, watching as Danyl hung up the heavy synthileather garment and tucked away the gloves and goggles and boots, the tool belt, and the backpack. Then he picked up Cark's rifle again and led her the rest of the way to the main living quarters.

As Erl had promised, Danyl could smell something good (although it would have smelled better without the overlay of sewage from Alania's filthy blouse and pants): probably stew made with vatmeat and whatever Erl had traded for at the Last Chance Market. Danyl still remembered the *real* meat he'd had after the trashslide when he was twelve; he could count on one hand the number of times he'd had it since.

"First things first," Erl said. "Get the docbot. Those cuts on Alania's forehead and cheek need attention."

Alania put a hand to her forehead as if she'd forgotten she'd been wounded. "It's already closed," she mumbled. "I heal fast."

Danyl said nothing; he would have expected any similar wounds on his face to close just as fast.

"I see that," Erl said. "But we should check them out just the same."

She nodded.

While Erl led Alania to one of the chairs at the dining table, Danyl leaned Cark's rifle against the wall beside the entrance, then went down the hallway to the metal cabinet containing the docbot. As a kid, he'd never questioned their possession of the thing, yet in some ways it was the most surprising item in their dwelling. Erl claimed he'd obtained it by bartering salvaged items at the Last Chance Market. Certainly Erl roamed the Middens solo, just as Danyl did, and so he *could* have discovered salvage Danyl knew nothing about, but finding anything valuable enough to trade for a docbot—even an old one—and keep it stocked with supplies seemed . . . implausible.

Finding something valuable enough to trade for a beamer rifle seemed downright impossible.

Danyl's current theory was that Erl had found a very unusual stash somewhere, perhaps a crashed aircar. When he was younger, he'd briefly convinced himself that Erl had found his way into one of the mysterious Cubes, but he knew better now. If there were any way into those things, they would have long since been emptied.

The docbot, a simple sphere about twenty centimeters in diameter in its dormant state, was far heavier than its size would suggest. Danyl carried it into the dining room, set it on the floor, and activated it. Its spindly legs sprouted from its sides, and the glowing blue scanner orb extended and turned to Danyl. "Please select a function," the docbot said in its girlish voice.

"First aid," Danyl said.

"Please identify the injured person."

"The only female present," Danyl said. The scanner orb surveyed the room, and then the docbot click-click-clicked across the stone floor to the table, where Erl was using a napkin he'd wetted in the kitchen to clean some of the blood from Alania's forehead. Sure enough, the wound had closed, but the flesh around it still looked red and puffy.

"Please remove the patient's clothing to permit diagnosis and treatment," the docbot said, and Alania's eyes widened.

"Unnecessary," Erl said crisply. "Examine head only." He stepped back from the table, and the docbot click-clicked into the space he'd vacated.

Alania blinked at it. "It's so . . . old-fashioned," she said. "We have a docbot in Quarters Beruthi, but it's nothing like this one. It's a full-body cabinet I have to climb into."

"Trust me," Erl said. "This one works just fine." He glanced at Danyl. "Danyl also heals fast, but he's still needed some fix-up work over the years. Not to mention regular checkups."

"I get them every six months," Alania said.

"So do I," Danyl said with a grimace, remembering being poked and prodded by the docbot while standing naked in a cold stone chamber.

"Silence, please," said the docbot. Then, "What is your name, female patient?"

"Alania," she replied.

"This may sting a little, Alania." A port popped open on the smoothly curving metal of its top, and a jointed arm reached out, the end spreading into a flat, flexible pad that the docbot pressed against the wound. There was a snicking sound and Alania flinched; then a hiss. The arm lowered. The wound now glistened, less angry-looking than before. The scanner orb lifted to it and bathed her forehead in an eye-hurting purple light. The light went out. The scanner orb retreated slightly. The jointed arm reached out again, and the docbot repeated the process on the cut on her cheek. "Wounds cleaned and disinfected. No stitches required," the docbot said. "Wounds sealed with analgesic artificial skin. No further aid required at this time. Please monitor for signs of infection." A pause. "Code Three."

"Code Three?" Alania said. "What's that?"

"It always says that after it's worked on me, too," Danyl said. "We don't know why." He glanced at Erl. *At least I don't.*

"Something in the programming," Erl said, which of course was no answer at all.

The scanner orb twisted to look at each of them in turn. "Are there any other injuries?"

"You're okay, Danyl?" Erl asked.

He nodded. "Not a scratch." Which was true, though he thought he might have pulled a muscle battling the twin he'd sent into the hazardous waste tank; his shoulder ached. Still, injuries like that never hurt him for long. By bedtime the pain would fade.

"Then I'll see to the stew," Erl said. "Show Alania the bathroom. She'll need clean clothes—she's a little smaller, so she can probably wear your last set of castoffs."

Danyl opened his mouth to protest, then caught a whiff of Alania's stink and thought better of it. He indicated the hallway to the bedrooms. "This way."

The docbot scuttled ahead of them. Beside its alcove, it turned back into a featureless sphere. Danyl lifted it back into its cabinet, grunting as his shoulder twinged.

"I don't understand," Alania said, but she wasn't looking at the docbot; her hand was pressed to the smooth reddish stone of the wall. "Why was a place like this built into the side of the Canyon? It obviously wasn't dug out by hand."

"Don't know," Danyl said. "Erl just says he was lucky to find it." *Like he was lucky enough to find something worth a beamer rifle?* He led her to the closed door near the end of the hall and opened it. "Here's the bath."

The bathroom was one of the glories of their tucked-away little corner of civilization. A proper toilet, a tiny shower—just a brick ring surrounding a drain with a showerhead above—and a tub big enough to double as a small swimming pool, lined with blue tile, constantly filled with ever-recirculating water from what Erl swore up and down was a clean source far away from the noxious pools of the Middens.

Danyl opened the cabinet under the sink to show Alania the motley collection of towels, crafted from bits of cloth scavenged over the years. He left her examining them while he went into his room and dug out from the trunk at the foot of his bed the last set of clothes he'd outgrown—now that he was twenty, maybe he'd stop doing that. He found a clean pair of drawers, an undershirt, and a patched pair of socks and put them on the low wooden bench at the foot of the tub. "Get cleaned up," he said. "Then it'll be my turn."

"How do I lock the door?" Alania asked as he turned to go.

He looked back at her. She stood, face pale beneath the dirt and drying blood, one hand on the wall as though it were the only thing keeping her upright—which it might well have been. "Why?"

"I'm in an underground cavern in the most lawless place in the Heartland with two strange men, and I'm about to take off all my clothes and get into a bath in which I'll be completely vulnerable to attack," Alania said evenly. "Why do you think?"

Danyl frowned. "Do I look like a rapist to you? Does Erl?"

"I don't know what a rapist looks like. It's my understanding that they can look like anyone."

Danyl felt a flash of anger, but took a deep breath to quell it. "There's no lock on the door, but you're safe here. And you're going to stay safe. Believe it or not. Be clean or be dirty. It's up to you. But hurry up either way. I want my own bath."

He left the bathroom and closed the door firmly behind him.

Erl had made it clear they wouldn't be trading Alania at the Last Chance Market. He clearly knew who she was and had other plans for her.

Well, whatever it is, the sooner we're rid of her, the better, he thought, and he went to see if Erl needed help in the kitchen.

TEN

FIRST OFFICER KRANZ looked up from the report he'd just been handed at the grim-faced Provost Commander who had done the handing. Achil Havelin stood straight as a lamppost, staring ahead, like a lowly recruit expecting a dressing-down from . . . well, from Commander Havelin, who excelled at such things.

"Four armed attackers somehow obtained a key that allowed them to board a personnel lift on First Tier, lock out all other passengers, and ride it all the way to Twelfth, where they attacked my ward and her escort—whose movements they had clearly been apprised of—as they were en route from Quarters Beruthi to Quarters Kranz," the First Officer said. Though he spoke in a flat, conversational tone, Havelin's jaw clenched. "The fortuitous arrival of four additional Provosts heading to the Core on a completely unrelated assignment meant that the attackers were all killed, but Alania, for some unfathomable reason, jumped into a freight elevator and was summarily dumped into the Middens. Have I correctly summarized events?"

Commander Havelin still did not meet his eyes. "Yes, sir."

"Have these killers been identified?"

"Yes, sir. Three were ordinary workers from First and Second Tiers who have not come to our attention before. We believe the fourth had connections to a First-Tier criminal organization. We're continuing to question suspects to try to determine how they obtained such a high-level access key."

"I should think that's obvious," Kranz said. "Someone among the Officers is a traitor."

"I . . . can't speculate about that, sir," Havelin said carefully. "Investigating such matters is outside my jurisdiction."

"I'm well aware of that," Kranz said sourly. It could hardly be otherwise, since investigating such matters was very much within *his* jurisdiction. He looked down at the report again. "According to this, the trash elevator delivered its cargo directly to the Middens with no stop for sorting or recycling along the way. Have you questioned the waste-disposal workers who made that unusual arrangement?"

"Yes, sir," Havelin said. "They were hired by relatives of the Officer who died and whose quarters were being emptied. They admitted after considerable . . . encouragement that they feared there might be incriminating evidence among the Officer's possessions that might fall into the wrong hands if those possessions were not summarily disposed of." He grimaced. "It concerned sexual perversion. Not related to the attack, so far as we can determine."

"I see." Kranz said. He found his heart beating faster and his hands wanting to tremble as he asked the next question, though of course he concealed it from Havelin by pressing his palms against the glass desktop and let nothing of it into his voice. "And what happened to Alania Beruthi when she fell into the Middens?"

"Security cameras are few and far between down there, sir," Havelin said. "But one did record her, alive and apparently uninjured, being rushed away by two men."

Kranz felt a surge of relief, followed by a surge of fury. "I presume you are going after them."

Havelin nodded. "Yes, sir. A retrieval team is being assembled."

"How large?"

"Six armed Provosts. And a medical team, of course."

"Expand it," Kranz said flatly. "That side of the Middens has been left undisturbed for too long. Use overwhelming force. Find my ward. Arrest everyone you find for questioning. Kill them if they resist."

Havelin saluted. "Yes, sir."

"I also want you to conduct thorough sweeps of every Tier below Tenth. We're looking for weapons, seditious literature, known agitators." Kranz reached out and picked up the ancient dagger, made of meteoric iron, that had graced the desk of every First Officer Kranz since the original, centuries ago. "I will oversee the investigation of Eleventh and Twelfth myself, of course."

"Yes, sir."

"Dismissed, Commander."

Havelin saluted smartly, turned on his heel, and went out the wood-sheathed double doors, which opened and closed automatically.

Once the Commander had left his office, Kranz stood and took half a dozen steps to the left, to one of the paintings that hung on the dark paneling. It showed a twilight view of the City from a distance, its curving metal skin shining in the last rays of the sun, diamond flecks of light beginning to glow here and there where windows and balconies had been cut through the skin. He reached up and tugged at the right side of the frame. The picture swung back from the wall, revealing a glowing screen. It was a medical monitor, though most City doctors would not have recognized many of its displayed readings, and they would've found it hard to believe that those they did recognize belonged to a living person. But even a non-doctor could see at a glance that the patient being monitored was not doing well—not with that many readings displayed in red.

Beneath the monitor was a small metal plate with a hole in the middle, into which an access key had to be

inserted to call the elevator whose doors, artfully illuminated by concealed lights, glowed gold not far to the
monitor's right. Ostentatious as hell, but then, it was
meant to be. It was visible proof to those select few who
were allowed into the First Officer's office that they
could ascend no higher, that he and he alone had access
to the Thirteenth Tier and to the Captain.

The Captain, whose vital signs were weakening day
by inexorable day.

Kranz frowned at the medical monitor for a long moment, then pushed the painting back into place and returned to his desk. He picked up the dagger again and
stared down at its dark, mirror-smooth blade. There was
a traitor among the Officers, someone who had attempted to subvert the plan he had put in place more
than twenty years ago, someone whose attempt to kidnap Alania threatened not only Kranz's personal power
but potentially the continued existence of the City itself.

Another traitor. Twenty years ago, Ensign Erlkin Orillia's attempt to subvert the plan had failed, but it had
come perilously close to success. Today's attempt had
come even closer, and the plan might *still* fail if something happened to Alania down in the Middens.

Kranz could do nothing more to rescue her than he
had already done. Havelin was a competent commander,
and his men would track her down and return her to
Quarters Kranz, where she belonged.

He thought of the monitor behind the painting.

Not just where she belonged, where she *had to be.*
Soon.

In the meantime, he intended to find out who the traitor was, starting with a thorough interrogation of the
family members of the recently deceased Officer, the
ones who had paid the workers to send their "sexually
perverted" relative's belongings straight to the Middens.
Perhaps the fact that the trash elevator had been open at
the moment of the attack had been coincidence. Perhaps

not. Either way, they were clearly guilty of subverting regulations, at the very least, and punishing those who broke regulations was one of the duties of the First Officer . . . a duty, and sometimes a joy.

Like this time.

Kranz put the dagger back on the desk, then touched the glossy surface next to it. The glass lit with an image of Ensign Bothnis, his secretary, ensconced in his own office three floors below Kranz's. The Ensign looked up. "Sir?"

"Order my bodyguards to meet me at the front entrance. I'm going out and may be some time. Cancel my appointments."

"Yes, sir."

Kranz left the office without looking back, but even so, the grim red readouts of the medical monitor hidden behind the painting seemed to follow him, hanging in the back of his mind like the first flickering flames of a coming conflagration.

The moment the bathroom door closed, Alania's knees gave way and she sank to the stone floor, trembling.

For the first time since she had landed in the Middens, she was alone. Only a little more than an hour had passed since the Provost's head had disintegrated and she had run for her life. She'd had almost no time to think. Now she did, and that, as much as shock, reduced her to a shivering lump on the floor. She wrapped her filthy arms around her stinking knees and tried to wrap her mind around everything that had happened.

The Middens. She was in the Middens. She'd heard the phrase "Go to the Middens" all her life from girls who had been brought up in polite society and thus were not allowed to use words like "hell." Now she actually had "gone to the Middens" and had even seen the part the *residents* called hell. *At least there's nowhere worse I could end up, is there?*

Is there?

She pressed her face into her knees. Of course there was. She could end up gang-raped, or dead, or both. She could be enslaved. Tortured. She gripped her legs even more tightly.

Maybe I should try to escape, run back to the City, find some way up to the Gate. They'd recognize me—the Provosts must be looking for me. I could be home by sundown...

Except "home" meant Quarters Kranz, not Quarters Beruthi, where she had lived all her life. And without a guide, she didn't have a chance of making it back to the City. You couldn't exactly lose it, not with it hanging above the canyon like a thundercloud, but that wouldn't help her navigate the torturous paths along which Erl and Danyl had led her after they'd fled the Rustbloods. And she already knew some of the hazards. She'd seen the tottering piles of trash threatening to collapse at any minute—and having already been buried in trash once, she had no desire to repeat the experience. She'd been covered in sewage and had almost plunged into a pool of flesh-melting hazardous waste. She wouldn't last twenty minutes on her own.

Here, at least, she was relatively safe ... and the more she thought about it, the better she thought she understood why.

The men who had attacked on Twelfth Tier hadn't just been thieves or killers out to murder some Provosts and loot some rich Officer's Quarters. They'd been after *her*, specifically. She had no clue as to why, but it was undeniably true.

It had to be tied to the change in her circumstances from ward of Lieutenant Beruthi to ward of First Officer Kranz. It had to have something to do with the test Kranz had performed on her, the same test that had been performed at regular intervals throughout her life; with the fact she'd never known her parents; with the way she'd lived her whole life as a virtual prisoner; with that mysterious half-overheard conversation four years ago. All that was clear, but she still lacked enough information to even begin to put those pieces together into something that made sense of why she was so valuable.

Of course, in the Middens, in this anarchic, violent realm, no doubt she had intrinsic value just by virtue of being female. Cark had made that clear. But if the attempt to kidnap her on Twelfth Tier was proof she had some value up above as well . . . then Danyl and Erl might value her for a reason besides the obvious one.

They think they can trade me for ransom.

It was the only possibility that fit the facts, and the thought both reassured and outraged her. It reassured her because it meant Danyl had been telling the truth and she could safely take a bath; it outraged her because it meant that as kind as he and Erl were being at the moment, they were doing so only because they thought they would be rewarded for it. If it turned out they were wrong and she had no value to the City, then she'd wager they'd be ready to trade to her to someone much nearer . . . like the Rustbloods or that other gang they'd mentioned, the Greenskulls.

She shuddered and pressed her lips together. *They won't find that easy!*

She hauled herself upright. Sitting there quivering like one of the gelatin desserts at her birthday party—had that really just been yesterday?—wouldn't accomplish anything. One step at a time. Get cleaned up. Get dressed. And then confront Danyl and Erl.

She tested the swirling water in the bath, found it pleasingly hot, and then gave the unlocked door another slightly uneasy glance before turning her back on it and peeling off her ruined blouse and pants, boots and socks and undergarments. She lowered herself into the steaming

pool, gasping a little at the heat but then sighing with relief as the warmth soaked into her body. There was a
bench built into the side of the bath, and she settled onto
it. She closed her eyes. Exhausted from her early rising
and everything that had happened since, she drifted into
a doze . . .

. . . *the Provost turned toward her as if he were going
say something, and his head burst like an overripe fruit,
spraying her with blood and brains . . .*

She jerked upright, gasping, gorge rising. She gulped
to keep from fouling her bath, and reached for the soap.
She scrubbed her hair hard, then every inch of her body
even harder, remembering everything that had sprayed,
dripped, or splashed onto her during the course of the
morning. She kept one eye on the door the whole time,
but it remained closed as promised, and finally she pulled
herself out and toweled herself dry.

She'd never worn boys' clothes before. She hesitated
before donning the drawers, but they looked clean, and
she could hardly go without underwear. She pulled on a
rather gray undershirt, then buttoned a black flannel
shirt on over top of that. The pants were dark green. All
of the clothes looked worn and oft-repaired, but they
covered her and were comfortable enough.

She pulled on the patched blue socks Danyl had provided, then, leaving her boots where they were, padded
in stocking feet to the door of the bathroom. As she
pulled it open, she heard Danyl and Erl talking in low
voices in the main room, the sound carrying clearly down
the stone corridor.

". . . told you, I didn't know she would be in the Drop,"
Erl was saying.

"Then why did you show up when you did? And with
a weapon I didn't even know we had?" Danyl sounded
angry. "Do you know how much more salvage we could
have claimed if I'd been armed as well as Cark the last
few years?"

"You're armed as well as Cark was now," Erl pointed out. "Literally."

"Yeah, well, as you've already pointed out, fat lot of good that will do us once somebody new gains control of the Rustbloods and decides to take revenge. They know where the hovel is."

"It doesn't matter."

"Because you think they can't get in here? All they have to do is camp out front until we run out of supplies."

"It doesn't matter," Erl said again. "After today, we're done with the Middens."

"What?" Danyl sounded shocked, and Alania, equally alarmed, ran down the hallway.

"What?" she cried in echo.

The two men were seated at the table; their heads swung toward her in unison. Erl got to his feet. "Sit down," he said. "Danyl, your turn to get cleaned up. You stink."

Danyl turned back toward him. "I want to know what you mean!"

"And I'll explain it," Erl said. "But not until you're clean and we're sitting down to lunch." He glanced at his watch. "An early lunch, but I think we could all use it."

Danyl glared at him, glared at Alania with those blue eyes so frighteningly similar to her own, and then stomped off to the bathroom, slamming the door closed behind him.

"Forgive him," Erl said. "He has had a rather unconventional upbringing and no opportunity to practice social niceties." He smiled at her. "May I offer you a cup of kaff?"

Alania stared at the older man. Dark eyes sparkled at her. His accent, his turn of phrase . . .

Her eyes widened. "You're an Officer!"

Erl's left eyebrow arched. "Very observant. Yes, I was. But as far as First Officer Kranz and the Captain are concerned, I've been dead for twenty years." He jerked his head toward the corridor. "As has he."

Alania looked in the direction of the bathroom. "Does Danyl know?"

"No."

She turned back to Erl. "Then why did you just admit it to *me*?"

"First, because you'd already guessed. Second . . ." Erl sighed. "Second, because it no longer matters. I will tell Danyl the truth, too . . . if time permits."

That sounded ominous. "If time permits?"

"I'm expecting a call. Then I'll know." He stood. "So . . . kaff?"

Alanis *had* had a proper upbringing, and there was only one answer to such a question. "Yes, please," she said. "Two sugars, no milk."

Erl laughed. "Sugar is worth more than gold in the Middens, and milk is entirely unattainable."

"Then how can you get kaff?"

"Well, that's different. Kaff is a staple of life." He grinned. "Will you still have it even though you have to have it black?"

Alania sighed. "Yes, please."

Erl disappeared into the kitchen.

Alania put her elbows on the dining table and her head in her hands, running a finger over the synthetic skin covering the wound on her forehead. It was still morning, but she wanted nothing more than to go to bed and sleep for hours.

It seemed unlikely she would get her wish, so she settled for gratefully accepting the kaff Erl brought her in a rather ugly brown mug with a huge chip on one side of the lip. She was sipping from it when the bathroom door opened and Danyl came out wearing only a towel. He was wiry and well-muscled, and even from a distance she could see several scars on his torso and legs.

Then he glanced her way, and she blushed and quickly focused her attention on her mug.

Danyl emerged from his room—thankfully fully clothed—a few minutes later and joined them at the table, pulling up one of the armchairs from the wall since there were only two dining chairs. Erl went back into the kitchen and emerged with bowls of stew. Alania found herself famished. Apparently terror and the imminent threat of death both whetted the appetite and exhausted the body. *You also threw up every last bit of breakfast*, she reminded herself. She took her first bite of the stew rather gingerly, since she wasn't entirely sure what the lumps of meat in it were, but then devoured the rest as she discovered that whatever they were, they were deliciously savory.

Erl and Danyl ate more slowly. For a few minutes none of them spoke. Danyl finally broke the silence, pushing the armchair away from the table, its legs squawking against the stone floor. He folded his arms and glared at Erl. "Now I want some answers. You said you would tell us over lunch. Where did you get that beamer, how did you know to come rescue us, how did you know Alania's name, and what did you mean when you said we're done with the Middens?"

Danyl probably wanted to look stern and determined, but since the armchair was much lower to the ground than the dining chairs, he looked more like a ten-year-old seated at the grownups' table, trying hard to pretend to be an adult. Alania's mouth twitched at the thought.

Having the urge to smile at *anything* after the morning's events rather startled her, and it was in that moment that she realized something she had surely already known but hadn't admitted: she was enjoying herself.

Well, maybe "enjoy" wasn't quite the right word. But the truth was that despite the terror and pain and shock and everything else, this had been the most interesting morning of her entire twenty years of life, the one morning when everything that had happened had been completely out of the ordinary and uncontrolled.

Although, come to think of it, perhaps the out-of-the-ordinariness had really begun the day before with First Officer Kranz's unexpected arrival at her birthday party and subsequent shocking announcement.

I should thank him next time I see him for making it possible for me to finally get out of the City. Her mouth quirked again.

"You seem . . . remarkably unfazed by this morning's events," Erl said to her, ignoring Danyl. (She supposed he'd had a lot of practice at that.) Old he might be—at least, old to her—but clearly he missed nothing. "Even amused."

She shook her head. "Believe me, I am *completely* fazed," she said. "It's just . . ." She paused to try to find exactly the right words, and finally decided upon, "It's just that for once in my life, I'm not bored."

Danyl snorted. "So glad we could provide entertainment."

Erl gave him a warning look, and he subsided. "You have asked me several questions," he said to Danyl. "But before I provide my answers, I think you need to hear from Alania exactly how she embarked on such an . . . unexpected journey." He looked at Alania, and her eyes widened as she saw in his face that he already knew what she was going to say. *How . . . ?*

Ex-Officer, she thought. *And he said he's expecting a "call." He must still have contacts up above. He's not just an old scavenger. He's something else.*

What else they would presumably find out in a few minutes.

"All right," she said. She leaned forward, elbows on the table, and told Erl and Danyl everything that had happened to her, starting with the arrival of First Officer Kranz at her birthday party.

Danyl's eyes narrowed. "Yesterday was your birthday?"

She nodded. "My twentieth. Why?"

He glanced at Erl. "It was my birthday, too. Twentieth."

"And no, that is not a coincidence," Erl said. "Alania, carry on."

Alania told the rest of her tale. When she'd finished, Danyl gave a low whistle. "You're something special for sure." He gave Erl a meaningful look. "Something *valuable*."

Alania sighed. "You don't have to keep speaking in code. I've figured out why you want me and why you're being nice to me. You think maybe you can get a good ransom for me from the City. I'm the best piece of salvage that has come your way in years. Am I right?"

Danyl's mouth fell open a little. Erl laughed. "Our young guest here," he said, "is not stupid, Danyl. Out of her element, yes, but definitely not stupid." He snorted. "She could not be stupid, being what she is."

"But what am I?" Alania asked. "Do you know?"

Erl leaned back. "Therein," he says, "lies a tale." He sipped his kaff, then put it back on the table. "To begin with, not everyone is happy with the rule of the Captain and First Officer."

Alania wondered if he meant that to shock her. "Even on Twelfth Tier that's true," she pointed out.

"Indeed," Erl said. "As I have reason to know. Twenty years ago . . ."

An urgent beeping came from down the corridor leading to the bedrooms and bathroom. Erl twisted sharply around. "Early," he said, sounding worried.

"*What's* early?" Danyl demanded.

"I have a call." Erl pushed back his chair and went down the corridor to his own room.

"A call?" Danyl shouted after him. "From who?"

"*Whom*," Alania corrected without even thinking about it. Danyl turned his fiery gaze on her, brows knitted, and she raised her hands defensively, palms out, with a little laugh. "Sorry. Well drilled. I have also been known to fly into a rage when confronted by an errant apostrophe, and I once killed a servant who dared to misplace a comma."

Danyl's eyes widened. "You . . ."

Alania sighed. "I'm joking. I only had him severely beaten."

Danyl stared at her, and then, suddenly, he laughed.

Alania smiled at him, but the moment passed as quickly as it had come. Danyl leaned forward. "There's something I need," he said fiercely. "Something I thought you could get for me . . . or that I might be able to get because of you. I was going to take you to the Last Chance Market and barter you for the one thing I've never been able to afford, the one thing even Erl hasn't been able to get: a City Pass."

Alania didn't know what that was. Her confusion must have shown on her face, because Danyl rushed on. "It's a . . . ticket, an entrance ticket to the City, granting permission to live and work there. Very few of them are granted to anyone who isn't born and raised in the City. But there's a trader in the Market who swears he can get me one if I find something valuable enough. And you are *definitely* valuable enough. The Market is this afternoon. But now . . ." He looked down the hallway. "Erl says I'll never go back into the Middens. I don't know what that means. And he clearly has something else in mind for you . . ."

"Yes," Erl said, appearing from his room. "He does."

Danyl twisted all the way around in his chair to face him. "And are you finally going to tell me what that is?"

"I will tell you what you need to know." Alania realized Erl had the beamer rifle in his hand again. "How much ammo in Cark's slugthrower?"

"Twelve rounds," Danyl said. "Erl . . ."

"It'll have to do," Erl muttered. "It'll hold them off for

a little while, at least." He looked at Alania and Danyl in turn. "Both of you get your boots on. Danyl, get your backpack. Then come to the kitchen." He left them.

"Hold them off?" Danyl shouted after him. "Hold off who?"

No answer. Danyl swore, shoved the armchair back, and stalked down the hall to his room.

"Hold off *whom*," Alania murmured to no one in particular. Then she sighed. "I guess a nap is out of the question."

She headed toward the bathroom to retrieve her boots.

ELEVEN

BY THE TIME Danyl got to the kitchen, Erl, a backpack and the beamer rifle on the floor beside him, was kneeling at the back wall as though praying—somewhat startling, since Erl had never shown any religious proclivities before. But then he stood up again, and a section of the wall that Danyl had always thought was solid rock swung outward, revealing a tunnel, a twin to the one at the front of their quarters. Danyl gaped at it, feeling a moment of confusion that was almost like vertigo. How many more surprises would this day hold?

"We don't have much time," Erl said as Alania came into the room. He reached down, picked up the pack, and held it out to Alania, who took it. "Put this on; it has supplies you'll need. Follow this tunnel. After about a hundred and fifty meters, it turns sharply right; follow it another couple of hundred meters, and you'll reach a ramp. It descends a few meters, then joins a stairwell. Going up, the stairwell leads to the Rim. Don't go that way, or you'll die. Take the stairs down all the way to the bottom of the Canyon. You'll find a boat on the River. Get into it and let it float you down to the River People. Ask for Yvelle. She will be expecting you. She will get you to Prime."

"Wait!" Danyl glared at Erl. "Have you gone insane? The River People? Yvelle? Prime? In twenty years you've never mentioned any of these things!"

"For twenty years you didn't need to know about them. Now you do. There's no time, Danyl. Do as I say."

"You keep saying there's no time. But you never say *why*. Who did you get a call from? What's happening?"

Erl took a deep breath. "Alania is not just valuable, she's *in*valuable . . . to a lot of people, but especially to First Officer Kranz. He knows she dropped into the Middens, and he knows she's alive. He's ordered the Provosts after her. I suspect they're already in the Middens. They'll hit the Rustbloods first, and the survivors will point them to us. If they're not already on their way to the hovel, they will be soon. The Rustbloods might not be able to recognize the entrance to our little hideaway here, and they certainly can't get through that door, but the Provosts can. They'll take Alania back to the City. That can't be allowed to happen. She wasn't supposed to end up down here, and she sure as hell wasn't supposed to end up with me . . . and especially not with *you* . . . but that's the hand we've been dealt, and that's the hand we have to play." He reached into his pocket and pulled out a familiar object: an old-fashioned data crystal, bright blue, six-sided, ten centimeters long and a centimeter wide. "Turn around."

"What?"

"Turn around!"

Danyl obeyed. He saw that Alania had put on the pack Erl had given her; now Erl tucked the data crystal into an outside pocket of his own backpack. "There's a reader in Alania's pack," Erl said as he sealed the pocket. "Use it when you have time. Which you won't until— *unless*—you make it to the River People."

Danyl spun to face him. He had suddenly realized where this was heading, and fierce denial welled up in him. "You're coming, too!" he cried, but as he had known he would, Erl shook his head.

"No. I have to delay the Provosts. I'll hold them in the tunnel, keep them from coming after you."

"They'll kill you."

"No," Erl said, "they won't. First Officer Kranz is going to want to talk to me. I'll surrender as soon as I'm out of ammo. I'll lie, tell them you fled the other way through the Middens, send them on a wild goose chase to the Greenskulls. I'll be fine."

"Talk to you?" Danyl stared at him. "Why?"

"There's no time. The data crystal will tell you. Now go."

Danyl felt panic rising in his chest, an unfamiliar sensation, something he hadn't felt since he was twelve and trapped in the trashslide. His panic then had done him absolutely no good. Struggling had only made the rubbish grip his body tighter. It wouldn't do him any good this time, either, but the thought of losing Erl . . .

"You're the only family I have! I can't—"

An alarm cut him off: a sharp, repeating squawk, so loud and piercing it hurt.

Alania flung her hands over her ears. "What's that?"

"Intruders in the hovel," Erl said. "The Provosts have arrived. It won't take them long to find the real entrance." He snatched up the beamer rifle from the floor and thrust it at Danyl. "Take it!"

Danyl stared at the weapon for a long moment, then seized it almost spasmodically and slung it over his shoulder.

Erl turned to Alania. "I'm sorry we didn't have an opportunity to get to know each other better," he said to her, and bowed, a courtly gesture that Danyl had never seen him make before.

Alania curtsied in response. "As am I, sir," she said. "But I do thank you for the kaff and that delicious meal."

"You are most welcome."

Danyl felt as if he'd fallen into some strange alternate universe. The Provosts were literally knocking on the door, he and Alania were supposed to flee for their lives along a tunnel he'd never even known existed until that moment, and Erl and Alania were exchanging polite chitchat?

Life at the top of the City clearly drove people bonkers.

The moment passed. Erl turned back to Danyl. "Now go!"

Danyl surprised himself by flinging his arms around the older man. "No time, boy!" Erl growled, but all the same, he returned the hug.

Danyl took a deep breath and released his guardian. As he had so many times at Erl's urging, he had a task to perform. Flight this time, not salvage or scouting, but Erl had never steered him wrong before. "Good-bye."

"Good-bye," Erl said. "I—"

Whatever he wanted to add was cut off by a new alarm, even higher-pitched and more frantic.

Erl's head snapped toward the dining room. "They've uncovered the door mechanism. Go!" He dashed out of the kitchen. Alania ran through the secret door and into the tunnel beyond. Danyl followed, then turned and hurriedly searched the wall for some way to close the door behind them. He found a pressure plate and pressed it.

As the door swung shut, he heard the unmistakable boom of Cark's ancient rifle.

Erl ran into the dining room and grabbed the late Rustblood leader's antique slugthrower from where Danyl had left it next to the door into the entrance tunnel. Twelve rounds, Danyl had said. Erl doubted he'd have the chance to use them all.

He opened the door into the tunnel, propped it open with the hunk of slag they kept handy for that purpose, then knelt and aimed the rifle down the corridor, waiting.

He wasn't particularly concerned about getting shot; the Provosts' heads-up displays would immediately identify him as an Officer from the implant he still carried in the muscle of his right arm. And not just *any* Officer, but Ensign Erlkin Orillia, a name from the past that should raise all *sorts* of interesting red flags.

He'd never removed the tag because it could only be read at very close quarters, and if any Provosts got *that* close, like now, he *wanted* them to be able to read it. His sudden reappearance twenty years after he was presumed dead would confuse them, slow them down. He'd surrender, then tell them some story about Danyl and Alania running away together through the Middens. These chambers, prepared secretly for him and the boy before Yvelle's raid on Twelfth Tier Hospital, didn't exist on any map. Nor was there any record of the back exit that led to the long-closed stairs from the East Rim to the bottom of the Canyon. Even though the stairs themselves—and the collapsed elevator shaft that ran parallel to them—certainly *were* in the City's databases, they hadn't been used for at least a century. Danyl and Alania should be able to make it to the River People safely, and Yvelle could take it from there. After the warning call from Prime, Erl had contacted her, passing along Prime's instructions for getting the young people safely to him. Even if the Provosts found the River People—no, not if, *when*, if he was honest with himself, though he wished like hell they could stay hidden—Danyl and Alania would be long gone, en route to Prime himself.

Erl didn't want to kill any Provosts if he could help it; hitting one of them might tempt them to shoot first and ask questions never, and he wanted to be taken alive and unharmed to the City, where he was quite certain Prime would find a way to free him. His biggest worry about Cark's rifle was that its aiming laser might be so far out of alignment that he'd shoot someone he was actually trying to *miss*.

He glanced around at the quarters he had shared with

Danyl for twenty years. They'd been good years, but they had already been due to come to an end as the plan he and Prime had put in place so long ago finally came to fruition.

Still, they hadn't meant things to end like *this*. Those lower-Tier idiots Prime had set the task of kidnapping Alania had screwed up royally, and now everything he and Prime had worked toward for so long was in danger. If the Provosts hadn't done the job for him, he would gladly have shot the feckless fools himself.

Erl's gaze snapped back to the tunnel as the front-door alarm suddenly cut off. The door had been unsealed.

Yvelle will get them to Prime, Erl thought, raising the rifle so the red dot of the aiming laser touched the stone just above the door. *She wasn't happy to hear from me, but she'll do it. She has no choice—or rather, she made her choice twenty years ago.*

And meanwhile, I'll get myself into the City. Prime will free me. Working together, we can salvage this. We've got both of the Cityborn, after all, and Kranz has squat.

The door to the hovel suddenly swung inward, revealing the hut's interior, apparently deserted. Erl fired anyway, the bullet striking right where the laser pointed, ricocheting off the ceiling in a spray of stone chips. *That'll make them cautious*, he thought. *They'll stick a sensor around the corner to scope out the situation, realize who I am, and then . . .*

Instead, some maniac burst through the door, spraying automatic fire.

Erl barely registered a massive blow to his head before his world went black.

Danyl, the beamer rifle clutched uselessly in his left hand, pressed his forehead and right palm against the closed door's smooth stone, trembling, that single shot echoing in his mind. The entrance tunnel was a death trap. Even if Erl intended to surrender—even if, for some unfathomable reason, First Officer Kranz wanted him alive—would the Provosts allow it?

Suddenly furious, he shoved himself away from the wall and spun to look down *their* tunnel, lit only by the pale-green light of eternals every five meters. He strode past Alania. "Come on!"

"Erl will be all right," she said from behind him.

"How would you know?" he snapped at her over his shoulder.

"He's an Officer. Provosts would never—"

Danyl stopped so suddenly Alania ran into him. He spun to face her. "He's what?"

"An Officer. He told me while you were in the bath."

"He told you . . . ?" Danyl stared at her, outrage and more than a little plain old *rage* bubbling up inside him. "You're lying. He's raised me since I was a baby. I've asked him thousands of times to tell me where he came from. He's never answered. He's known you for a couple of hours, and you want me to believe he told you his life story?"

Alania took a step back, her expression wary. "He would have told you just now, if that call hadn't—"

"A call." Danyl clenched his fists so hard his nails dug into his palms. "I knew he had contacts in the City because he knew when Drops were coming—like the one today—but I never knew how he knew. I figured some trader was passing him information at the Last Chance Market. Now I find out he's been in direct contact with someone high up the City all this time. And then just like that, we're on the run." He looked back down the corridor. "What the *hell*, Erl?" he shouted. His voice echoed back, but no one answered.

"I guessed before he told me by the way he talked,"

Alania said. "He just confirmed it, if that's any consolation."

"I don't need consolation," Danyl snarled. "I'm not a child." He shook his head. "He's an *Officer*. And now Provosts are after us." He shot her a look. "After *you*. The First Officer wants *you*. You're his *ward*."

"As of this morning," Alania said. "For twenty years he's ignored me. I don't know what's going on any more than you do, Danyl."

He stared at the closed door into the kitchen for another long moment, then turned and hurried on. "*Damn him!*"

"At least you care about him, and he cares about you," Alania said in a soft voice behind him. "I'd give anything to have that."

Danyl didn't turn around.

They reached the right-angle turn, then jogged along the new tunnel. Two hundred meters really wasn't very far, but it seemed to take forever to travel. At last they reached a ramp sloping down. At the bottom there was another long, straight corridor, and at the end of that they emerged through an open, red-painted door into the promised stairwell.

The metal landing, the stairs leading both up and down from it, and the supports for the stairs bolted into the stone were pitted and rusted. And unlike the eternals in the corridors they'd just traversed, which had burned as bright as eternals ever got, the lights in this stairwell, a square, smooth-walled shaft about fifteen meters wide, were dim or entirely absent. In the uncertain light, it was impossible to ascertain how far the stairs extended in either direction. Danyl stared up. Erl had said the stairs led to the Rim, which in this location meant they also led to the mysterious, impenetrable Cubes . . . but why? Had these stairs been built at the same time as the Cubes?

He looked down. The Canyon was half a kilometer

deep; the stairs simply disappeared below them into darkness the failing eternals could not penetrate. "I had no idea these existed," he said. "But they must have been here for decades . . . maybe centuries. Stick close; we don't know how sturdy the—"

With a sharp *crack!* a puff of dust and chipped stone erupted from the wall just outside the red-painted door. Danyl grabbed Alania and hustled her down the metal stairs. "Provosts!"

"They won't shoot *me*," Alania said. "If I give myself up—"

Danyl's rage surged again, and he swung the beamer toward her. "Erl wanted *both* of us to escape," he snarled. "He said it was important . . . so important he may have . . ." He couldn't say it. He gave Alania a shove toward the stairs. "You're *not* going back to them. *Move!*"

Alania glared at him, then gave a jerky nod, turned, and clattered down the rusty stairs. He followed.

Above them, the slap of booted feet on stone mingled with hoarse shouts. He and Alania were no more than twenty meters down the stairs when the shouts suddenly shifted from faint and muffled to loud and clear: the Provosts had entered the shaft directly above them. Danyl grabbed Alania again and thrust her back against the wall, one arm pressed across her chest, his other hand clutching the beamer rifle.

"Are you sure you saw something, Jerrik?" a man called.

"Can't be certain, sir," a second replied, "but I thought I saw movement."

A moment's silence. Then a light flashed on, flickering through the metal grids of the stairs above them. "What the hell is this place?"

"Shaft to the bottom of the Canyon in one direction, looks like." The light flashed up. "Goes up to the Rim and the Cubes in the other, I'd guess. It's old. Old as the City, maybe."

"Corridor we just came through wasn't old," the first man said. "Somebody cut that to join up with this." The lights flashed around some more. "This shadow you shot at, Jerrik. Did it go up or down?"

"Can't say, sir."

A moment's silence.

"All right." A crackling sound: a communicator. "Corporal Storlin, Captain Mirral here. Status, please."

"The old man's on his way to the City, Cap," a voice came back. "Bit of a firefight happening over on the other side of the Canyon, but shouldn't be a problem on this side."

Danyl's heart skipped a beat. The old man? Erl? On his way to the City? But . . . alive, or dead?

"All right, then. Preskot, Torgan, head up the stairs. Jerrik and Xarver, you're with me. We'll head down. Helmet lights, everyone."

Shit, Danyl thought. He turned his head and barely breathed into Alania's ear. "Move when they move. Quiet as you can, but we have to stay directly underneath them or they'll spot us and be able to shoot at us." She turned to resume the descent, but he pinned her where she was a moment longer. "Wait . . ." He listened. Footsteps, lights flickering, maybe four or five turns of the stairs above them. "Now."

Around and around the shaft they went, always directly below the descending Provosts. The air grew cooler as they descended, and the walls dampened. The stairs, which had seemed solid enough when they first stepped onto them, now occasionally quivered as though their anchors to the shaft walls had loosened.

Then they rounded the shaft for the thirty-third time, and with a groan and a bang and a squeal of tortured metal, the stairs fell away beneath their feet and pitched them forward into darkness.

TWELVE

ALL I HAVE TO DO is let the Provosts catch me, and I *could be back on Twelfth Tier by dinner.* The thought circulated in Alania's mind in time with their revolutions of the shaft. "They won't shoot me," she'd told Danyl, and she knew that was true. Kranz, for some utterly inexplicable reason, valued her so highly that he'd sent Provosts into the Middens after her.

Erl, for some equally inexplicable reason, considered her so valuable that he might well have given his life to give her the chance to get away.

Well, considered her *and Danyl* that valuable: both of them, as Danyl had pointed out. But whereas she could understand Erl's concern for the boy he'd raised from infancy, he'd had no clue she had even existed until today ...

Until he was told by his mysterious contact on high, and she didn't mean God.

She remembered the surveillance cameras she'd found in her bedroom. Lieutenant Beruthi hadn't been her guardian—he'd been her *warden*, enforcing her house arrest. She clenched her fists in renewed anger at that violation. So, yes, she could turn herself in to the Provosts and return to Twelfth Tier, just like any escaped prisoner could turn herself in and be returned to prison.

Funny thing was, she didn't want to go to prison. No matter how pleasant a prison it might be. No matter how uncomfortable freedom might be ... and so far, she thought, her calves aching with the constant descent, it had proved pretty uncomfortable.

There was another thing. Erl wasn't the only one who had risked his life so she could escape. Men had died in the raid on Twelfth Tier. She hadn't asked for any of it, but those deaths were at least partly on her shoulders, and to go meekly back to the First Officer and whatever fate he had in store for her, certainly never to escape again, would make a mockery of those deaths. She had to find out what was going on. She had to know why everyone wanted her so badly. She had to learn what her connection with Danyl was. She had to ...

She had to get to the bottom of this bloody staircase. Was there no end to the damn thing?

Almost as she thought that, it ended. Suddenly. It collapsed beneath them, and she and Danyl toppled forward. It happened so fast she had no time to react, and then she slammed onto the still-solid next landing—not a long fall, but enough to drive the breath from her body. For a moment she couldn't move, paralyzed with pain and shock. Then Danyl jumped down beside her; he must have managed to grab something as the stairs came apart. "Are you all right?" he asked anxiously. "Can you move?"

She managed to gasp in a tiny, tiny amount of air. "Breath ... gone ..."

"Any broken bones?"

She tried to consider that as spots danced in her vision. "I ... don't think so." Her breathing eased. Her vision cleared. "Not ... arms and legs, anyway. Ribs ... I can't tell."

"You're bleeding."

"Again?" Alania raised her hand to her head. Her fingers came away dark with blood. *At least it's in a different spot than the last cut,* she thought inanely.

"Someone below us!" came a shout from above them, where the lights flashed.

"Alania Beruthi!" called the voice of Captain Mirral. "Is that you?"

Danyl raised a finger to his lips, but Alania wasn't about to answer. Even if she'd had the breath.

"Sounded like the stairs collapsed, sir," the first voice said. "She could be injured."

"Keep moving. But spread out. These things clearly aren't safe."

Understatement of the year. Alania pushed herself upright, wincing. Bruises, scrapes, and her bleeding forehead seemed the worst of her injuries. In fact, she already felt better than she had a moment before.

"We can't stay directly below them if they spread out around the shaft," Danyl whispered. "We have to move now!"

"So help me up, idiot," Alania whispered back. Danyl looked startled, then grabbed her arm and pulled her to her feet.

They'd only gone a few more steps before someone shouted, "Halt!"

Danyl didn't hesitate. He flung himself against the wall, raised the beamer rifle, and fired at the bright spot of light above them and across the shaft. A man cried out, and the light bobbled and dropped. "Run!" Danyl shouted to Alania, and the two of them pounded down the stairs, which shook and trembled beneath their feet.

A flash lit the shaft, and a bullet whined off the railing to their left. "Cease fire, you idiot!" roared Captain Marril. "You might hit the girl!"

"They shot Xarver!"

"Grazed him. He's out of commission but he'll live. But we won't if we kill the First Officer's ward. So stop shooting, turn off your helmet light so they can't shoot you, too, and keep going down! We'll catch them at the bottom. It must empty out onto the Canyon floor, and there's nowhere for them to run down there."

There'd better be, Alania thought. Stumbling, aching

with every step, she pressed on down the stairs. *Erl sent us this way. Told us to find the River People. Some woman named Yvelle. There must be a way out.*

Or at least there used to be. The stairs were starting to fall apart. Who knew what shape the exit might be in? What if it had collapsed and they found themselves trapped at the bottom of the shaft?

The stairs weren't the only thing deteriorating. Only a few eternals still burned down here and only with the faintest green glow. On the plus side, it was too dark for their pursuers to see them. On the minus side, it was too dark for them to see what might—

Danyl gasped and grabbed her right arm, making her grunt with pain as her already abused muscles were abused still more. But she forgave him as she realized he'd just saved her life.

They had come to the end of the stairs . . . but not the bottom of the shaft.

The last two turns of the spiral were simply *gone*. Or not *exactly* gone—looking over the final step past the torn metal bracing, Alania could just make out a dark mass of twisted metal beneath them, where a single eternal still managed to glow. "Dammit," Danyl muttered. He turned and looked up. "From the sound of it, they're farther back than they were. That gap in the stairs probably slowed them down. But they're coming." He lifted the beamer. "I'll have to take my shot when I—"

"Wait," Alania said, peering into the dimness below. "I think we can get down there."

Danyl turned. "What?"

"Look." She pointed. "The braces . . . brackets . . . whatever you call the things that hold the stairs to the wall. They're still there. The stairs came off the supports, but the supports didn't come out of the wall. We should be able to use them like stairs." *Very skinny, bendy, uncertain stairs. Are you crazy?* part of her wanted to know.

She ignored it.

"Are you crazy?" Danyl echoed her inner critic. Unfortunately, she couldn't ignore *him*.

"They know you have a beamer," Alania said. "They've turned off their lights. They won't present a target until the last minute. There are two of them left. Even if you get one of them, the other one gets you, and I just get . . . gotten."

Danyl stared up the shaft a moment longer, then shouldered the beamer and turned back to Alania. "All right," he said. "You go first. If they get here before we find a way to the bottom, I might get a shot."

"I think you're going to need both hands," Alania said, already wishing she hadn't thought of doing what she was about to do. But there was no time for second thoughts, and so she stepped down onto the first torn support, no more than half a meter in length and bent downward. She expected it to flex, but then again, she weighed far less than the stairs it used to support. It didn't move.

Much.

Leaning against the wall as if her life depended on it, which of course it did, she took another step. And then another. After half a dozen, Danyl started down behind her.

Step by step, they descended. About twenty steps down, a bracket had torn out of the wall, leaving a gap. Alania took a deep breath and an extra-long step. For a frightening moment she felt herself overbalancing, but she lurched toward the wall and slammed her already bruised shoulder against it. Wincing, she pressed on.

One and a half turns around the shaft, and she reached the tangled metal of the fallen stairs. She stopped for a moment. Her eyes had adjusted to the darkness as she descended, and the single eternal burning below provided just enough light for her to see the general shape of things. It looked like she should be able to climb down through the maze of metal bars and twisted steps to the ground . . . if it *was* ground. It glistened. *What if the bottom of the shaft is full of water?* she thought. *It could be meters deep.*

Shouts from above. She looked up.

The Provosts, barely visible silhouettes in the gloom, had reached the end of the steps. They'd have to descend the same way she and Danyl had, and they wouldn't be able to use their weapons as they did so any more than Danyl could use his beamer now—not that the Provosts presented very good targets, with both the poor lighting and the metal stairs protecting them.

Or did those thin slabs of metal matter to a beamer? She knew nothing about weapons. Until today, she'd never expected to need to.

She took a deep breath and stepped tentatively down onto the jumbled, jagged mass of metal that had once been stairs. It gave under her weight, but not much. Carefully, she felt her way lower and lower. Danyl followed close behind.

Something dropped from above, hitting the metal with a clang and then bouncing its way down to the bottom of the pile. She barely had time to wonder what it was before it exploded.

Light blinded her wide-pupiled eyes, stabbing into her head like diamond daggers, and the blast stunned and deafened her. Her fingers slipped from the bit of railing she clung to, and she dropped the rest of the way to the bottom of the shaft.

She hit the icy water with a splash, floundered, found her feet, and stood up, gasping, still waist-deep. Something thudded onto a bit of staircase over her head and hung there: Danyl's beamer, stopped from falling into the water by its strap. She couldn't see Danyl—she could hardly see anything after that flash except the lights of the two Provosts, who must have switched them on again to check the results of their explosive device. One had moved off the final hanging step and was slowly descending the broken supports that Alania and Danyl had just negotiated. The other remained where the stairs ended, presumably with his rifle pointed into the shaft, his target Danyl . . .

. . . who was either unconscious or dead.

Alania didn't know where the impulse came from. All she knew was that suddenly she felt enraged: furious at the Provosts pursuing them, at her erstwhile guardian Lieutenant Beruthi, at First Officer Kranz. She ripped Danyl's beamer rifle from where it hung and raised it.

The Provost who had remained on the steps was still almost directly above her; she couldn't get a clean shot at him. But the other one was on the other side of the shaft from her, halfway down the failed supports.

The beamer, she discovered, painted a red dot on its target. She aimed above the headlamp, slid the dot down the Provost's helmet, his chest . . .

"Beamer!" the man above screamed, but Alania had found the Provost's leg with the bright red dot and pressed the firing stud.

A flash, a pop, a sizzle, and the man screamed and dropped from the wall, slamming into the metal tangle below so hard that all the wreckage trembled . . . and Danyl also dropped from somewhere up above, drenching Alania anew as he splashed into the water. Alania, suddenly shaking—*I shot a man!*—slung the beamer over her shoulder and knelt, feeling for Danyl, afraid he might be unconscious and drowning. But when her fingers touched his shoulder, he grabbed them suddenly and tightly and then exploded upright, coughing and sputtering. "What . . ."

"Flash. Bang. I don't know."

"Flashbang."

"That's what I said," Alania said, confused.

"No, that's what it's called. A flashbang. A stun grenade." Danyl sounded shaky. "Are you all right?"

"Blinded me. Deafened me. For a minute."

"Knocked me right out."

"Captain Marril!" shouted the remaining Provost directly over their heads. "Sir! Talk to me!"

Danyl's head jerked up, then back to Alania. "What happened?"

"Got the beamer. Shot the other one as he came down." Alania tried to say it matter-of-factly, but it didn't sound matter-of-fact. "He fell. Over there." Now that she looked, she could see the fallen man's headlamp glimmering through the tangle of metal. It wasn't moving.

"Good," Danyl said. He turned toward the wall. "There has to be an exit . . . oh. Of course."

Alania saw what he'd just spotted: a metal door at the end of a short tunnel a few feet higher than the floor of the shaft, which began beneath the lone eternal still burning down here. But that short tunnel was on the opposite side of the shaft from them . . . where they would provide an excellent target for the Provost still lurking above them, rifle in hand, calling for his fallen officer.

THIRTEEN

DANYL STILL FELT a little fuzzy-headed from the effects of the flashbang, but it didn't dampen his newfound respect for Alania. Who'd have thought a sheltered Officer girl from Twelfth Tier would have it in her to beam down a Provost?

He just hoped he'd live long enough to tell her how impressed he was. "We're going to need to distract him, get him looking the wrong way," he whispered. "I'll do that. You make for the door."

Alania peered at the exit. "Looks like there's just enough room to duck under the wreckage," she said. "All right. Do you want the beamer?"

Danyl started to say yes, of course he wanted the beamer . . . but then he realized that made no sense. If anyone was going to have a shot at the Provost still above them, it would be Alania. "No," he said. "Keep it. If this doesn't work, it may be your only chance."

Alania didn't argue, just nodded. Even allowing for the dim light, she looked pale. *Well, she just shot someone. She's got a right to.*

"All right," he said. "Here we go." Keeping as close to the wall as he could—which, thanks to the wreckage, wasn't very close—he crept slowly through the water. He could see the Provost up above, and he knew all the man had to do was flick his light toward Danyl and he'd be seen (and likely shot). But the Provost was peering in the direction of his fallen commander, whose own light had started to move as though he were turning his head from side to side.

"Captain Marril!" shouted the man up above, and Danyl took advantage of the noise. He plunged under the water, surfaced close to the wreckage, raised his arms, and brought them splashing down as he let out a horrendous moan. *Overacting much?* he thought as he submerged again and moved. And not a moment too soon—a tremendous flash lit the shaft, and bullets zipped into the water where he had been two seconds before.

In that same instant, Alania splashed under the wreckage, scrambled up the steps leading to the tunnel, and dashed into it. In her wake, bullets chipped the stone at the tunnel's mouth. Danyl dove under the black water, swam blindly for several strokes, emerged with another moan, and plunged to the side again as the rifle blasted in his direction. The light from the Provost's lamp flashed wildly across the water where he had been while he lunged for the tunnel in the shadows. Alania waited there, just out of the line of fire. Danyl scrambled up the steps and in beside her just as the Provost got his bearings again. Bullets shattered stone and struck sparks off metal, but none found their targets.

Breathing hard, Danyl nodded to Alania. "Good work," he said. "You sure you haven't done this before?"

She smiled, though her face looked as pale as ever in the dim light. "I think I'd remember."

"He'll be heading down after us, or at least to help the other guy. Let's get out of here."

He splashed down the tunnel through water just a few centimeters deep. The metal door looked forbidding, but when he pushed down on the latch, there was a solid, satisfying click, and the door swung smoothly and silently outward. Someone had clearly been maintaining it, although he wondered if they'd bothered to open it, since they hadn't done anything about the twenty meters of metal staircase that lay in ruins on this side of it.

With water foaming around his feet and pouring down three steps to spread out on a stone floor, Danyl, blinking in what seemed painfully bright light after their long descent in the dark, found himself looking into another stone chamber. Although the floor had been smoothed, this one was clearly natural, the reddish rock above them rough and green with slime. Past the mouth of the cave flowed a river, the water slick and oily, covered with an iridescent sheen.

A wooden pier thrust into that black water, and tied up to it was a boat, if you could call it that. Flat-bottomed and graceless, it looked to have been cobbled together from stray pieces of wood and plastic, as it almost certainly had been. What other raw materials could these "River People" have except for rubbish they salvaged from the lowest reaches of the Middens?

"That's our ride," he said to Alania. She mutely held out the beamer rifle, and this time he took it. Then he took hold of her arm and helped her limp toward the boat.

They emerged from the cavern, and for a moment Danyl forgot everything else.

The Black River flowed to their left, south along the Canyon, disappearing around a bend. Sheer walls of red stone towered above them, boulders the size of aircars scattered at their bases. The River slithered around the half-submerged rocks like an oily snake, leaving behind a greasy gray residue.

To their right rose the Middens.

Centuries' worth of rubbish hundreds of meters deep had compressed here at the base into a black, greasy conglomerate. A steep slope covered with a sickly green sheen of weeds stretched up and up to the City, though all Danyl could see of the vast structure was its rounded top—the opalescent dome of the Thirteenth Tier, home to the mythical Captain.

Alania followed his gaze, and he wondered what she was thinking as she looked up at her old home.

Probably hating you for not letting her turn herself in when she had the chance. But he couldn't betray Erl that way. He had no idea why his guardian wanted them down here, wanted them to find Yvelle and the River People, but Erl had been willing to risk his life to make it possible, and Danyl was damn well going to try to carry out what might've been his final wishes.

Tunnels had been driven into the bottom of that massive heap of refuse, the openings shored up with beams of wood, metal, and plastic. Eternals glimmered in the depths of those tunnels.

Mines, he realized. *These "River People" are mining the Middens.*

He thought he heard a sound in the cavern behind them. *Enough sightseeing.* He turned away from the Middens and stepped down into the boat. It rocked under his weight, the movement sending long, slow ripples across the oily water. In the boat's flat bottom he found two paddles. He held out his hand to help Alania down into the ungainly craft, then handed her a paddle. She took it gingerly. "What do I do with this?"

"Paddle," Danyl said.

She gave him a withering look. "I know *that*. But . . . how?"

"Do I *look* like someone who's done a lot of boating?" Danyl said. "Do the best you can." He used the paddle to push the boat away from the pier, and it drifted out into the River, moving farther away from the shore as the current took it.

From the center of the Canyon, the Middens looked even taller, and he could see that in the very middle of the slope was a long, wide gouge, a scar where no weeds grew and the rubbish looked fresher, as though it had arrived recently or been flipped over. Danyl recognized the signs—sometime recently, a trashalanche had roared down that slope, plunging down into the River . . .

. . . right where they currently drifted.

Danyl remembered being trapped in the trashslide when he was twelve, the day he'd followed Erl to the Last Chance Market. He'd been lucky he'd only been injured, even luckier that Erl had scavenged the docbot that had fixed him up and managed to keep it stocked over the years with—

Scavenged?

Danyl suddenly felt like an idiot. Whatever Erl had been doing for the last twenty years, it clearly had involved far more than scavenging. *He must have been getting supplies directly from his contact in the City*, Danyl thought. *He probably just had to make a call to get whatever he needed.* It hadn't just been *Erl* protecting him his whole life; it had been a whole network of people, people he didn't even know, all trying to keep him safe.

It had to be the same people who had tried to kidnap Alania from the First Officer. But why?

What's going on?

The River gave no answer, slithering unhurriedly along between the towering Canyon walls. Danyl looked at the gray scum covering his paddle each time he drew it from the water and hoped like hell neither of them fell in.

The boat, with its shallow draft and flat bottom, seemed designed for someone to stand up and drive it along with an oar or pole from the rear. Danyl kept *his* bottom firmly planted on *its* bottom instead and paddled away, trying really, really hard not to splash any of the foul liquid on his skin or Alania's. They both had multiple scrapes, and though Alania seemed to heal as quickly as he did and might even be as resistant to infection, they still needed clean water, antiseptic, antibiotics, and bandages as soon as possible.

He snorted. Why not hope for a Twelfth-Tier hospital while he was at it? It seemed about as likely.

They reached a bend in the River and slipped silently around it, the Middens and the City vanishing from sight. They floated down another long stretch and rounded another bend, then another and another. Danyl had never before been out of sight of the City. It was a strange feeling. He supposed it should have been liberating, but it was hard to feel liberated while trapped in this strange boat with no place to land beneath the sheer walls, accompanied by the certain knowledge that sooner or later Provosts would follow them down the ugly River.

His watch still worked. It was approaching 1300—midday. They'd been on the River for a bit more than an hour when they rounded another bend ... and everything changed.

The walls of the Canyon closed in. The current sped up. Worse, the water began to heap up into oily black hummocks, which could only mean there were rocks beneath the surface. There was no white water—Danyl doubted this river could *form* white water—but a greasy gray foam began to collect on the surface.

"Stop paddling!" Danyl called to Alania. He pulled his paddle from the water as Alania shipped hers, then stuck it over the stern of the boat, hoping to use it as a rudder. His mouth had gone dry. If they hit one of those rocks and tipped into the River, neither of them would come up again.

Fortunately, for all the turmoil in the water, there seemed to be a deep channel right down the center of the stream. Danyl suspected it was man-made—it acted almost like a rail along which the boat sped, the water pouring around the boulders to either side forming a kind of cushion, keeping them right where they needed to be.

They raced downstream now rather than crawled. As they neared yet another bend, Danyl began to hear a roaring, rushing rumble.

He looked desperately around, but there was no escape. The walls rose as steeply as ever. Far overhead, blue sky mocked them. Bright sunlight lit more than half of the western wall. Soon the sun would shine directly down onto the River, however briefly.

Danyl doubted either of them would see it. That noise could only mean one thing:

A waterfall. Their deaths.

Gripping his paddle so hard his knuckles whitened, he cried, "Hold on!" to Alania and waited helplessly to see what the River had in store.

FOURTEEN

"HOLD ON!" DANYL CRIED to Alania, but of course there was nothing to hold on to but the thin walls—transoms? ransoms?—of the boat, and they felt like they might snap off in her white-knuckled hands at any moment.

She could hear the thunder of falling water and knew Danyl had come to the same conclusion as she: that just out of sight around the next bend, the River plunged into a waterfall. If they went over the edge and fell into this dark water, that would be the end. Even if the fall didn't kill them, as it almost certainly would if there were rocks at the bottom, the water was foul, and the backpack Erl had provided would drag her down. She felt as helpless as she had in the elevator that had dumped her into the Middens.

Surely Erl hadn't meant for this to happen. Had he not known about the waterfall? Or had they misunderstood his instructions? Were they supposed to have gone the other way, into those shadowy mineshafts dug into the bottom of the Middens? Or had there been some other place they were supposed to disembark, some landing spot they'd overlooked . . . ?

They swept ever closer to the bend. The roar grew louder. Sunlight raced down the western wall of the Canyon with astonishing speed, and just as they reached the bend, it cleared the eastern wall and lit up the River like a spotlight. It wasn't an improvement; the water suddenly looked black as ink, covered with an iridescent sheen of poisonous colors.

Then they rounded the bend, and Alania's heart leaped into her throat and fluttered there like a trapped bird when she saw the waterfall a hundred meters away. They swept toward it at a terrifying velocity, but as they neared the spot where the River plunged out of sight, a smooth, curving drop-off where the sun had turned the water the purple-black of an old bruise, something exploded into view in a cloud of spray.

Danyl yelped, and Alania screamed, convinced for a terrifying instant that some nightmarish creature, all dripping tentacles and antennae, had burst from the water to seize them. But then suddenly her brain reinterpreted what her eyes were registering, and she realized it wasn't a creature at all, but a net—a vast net strung from one side of the Canyon to the other.

And then they slammed into it.

The impact pitched Alania forward. She grabbed the slimy netting—rope with a core of wire—and climbed up it, trying to avoid the rushing water. Danyl clung to the net just below her, the capsized boat bobbing beneath his feet.

Then the netting began to move, carrying them up and away from the water, tightening at the same time. In a moment they were no longer hanging like insects in a spider's web but instead lay on a kind of mesh bridge, staring down at the depths into which the River plunged, carrying the boat with it. It tumbled into a swirling black pool full of multicolored foams and giant shimmering bubbles, vanished from sight for a few seconds, then bobbed to the surface in the calmer water several meters downstream.

"What's happening?" Alania cried to Danyl.

"How would I know?" he shouted back.

"Hold still!" a new voice called. Alania raised her head, staring along the length of the netting instead of down into the Canyon depths. The net, she saw now, was attached to a post, and the post to a wheel whose axle was set in a slot. The net could clearly be raised, lowered, and tilted, which meant that if the operators wanted to, they could rotate the net back to a vertical position—or flip it over completely and dump both of them to their deaths.

Apparently they didn't want to. Three figures covered head to toe in shining black, gloved, booted, and helmeted, eyes encased in bubble-like goggles, had clambered out onto the netting from the eastern wall and were swiftly approaching, looking for all the world like four-legged spiders . . .

Now *there* was an image Alania could have done without.

Trapped in a web, she thought. Of course, it seemed she'd been trapped in a web her whole life, a web of intrigue and secrets and lies with Lieutenant Beruthi and the First Officer at the center of it. Maybe that was why she'd always hated spiders: she'd somehow sensed she was nothing more than an insect at the center of a web, waiting to be devoured.

Now the metaphor had become literal. She twisted her head around and wasn't surprised to see two more black-clad figures skittering over the net toward them from the other direction. "We were sent to meet Yvelle!" Danyl shouted at them. "She's expecting us!"

No answer from the approaching spider-people. The trio from the eastern end of the net and the duo from the west arrived at the same moment. The three grabbed Danyl. He tried to struggle, yelling curses, but the net provided no purchase, and in moments they had relieved him of the beamer rifle, bound him hand and foot with black cords, and gagged him with a strip of white cloth . . . all of which Alania saw only in flashes, since the duo who had come up behind her were busily trussing her in the same fashion, minus the gag. Feeling more like a spider's prey than ever, unable to struggle, she was dragged over the net in Danyl's wake toward the eastern wall.

Just as they reached it, the sunlight vanished as the sun slipped behind the western rim of the Canyon.

Her captors dumped Alania unceremoniously onto a cold floor. Her cheek was not pressed against rough stone, as she might have expected, but ceramic tiles that formed an intricate mosaic of blue and green and gold. Though cracked in places and missing tiles in others, it was still the kind of floor that would not have looked out of place in the Twelfth-Tier residence of one of her girlhood "friends," or in Quarters Beruthi, for that matter, though Beruthi's taste in floors ran more to stark black and white.

The mechanism for lowering and rotating the net, on the other hand, was *exactly* what she would have expected: rough wooden beams, wooden gears, and a capstan—was that the word?—to power it all.

Her captors rolled her over, the backpack a painful lump beneath her back, and untied her feet, though not her hands. The smallest of them hauled her upright, then reached up and pulled off her black helmet—greased synthileather, it looked to be made of—and goggles, tucking both into a pouch at her belt.

Alania found herself looking at a young woman about her own age with blond hair cut severely short. "Did you get wet?" the stranger asked urgently. Her eyes went to Alania's forehead and widened. "A *cut*? Did it get wet?"

"I . . . maybe? A little?"

"This one, too," said another of their . . . rescuers? Captors? Both? He held the beamer rifle and had just pulled Danyl, still gagged, to his feet. The rest of their captors removed their helmets and goggles in turn, revealing two women and three men. Alania's interlocutor was the youngest woman, though the male who had confiscated the beamer looked like a teenager. The other woman had gray in her hair, as did one of the men. The third was bald as a boulder.

"Ungag him," the young woman said. Despite her youth, she seemed to be in charge. "That really wasn't necessary, Nobu."

"He was swearing at us," the teen said.

"I'm sure you've been sworn at before," the young woman replied dryly. "I seem to remember doing it myself."

Nobu grinned. "I remember that, too. Fair enough." He undid Danyl's gag.

Danyl spat fluff from his mouth, glared at the boy, then turned toward the woman. "We were sent here to see Yvelle. By Erl."

"We know," said the woman. "We were watching for you. And I *will* take you to see Yvelle. But first you have to be decontaminated, and any wounds must be cleaned and sterilized immediately. Come with me. Nobu, take Danyl."

"There's no time for this," Danyl said. "There are Provosts after us." Then he blinked. "You know my name?"

"We know both your names," the young woman said. "And there is time. Well, assuming you want to live."

"So you know our names," Alania said. "What's yours?"

"Chrima," the young woman said.

"What do I do with this?" Nobu said, holding up the beamer rifle.

"I'll take it to Yvelle," Chrima said. Nobu passed it over to her, and she hefted it. "Nice." She slung it over her shoulder, then led Alania across the tiled floor to ... Alania blinked. Elevator doors, of all things, mirrored gold framed in white marble, set into a tiled wall that shaded from dark blue near the floor to light blue as it met the white ceiling. A crystal chandelier hung dark above them.

Chrima pushed the single button to the right of the

elevator. The doors opened at once. Inside, an eternal had been bolted into a metal box in the ceiling clearly intended for a much larger fixture, filling the elevator with its green light. Alania was heartily sick of that color and of the eternals. *Why do they have to be green?* In that light, every one of them—the five whoever-they-were, Danyl, and undoubtedly Alania herself—looked like they had been dead for a week.

In a week we may *have been dead for a week*, Alania thought, then wished she hadn't.

She half expected music to play as they descended; had the elevator been better lit, it might have been in one of the multistory Twelfth-Tier shops near the Core or in the home of one of the richer girls whose birthday parties she was forced to attend year after year. (Quarters Beruthi had an elevator in addition to the secret one she, Sandi, and Lissa had ridden down to Fifth, but it was strictly utilitarian, used by the robot staff. Beruthi had always forbidden Alania from using it, supposedly to ensure that she didn't accidentally get hurt by a robot but also, she suspected, because he thought climbing stairs built character as well as calf muscles.)

No one said anything as they descended. When the elevator stopped at last and the door opened, she gasped.

They stepped out into a vast semicircular space, the far side enclosed with glass so clear she thought it was open to the outside air until a slight reflection revealed the truth a moment later. Beyond the glass was the pool, gray and foaming, into which the waterfall plunged. On the far side of the pool, Alania saw another opening in the Canyon wall, though it didn't look like it was glassed in like this one. Pillars were spaced along the curving wall in which the elevator was centered, other doors and arches lurking between them. On the tiled floor, concentric semicircles of blue and green ran from the pillared wall to the glass one.

"What *is* this place?" Alania almost whispered.

"Later," Chrima said. While three of the escort members departed, she and Nobu led Alania and Danyl through one of the archways to the left into a blue-and-green hallway lit by more annoying eternals. The corridor ended after ten or fifteen meters in a white-tiled wall holding a golden basin with a spigot above it. Clearly water had once poured into it for decoration, though it was now dry as dust.

A sign above the bowl read, simply, "The Pool." To either side of it were doors, the one to the left labeled "Men," the one to the right labeled "Women." Chrima took Alania through the women's door as Nobu took Danyl through the men's.

Inside the swimming pool changing room, Chrima carefully set aside Danyl's beamer. She stripped off her outer rubbery suit and dumped it into a wheeled bin of blue metal, then without a trace of shyness pulled off the underwear that was all she wore beneath it and put that in another bin. Her nude body looked painfully thin to Alania.

Feeling self-conscious—Alania had rarely been naked in the company of anyone (*other than whoever was watching me through those cameras in my room!* she thought with a surge of anger)—she took off her backpack, set it next to the beamer, and stripped off the green pants and black shirt and boys' underwear Danyl had given her. At Chrima's instruction, she put them in the second bin. Then Chrima led her into the next room, tiled green, where there were eight showerheads set into the wall, each with a knurled knob beneath it. She pointed Alania to one and stood under another, facing the wall. "Keep your eyes closed," she said over her shoulder. "This isn't just water, and it stings even unbroken skin. It's going to hurt like hell in any cuts." Her lips curved in a small smile. "It also tastes terrible, so keep your mouth shut tight, too." She twisted the faucet knob.

Alania turned on her own shower, squeezing her eyes

shut as she did so. She gasped as liquid, heated to just below the threshold of being unbearable, doused her body. The fluid had an acrid, acidic smell to it, and despite holding her lips pressed tight, Alania got a mouth-puckering taste of its bitterness. But remembering the foul water of the River, she welcomed its astringent touch, turning this way and that to be sure it reached every square centimeter of skin. Chrima hadn't been kidding—it burned like hot metal in every scrape and cut. But she embraced that pain as a small price to feel truly clean again.

"It will switch to water in a second," Chrima said, and sure enough, the spray suddenly lost its strange smell. Alania raised her face to it, and when it ended a couple of minutes later, she opened her eyes and brushed lank hair from her forehead.

"That felt wonderful," Alania said. *Second bath today*, she thought. Being really filthy was something of a new experience for her; it just didn't happen on Twelfth Tier.

Chrima smiled. It made her look like a teenager. "Even when I've been wearing that dry suit I'm glad to get decontaminated after net duty," she said. "Mining is even worse." She led Alania back into the room where they had stripped. Lockers lined the walls, and from one she took out clean clothes for herself; she offered Alania clothes from another. Chrima's, black pants and a black vest over a dark-green turtleneck, were obviously her own. Alania's didn't fit nearly as well and had clearly been sewn and patched multiple times, but she donned them gratefully all the same, beginning with proper underwear. Over that, she pulled on khaki-colored pants, rolled up at the cuffs because they were too long, a rather baggy long-sleeved blue shirt, and thick gray socks. There were several pairs of shoes to choose from: she found some comfortable canvas ones that fit, though she gave her own fouled boots a fleeting glance of regret—she'd loved those boots.

"Now let me look at that cut on your head."

Obediently, Alania sat on a worn wooden bench. Chrima opened yet another locker and took out a metal box. "We keep a first aid kit in here so we can treat any minor wounds as soon as possible," she said. She leaned forward, frowning. "That's . . . odd. When did you get that?"

"A couple of hours ago," Alania said. "In the stairwell."

Chrima's eyes widened. "But it's almost healed. Kind of red, but it's closed."

Alania shrugged. "I've always healed fast." She touched her cheek; the synthiskin there had fallen off. The piece on her forehead covering the cut she'd sustained when she'd landed in the Middens was still in place, but it, too, had started to peel away. She took hold of one edge and pulled it off completely. "How's that wound look?"

"What wound?" Chrima said. She bent closer. "A faint scar . . . When did that happen?"

"This morning." Alania pointed at her unmarked cheek. "I was cut here, too."

"That's not just fast, that's miraculous," Chrima muttered. She shook her head. "Well, just to be safe, I'm going to treat the one that's still red." She rummaged in the first aid kit and drew out a small spray can. "Hold still."

Alania obeyed. She heard the hiss of the can and yelped; the decontamination shower had burned like fire, but this stuff burned like ice. "Antiseptic," Chrima said. "And an analgesic, too." Sure enough, the pain had already vanished. Chrima dug around in the kit some more, pulled out another synthiskin patch, and stuck it over the cut. "There," Chrima said. "I hope this fast-healing trick of yours helps prevent infection, too." She closed the kit. "You're lucky—right now we have medical supplies, thanks to Erl. We don't always."

"What happens if the cut becomes infected?" Alania asked.

"Don't think about it," Chrima advised. She stowed the first aid kit back in its locker, then picked up the beamer rifle. "Grab your backpack."

Rather reluctantly, since the pack still looked gray from being dunked in the River and *hadn't* gone through decontamination, Alania obeyed. Then Chrima led her out of the change room and back down the hall to the pillared, semicircular chamber into which the elevator had originally deposited them. Danyl was already there, dressed in black pants and a faded red shirt. "Now," Chrima said, "you can see Yvelle."

She turned left and walked across the semicircular room to a hallway that opened where the curving wall met the long window, so that one wall of the corridor beyond was also made of glass. Like the rest of this very odd place, the hallway was strangely ornate, though the blue carpet had worn to nothing but gray rubber down the middle. Nude statues in athletic poses, each about fifteen centimeters tall and carved from pale green stone, graced gilded alcoves on the inside wall, although about half of the alcoves were empty and in one or two only half a statue remained, a pair of muscular legs cut off at the thigh or a woman missing both arms. Outside the glass wall, the waterfall pool stretched, less turbulent this far from the cascade. The odd thing was that the River didn't seem to continue past the pool; the southern wall of the vast open space into which it plunged was solid. Concrete balconies and black, blank windows stretched several stories up it. *But the water has to go* somewhere, Alania thought. *It must plunge underground.*

She glanced back at Danyl. He stared back with a slight scowl, though she didn't think that had anything to do with her. *He's worried about Erl.*

So was she. And she was still wondering what was going on.

Maybe Yvelle would tell them . . . something.

The corridor ended in a door marked "Administration." Chrima knocked, and it swung open from inside. The glass wall continued into the office beyond, which Alania could only glimpse past the tall, thin, dark-skinned woman dressed in black who blocked the way. She wore a sheathed knife on her left hip.

"Hello, Idell," Chrima said. "I've brought them."

Idell nodded and stepped aside. "Yvelle is in the inner office," she said.

The antechamber Idell guarded had the same thread-bare blue carpet as the hallway. Gold-speckled white stone sheathed the three walls that weren't made of glass. Instead of statues on the inside wall, there were paintings. One showed the Canyon, the River rushing over rocks, the water sparkling blue and white in the sunshine streaming down from high overhead. Another showed the City perched above the Canyon, likewise sparkling in morning sunlight. No garbage filled the chasm below it, the walls of the lower Tiers weren't stained with rust and oil and nameless gunk, and it didn't smoke and steam the way the real City did.

Dull metallic letters bearing flecks of gold paint stretched across the farthest wall behind a curved desk of scarred dark wood. "Whitewater Resort," Alania read, though some of the letters were only outlines marking their former placements; the remaining characters really read "hite ate sort." The desk beneath the crumbling sign bore its own sign: "Rec ptio."

Idell led them to the inner door, knocked once, and then swung it open. Chrima urged Alania forward.

She and Danyl stepped into the presence of the mysterious Yvelle.

FIFTEEN

FIRST OFFICER KRANZ glared down at the man in the hospital bed—the man who shouldn't have been there. The man who shouldn't have been *alive*. He shouldn't have been hiding in the Middens, and he *definitely* shouldn't have been involved in the kidnapping of Alania. The fact that he had been—and the fact that he had apparently had company in the form of a young man the same age as Alania—made Kranz want to kill someone.

The man in the hospital bed would have been the logical choice, but unfortunately, Kranz didn't want him dead—at least not until he'd had a chance to question him.

Which he might or might not have the opportunity to do. Medical Officer Saunders, Twelfth Tier Hospital's Chief of Medical Staff, who had been a mere intern twenty years before when Ensign Erlkin Orillia had abducted one of the very special infants from the nursery, stood deferentially at Kranz's right side, giving him an update on Orillia's condition.

"... perforating bullet wound ... passed through the tip of the right frontal lobe ... no vital brain tissue impacted, but there's swelling ... deeply unconscious ... time will tell."

Phrases from the Medical Officer's report on the damage caused to Orillia's brain by the ricocheting bullet that had taken him down floated through Kranz's own undamaged brain without taking purchase. He latched on to that last phrase, though.

"How much time?" he growled.

"There's no way to know, sir," Saunders said. "Head trauma is a tricky thing. Wounds that appear survivable often aren't, and sometimes wounds that appear fatal prove survivable. Until he wakes up—*if* he wakes up— we can't even tell how much impairment he will suffer. Even if he survives, he may not be able to provide you with the ... intelligence ... you require."

Nobody in this whole City can provide me with the intelligence I require, Kranz thought savagely. *Nobody in this City appears to* have *any. What the hell did that Provost think he was doing, firing down the tunnel when he knew Alania might be at the end?*

"Keep me posted," he said, then turned and left the room, not bothering to return the salutes from the two Provosts stationed in the hall or the additional six, his ever-present bodyguards, who fell in behind and beside him as he made his way out of the hospital and back toward Quarters Kranz. He hoped all of them were more competent than the Provosts who had gone after Alania ... and failed so spectacularly to retrieve her.

When he reached his office on the fourth floor of Quarters Kranz a few minutes later, he found Commander Havelin waiting for him in the marble-tiled hallway outside the double doors. The doors opened automatically at Kranz's approach; he waved Havelin through and sat down at his desk. He didn't invite the Commander to sit. He'd already torn a strip off Havelin for what had happened in the Middens, so there was no need to rehash *those* events. "Where did they go?" he asked without preamble. "I'm assuming they didn't drown themselves in the River."

"Where they exited, there are ... mines ... in the lower reaches of the Middens," Havelin said. "We thought they might have gone in there, but we explored them thoroughly, and they're empty of life, though someone has been working them recently. There was also a pier, but no boat. That suggested a River escape, so we sent a drone down the Canyon. We didn't spot Danyl or Alania, but we did find something unexpected: squatters in the old Whitewater Resort."

Kranz's eyes narrowed. "Whitewater? That place hasn't been occupied since the River turned into the *Black* River. Who would live there?"

"Middens-dwellers who just kept going down," Havelin said, contempt in his voice. "Scavenging garbage from the River, most likely. We saw some makeshift greenhouses where they must be growing food, and obviously they're also the ones mining the base of the Middens."

"And that's where this mysterious youth and my ward are currently hiding?"

"I can't confirm that, sir," Havelin said. "But if they aren't there, they're dead. There's a waterfall. And the water is foul. If they fell into it, I don't believe they would've survived for long."

"I hope for your sake," Kranz said, "that that didn't happen." *For all our sakes. If Alania is dead . . .* He took the meteoric-iron dagger from his desk and turned it over and over in hands, which were otherwise inclined to tremble. "Assemble a force . . . an *overwhelming* force. Evict the squatters. Use whatever means necessary. Bring back any survivors for questioning. Rescue my ward and the boy she is with."

"Yes, sir."

"And I want live vid of the operation streamed to my office."

"Yes, sir."

"Dismissed."

Havelin saluted, spun smartly on his polished boot heel, and marched out.

As the doors closed behind him, Kranz sat back. His

hand clenched on the dagger's hilt. Ex-Ensign Orillia, far from perishing in the Iron Ring, had clearly been hiding out in the Middens with Danyl, the candidate baby kidnapped two decades earlier and also presumed dead until that very morning, literally under the feet of Kranz and the Provosts. Kranz's lips tightened. *I've ignored the Middens too long.*

Oh, there were reasons. Malcontents and troublemakers who fell out of the City and onto the garbage heap where they so richly deserved to be neatly ceased to be problems. They could not reenter the City without Passes, and their short, miserable existences trying to survive by scavenging trash seemed punishment enough. But now it seemed his laissez-faire attitude had come back to bite him. *When I have Alania—when we have a new, improved Captain—we will deal with the Middens once and for all. I may not be able to empty the Canyon of trash—not yet—but I can damn well get rid of the parasites infesting it.*

He tossed the dagger onto his desk and leaned forward again, flipping up one of the hidden display screens. Even with plans decades in the making and the future of the City hanging in the balance, he had a thousand administrative details to deal with.

The people of this City, he thought, *just don't appreciate how much I do for them.*

Danyl followed Alania into the inner office of the exceedingly strange place in which they had found themselves, anxious to see the mysterious Yvelle, who clearly knew Erl. He couldn't imagine who she was or why she would know anything about him, and his first sight of her did not enlighten him. She looked to be a perfectly ordinary woman, younger than Erl—perhaps in her mid-forties—with a few streaks of gray in her black hair but a mostly unlined face. She was shorter than Alania and, like Chrima, slim to the point of emaciation.

She wore a plain white blouse and a silver chain around her neck. She fingered a locket hanging from that chain as she watched Alania and Danyl enter her inner sanctum. Like the reception room, the corridor, and the large semicircular chamber, it had one glass wall showing the waterfall and the foaming black pool below it. The other walls were the same gold-speckled stone as the outer room, the carpet the same threadbare blue. The wall behind Yvelle was blank, although there were holes in it that had probably supported artwork once upon a time. The wall to their left had a row of metal cabinets missing a few doors and a sink. Two chairs of dark wood, upholstered in white, stood between them and the desk.

"Take off your backpacks and sit down," Yvelle said without smiling.

Alania slipped out of the backpack Erl had given her—they still hadn't had time to look inside it—and set it on the floor. She took the chair to the left, so Danyl, shrugging out of his own pack, took the chair on the right. The cracked synthileather felt hard and brittle beneath him. He wondered if either the data crystal Erl had given him or the reader that was supposedly in Alania's pack had survived the harrowing descent down the stairs and along the River. If they had, would they really answer all his questions?

He doubted it. He doubted there was a data storage device in the world with enough capacity to contain answers to all the questions he had.

Nobu and Chrima lurked behind them. The imposing Idell continued to guard the door.

"Danyl," Yvelle said. "It's been a long time."

"It must have been," Danyl said, "since I didn't know you existed until today."

"You were a baby when I saw you last." Yvelle turned

her dark brown eyes to Alania. "You I have never seen before. Fortunately for you."

"That sounds . . . ominous," Alania said.

"It was meant to." Yvelle returned her gaze to Danyl. "What did Erl tell you about me?"

"Nothing," Danyl said. "The Provosts were at the door."

"As they soon will be again," Yvelle said. "A drone flew over fifteen minutes ago. Erl promised me they would not find us, but in truth I knew the moment I heard from him that this would happen. I do not expect an attack today—it will take time to organize—but I expect one tomorrow, probably as soon as it's light."

Danyl heard a rustle behind him and knew Nobu and Chrima had just exchanged glances.

"It's because of me," Alania said in a small voice. "I don't understand any of this, but I know it's because of me. There was an attack on Twelfth Tier, people trying to kidnap me. I ran away and ended up in the Middens by accident. Danyl and Erl rescued me, and then the Provosts came. They followed us all the way down here. I don't know why, but they're determined to get me back." She took a deep breath. "Let me turn myself in."

"No!" Danyl shot her an angry glance.

"It's too late for that anyway," Yvelle said in a flat voice. "By now First Officer Kranz knows that Erl hid Danyl right under his nose for twenty years. It's no longer just about getting you, Alania. It's about getting both of you. And he'll stop at nothing."

"I don't suppose you'll tell us why?" Danyl growled.

"I can't," Yvelle said.

"Can't or won't?"

"Can't. No one has ever told *me* why you are so valuable. I know nothing more now than I did twenty years ago when I stole you from Twelfth Tier Hospital and handed you over to Ensign Erlkin Orillia . . . the man you know as Erl."

Danyl felt as if he'd been sucker punched. "Twelfth Tier . . . you mean . . . I was born to an Officer?"

"I don't know your parentage," Yvelle said. "All I know is that there were seven candidate babies, and I was ordered to abduct the first one I found who carried certain genetic tags, as identified by a scanning device I was given. You were the first baby who tested positive for those tags, and so you were the one I abducted."

"What about me?" Alania said.

Yvelle glanced at her. "You were missing that evening. I don't know why."

"That's two of the seven," Danyl said. "What about the other five?"

"They don't matter," Yvelle said flatly, but Danyl thought he saw a flicker of a shadow cross her face. *She's hiding something.*

"What was the significance of the genetic tags?" he asked.

"I wasn't told."

"Who gave you your orders?"

"There are those," Yvelle said, "who believe there should be a change in the way the City is governed, who do not believe we should live and die at the whim of the Captain and her hatchet man, the First Officer."

"Rebels?" Danyl asked. His heart beat faster, and he leaned forward. "They really exist?"

"They exist," Yvelle said. "They existed twenty years ago. They still exist. They call themselves the Free Citizens—the Free, for short. Erl was one of them, much higher up than I. He received word this morning from someone in the City—I don't know who—about the failed attempt to abduct Alania and her completely unexpected descent to the Middens. Erl was ordered to pass you along to me . . . and I was given new orders as well, instructions for getting you to the leader of the Free, the man who gave me my mission twenty years ago. I know him only as Prime." She looked at them both, unsmiling. "By sending you to us, Erl signed the death warrant for our little corner of freedom. We cannot stand against the Provosts. If we fight, we will die. If we flee, we will be hunted down. Our only hope is to hand both of you over to the Provosts when they arrive."

Danyl stiffened. Nobu's hand descended on his shoulder, pinning him to the chair. "You said it's too late for that," Alania said.

"I said it's too late for you to give *yourself* up," Yvelle corrected. "That wouldn't help us; we would still be punished. But it might not be too late for us to give up both of you in exchange for leniency."

"Erl wanted you to help us!" Danyl protested.

"I met Erlkin Orillia exactly once, the night I handed you over to him," Yvelle said. "In twenty years, we have exchanged only a handful of messages. Occasionally his contacts in the City have provided us with necessities we could not scavenge. Occasionally he has guided someone to us whom he thought could be of help to us, someone who would otherwise have been lost to the gangs. But *I* built this community, not him. It's a mean existence, scouring the Black River for whatever detritus finds its way down it from the Middens, mining the lowest levels of the garbage heap, growing what food we can in greenhouses and meatvats, but at least it's an existence free from the heavy hand of the First Officer. For twenty years, we have been as free as any people *can* be in the shadow of the City. So the question I must ask myself is this: is what I have built here in the last twenty years more important than the cause in which I enlisted when I agreed to steal a baby from Twelfth Tier?"

"What will happen to us if you turn us over to the Provosts?" Alania asked.

"I don't know," Yvelle said. "They clearly want you alive. That does not mean you will enjoy whatever plans they have for you."

"Then you *should* turn us in," Alania said. "You should save your community."

"No!" Danyl glared at her, then turned back to Yvelle. "No," he repeated. "Yvelle, if we're somehow important to the effort to overthrow the City government—I admit I don't understand how that can be true, but clearly someone in the City thinks it is—then you *can't* turn us over. Do you think Kranz will let you just sit down here in peace and quiet now that he knows you exist? If you hand us over, he'll take us, say thank you, and then march you all back to the City as prisoners. You're right—by sending us here, Erl has guaranteed the end of this place. But at least if you help us escape, send us on to this Prime person, then maybe the world gets that much closer to a time when *no one* has to fear the Provosts or Kranz's 'justice.'" He leaned forward. "You'll only be buying time if you turn us in, and probably not very much of it. But if you help us escape, you may be buying freedom for everyone." *Though I can't imagine how . . .*

Yvelle lowered her eyes and fingered the locket at her throat. "I was young when I abducted you," she said in a soft voice. "Not much older than you are now. And I did not do what I did out of any noble commitment to the cause of freedom. I did it to exact revenge. I did it because the City killed my husband, aborted my child, destroyed my life. I would have done anything to take that revenge. I *did* do . . . anything . . ." Her voice trailed off. She released the locket. She raised her head. "It is not entirely up to me," she said then, her voice stronger. "I founded this community, but I am not a Captain or First Officer who rules by dictate. We must have a meeting." She looked past him. "Chrima, will you see to it? Half an hour. No more."

"I'll spread the word," Chrima said from behind them. Danyl didn't turn around, but he heard her exit.

"Have you eaten?" Yvelle asked then.

The question startled Danyl because he realized they

had; not more than three hours ago, probably less, he'd been sitting at the dining table in the quarters he shared with Erl, as he had every day of his life. Three hours and everything had changed—though the change had really started the moment Alania fell into his world. That must have been all of *five* hours ago.

"Yes," he said. "We have."

"Then I suggest you wait here," Yvelle said. "Nobu, stay with them. Guide them to the meeting room in half an hour." She stood. "I need to think." She walked past Danyl and out the door.

Danyl looked at Alania, who raised her hands in a "what now?" gesture. Then he twisted around in his chair to look at Nobu, who had said nothing to him even while they were in the shower together being disinfected. He still didn't, staring at Danyl impassively. He was remarkably self-controlled for someone who couldn't have been older than seventeen.

Danyl turned back to Alania. "How are you doing?" he asked.

She smiled a little. "I haven't had enough time to think to figure that out."

"Well," he said, "you've got half an hour. As for me . . ." He sat back in the chair, rested his head on it, and closed his eyes. It had been a very strange day, and right now the best thing he could think to do was try to take a nap.

Amazingly, he succeeded.

SIXTEEN

ALANIA STARED AT the dozing Danyl and envied him. He sat with his head lolled back on the cracking white synthileather of the ancient chair, mouth slightly open, chest rising and falling steadily. She knew she could not emulate him. She fizzed with nervous energy, so much that her hands trembled.

The attack on Twelfth Tier . . . the fall into the Middens . . . the flight from the Rustbloods . . . the journey to Erl's . . . the renewed flight down the stairs, pursued by Provosts . . . the journey down the River . . . It had all taken place over a single morning, but already her old life seemed a million miles away and a million years in the past. As for her future . . .

Her future, it seemed, was all tied up in a past she had never even known existed. Twenty years ago, if Yvelle was to be believed, she and Danyl had been babies together in Twelfth Tier Hospital with five other candidate babies. Candidates for *what?* Yvelle claimed not to know. Apparently Danyl had certain unspecified genetic tags. She had to assume she had them, too—presumably that was what the familiar little scanner Kranz had used on her when he'd taken her aside at her birthday party (just *yesterday*) determined. Somehow, those genetic tags had justified an elaborate kidnapping scheme undertaken twenty years ago. *They didn't get me back then, so they tried this morning*, she thought, but then she frowned. On second thought, that didn't seem likely. Why wait twenty years?

If she had been there in the hospital two decades ago, would Yvelle have taken her, too? Would she and Danyl have been raised as brother and sister?

And then she blinked. *Oh, crap. We probably* are *brother and sister!*

The thought made her feel distinctly ... odd. She'd only known Danyl for a few hours and hadn't even had time to decide if she liked him ... but he was a young male, and there'd been a definite shortage of young males in her life. The thought that the first one she'd been able to spend time with might be her brother was just plain weird, not to mention ... disappointing.

Worry about that later, she told herself firmly. *First worry about this "meeting."*

She'd offered to turn herself over to the Provosts to save Danyl. She'd offered again to save the River People. She was still prepared to do that if it would prevent more people from being hurt. But it sounded like it wouldn't, and secretly, shamefully, that relieved her. She didn't *want* to turn herself over to the Provosts. She didn't want to return to Twelfth Tier and her stultifying life as a prisoner. She didn't want to meekly submit herself to Kranz and whatever plans he had in mind for her.

In truth, the adrenaline singing in her veins intoxicated her. She liked being free. She'd never felt more alive—ironic, considering how close she had come to death several times that morning. And the thought that she might have some greater purpose, that somehow she might be able to help liberate the City from the Captain, Kranz, and the Officers ... that was even more intoxicating.

She'd never thought she *mattered*. She'd never thought she *could* matter. And now, though she had no clue how or why, it seemed she mattered more than anyone she'd ever met ... except, apparently, Danyl.

Seven candidate babies. One abducted. One—her—absent the night of the abduction. What had happened to the other five? Did she and Danyl have other unknown could-be siblings hidden away somewhere?

She frowned. Yvelle had clearly not told the entire story of that night in the hospital, and Alania had a very bad feeling about that. *"I would have done anything to take that revenge,"* Yvelle had said. *"I did do . . . anything . . ."*

Outside the window, the water foamed in the black and murky pool at the base of the cascade. Some of that was liquid from the City, seeping through the mass of garbage piled in the Canyon over centuries. Eventually it all flowed downstream. Just because you threw something into the Middens didn't mean it vanished forever. At any moment it could surface. And so, it seemed, could events from her past, even if it was a past she'd had no clue existed until today.

Danyl continued to nap. Alania continued to quiver. And then, finally, Nobu said, "Time to go."

Danyl came instantly awake. He got up from the chair. "Ready?" he asked Alania.

"How can I be?" she asked.

His mouth twitched into an almost-smile. "Point."

"This way," Nobu said. He waited while they donned their backpacks again, then led them back out through the reception area and down the hall to the big colonnaded room they had entered from the elevator. It now held perhaps seventy people—all, or nearly all, of the River People, Alania assumed. Like Alania and Danyl and everyone else they'd seen, they were mostly dressed in a motley assortment of clothes, much patched and of wildly different styles, except for the few like Idell—soldiers, she guessed she'd call them—who wore all black, like Chrima and Nobu and the others had when they'd retrieved Danyl and Alania from the net. Only a couple of the River People looked older than Yvelle; most looked much younger. There were even a handful of children among them, from toddlers to teens, and one babe in arms, suckling quietly at the breast of its mother.

Yvelle stood with the elevator at her back on a simple dais made of an old packing crate, her face illuminated by the bluish light from the shadowed Canyon streaming in through the glass wall. The River People stood silently around her, without the chatter Alania would've have expected—but then, in a community this small, discussions and rumors must have already spread like an infection, and now the denizens of the former resort were waiting to hear the truth. Nobu led Alania and Danyl to the back of the group, so unobtrusively that no one even turned toward them.

"Earlier this morning," Yvelle said without preamble, "I received a transmission from Erlkin Orillia, warning me that he was sending two young people our way." She indicated Alania and Danyl, and as every head turned to look at them, Alania suddenly felt very small and exposed. Without even thinking about it, she reached out for Danyl. He flinched a little at her touch but then gripped her hand firmly and squeezed it.

"Not quite twenty years ago," Yvelle continued, "I abducted that young man, Danyl, from a hospital on Twelfth Tier. I did so at the behest of the revolutionary organization that calls itself the Free Citizens, dedicated to overthrowing the leadership of the City. Some of you, I know, are familiar with the Free. Their leader, a man known to me only as Prime, told me that Danyl was vital to their goals—that once grown, he might free *everyone* from the tyranny of the Captain and her Officers."

She paused. "Some of you already know that tale," she continued after a moment. "But this is what you do not know. My orders were to test all seven of the babies in the hospital ward that night for certain genetic tags. The first baby who tested positive—Danyl, as it turned out—I was to abduct. Any baby who did not have the tags, I was to leave alone." She paused again, and when she continued, it was as if she were forcing each word out through a throat so constricted that even air could barely escape. "And any baby after the first who *did* have those tags . . . I was to kill."

Alania felt as if she'd been punched. There were a few gasps and one muffled "No!" from the River People, but then they stood silent and still, as if frozen in place by the enormity of what they were hearing.

"And so," Yvelle continued softly, "I killed a baby that night, a baby of the City, as revenge for the death of my husband and my own unborn child." Then she looked straight at Alania. "And I would have killed a second one, had she been there."

Alania swallowed hard.

"I delivered the boy to Erlkin Orillia—Ensign Erlkin Orillia, he was then," Yvelle continued, and that revelation elicited more gasps. "He created an elaborate scheme to make it appear that he and the child had vanished into the Iron Ring. In reality, he descended to the Middens, where he has raised Danyl ever since in quarters Prime had secretly prepared for him, through which many of you have passed. The child I failed to kill—Alania—was raised by Lieutenant Beruthi at the behest of First Officer Kranz. She, like Danyl, turned twenty yesterday. This morning she was to become the ward of First Officer Kranz—for what purpose, I do not know. The Free Citizens somehow knew of this transfer and attempted to kidnap her while she was en route to Kranz's Quarters. But the attempt failed. Alania took refuge in a trash elevator, one that, by chance, was dumping its contents directly into the Middens. There Danyl found her.

"Erl, told by Prime what had transpired, understood that the Provosts would soon descend on the Middens to attempt to capture her. He sent her to us, along with Danyl. He hoped his secret entrance into the old staircase from the Rim down to the River would not be discovered, that he would simply delay the Provosts and then surrender to them. But I was certain it was a vain hope, and I was right; the Provosts found the stairs and pursued Danyl and Alania as far as the Canyon floor. As for Erl . . . I do not know if he still lives."

Another general murmur of distress.

"Those same Provosts will soon attack our haven," Yvelle continued, voice flat and harsh. "Most likely first thing in the morning. They have already sent a drone. Our time here is at an end."

A falling drop of water would have sounded as loud as the waterfall outside in the silence *that* statement produced.

"Alania has offered to surrender herself to the Provosts," Yvelle added after a moment, and Alania felt even more like an insect under a magnifying glass as heads turned in her direction again. "A noble gesture, but it will do no good. Kranz will never allow this community to remain intact now that he is aware of its existence. He cannot permit anyone to live free of the control of the Officers. As I see it, we therefore have three possible courses of action.

"One: we can turn Danyl and Alania over to the Provosts in exchange for leniency. We might be permitted to return to the City, no doubt to do manual labor in the lower Tiers, closely watched our entire lives and subject to arrest at any time for any perceived missteps."

The mutter that ran through the gathered River People this time sounded angry.

"Two: we can flee. Prime has told me of a way to get safely into the Heartland, but it would take days for everyone to get out that way, and we do not have days. Even those who escaped could only hope to remain free for a short time. There is nowhere to hide in the Heartland, as we well know." Yvelle paused and surveyed the crowd. Then, "Three: we can send Danyl and Alania on to Prime, as Erl requested."

"And then what do *we* do?" Chrima called. She still wore the beamer rifle Erl had given Danyl strapped across her back.

Yvelle spread her hands. "We fight."

"We *die*, you mean!" shouted a different woman. "What about the children?"

"Even the Provosts won't murder children," Yvelle said.

You did, Alania thought.

"Children and mothers and any others who wish may withdraw to the farthest reaches of the complex and await the outcome of the battle."

One of the few men older than Yvelle, his face marred by a gnarled red scar slashing from his throat to his empty right eye socket, shouted, "The Provosts have rifles and beamers. We have bows and arrows and a few knives. The 'outcome of the battle' is already certain. We can't win!"

Yvelle didn't deny it. "There are still the first two options," she said quietly.

Arguing broke out around the chamber. Unfriendly gazes turned toward Alania and Danyl. She squeezed his hand tighter.

Chrima's voice cut through the babble. "What do you recommend, Yvelle? You founded this community. You gave us sanctuary, each of us."

The arguing died away, and all heads turned in Yvelle's direction. She said nothing for a long moment. She looked down at the floor, once again fingering the locket around her neck. She stared at the tiles. Her fingers quieted. She dropped her hand and raised her head, and the light from the window kindled sparks in her eyes.

"I say we fight," she said, voice clear and cold. "I killed an innocent baby to take my revenge, and I have regretted it ever since, but I will *gladly* kill Provosts, the thugs of the Captain, may she rot in hell. For twenty years I have lived free of them. Now I will *die* free of them on my own terms, protecting my home. I will not flee like a skitterbug across the empty farmland. I will not starve in the Iron Ring. I will not meekly submit to torture and degradation in Tenth Tier. I will *fight*." Her gaze swept across the assembled River People like the ray of a beamer. "What about the rest of you? Do we fight? Vote!"

Some hands went up at once—Chrima's, Nobu's. Others followed more slowly. A few hesitated until the last moment . . . but in the end, every hand in the giant chamber was raised except Danyl's and Alania's.

Yvelle nodded once. "The Provosts will not attack today," she said. "They will need time to organize. Again, dawn is the most likely hour, which gives *us* time to prepare a welcome. I will meet with the section leaders in my office in twenty minutes." She looked through the crowd then, her bright eyes finding Alania and Danyl. "You two come with me. Chrima, accompany us."

"Yes, Yvelle," Chrima said.

The River People scattered, disappearing through the doors and archways leading out of the semicircular room. Yvelle crossed the tiled floor, boot heels clicking. Alania watched her approach and didn't know whether to hate or pity her.

"You killed a baby," she said when the leader of the River People reached them. She hadn't known she was going to say it until the words came out of her mouth. "A *baby*." She had held a baby once at one of the interminable birthday parties, the little brother of one of the girls, and she remembered the awe she had felt as she looked down at that tiny, perfect human being. So much potential, so much future, wrapped up in such a fragile bundle. The thought of snuffing out that infant life when it had barely begun . . . "*How could you?*"

Yvelle's mouth twisted. "You can do anything if you hate enough. And I *hated*. More than I hope you can ever imagine. *My* baby had been killed in my womb by the City's butchering doctors. My husband had been killed on Tenth Tier. The Free gave me a chance to strike back. I had hoped I wouldn't have to kill any of the babies. But it didn't stop me from doing what I had to to take my revenge."

"You would have killed *me* if I had been there."

Yvelle met her gaze squarely. "Yes."

"Who is this Prime?" Danyl demanded. His tone implied that dead babies from twenty years ago didn't really concern him all that much, and Alania, stung, pulled her hand free of his for the first time since the meeting had started. He didn't seem to notice. "Erl has never mentioned him to me." He frowned. "Just like he never mentioned *you*."

"I don't know who he is. But Erl has provided detailed instructions from him about how you are to make your way to him."

"You didn't have to take us in at all," Alania said. "You could have drowned us in your waterfall net, put our bodies somewhere upstream for the Provosts to find so they'd never send a drone down here. You might have stayed hidden for years more. So why didn't you? In my case, it would only have been the twenty-years-delayed fulfillment of your original orders."

"The thought crossed my mind," Yvelle said evenly.

Chrima, who had been listening silently, shot her a startled look. "A *fourth* option. But you didn't mention it in your speech."

Yvelle shrugged. "It hasn't been an option since the drone flew over. The Provosts know Danyl and Alania aren't dead in the River. And even if they *were*, Kranz would still send his Provosts down here now that he knows we exist."

"So we have to be gone before the Provosts arrive," Danyl said.

"And you cannot go until morning," Yvelle said. "Prime's instructions make that clear."

"But what if you're wrong and the Provosts attack *today*?"

"Then they'll catch you," Yvelle said. "Your escape route will not be open until morning."

"But it's a path to the Heartland, from what you said," Danyl argued. "It must be a long way downstream if it avoids the Rim defenses. Why couldn't we start along it now?"

"It doesn't go downstream," Yvelle said. "It goes straight up the western wall." She pointed across the cauldron of the waterfall. "Right there."

Danyl's eyes widened. "That's suicide!"

Alania said nothing, but she suddenly felt cold. She knew perfectly well what guarded the Rim this close to the City, and she knew exactly how impossible it was to get by such guards, because she'd been surrounded by their counterparts all her life.

The Rim was guarded by robots. *Killer* robots.

And, ironically, her former guardian had built them.

SEVENTEEN

"**IT IS NOT** suicide," Yvelle said in response to Danyl's outburst. "At least, not according to Prime. Across the River there are stairs very much like the ones you descended from Erl's. But whereas that one and the collapsed elevator shaft that runs parallel to it once provided access to a research facility devoted to the study of the Cubes—useless, as it turned out—this one climbs to what was once a garden."

Danyl blinked. "A garden?"

"Once," Yvelle said. "But it's not there any longer. Now it's a . . . nest, I suppose you'd call it. For the Rim Guardians." She reached into her pocket and drew out a folded piece of paper, which she handed to Chrima. "I went over these instructions with Chrima before you even reached the Net," she said. "She'll brief you once you get to the other side of the River."

"You want us to climb up half a kilometer of stairs just to end up inside a Rim Guardian nest?" Danyl pointed at the beamer rifle—*his* beamer rifle—which Chrima still wore slung over her back. "She might as well shoot us now and save time!"

"Prime's instructions can get you across the Rim safely if you time it right," Chrima said. She held up the folded paper, then tucked it into her own pocket. "Supposedly."

"*Time* it right? What does *that* mean?"

"You have to reach the nest at precisely 1000," Chrima said. "There are two shifts of Guardians. Prime says that's when Shift One transitions to Shift Two and enters the nest for recharging. For five minutes, both shifts are out of the nest, exchanging data. If you enter the nest during those minutes, you can initiate maintenance protocols that will open up a safe passage out of the Rim, through a gate, and into the Heartland."

"'Prime says,'" Danyl mimicked. "We don't even know who he is!"

"But you know Erl," Yvelle said sharply, "and it was he who passed along these instructions. Erl promises they will see you safely past the Rim. Once you are in the Heartland, there are more instructions, which will guide you to Prime." She shook her head. "It doesn't matter whether you believe the instructions are valid or not. They're your only hope of escape. Your other choices are to surrender to the Provosts or join us in fighting them."

Danyl glanced at Alania. She gave him a tiny shrug, as if to say, *She's right.*

I know she's right, dammit. But that doesn't mean I have to like it. Because he *had* trusted Erl all his life, and Erl had told him more than once that there was no way past the Rim Guardians. Now, suddenly, there *was.*

He took a deep breath. "Fine. So once we get past the Rim, we have to somehow find our way through the Heartland. I've never been out of the Canyon." He glanced at Alania. "Have you?" *She's a rich girl from Twelfth Tier, so maybe . . .*

She shook her head. "Lieutenant Beruthi has an Estate not far from the City and a retreat in the northern foothills of the Iron Ring, but he never took me to either one. Until today, I'd never been outside the City."

"None of this matters," Yvelle snapped. "What do you want? Someone to hold your hand and pull you along like a toddler?"

Danyl felt a flash of anger. "I'm not asking for anyone

to hold my hand. I'm just trying to figure out what the hell this is all about!"

"I've already told you, I don't know," Yvelle said.

They glared at each other for a moment, and then Alania touched his arm. He looked at her. Her pale blue eyes, so much like his own, met his. "We'll find our way," she said, voice determined.

He stared at her a moment, then jerked a nod. She squeezed his arm, then released him.

"Very well, then," Yvelle said. "Chrima will accompany you under the River and to the stairs." She looked at Chrima. "Grab rations from the dining room on your way. Get them headed up the stairs at first light. If — *when*—the Provosts attack, they'll be focused on this side of the River, so Danyl and Alania should have a good head start."

"Not to mention that over there they'll be out of sight all night of any of our people who have second thoughts," Chrima said dryly.

"Not to mention," Yvelle agreed.

Chrima turned away from her. "Follow me, you two."

Danyl said, "Wait," and stepped closer to Yvelle. He looked down at her and noted, as he hadn't before, the fine lines at the corners of her eyes, the furrows at the corners of her mouth. *Twenty years of freedom, but also twenty years of carrying the burden of what she did*, he thought. *She was only a little older than I am now when she . . .*

He cleared his throat. "Thank you for helping us," he said softly. "We thank you, and Erl thanks you. And thank you, too, for . . ." He hesitated; it seemed an odd thing to say, and yet he felt he had to. "Thank you for abducting me when I was a baby."

Yvelle's eyes flashed, and her lips tightened. "Don't you *dare* thank me for that. You might have lived a life of luxury like Alania if I hadn't. You might have been groomed to be First Officer, for all I know. And I only abducted *you* because you were the first one to test positive for the genetic markers. It could have been Alania. It could have been the little girl I . . ." Her voice trailed off. Her mouth worked for a moment. "Don't thank me," she rasped out at last.

"*I* don't," Alania said, and Danyl shot her a glance, startled by the coldness in her voice. She turned her back on Yvelle. "Lead on," she said to Chrima.

"As I said, it's this way," Chrima said. She glanced at Danyl. "Coming?"

Danyl met Yvelle's eyes. They looked back at him, brown like Erl's, but somehow much older and sadder. Then they dropped. Yvelle's hand went to the silver locket around her neck. And then she turned and walked away, back toward her office.

She's going to fight. They're all going to fight. And most of them are going to die just so Alania and I can reach this Prime.

It was an uncomfortable thought, so he turned away from it and said to Chrima. "Well, what are you waiting for?"

She snorted and led them in the opposite direction from Yvelle, parallel to the glass wall, to a doorway directly across from the hallway they'd followed to Yvelle's office. The door opened into a short, utilitarian corridor at the end of which stairs led downward. For a change, the stairs weren't lit by eternals but by honest white lights. "Wait in here," Chrima said, and then she went out again, closing the door behind her.

After a moment's silence, Danyl looked at Alania. "How are you holding up?"

"All right, I guess," she said. "Do you really think we were babies together on Twelfth Tier?"

"I don't know what to think," Danyl admitted. "But why would Yvelle lie?"

"I don't know." Alania stared at the floor for a moment, then looked up. "Has it occurred to you that if all this is true, we're almost certainly brother and sister?"

"Yeah," Danyl said. He didn't let the regret he'd felt at that realization color his voice, but it was there all the same, like he'd lost something before he'd even had a chance to have it.

And yet . . . he kind of liked the idea of having a sister. *A twin sister, at that—or a septuplet sister, anyway. Actual flesh-and-blood family.*

He didn't say any of that out loud. They waited in silence.

Chrima returned within ten minutes. "Rations," she said, holding up a cloth bag. "I'll divvy them up when we get to the other side of the River. Come on." She set off down the stairs.

Danyl followed, and Alania brought up the rear. They walked down the first flight of stairs, turned right, walked down another, turned again, and again, descending a squared-off spiral, though a tighter one than in the shaft that had led them down to the River. "How do we know," Danyl asked the beamer bouncing on Chrima's back—*his* beamer!—"that you aren't simply taking us down here to execute us and dump our bodies in the River for the Provosts to find in the hope they'll let you all off easy?"

"You don't," Chrima said without looking around. "How do I know you're not going to push me down the stairs, steal the beamer, run back and assassinate Yvelle, and then turn yourselves in?"

Danyl laughed. "You don't."

"Well then," Chrima said, "let's all just pretend we're going to do what we said we're going to do, and before you know it, we'll have done it."

It took Danyl a couple of more flights to untangle that sentence.

At last they reached the bottom, another plain corridor. To their right was a door labeled "Hell's Cauldron: Maintenance Access." To their left, another read "Sub-River Tunnel Access." Chrima opened that one, revealing—hardly a surprise—still more stairs. Alas, these *were* lit by eternals, faded and failing. They descended another thirty meters, and as they did so, the walls changed from concrete to red stone glistening with moisture.

They reached the bottom of the stairs. "Why is there a tunnel under the River?" Danyl asked. He ran a hand over the damp rock. "And why is it leaking?"

Chrima shrugged. "The rock is a bit porous. Sometimes you have to wade down here. I hope you're not afraid to get your feet wet."

"In that River? Yes," Alania said.

Chrima laughed. "Fair point. But by the time the water makes its way down here, it's much cleaner—the rock filters it. It won't kill you . . . well, unless this is the day the tunnel finally collapses entirely. That'd be bad luck."

"Considering the way things have gone downhill since my birthday party yesterday," Alania said, "don't even joke about it."

Chrima laughed again.

The tunnel was not only dank and cold, but it also smelled like a sewer. Danyl thought Chrima was overestimating the stone's effectiveness as a filter. But they made good time along it, and although they did have to splash through a few puddles, the water never rose higher than his ankles and thus never overflowed his boots, which made him very happy.

At the far end, they trudged up steps identical to the ones they had trudged down and emerged through a metal door into a long corridor running deep into the rock. To their right was a closed door of bare metal. At the far end was another door, painted red. An eternal—rather bright, for once—still burned faithfully above it. "Rim Garden Maintenance Access" white letters proclaimed on a door which seemed to be red as much from rust as from paint. There were two other doors opposite each other just shy of the red one.

Chrima led them to the one on the left and opened it inward, revealing a small chamber with four cots and a food preparation area, lit by an ancient light fixture. Thankfully, it was not an eternal; this one gave honest white (well, yellow) light. "We'll spend the night here." She pointed to the door across the hall. "Toilet. It works. More or less."

Danyl looked at the red door at the corridor's end. "Why on earth was there a garden on the Rim?"

Chrima shrugged. "Place was a resort. I think they had dances and dinners up there. They ran guests up to it in a big elevator."

"Which there's no chance we could take, I suppose? I mean, it was one thing to come down a few hundred meters of stairs, but going up them's going to be . . ."

"Challenging," Alania put in.

He flicked a quick smile in her direction. "One word for it."

"It's out of commission," Chrima said. "Cable broke at some point. I've seen the shaft. There are some old bones mixed in with the rusty metal. It wasn't empty when it failed. Must have been long after the resort closed—squatters, probably."

Danyl winced at the image. He turned back to the room with the cots. "And what was this for?"

"Maintenance workers' lounge, we think. Where they took their break. We put the cots in." Chrima pointed back down the hall to the unmarked door they'd passed at the top of the stairs. "That leads to stairs up to the ledge where this end of the net is anchored. Nobody on duty there now, though. Nobody ever again, I guess."

Alania sat down on one of the cots. "So," she said. "We have the rest of the afternoon and all evening to wait. Anyone for bridge?"

Danyl blinked at her, confused. "There isn't any bridge. That's why we took a tunnel."

Alania chuckled. "It's a card game."

"Erl and I didn't play cards," Danyl said.

Alania's grin spread wider. "We'd really need a fourth, although I know a three-handed version where the fourth is a dummy."

Danyl blinked again. "The fourth is a what?"

Alania laughed. "Never mind."

Danyl looked at Chrima. "Do you know what she's talking about?"

"Not a clue," Chrima said. She sat on another of the cots. "Did you really grow up on Twelfth Tier?" she asked Alania. She unslung the beamer and put it on the bed beside her. Danyl eyed it. He didn't intend to go in search of the mysterious Prime without it.

Alania nodded. "What about you?"

"Born on First. My parents got into trouble . . . I don't know what, exactly. I was eight when they fled to the Middens. Rustbloods found us. Mom and Dad hid me inside an old crate. They were dragged away. I hid for two days, too scared to leave, waiting for them to come back. But they never did. Instead, Erl found me and sent me down to Yvelle." She sighed. "I owe him my life. A lot of us do."

"He never mentioned any of this to me," Danyl said. "Not once. I never knew he was rescuing other people from the Middens, never saw him do it, even though they must have passed right through our quarters . . ."

"In case you haven't figured it out," Chrima said, "Erl is very good at compartmentalizing information and keeping secrets."

Danyl shook his head. He still found it hard to believe that Erl, the old scavenger he'd thought of almost as a father, was in fact a revolutionary, a leader in a decades-long effort to overthrow the Officers and Captain. He found it even harder to believe that he, and apparently Alania, too, were vital to that effort.

Did Erl ever really care for me at all? he wondered, and the thought burned like acid. *Or did he look after me only out of a sense of duty?*

He didn't want to believe that; he found it *hard* to believe, since he had so many memories that seemed to belie the notion. Erl tucking him into his bed, birthdays celebrated with cake and other delicacies traded for at the Last Chance Market (or so he'd thought—now he wondered if Erl had had them sent by his contacts in the City), endless hours of teaching and training and playing games and . . .

But it seemed clear that Erl would have been an equally supportive guardian to some entirely different child. To Alania, if Yvelle had found her. To that other baby . . . the one Yvelle had murdered.

He felt a little sick thinking of what the woman they had left behind in the resort had been willing to do, not even for the supposedly noble goal of overthrowing the Officers but simply because she had been angry and vengeful.

Then another thought struck him, even more sickening: if Erl had been a part of this revolutionary effort for as long as it seemed he had, then he must have *known* about the plans for the seven babies. He must have *approved* of the plan to murder all but one of those who had the mysterious genetic tags.

And that made his "love" for Danyl even more suspect. How loving could a guardian be if he had no compunction against the murder of a baby?

Can any *supposed greater good be worth the murder of a baby?* Danyl thought, but had no answer. He swiped the back of his hand across his suspiciously watery eyes. *Maybe that's why Erl has worked so hard to save children like Chrima. To try to salve his conscience for what he'd agreed to twenty years ago.*

I wonder if he succeeded?

Enough! Almost violently, Danyl pulled off his backpack. He opened the outside pocket into which Erl had placed the data crystal and drew it out. It glittered in the light from the overhead fixture.

"Very pretty," Chrima said from her cot. "But what is it?"

"It's a data storage device," Danyl said.

"I saw Erl give that to you," Alania said, "but I've never seen one before."

"Erl had a few of them," Danyl said. "He said they were 'archaic technology,' which was why they were thrown into the Middens." He held the crystal up to the light. It looked undamaged, but that didn't prove anything. "He said I should read it when I had time. It looks like we have time."

"And he said the reader's in my backpack," Alania said. She shrugged out of it and put it down on the stone floor by her cot. "I haven't even looked in this thing." She unzipped the top, peered inside, and grimaced. "Uh-oh. I thought it was waterproof, but everything in here is . . . sludgy."

"Everything?" Danyl put the crystal down on the bed and went to her side. Kneeling, he peered into the pack. "Shit," he said, which was certainly what the inside of the pack smelled like. He pulled out the reader and recognized it immediately as the one he'd used a million times growing up. Black water . . . or something . . . dripped from it. "That can't be good."

"Maybe it will still work," Alania said, but not as if she really believed it.

Danyl put the reader on the floor and gingerly touched the power button. No lights sprang to life. The reader just sat there, inert as a rock and twice as useless.

"Shit," Danyl said again. He looked into the pack. "Clothes, ruined . . . bottled water, should be all right . . . maybe a dozen mealpaks. They should be all right, too, if we wash them off." He pulled things out, and at the very bottom, he discovered a sealed black pouch. He lifted it;

it was heavier than he expected. He put it on the floor and unzipped it.

A slugthrower in a black synthileather holster gleamed at him. "That's more like it!" He lifted it out and pulled it from the holster. He'd never handled one in real life before, but it was weighted the same as the mock one he'd used to train with in Erl's "scavenged" simulator, just as he'd trained with so many other weapons. Underneath the weapon was another black pouch containing three ammunition clips, each holding ten slugs. Thirty shots. Not a lot, but better than nothing.

He pulled out a clip, popped open the bottom of the slugthrower's grip, slipped the clip inside it, and closed it up again. He thumbed the power button. A red light sprang to life on the opposite wall. He thumbed the power off again.

"Nice," Chrima said. "Guess I can keep the beamer, then."

"Guess again," Danyl said. He didn't point the slugthrower at her, but he didn't exactly *not* point it at her either. "Erl gave it to me. Not you."

Chrima studied him for a moment. "Fair enough," she said at last. "But I'm going to keep it until you reach the top of the stairs. Just in case."

Danyl didn't have to ask, *in case of what?* He knew what Chrima was thinking. If things went badly, Provosts could come charging along the River tunnel before they'd gotten very far up the stairs and be in the stairwell with them moments later. In which case both he *and* Chrima had better be armed.

Alania deserved a weapon, too, but there wasn't one to spare, and unlike him, she hadn't trained with even simulated versions. He wouldn't have hesitated to arm her otherwise; she'd shown remarkable grit from the moment he'd encountered her, far more than Danyl would have expected from a girl raised in the lap of luxury.

The lap of luxury.

He wondered for an uncomfortable moment if that was just a figure of speech. A beautiful girl raised by an Officer . . . her guardian, sure, but not really *family*. Had this Beruthi been tempted? Had he taken advantage of his power over her? Alania hadn't said anything to indicate it, but Danyl couldn't help wondering.

He didn't like the idea, so he shoved it out of his mind. He wasn't about to ask Alania. Instead, he said, "Agreed," out loud to Chrima. He pushed the filthy clothing and ruined reader back into the pack and kicked it under the bed. The rations would fit into his pack with the rope and spare knife and pocket toolset and canteen and clothes he always carried. No need for Alania to continue to be burdened with them.

He put the data crystal inside the pack this time, where it was less vulnerable to breakage. It would have to wait, infuriating though that was. He felt woefully ignorant, and he hated that feeling. He undid his belt, slipped the holster onto it, did the belt up again, and put the spare clips of ammo into his pants pocket.

Chrima lay back on her cot. "I never have an afternoon to do nothing," she said. "I think I'll take a nap." She closed her eyes.

Danyl looked at Alania. Sometime in the last few minutes, she had also lain down. Not only were her eyes closed, she was breathing deeply and regularly.

"I'll keep watch," he said to no one in particular.

He made cautious use of the promised toilet across the hall—while it did indeed work, he suspected it hadn't been cleaned since the River People found it—and then reemerged into the corridor. He looked toward the steps leading up from the tunnel beneath the River. A spectacularly deep silence reigned in that direction, but within hours, Provosts might be storming through it.

He put his back to the door that would take them to the Rim and beyond, to the mysterious Prime, if all went well, and slid down to sit on the floor. With the slugthrower in his hand, he stared down the silent corridor, his thoughts flowing in dark, sluggish currents like those of the River. But unlike the River, from which useful things could occasionally be salvaged, nothing of worth or note surfaced as the long hours dragged by.

EIGHTEEN

YVELLE STOOD on the balcony of one of the topmost decaying guest rooms of the Whitewater Resort, twenty-five stories above the swirling water of the basin into which the waterfall plunged, fingering the locket around her neck, awaiting the end of her world. Above the Canyon, the sky had lightened to a cold gray, and rain sluiced down on the Black River. It would do nothing to stop the impending attack.

She remembered climbing the ladder to Twelfth Tier twenty years ago. She remembered taking Danyl from his crib, discovering Alania was missing. And she remembered—God, she remembered—how the baby girl's mouth and nose had felt beneath her hand, the feeble struggles. She had felt the moment the spark of life had left the child. She had felt it night after night since in her nightmares.

She had no fear of death. If there were any justice in the universe, she would have died long ago for what she had done that night. But then, if there were any justice in the universe, the Captain and First Officer and all the Officers would have died long ago for what *they* had done to her husband and so many others. At the time, she had thought she was hastening that long-delayed justice with her actions, that somehow she was wreaking righteous vengeance. But as the years had slipped away, nothing, so far as she could tell, had changed in the City, out of sight of the old resort but still casting its dark shadow and excreting its noisome outflows.

She and her community had scooped what they could from the River, mined the lowest reaches of the refuse heap, and occasionally accepted a refugee or a desperately needed crate of supplies sent their way by Erl. Some couples had produced offspring, children who had never known anything other than life with the River People, for whom the old resort was simply home. Last night those children had been sequestered deep within the complex to await the results of the expected raid.

Yvelle had told the River People that even the Provosts would not murder children. She hoped she was right, but as she knew only too well, the murder of a child was never truly unthinkable.

Even from her vantage point, she could not see the hidden fighters waiting in the glass-walled lobby, armed with the handful of crossbows they had managed to construct over the years, the most powerful weapons they could muster. The River People had abandoned the far side of the waterfall pool to focus the Provosts' attention on the side where Alania and Danyl *weren't*. Chrima had taken the beamer rifle Danyl had been carrying, but a single beamer would hardly make a difference against the kind of firepower the Provosts would soon unleash. Better she used it to ensure Alania and Danyl made it to the Rim, then gave it to them so they could have at least some slight chance of reaching the mysterious Prime.

And then? To what use would Prime put the two surviving candidate babies? Could one or both of them truly bring about the long-awaited revolution?

I'll never know.

Yvelle picked up her own crossbow from where it leaned against the railing of the balcony. It was the finest they had constructed; it even had a scope, a miraculous find in the bottom layers of the garbage, its lenses scratched but serviceable, its tube once dented but carefully straightened. It must have fallen into the Canyon rubbish dump centuries ago, no telling how or why.

There are so many things I will never know the reasons for, Yvelle thought. *I'll never know where the City came from, why it crouches where it does above the Canyon, how the Officers took power, if the Captain has truly lived for centuries, or if she is mere myth.*

Children were taught that the City had been placed where it was by the will of the blessed Captain, "may she live forever," and that the location had been carefully chosen: the center of the vast circular plain called the Heartland, surrounded by the impassible Iron Ring, mountains so high that no aircraft could fly over them and no human could ever scale them, teeming with deadly (and inedible) wildlife and plants. Children were taught that the first inhabitants of the City had awakened, full-grown, with no memories of whatever had come before. They were taught that the Officers had been appointed by the Captain to rule the City and order its affairs and that the Provosts were the Captain's right hands, ensuring her will was done.

They were *not* taught why the City had become such a miserable place to live; why nothing seemed to work; why raw sewage and industrial waste and refuse dropped like excrement from the City onto the Middens day after day; how the Officers continued to live in luxury despite the ever-worsening conditions in the Tiers beneath their lofty perch.

Yvelle used to think the teachers knew the answers but weren't telling anyone. Later she had become convinced the teachers knew no more than they taught, that no one in the City apart from the Captain (if she truly still lived) and perhaps the First Officer knew the truth about its founding and ongoing decay.

Perhaps Prime knows, she thought. Somehow, all the mysteries of the City had to be connected to those candidate babies. To Alania and Danyl.

To our imminent destruction.

A siren sounded: an alarm salvaged from an aircar wreck, triggered by the lone scout she had posted at the bend in the River upstream from the falls. But it was hardly necessary. Almost at once, she heard the beat of rotors.

She raised the crossbow scope to her right eye.

She'd been certain the Provosts would arrive by helicopter. They could do nothing else—it was impossible to get boats to the River from the Middens or down the stairwell behind Erl's quarters. Nor was there any place to land a boat, since Yvelle had ordered the landing stage destroyed; they simply would have been swept over the waterfall. The reconnaissance drones must have made that clear to them.

The first 'copter, sleek and black, thundered around the bend, then hung in place, thirty meters lower than her balcony perch but well above the cauldron of the waterfall. An amplified voice boomed from it, echoing off the walls. "Lay down your weapons and show yourselves! By order of the Captain, this illegal community is to be dismantled. Comply, or we will use deadly force to make you comply!"

No one appeared in response to that command. Yvelle had counted on the Provosts offering surrender before attacking, since their primary purpose had to be to capture Alania and Danyl alive. Her own fighters stayed out of sight; they wouldn't attempt to fight aircraft, saving their bolts for the men who would descend from them.

Only Yvelle was in the open. Only Yvelle had a crossbow with a scope.

And only Yvelle had the two special crossbow bolts crafted with care by a particularly bitter engineer who had fled from the City to the Middens and been immediately recruited by Erl, who had somehow known he was coming. Strake Hanning had been his name, and he was long dead, poisoned by a River-contaminated cut—one that would have been too minor to worry about in the City—during a time when they were short of medical supplies. But during the two years he had lived as one of the River People, he had managed to concoct explosives from supplies carefully obtained through Erl. Most had been used to open collapsed tunnels and blast new spaces out of the Canyon walls. Only a few of those demolition charges remained, scattered amongst the fighters to use as they saw fit. Yvelle had made sure Chrima, for one, had one tucked away in her backpack.

But Strake Hanning had been interested in blowing up things other than rock. Just before he'd died, he had constructed two experimental crossbow bolts with blunt metal tips. One of those bolts was already loaded into Yvelle's crossbow. The second waited beside her on the balcony floor.

Peering down through her scope at the hovering 'copter, she had a clear view of the pilot's helmeted head through the transparent canopy of the cockpit.

She fired.

The bolt punched through the canopy, shattered the pilot's helmet and skull . . . and exploded.

Orange flame devoured the front of the 'copter. It twirled crazily out of control and fell, trailing smoke, chasing the shrapnel and bits of bone and flesh that were all that was left of its forward quarter. With an enormous splash and gout of steam, it plunged sideways into the black pool at the bottom of the waterfall. Its spinning rotor shattered. Some pieces hurtled skyward: one, a chunk of metal as long as Yvelle's leg, whirled over her head so fast she barely registered it, smashing into the edge of the balcony ceiling and spraying her with shards of concrete.

She reset the crossbow, reached for the second and last of her explosive bolts. She was just nocking it when the second 'copter thundered into sight.

The pilot of this one had seen the fate the first machine. He came in much higher. The black barrels of the machine guns on the 'copter's nose swung toward Yvelle. Through her scope, she saw the pilot's goggled face. She fired her second bolt at the same instant the machine guns spat fire in her direction.

The bullets traveled much faster than the bolt, but the bolt traveled fast enough. Even as the slugs tore through her body in a spray of blood and shattered bone, Yvelle felt the flare of heat and light as her second bolt blew the second helicopter and all the Provosts aboard it into the same oblivion that engulfed her.

In its final instant of consciousness, Yvelle Forister's dying brain produced a faint flicker of satisfaction.

Alania woke and wasn't quite sure why.

She stared up at a stone ceiling. Not her room in Quarters Beruthi. Where . . . ?

Everything that had happened the day before hit her with the force of an aircar dropping on her head. She sat up, gasping. *The attack . . . the Middens . . . Danyl . . . Erl . . . the stairs . . . the River . . . Yvelle . . .*

She'd slept all afternoon, as had Chrima, while Danyl kept watch. For supper they'd shared some of the rations from the River People's dining room: surprisingly good, thanks to the greenhouses she'd seen earlier and a meatvat provided, Chrima said, by Erl. No one had seemed interested in learning how to play bridge—not that they had cards to play it with, anyway. Instead, Chrima had gone over and over exactly what they would have to do, once they reached the robot "nest" high above, to evade the Rim defenses and slip out into the Heartland. It seemed simple enough. She suspected that was an illusion.

Despite sleeping all afternoon, she'd had no trouble

at all sleeping again that night, though her dreams did tend toward falling and drowning and exploding heads and other unpleasantries.

But neither memories nor dreams had awoken her. Something else . . .

"An explosion," Chrima said. She was at the door, peering around the corner in the direction of the stairs down to the tunnel beneath the River.

Danyl was sitting up now, too. He rubbed sleep from his eyes. "Provosts?"

Chrima gave him a withering look. "You think?"

"Then let's get moving," Alania said. She swung her feet over the side of the bed. "I get the toilet first."

She was crossing the hallway to the nasty bathroom when she heard the second explosion. The rock didn't tremble—they were too deeply embedded in the Canyon wall for that—but the air somehow quivered. She gasped, then hurried on to complete her business. When she emerged, Chrima went in, then Danyl. As he came out again, Chrima turned to the rusty red door. "It's a long climb to the Rim, and you can't enter the nest until 1000 precisely. Any sooner and the Guardians will take your head off. Does either of you have a working watch?"

Alania looked at her wrist. She still wore the decorative silver-and-glass timepiece Beruthi had given her three birthdays ago. It hadn't been designed for dropping out of the City into the Middens, floating down the Black River, and plunging over a waterfall. Neither had Alania, come to think of it, but she'd held up better than it had— its display had gone dark. "Not me."

"Mine's working," Danyl said.

"Is it accurate?"

"Sets automatically to the City time signal," he said. "Not that it's connected to that here, probably, but it shouldn't have lost time since yesterday morning."

"Good." Chrima dug a key-rod out of her pocket and inserted it into the hole in the door's lockplate. A bolt released with a bang. Chrima pushed at the door, and it opened inward, though it groaned as if it would have much preferred to stay closed.

The staircase beyond was, of course, lit by green eternals. Alania sighed.

"You'll need this at the top," Chrima said, holding out the key.

Danyl took it. "What about my beamer?"

"I'll be right behind you, protecting your rear," Chrima said. "I'll give it to you at the top if we all make it that far."

"You think we won't?" Alania asked. She looked back down the corridor toward the tunnel.

"I don't know what those explosions were," Chrima said. "What I do know is that the assault has begun. If there aren't Provosts inside the resort already, there will be soon. And if they've done their homework, they know the layout—at least the parts that the River People haven't modified." She grinned viciously. "And booby-trapped. That means they know about this tunnel. They may not consider it very important, since it only leads to the Rim, and they don't know you have a way through the Rim defenses. But sooner or later they *will* come this way, especially when they don't find you anywhere else." Her momentary smile faded. "My friends may be dying back there. My *home* is dying. They're dying so you two can escape, because Erl said it's important, because Yvelle said it's important. So you two are damn well *going* to escape. You're going to make it across the Rim and into the Heartland and do whatever the hell it is you have to do to bring down the Officers, because if you don't I'll kill you myself, even if I have to come back from the dead."

Alania swallowed. People were dying—people had *already* died—because of her, because of Danyl, because of whatever they were, whatever they represented to the First Officer, to the shadowy figures of the supposed revolution she'd never even dreamed existed. She hadn't wanted any of this. She didn't want it now. She hadn't chosen it; it had chosen her. And there was nothing she could do to stop it.

She remembered how free she'd felt just yesterday. But she knew now that she was no freer than when she had been imprisoned in Quarters Beruthi with hidden cameras watching her every move. She was still trapped by the strange circumstances of her birth.

Maybe she always would be.

"Let's move," Danyl growled.

They passed through the door. Alania and Danyl began to climb while Chrima hung back. After eight flights, Alania glanced down to see Chrima closing and locking the door, then following them up the stairs at last.

The dank, stale air in the stairwell didn't seem to contain as much oxygen as it should. Alania's lungs were laboring before she'd climbed fifty meters, a tenth of the total distance. "Slow down," she gasped up to Danyl. "We'll never last at this rate."

"We have to be there by 1000," he said, but he slowed all the same.

"What time is it?"

Danyl checked his watch. "0812."

"Then we have time. We have to conserve our strength, or we won't be able to do what we have to at the top." *If we reach the top*. In many places, the stairs no longer had handrails—another reason to slow down. A stumble or a faint, and . . .

Alania pushed a little closer to the stone wall and kept climbing, trying to ignore the growing ache in her calves.

Up and up . . . and up and up. Just as in the stairwell they had descended on the far side of the Canyon, the eternals barely burned in parts of the shaft, so at times they climbed in near darkness, faint green glow above them, faint green glow below them, neither doing much to light where they were at the moment.

Up, and still up. Time and consciousness collapsed into the endless now of climbing, climbing, climbing. Alania didn't know exactly how long they had been on the stairs or how much farther they had to go when there was a flash of light and an enormous bang below them—and then a shockwave ripped up the narrow chimney of the stairwell, so powerful it threw her from her feet. Her right hand dropped into the void, and she hastily rolled over onto her back, then hauled herself upright. Her ears rang, and when she swiped the back of her hand across her suddenly runny nose, it came away with a smear of red. Above her, Danyl was likewise pulling himself to his feet. He drew the slugthrower, shook his head as though trying to clear it, then turned and peered downward.

"They're in the stairwell!" Chrima shouted up from an indeterminate distance below them. "Move! I'll hold them off with the beamer."

But for how long? Alania wanted to ask, but she didn't really have the breath for it. Danyl swore, slammed the gun back into its holster, and resumed climbing, Alania on his heels.

They climbed in silence—ominous silence, Alania thought—for several more minutes. And then . . .

Light. Blinding white light streaming up from below. They had climbed so far it barely reached them, but looking down through the metal mesh of the stairs, Alania saw Chrima silhouetted against it, taking aim with the beamer.

The light flashed out.

They climbed two more turns of the stairs. Alania's heart pounded in her ears harder than even the exertion itself could account for, but she could still hear Chrima's footsteps clattering *down* the stairs, farther and farther away from them. She heard her shout something, heard the barest whisper of answering shouts.

Silence for four more turns of the stairs.

Then a single rifle shot rang out from far below.

An instant later, the bottom of the shaft exploded.

This shockwave made the previous one seem like the gentle breezes that blew from the Twelfth Tier ventilation shafts. It not only hurled Alania from her feet, it blasted her into the air. She slammed against the wall, knocking her forehead on the stone, then crashed down on the stairs on her back.

"Help!" Danyl gasped out above her, through the renewed ringing in her ears. She opened bleary eyes that didn't want to focus, turned her head, and saw that he was dangling in space, barely hanging on to a twisted balustrade, all that remained of the long-gone railing, that stuck out from the steps. She rolled over and lunged for him, reaching out her hand. He let go of the balustrade with one hand to grab it and then was able to shift the grip of the other hand closer to the stairs. A few moments later she was pulling him back to safety . . . if you could call it that. She collapsed against the inside wall, breathing heavily. He sat beside her.

"What happened?" she asked. Her ears still felt stuffed with cotton, if cotton could ring like a bell, and the front of her borrowed blue shirt was spattered with fresh blood from her nose.

"Chrima," Danyl panted. "When she opened her pack yesterday, I saw something . . . didn't know what it was. A rectangular package. Now I know. A demolition charge."

"A demolition . . ." Alania peered down but could see nothing; the bottom of the shaft was filled with a cloud of dust. There was no sign of Chrima. "You mean . . ." Horror gripped her throat. "She blew herself up?"

"Herself, and the stairs, and any Provosts who were in the shaft—if the blast didn't get them, the falling rock and debris must have. If we're lucky, they can't even get into the shaft anymore."

Alania felt sick. "How could she do that?" She'd just met Chrima the day before. She'd liked her, they were almost the same age, and now, just like that, she was gone—and she'd done it to *herself*?

So we can escape, Alania thought. Guilt mingled with her horror.

"I wish I knew," Danyl said. "I wish I knew why so many people are dying for us." He looked down at her, his face corpse-gray in the green light. His nose had started bleeding after the explosion, too, and the blood glistened almost black on his upper lip and chin. "Alania, who are we? *What* are we?"

"I don't know," Alania said. "But whoever we are, *whatever* we are, how can we possibly be worth . . ." Her throat closed as she looked down into the billowing dust and smoke.

She felt Danyl's hand on her shoulder, squeezing. She looked up at him through tear-blurred eyes. "All we can do," Danyl said, his voice soft and yet somehow hard at the same time, "is to press on. To try to get to this Prime. To find out what makes us so important. And hope like hell it really is worth all this."

Alania took a deep, shuddering breath. "At least we're on our own now. Nobody else will die because of us."

"Except for however many are dying in the resort," Danyl said grimly. He struggled to his feet, wincing. "No bones broken . . . I don't think." He held out his hand. She took it, warm and strong in hers, and let him haul her to her feet. She felt a twinge from her left ankle, but it bore her weight, so she didn't mention it.

Danyl glanced at his watch. "0903. Less than an hour to get to the top." He looked up, and Alania followed his gaze, but the dim lighting from the eternals gave no clue how much farther they had to climb. "Onward and upward?"

"Onward and upward," Alania agreed. She closed her eyes. *Goodbye, Chrima*, she thought. *Thank you.* Grief closed her throat. She swallowed hard, opened her eyes, and resumed climbing into the unknown.

NINETEEN

FIRST OFFICER KRANZ watched the assault on the River People from the comfort of his office. He watched the first helicopter crash, then saw the second one suffer the same fate, but he also saw the sniper be obliterated. The remaining four helicopters reached the old resort unopposed. Provosts swarmed down lines, entering the resort through the shattered windows that overlooked the once-scenic waterfall and pool—now cesspool. With a twitch of his finger, he switched from helmet cam to helmet cam. He saw a handful of his soldiers fall to crossbows and booby traps, but not very many, and one by one, the defenders were eliminated or arrested.

But there was no sign of Alania, no sign of Danyl—no sign of the two people the raid was intended to capture.

He watched a door be forced open, saw children and their mothers cowering wide-eyed in the chamber beyond. The Provosts rounded them up. They'd be questioned, of course, but he doubted any of them knew where Alania and Danyl had gone. The leaders, whoever they were, would not have shared that information with the people most likely to survive the assault.

Kranz's fingers dug into the arms of his chair as the assault wound down. *Damn it. Where the hell could they be?*

The final "battle" of the raid took place in a stairwell leading up from the resort to the Rim, where there had once been a garden, now a nest of deadly robot Guardians.

What the woman fleeing up those stairs thought she could accomplish at the Rim, Kranz would never know; she blew up herself and much of the staircase, the debris crushing three Provosts at the bottom of the shaft and effectively closing it off.

The River flowed underground from the waterfall's pool, which had been artificially created with a dam when the resort was built. Could Alania and Danyl have fled along it somehow? It seemed unlikely—old records did not indicate any sort of traversable cavern down there, and the River remained underground for a kilometer before emerging through a spillway. But it would have to be checked out once divers could be brought in, equipped with sonar to penetrate the murk of the water.

Kranz frowned at the resort's plans, summoned from the City's database. It showed only two ways out of the Canyon. There was a main elevator shaft and accompanying staircase up to the Rim above the resort's glass-walled lobby in the Canyon's east wall, and there was a matching elevator shaft and staircase on the far side of the pool in the west wall. The elevator on the lobby side still worked, but while its mechanism was intact, there was no longer an exit up on the Rim; the once-grand main entrance to the resort had long since been demolished.

The elevator in the west wall had failed years ago, the Provosts had reported. Even its mechanism no longer remained atop the Rim. Now the woman they had pursued up the western stairs had blown herself up and brought the bottom half of them crashing down. Even if someone higher up had survived the blast and made it to the top, they would find themselves in what was once a pavilion offering resort guests pleasant dining in the Rim Garden but was now a Rim Guardian nest. Entering *that* would be suicide.

And yet, unless Alania and Danyl turned up cowering in one of the dozens of guest rooms in the old resort—which had not all been cleared, so that *was* still possible—the western staircase was the only route they *could* have taken, presumably ahead of the self-detonating woman. Which would at least explain why someone had been willing to destroy it so spectacularly, permanently . . . and fatally.

Kranz continued to watch the cleanup operation for some time. As door after door was kicked in and Alania and Danyl remained missing, he became increasingly convinced he was right. He touched a control on his desk, opening his direct link to Commander Havelin. He'd refrained from speaking to the Commander until that moment; micromanaging a battle from afar was hardly a recipe for tactical success, and it was a very good way to damage morale.

"Havelin here," came the Commander's voice in response to his signal.

"First Officer Kranz here, Commander," Kranz said.

"Yes, sir?" Havelin's voice sounded crisp, professional . . . and very slightly guarded.

"Excellent work," Kranz said. *Except for losing two helicopters within five minutes of each other to a bloody sniper*, he thought, but there was time enough for *that* discussion later. For now, he wanted the Commander entirely on his side.

"Thank you, sir," Commander Havelin said, and Kranz thought he sounded a little less guarded and a lot more relieved.

"I've been studying the plans of the resort," Kranz said. "Since our quarry has not turned up anywhere within the complex, I think they must be in the western stairwell leading to the old Rim Garden."

"As do I, sir," Havelin said. "I have already had Rim Control deactivate the air defenses so I can send a helicopter up there, and I recalled a squad from the cleanup operation in the guest rooms. They're resupplying as we speak and should be at the top within fifteen minutes. Rim Control is standing by to deactivate all other defenses once we're ready to move in and enter the stairwell from the top."

"Excellent," Kranz said again. Perhaps he would not have to have the Commander stripped of his rank after all. He glanced at the chronometer on his desk: almost 1000. "I will be observing with interest. Carry on."

"Yes, sir. Thank you, sir. Havelin out."

Kranz called up the camera feeds, selecting one that showed Provosts emerging onto the shelf of rock outside the now-shattered glass window of the resort lobby to be lifted one by one to the hovering helicopter. A thunderstorm had rolled over the Canyon. Rain sleeted down all around them.

If Alania and Danyl *had* made it to the Rim, they wouldn't be able to get past the robot sentries. They were trapped. Just a few more minutes, and this whole ridiculous and costly charade would come to an end.

Kranz allowed himself one glance at the frightening array of yellow and red lights on the Captain's medical monitor, which he now kept uncovered whenever he was in the office alone, and fought down the familiar surge of near panic that gripped him whenever he allowed himself to think too hard about the stakes involved in the search for Alania and Danyl. Then he went over to the bar that ran along one wall of his office, poured another cup of kaff, and returned to his desk. Sipping the hot, bittersweet liquid appreciatively, he settled in to watch what he desperately hoped would be the endgame of that search.

Danyl and Alania reached the top of the stairs with five minutes to spare. It gave them little time to rest. "You remember the plan?" he asked Alania, panting.

She gulped air, then nodded. "There's a five-minute interval during which there are no robots in the hut beyond that door. We have that long to activate the safe passage to the nearest Rim gate. It will last for ten minutes, during which time the robots will not register our presence as long as we stay within the passage's boundaries. Once that time is up, they'll kill us on sight."

"Right. Although I don't understand why this 'safe passage' protocol even exists."

"I do," Alania said, and Danyl raised an eyebrow at her. "Normally techs carry transmitters that identify them as harmless to the robots," she explained. "But if something went so seriously awry that the robots no longer accepted the transmitted security codes, you might need a safe way in and out of the nest. No doubt the protocol can be activated from the City as well."

"You seem to know a lot about robots."

She smiled briefly. "Misspent childhood. My guardian's factory probably built these. He insisted I study robotics. Among other things." Her smile faded. "I used to think he meant for me to take his place, since he had no children of his own. Then he handed me over to Kranz."

"Another part of the puzzle," Danyl said. "All right, expert. Why do we have only ten minutes to get out? Why can't we just shut down the robots completely and take our time?"

"Because Prime didn't tell us how," Alania said. "He must have had a reason. Maybe it requires security codes he doesn't have. Maybe it would raise alarms we don't want to raise." She looked over the side of the landing, back down the long, long shaft they had just climbed so laboriously. Danyl knew what she was thinking, because he was thinking it, too: *Chrima's grave*. "The Provosts may have guessed where we've gone. Even if we get across the Rim, they may be waiting for us just beyond the Fence."

"I know," Danyl said. He pulled out the slugthrower, checked it over, and then holstered it again. Ten shots before he'd have to reload. If the Provosts *were* waiting . . .

They don't want to kill us, he thought. *They want to capture us. That gives us an edge.*

But not much of one.

He checked his watch again. "One minute." They were sitting side by side on the landing. He climbed to his feet, held out his hand to Alania. She took it. *My sister*, he thought with a sense of wonder. *Probably*, honesty compelled him to add, but in truth, he was certain of it. Her eyes, if nothing else, told the tale.

He felt ashamed of how he'd originally seen her as nothing more than another salvage prize, his ticket to the City. She was clearly far more valuable than he'd ever dreamed — as was he, apparently (and astonishingly) — but whatever her value to the First Officer, she was even more valuable to *him*.

He pulled her upright, then released her hand and took out the key Chrima had given him. He held it at the ready in front of the key-port in the lockplate to the right of the door. The green numerals on his watch flicked to 1000 — and he thrust the rod into the waiting receptacle. The locking mechanism groaned and clanked, and then the door swung inward of its own accord.

What Danyl had been imagining as a utilitarian shed proved to be nothing of the sort. Extending twenty meters to both the left and the right, it boasted a fancy (though badly scarred) parquet floor, three more-or-less-intact (though dark) crystal chandeliers, and a high ceiling bearing a painted and peeling representation of clouds. There were pillars half buried in the walls, as though the pavilion had originally been open to the Rim Garden on all sides. Had guests dined and danced here once upon a time?

Danyl had never been to the Rim before, but he knew no gardens remained there now. Or anything else green and growing. The maps he had studied in the teaching machine showed that the Rim Defenses extended twenty kilometers to the north and south of the City, on both sides of the Canyon: hundred-meter-wide no-go zones of smooth concrete patrolled by the Guardian robots. Three-meter walls topped with razor wire and their *own* defense and surveillance systems enclosed the robot-defended strip on both the Canyon and Heartland sides: the one on the Heartland side was called "the Fence." The defenses were broken only on the west side of the City, where the main gate and the warehouses and other structures surrounding it stood. Provosts guarded those, of course. The ladder and cargo crane associated with the Last Chance Market also stood within that gap.

Danyl had asked Erl about those defenses, which seemed like ludicrous overkill just to keep Middens-dwellers from escaping into the Heartland. Erl had replied they'd been there for more than two centuries because of a failed attempt to overthrow the Officers, led by rebels from the farm villages before they were as tightly controlled as they now were. "Like most things in the City, the Rim Defenses took on a life of their own," he'd said. "Once something like that is created, it must continue. The Officers do not like change."

The defenses might have served little practical purpose, but that did nothing to lessen the problems they posed for him and Alania. And if the instructions provided to them did not work, the *best* they could hope for was to be trapped in the shaft they had just so laboriously climbed, awaiting the eventual arrival of the Provosts.

At worst, of course, they would be laser pincushions. *Guess we're about to find out.*

A silvery cylinder about a meter in diameter punctured the ancient parquet floor at its center: the control station. Danyl looked both ways before stepping through the door, though the gesture was futile—if the robot sentries or some other automated defenses were active, they would react to his presence before he could even begin to register theirs.

But his head remained firmly on his shoulders, and no

smoking holes appeared in his body. "So far, so good," he said over his shoulder to Alania, who followed him as he strode to the control station. The top of the cylinder was a blank gray screen; he touched it, and it lit with a series of numbers, meaningless to Danyl, presumably showing the status of the Guardians stationed in the pavilion "nest." In the center of the screen glowed eight icons, abstract shapes that again conveyed no information to Danyl. From his pants pocket, he pulled Prime's instructions as recorded by Yvelle, and he held the piece of paper out to Alania. They'd both studied it carefully in case something happened to that sheet of paper, but now he wouldn't have to rely on his memory.

"Rotating cube icon," Alania read.

He located it, touched it. The display changed. The new one was labeled "Maintenance Options."

"Green circle."

Danyl touched it. A new window opened. "To grant Temporary Security Zone Access, enter security code," he read out loud.

"842XRCI22133," Alania read, and he carefully punched in the apparently random mixture of numbers and letters. The instructions warned that he'd only get one chance, and he held his breath until the screen blinked "Temporary Security Zone Access granted."

The screen returned to the Maintenance Options screen, but now the green circle glowed red. Beside it, a countdown had already begun: 9:58. 9:57. 9:56.

"We should move," Danyl said, but Alania was staring at the screen.

"There's another red icon. That V-shape. Something else is turned off."

Danyl frowned at it. "You're right. Let's see what it is." He touched the icon.

A new window appeared. "Air defenses currently inactive. Reactivate air defenses?" Below that, the red V-shaped icon appeared again.

"Air defenses?" Danyl stared at the screen. "Inactive?" He suddenly realized what that had to mean. "They know we're up here. They're sending aircraft!"

"Well then," Alania said, and she reached out and touched the V-shape.

The icon turned green. "Air defenses reactivated," the screen read for a moment before it blinked back to the Maintenance Options screen.

The countdown continued. "9:24. 9:23. 9:22."

"Now," Alania said, "we *really* should move."

Danyl nodded, though he felt a surge of admiration . . . mingled with maybe just a little irritation. Alania kept acting without asking his permission, or sometimes even his opinion. It offended his male ego just a little — hence the irritation — but the admiration outweighed that. In the Middens, he would have been the natural leader, but . . .

You're not in the Middens anymore, he reminded himself. *You're both on the same footing up here. And if you get to the City, she'll know more than you do.*

Together they hurried across the parquet floor to a featureless door. Danyl slowed, wondering how to open it, but it opened on its own, revealing rain-spattered concrete. Overhead, lightning flashed, followed by the rumble of thunder.

Just as described on their instruction sheet, solid yellow lines marking the safe corridor ran straight from the shed to a wall fifty meters away: the Fence. Made of concrete topped with opalescent domes, which Danyl knew contained its cameras, sensors, and weapons, it was a forbidding sight. The outlined path crossed a two-meter-deep trench just inside the Fence via a metal bridge, rainwater pouring from it, which Danyl suspected only extruded when the safety corridor was activated. As they hurried toward the Fence, he looked both ways again and almost stumbled: six Rim Guardians watched them, three on either side of the corridor, black oval bodies on multidirectional wheels. Turreted weapons, both beamers and slugthrowers, tracked them as they moved.

He couldn't see the countdown, but there had to be several minutes left before the safety corridor stopped being safe. *Lots of time*, he thought. *Lots of time*.

But even as he thought that, he heard the beat of a helicopter's rotors rising out of the Canyon. He stopped and twisted around, as did Alania. The first time he'd seen a helicopter, when he was eight, he'd thought it the most wonderful thing ever. Even though he'd seen many aircars come and go from the City before that, there had been something about the beat of helicopter rotors that had truly seized his imagination. He'd dreamed of roaming the Heartland in one of the sleek black vehicles, exploring the rivers and lakes and farms and valleys, flying to the foothills of the Iron Ring itself, announcing his presence everywhere he went with that glorious pounding thunder.

He'd talked about it so much that Erl had sat him down and explained firmly that only Provosts used helicopters, so the only way he could ever ride in one would be to either be a Provost—and since he did not live in the City and thus could not enlist, that would never happen—or to be *arrested* by the Provosts, in which case he would have a very short flight to the helipad on Tenth Tier and never be heard from again.

After that, Danyl had decided that maybe helicopters weren't so wonderful after all. The sight of this one confirmed that negative opinion.

"Run!" he shouted at Alania as the whirling rotors appeared above the roof of the pavilion. He needn't have bothered; she dashed past him as the word left his mouth, splashing through the puddles created by the driving rain. He bolted after her, running between the yellow lines toward the metal bridge.

"Halt in the name of the Captain!" an amplified voice boomed, echoing weirdly off the Fence and across the pavement. "Provosts will—"

The voice cut off. The helicopter's thunder swelled from merely loud to earsplitting. It sped forward, gaining altitude ...

... but not fast enough to avoid the beamers of the security robots, all of whom fired at it simultaneously.

The 'copter came apart in midair in a spray of oil and fuel that instantly ignited, the fiery blast slamming into Danyl and Alania just as they reached the bridge, hurling them off of it and into the ditch. They splatted into thick, soft mud as heat and smoke and steam and shrapnel drove like a deadly hailstorm across the open space above them. A second later, the largest chunk of the helicopter—probably the crew compartment, though all Danyl saw for sure was black, twisted metal trailing flame and smoke—tore through the concrete of the Fence like paper. Danyl flung himself on top of Alania and pressed her down into the mud while hell exploded above them. Only the steep walls of the ditch saved them—that, and luck: a lump of twisted metal the size of Danyl's torso thudded into the muck a hand's breadth from his head.

Then, just like that, it was over, except for the stench of burning fuel and the hiss of rain falling on flaming wreckage.

Alania made a muffled noise, and Danyl rolled off her. She sat up, plastered with mud, and swiped a hand across her face to clear her eyes, nose, and mouth. "I guess the air defenses worked," she said in a shaky voice.

"Yeah," Danyl said. "Good call, turning them on. Well ..." He looked pointedly at the half-buried chunk of steaming metal. "... kind of."

"We need to get out of here," Alania said. "Now. This is our best chance to get away. Maybe our only chance."

Danyl blinked at her. His ears still rang from the noise of the helicopter's sudden demise, and his head felt stuffed with oily rags. "What?"

"Anyone watching will have seen the helicopter go down apparently right on top of us. With luck, they'll think we're dead. And all the sensors and cameras on the chunk of wall the helicopter just took out means we're in a blind spot."

Danyl felt his brain click back to life. "Right," he said with sudden excitement. He scrambled to his feet. The edge of the trench was just above the top of his head. "Boost me up, then I'll pull you up."

Seconds later they dashed across the road beyond the broken Fence and threw themselves down into a wheat field, the tall stalks offering some cover while they stared back at the destruction wrought by the crashing helicopter. It had torn a fifteen-meter-wide gap in the Fence, now shrouded in smoke and steam. Flames still poured from the shattered hull, which had ripped a gouge in the wheat field some thirty meters from where they lay. Bits of metal—and of men, Danyl realized sickly—covered the wet road.

To their left, the City rose in the distance, dimmed by the rain. He had never seen it from any vantage point but underneath, where its vast mechanical underpinnings dominated everything and the Tiers above were all but invisible. Now he could see all the Tiers at once, and the City was revealed as a gigantic, elongated ovoid, flattened on the bottom, topped by a silver-gray dome, home of the mythical Captain. Danyl only spared it a glance before looking the other way, to the south, where a windbreak ran east-west along the edge of the field, a thick line of trees and brush running up and over a slight rise. "That way," Danyl said. "Let's get as far away from here as possible. Then we'll worry about getting to Prime."

Together, they ran through the rain for the shelter of the trees.

TWENTY

THE DESTRUCTION OF yet another helicopter was so sudden that First Officer Kranz stared at the screen for several seconds before he fully registered what had happened.

He'd heard the calm chatter as the helicopter rose above the Rim, saw Alania and Danyl running for the wall through the 'copter's cameras, heard the Provost's squad leader say, "Halt in the name of the Captain! Provosts will—"

And then he'd heard another voice, calm no longer, ringing with panic: "The air defenses are active! The air defenses are active!"

The helicopter had roared, trying to leave the Rim airspace, but no human could react faster than robot sentries. Beamers had sliced it apart, it had burst into flame, and seconds later it had crashed and exploded . . .

. . . right where Alania and Danyl had been standing seconds before.

The loss of a third helicopter and crew meant nothing to Kranz compared to the catastrophe the deaths of those two represented. They were the culmination of three decades of preparation for an event that could not be postponed much longer. If they were truly lost . . .

If they're lost, all is lost. If they're lost, the City will die, and everything the First Officers have worked for since the beginning will die with it. If they're lost . . .

If they're lost, I am lost.

Patrols were already racing to the site. He'd know soon enough.

He sat back in his chair, stomach churning, staring at the smoke and flames rising from the burning wreckage of the 'copter, the perfect visual metaphor for what might have just happened to everything he had worked toward for so long. If Danyl and Alania had died, the City *itself* would soon be nothing but a burning hulk.

He clenched his trembling hands. Then he took a deep breath, leaned forward, and began calling up other camera feeds. He needed to see *exactly* what had happened to Alania and Danyl. Until their bodies were discovered, there was hope.

There had to be.

By the time they reached the windbreak and plunged into its welcome shadow, Alania's heart was pounding, and her legs, already worked to their limit by the long climb from the base of the Canyon, felt like they were on fire. She collapsed on all fours on the wet ground in the middle of the windbreak, where there was a kind of corridor between the two rows of trees and shrubs that formed it. "We can't stop," Danyl said, but he stopped anyway and helped her back to her feet.

She remembered how he had thrown his body over hers as he tried to protect her from the inferno of fire and metal screaming over their heads. Of course, he'd almost drowned her in the mud, and she wondered exactly how he thought his body would have saved her had the wreckage landed on top of them, but it was the thought that counted. Just yesterday, he'd seen her as nothing more than a way to get a pass into the City. Now he was willing to risk his life to keep her safe.

He's my brother, she thought. She was certain of it now,

and despite everything that had happened, it made her unreasonably happy. *So this is what it's like to have family.*

And there might be more. Seven candidate babies . . . though candidates for what, she still didn't know. Yvelle had murdered one, and Danyl and Alania made two more; that meant there should be four young people out there who were also their siblings.

She wondered how it had been done almost as much as *why* it had been done. *In vitro fertilization, artificial wombs,* she thought. She knew from her study of City technology that artificial wombs existed and had been used more than once to ensure an heir for a great Officer family, and you couldn't coordinate ordinary pregnancies closely enough to have seven identically aged babies in the hospital at the same time.

She frowned. *Or could you?*

She thought about it. The mothers—presumably surrogates—would all have had to be implanted with embryos at the same time, then all the births induced or C-sectioned at the same time. The thought made her shudder: seven women treated like so many brood cows. Maybe it wasn't impossible, but it seemed unlikely, especially given the existence of artificial wombs.

Whatever the mechanism of their births, she was sure she and Danyl were brother and sister. While in a way it was disappointing that the first young man she'd had the opportunity to spend time with (even if most of that time had been spent running for their lives) was not someone with whom she could kindle a romantic relationship, she still liked having a brother. And there would always be time for romance later.

Well, if there *was* a later.

Danyl pulled the creased piece of paper bearing their instructions from his pocket, bent over it to shield it from the water dripping through the trees above their heads, and opened it up so both of them could look at it. "We're off to a good start," he said. "I wasn't thinking about it when we ran this way, but this windbreak is the first landmark."

Alania studied the notes and distances given. She added them up in her head and blinked in dismay. "That's fifty-six kilometers. That'll take us . . ."

"All of today and most of tomorrow," Danyl said. He looked down at their feet. "I foresee blisters."

Alania sighed. "So let's get started making—" She stopped and spun around as a sound penetrated her consciousness. *Rotors!* "There's another helicopter coming!"

"Can you run some more now?" Danyl asked.

"Oddly enough, I think I can."

They splashed off down the muddy corridor between the windbreak's trees and bushes. The surge of adrenaline the sound of the helicopter sent through Alania's veins masked the pain in her legs (and other places—she suspected she had black and blue patches all over her body), but not for long. Eventually the ache returned, and her pace slowed. Danyl was clearly struggling, too. But though they were eventually reduced to a shambling walk, and though the fire in her legs was more than countered by the chill of the rain that had soaked her to the skin, they kept moving.

Alania kept expecting the sound of the rotors to swell behind them, for the new helicopter with a fresh squad of Provosts to come screaming by overhead, searching for them among the trees. But instead the sounds from the crash site diminished as they ran and were silenced completely by the time they crested the small hill and started down the other side.

The windbreak ran for five kilometers, after which they turned left and continued another five kilometers along a second windbreak, following Prime's instructions. This one brought them to a river flowing along a deep gully toward the Canyon, where Alania thought it must make a spectacular waterfall as it leaped into the depths somewhere downstream from the Whitewater Resort.

The last place they wanted to return to was the Canyon; they scrambled down the side of the gully to the rock-covered bank and turned upstream instead. For the rest of the day they followed the stream's winding path, hidden from above by overhanging trees with long, trailing branches. The scattered rocks made for uncertain footing, and Alania worried what would happen if one of them turned an ankle.

But they survived unscathed until nightfall, though they were drenched periodically by a series of thunderstorms chasing each other across the Heartland. By then Alania was so tired she could hardly see straight, and she definitely couldn't walk straight. The sky finally cleared as the sun neared the horizon. Danyl looked around uneasily. "It's about to get a lot colder," he said. "We can't stay down here. We have to find shelter. We could die of exposure."

Alania tried to reply, found her teeth chattering, and clenched them for a moment before managing, "There . . . may not be any shelter up there, either."

"There's got to be something," Danyl said. "It's all farmland. An equipment shed. Something . . ."

Hoping he was right, Alania followed his scramble up the muddy side of the gully.

They'd had no view of the surrounding countryside since they'd started following the river, and when they reached ground level, they found things had changed. Contrary to Danyl's assurance, it *wasn't* all farmland. Instead they were in a forest, a thick tangle of small trees and brush growing up around massive tree stumps, all that remained of the long-since-harvested first-growth trees. The welter of greenery competing to fill the ecological niche had created a barrier Alania and Danyl would have difficulty forcing their way through and would probably get lost in if they tried, especially with night coming on.

"Shit," Danyl said, summing up the situation perfectly.

"No shelter," Alania pointed out completely unnecessarily. She felt she should contribute something other than another swear word, although that was her first inclination.

"We were better off down by the river after all," Danyl said. "Maybe we can find a cave."

"It's almost dark."

"I know." Danyl turned and half slid, half stumbled back down the muddy slope to the stony riverbank. Alania slid down on her rear end and stood beside him. He stared around in the fading light. "There," he said suddenly, pointing. "Maybe among those rocks?"

"Those rocks" were a pile of boulders tangled with dead trees at a bend in a stream: a remnant of a long-ago flash flood, Alania guessed. They reached the rocks as the last of the twilight faded. There was just enough room for the two of them to squeeze in among three of the largest boulders. The branches overhead would have done nothing to keep out the earlier rain, but fortunately the sky remained clear. Alania was still wet and shivering, though, and so was Danyl. "We'll have to . . . um . . . share body heat," he said diffidently.

Alania had already come to that same conclusion and saw no reason to be shy about it, not with survival at stake. *Besides,* she thought, *he's my brother . . . right?*

She wasn't entirely sure her body would register him that way, though, given how deprived of male companionship it had been her entire life. And perhaps it would have been a problem, under different circumstances. But cold and wet and miserable as she was—and Danyl, too, no doubt—her only interest in the nearness of a male came from the fact said male was giving off heat. She spooned with Danyl, pressing her body against his back while holding him tightly in her arms. The backpack beneath their heads made a totally inadequate and very lumpy pillow, but it was still better than nothing.

Barely.

Still, there was one thing to be said for climbing half a kilometer up a staircase, running for your life from exploding helicopters and killer robots, and then fleeing cross-country on a multikilometer walk: suddenly finding itself motionless, her body made another sound decision and promptly went to sleep.

The video from the destruction of the helicopter atop the Rim proved inconclusive. Kranz tamped downed the panic bubbling just under his carefully maintained calm surface and stared again at the last clear image of Danyl and Alania, which showed them running onto the bridge over the ditch inside the Fence. Smoke and flame obscured them in the next frame. When there was a clear image again, there was no sign of them, but there were also enormous blind spots in the surveillance footage; the cameras that would have provided a view down into the ditch had been obliterated along with many others.

Kranz could do nothing but wait for a report from the Provosts at the scene. Among them were search-and-rescue experts, but it was already clear there wouldn't be anyone to rescue; everyone who had been on board the helicopter was obviously thoroughly deceased. His heart thumped in his chest. If Danyl and Alania were dead, then the City had just died with them, though its death throes would be far more prolonged than theirs. Thanks to the nanobots within his body, which had given him access to the thoughts and plans of the original First Officer, Kranz—and Kranz alone—knew how to salvage the failing City and the dying Captain, how to prevent the final and fatal failure of all the City's systems and the carnage and chaos and civil war that would surely follow.

But to do it, he needed Alania.

Kranz shouldn't have been alone in his knowledge.

His clone, Falkin, should have been at his side. The boy's loss had hit him hard. To his shame, he had even tried to convince Beruthi to advance the timetable, to let him have Alania when she was only sixteen. Without his backup in place, it would take only one accident or assassination attempt, something that damaged his body more severely than his nanobots could repair, to bring their only hope for saving the City crashing down. But Beruthi had forcefully reminded him that until the girl was twenty, her brain would not be developed enough to do what would be demanded of it. He had, in a way, talked Kranz down from a ledge. Kranz had doubled his bodyguards and taken very special care of himself ever since, rarely leaving Twelfth Tier. He had survived the last four years unscathed, waiting for Alania to come to him . . .

. . . only to have her snatched from his grasp and thrown into the Middens in the company of the boy he'd thought dead twenty years ago. If she had died now . . .

He shook his head, his black thoughts of imminent disaster having circled right back to where they'd started, as they so often did.

An hour passed. Two. Then he heard the chime he'd been waiting for, and his heart raced. He slapped his palm down on his desk to answer the call.

Commander Havelin's sweaty, black-grimed face filled the screen, framed by rising smoke. "We've searched the crash site thoroughly, sir." Havelin coughed and grimaced, then continued, "We've recovered the remains of the helicopter crew and the Provosts who were aboard. They were good men, sir."

"I'm sure they were, Commander," Kranz said, though he wasn't sure of any such thing; it seemed to him the Provosts who had died must have been drooling idiots to have allowed such a thing to happen. "And I will personally talk to the families of each of them." No, he wouldn't, but he'd have someone do it for him. "But what about your main quarry? What about . . ." His throat closed, and he had to clear it before he could finish. *"What about Alania and Danyl?"*

"No sign of them, sir. Nowhere near the bridge. If they made it to the ditch, they might have survived the blast, and they could have escaped into the farmland after that."

Kranz felt as if the giant fist that had been clenching his heart had suddenly released. *They're alive!* "Then I suggest you send out patrols to find them," he snapped.

"Done, sir, but if they're out there, they have a huge head start, and there are a lot of different directions they could have gone. And it's been raining heavily; any tracks they might have left will be very hard to find."

"Find them, Commander," Kranz said, and he put every bit of threatening urgency he could into that simple command.

Havelin stiffened to attention. "Yes, sir!"

"I will issue a call to the Officer Estates to be on the lookout. Keep me informed."

"Yes, sir!"

"Kranz out." He blanked the screen, then sat back, his mind boiling with relief that the Cityborn still lived, mingled with fury that they had once again eluded him.

But not for long, he thought. *There's nothing out there but Estates, and there are cameras everywhere, on every robot tilling a field or harvesting potatoes or maintaining a road. It's only a matter of time. Even if they aren't seen right away, they'll get hungry soon enough. If we don't find them by nightfall, they'll spend a cold, miserable night in the open and be desperate for shelter in the morning . . . and then I'll have them. I have only to wait.*

Ordinarily, he was very good at waiting. He'd waited twenty years for Alania to come of age, after all. But *this* wait . . .

He glanced at the Captain's monitor, grimaced, and then turned back to his desk and the endless trivia of administration. *At least it will pass the time.* He glanced over the list. The usual litany of system breakdowns on all Tiers and crime and squalor on the lowest ones; a series of execution orders to approve; the latest crop reports; it went on and on and never changed—worse, never *improved*—day after day, year after year.

But it will, he thought. *Once I have Alania back. It will.*

He keyed up the first item and set to work.

Not even her exhaustion could keep Alania asleep when another helicopter came thundering over their hiding place in the middle of the night. She went from oblivion to trembling wakefulness in an instant, and her arms tightened around Danyl's chest. He put his hands on hers. "Are they looking for us?" she whispered.

"I don't know," he said. "I don't think so, at that speed. They're trying to get somewhere in a hurry. Might not have anything to do with us."

"What time is it?"

Danyl's body shifted as he raised his arm to look at his watch, a faint rectangle of green illumination in the otherwise pitch dark. "Still an hour until dawn. We should be ready to move the moment it's light."

Alania groaned. "I don't know if I can." Now that she was awake, she could feel how stiff and sore her muscles were from the previous day's exertions and a night on the ground. Her stomach suddenly and embarrassingly growled with hunger, and she felt an increasingly pressing need to relieve her bladder. But there seemed no hope of that until it was light. If she tried to get out of their shelter in the dark, she'd probably break her leg or fall in the river.

More sleep seemed unlikely, too, however. So she stayed where she was, miserable, while Danyl, to her envy, slipped back into a doze, signaled by his deep, even breathing. She felt his chest rising and falling within the circle of her arms, and a wave of tenderness washed over her.

Brother.

And as the last hour of the night wound slowly past, as she lay there, uncomfortable, chilled, and aching, she realized a surprising truth: there was nowhere else she would rather have been. Certainly not in her comfortable bed in Quarters Beruthi with the hidden cameras watching her while she slept. She used to think she'd been a prisoner there, but now she realized she'd been even less. She'd been a lab animal, always under observation, while Kranz and Beruthi waited for her to turn twenty, old enough for Kranz to haul her away and do whatever it was he intended to do to her, or get her to do whatever it was he intended for her to do. Had Kranz gotten his hands on her as intended, would he already have carried out his plans? And if he had, where would she be right now?

She shuddered. Having seen the lengths Kranz would go to to get her back, she really didn't want to *be* in his hands.

At least none of this seems likely to be because he has a thing for girls less than half his age, she thought. *Despite the cameras in my room. Not even Kranz would use all the resources of the City just to have sex with me.*

Would he?

She snorted. *Get over yourself. No, he wouldn't.*

Danyl stirred again, and she realized she could kind of see him now—just a black blob, but somehow blacker than the blackness around him. She twisted her head and could make out against the sky the silhouette of the tangle of tree trunks and branches over their heads. Dawn at last!

Danyl reached up and gently pulled her arm away from his chest. She withdrew it, and both of them sat up. The movement made her gasp involuntarily and put more pressure on her bladder. "Getting light," Danyl said.

"Yes," Alania said. She rolled over onto her hands and knees and crawled out of their impromptu shelter onto the water-smoothed stones of the riverbank. Danyl followed her. They both got stiffly to their feet. The sound of rushing water made the chill morning air somehow even colder and made bladder-relief even more imperative. Alania could now see well enough to spot a screen of bushes just a little ways upstream. She pointed at it. "I need to . . ."

"Me, too," Danyl said hastily. "I'll go the other direction."

A few minutes later, with the light waxing all the time, they reconvened at the rocks. "That helicopter," Alania said, holding her arms wrapped around herself, desperately missing the warmth of Danyl's body against hers. "Are we sure it wasn't looking for us?"

"Can't be *sure*," Danyl said. He was digging in his backpack, and from it he produced two rectangular, foil-wrapped packages. He tossed one to her. "It didn't have a searchlight, so it wasn't looking for us visually. Could have been using a heat sensor of some kind, but it went by awfully fast. Anyway, it didn't land."

Alania examined the package. STANDARD RATION PACK read a white label with a string of numbers and a convoluted swirling pattern below the letters. "How do I . . . ?"

"You've never seen a mealpak?" Danyl asked, sounding astonished.

"They're not exactly in vogue on Twelfth Tier," Alania pointed out.

Danyl laughed. "Guess not. They're a staple in the Middens. I don't know how the traders get hold of them, since they're normally issued to Provosts, but they always seem to have plenty to offer. Probably some kind of bribery/kickback scheme going on." He held up his own ration pack. "Pull this tab." He tugged. The top of the mealpak unfolded itself, and steam rose into the chill morning air. "It's kind of tasteless," he said, tugging out a plastic fork set diagonally across the top of the yellowish, mush-like contents, "but it's supposed to provide enough calories and other nutrients for a day's march. And it's hot."

They sat side by side on the ground as they ate with their backs to the boulders that had sheltered them through the night. Privately, Alania thought "tasteless" would have been an improvement. The stuff was more bitter than bland and had a grainy texture she found off-putting . . . but three minutes later, she found herself scraping out the last yellow blob with her fork, licking the interior of the mealpak, and wishing there was more.

At least they weren't short of water. The stream here flowed clear, unlike the noxious River into which it would eventually plunge, and they both drank deeply of it before at last, beneath a sky feathered with long, wispy clouds tinged pink, they set out once again along the gully.

Remembering the helicopter, they kept as much under the screen of overhanging branches as they could, but there were fewer trees now, leaving long stretches of the river gully naked to the sky. They scurried across those like skitterbugs surprised by the light, scuttling back into the protective shadows the moment they could.

Late in the morning, they came at last to their next landmark: a bridge spanning the river, a single concrete arch cracked and stained with age. As they watched, a transport—a featureless black box on twelve wheels— hummed over it.

Danyl again consulted the folded piece of paper in his pocket. "We're supposed to go under the bridge, then climb out of the river cut and follow the road, keeping to the trees, for another ten kilometers," he said, confirming what Alania remembered. "A side road will cross our path. We'll follow it east for five more kilometers. There'll be a gate. We're to stop there and wait for transportation."

He looked up at Alania. "And that's where the instructions end."

"Transportation to *where,* is what I'd like to know."

"You and me both."

There was nothing in the instructions about how or where Prime would contact them. It made Alania uneasy, but it wasn't as if they had any choice. They couldn't go back. They could only go forward.

She hadn't escaped being a lab animal after all. Not yet. *We're rats in a maze, scuttling along blindly, turning corners at random, hoping there's a reward and not dissection waiting at the end.* She winced. *Well, that was an unfortunate metaphor.*

They passed under the bridge and scrambled up the bank without difficulty. The road they now followed ran through uncleared land, and the importance of keeping to the forest was brought home immediately when another transport zoomed by. Another followed fifteen minutes after that, and another fifteen minutes after that. They stayed as deep among the trees as they could without losing touch with the road, and right where the instructions promised, they found a side road crossing their path, narrow but well paved. It wound through the woods in what Alania assumed was intended to be a picturesque fashion rather than slashing through them straight as a laser, even though the terrain would have permitted that. They hurried along it, again keeping to the trees, but no vehicles came their way at all.

At last the path straightened, running between two lines of equidistantly placed trees whose branches reached over the path to form living arches. It led them to a closed gate of black metal bars set in a three-meter-tall brick wall, then ran on into the land beyond. Stymied, Alania and Danyl stood side by side at the gate. Nothing moved beyond it. The mid-afternoon sun, burning overhead in a clear blue sky, made Alania feel a bit less like a lab animal and more like a specimen on a microscope slide, awaiting examination.

Examination or extermination? her brain insisted on asking.

Shut up, brain, she told it.

"Wait for transportation," the instructions had said, but they hadn't said how long the wait might be. Minutes passed, and nothing happened. Alania stared through the gate, wondering where the path led. A slight rise not far beyond the wall hid whatever might lie behind it. The trees were far more widely spaced on the other side of the wall, the grass surrounding them neatly trimmed . . .

She stiffened. "What was that?"

Danyl looked up from where he sat on the ground with his back to the wall, idly stripping the bark from a twig. "What was what?"

"I saw something move." Alania stared hard into the green shadows of the trees beyond the gate.

Danyl scrambled up and stood beside her. "Where?"

She pointed. "By that flowering bush over there."

Danyl followed her finger. "I don't see any—oh!"

A robot suddenly popped into view, a fat cylinder about half as tall as Alania with four spider-like legs emerging from the bottom and four arms extending from the top, fitted with clippers and spouts and trowels. "Oh!" Alania exclaimed. "It's a Beruthi 2900."

Danyl stared at her. "A what?"

"A Beruthi 2900 gardening robot." She felt almost homesick at the sight of it; one had tended the garden in front of Quarters Beruthi for as long as she could remember.

"Who has a robot as a *gardener*?" Danyl demanded.

"Officers. Every one of the families of the girls I knew growing up has an Estate in the country, and you can't expect Officers to do their own gardening."

"Don't they have servants for that sort of thing?"

Alania shrugged. "Some do, some don't. Robots are less expensive."

They watched the little green robot roll through the woods, clipping grass around the trunks of the trees. Then came a whisper of sound from behind them. Alania turned to see one of the big black transports they'd watched zipping along the main road rolling along the path toward them. "Danyl," she said, touching his arm.

He turned around.

"Our 'transportation'?" she asked.

"Presumably."

"They don't have crew compartments, do they?"

Danyl shook his head. "No. They're just boxes with wheels and computers to drive them."

The transport rolled up to the gate. The front of the featureless container lowered, becoming a ramp into the empty interior. A band of illumination a hand's-breadth wide ran its length. Danyl looked at Alania. "I guess that's our invitation."

Alania chewed on her lower lip. "Once we're in there, we won't get out again until it opens itself or someone opens it for us. And we won't have any way of knowing where we're going."

"I know," Danyl said. He spread his hands. "But what choice do we have? There's nowhere to hide. The Provosts will track us down soon enough if we stay here. Some hidden camera has probably already spotted us standing at this gate. We can't go back to the River People—they don't exist anymore. We can't go back to the Middens. And we can't get into the City . . . well, maybe *you* could, if you turned yourself in."

"No," Alania said instantly. "Not anymore. Not after what we've learned. And anyway, I wouldn't do that to you." She grinned at him. "Brother."

His face reddened; it was endearing. "Thanks . . . Sister."

"You're welcome." She turned back to the transport. "Two days ago, I would have said it doesn't look very comfortable," she commented, "but after last night, it actually looks pretty great. At least it's clean and dry." She walked up the ramp.

Danyl followed. The moment he was inside, the hatch swung smoothly closed. Alania half expected to be plunged into darkness, but the lights stayed on.

The transport started to move. Alania sat down against the wall, Danyl beside her.

A few minutes in, the transport turned left, presumably off of the side road they had followed to the gated Estate and back onto the main road. That meant they had turned north, but after that there was little sensation of movement at all, and Alania knew she wouldn't be able to feel a more gradual turn. They could end up heading in literally any direction.

"Do you know how fast these things move?" Danyl asked her.

She thought about it. She'd studied the Heartland transportation system, but the details were fuzzy. "I'm not entirely sure . . . Eighty kilometers an hour, maybe? They're designed to go a lot faster, but I know the roads have deteriorated so much that they keep the speeds down."

"A few hours in here, and we could end up anywhere in the Heartland, then," Danyl said.

Alania nodded without speaking. She found her eyelids growing heavy now that they were safely out of sight . . . well, presumably safely. She also found that she was surprisingly comfortable leaning up against the wall of the transport. *Well, why not?* she thought. She rested her head on Danyl's shoulder and let herself doze off.

She woke disoriented. Something had changed. She straightened. Danyl blinked at her; from his confused, rather frazzled expression, she gathered that he'd slept, too. "We've stopped," he said. He looked at his watch. "More than three hours since we boarded. It's late afternoon."

Alania stretched, opening her mouth wide in a yawn that snapped shut abruptly as something banged against the outside of the container. Heart pounding, she leaped to her feet, Danyl scrambling up beside her. Together they faced the end of the container through which they'd entered.

Naturally, the opposite end opened this time, letting in a flood of daylight and cool air along with a strange nose-tingling, invigorating scent Alania didn't recognize. She spun.

Two robots waited at the bottom of the ramp. They were almost identical to the Beruthi gardening robot they'd seen earlier . . . except each of *these* robots' four arms ended in weapon barrels, not gardening tools.

Beyond them a short driveway led to a large house with walls of natural stone, windows framed by rough-hewn timber, and a steeply pitched roof supported by massive beams of the same golden wood as the window frames. Smoke drifted from a tall stone chimney. Behind the house rose a steep slope covered with forest, and beyond that slope, more hills marched away, each ridge higher than the last, toward the awe-inspiring wall of the Iron Ring. Whisps of cloud clung to its steel-gray face, below the massive glaciers that topped its sawtoothed peaks. The shadows of the robots and the house stretched to their right, which meant the sun was sinking off to their left. They had to be at the northernmost edge of the Heartland . . . but why?

It didn't seem to be a good idea to move while killer robots were staring at them, and Danyl apparently concurred, since he stood as stock-still as she as they waited for whatever would happen next.

What happened next was that a *third* robot appeared, coming into sight from their left, moving on wheels instead of legs. Taller and more slender than the others, it had only two arms, ending in simple claw-like manipula-

tors. It rolled up the ramp and stopped a couple of meters away.

"My apologies for the rather unfriendly greeting,"
said a deep voice. "I had to be certain of who was in the
transport."

Alania's mouth fell open. She *knew* that voice. *It can't
be . . . !*

"Welcome to Retreat Beruthi," said her former
guardian.

TWENTY-ONE

DANYL WAS JUST starting to realize what that name meant when Alania grabbed his arm so hard it hurt.

"It's a trap!"

"Please don't be alarmed," the robot said, or rather the man speaking through it said. Alania squeezed Danyl's arm even tighter. Her face had gone pale, but two spots of red flamed in her cheeks, and he realized she was more furious than afraid.

"Why not?" she snarled at the robot.

"I understand that you find this disconcerting, Alania, but you are in absolutely no danger." A pause. "I see you're armed, Danyl. I would appreciate it if you would place that slugthrower on the ground before I approach in person."

Danyl looked at Alania. "Your guardian?"

She nodded. "I'd know that voice anywhere!"

Danyl turned back to the robot. "I don't think so," he said. He put his hand on the sidearm. "If I'm in no danger, there'll be no reason for me to shoot you. But you'll understand why I don't want to take your word for that."

Another pause. "Very well. I suppose that after the past two days, asking you to disarm yourself unilaterally *is* rather tone-deaf. One moment."

"Don't trust him," Alania said in a low whisper to Danyl. "He'll hand you over to the Provosts and me over to Kranz."

Danyl's hand tightened on the slugthrower's grip. "Not if I can help it."

The robot rolled away from them, down the ramp and off to one side. Then the door of the house opened, and a figure came down the half-dozen stone steps: tall, thin, tanned, black hair just beginning to go gray at the temples. He wore simple work clothes: a plaid shirt above black pants and sturdy boots. He held his hands slightly outspread, palms up, and approached slowly.

"That's far enough," Danyl said as he reached the top of the ramp. The man stopped. "Is that him?" Danyl asked Alania.

"Yes," Alania said. "My *guardian*." She made the word sound like a curse. "Lieutenant Ipsil Beruthi."

"Lieutenant Commander," the man said mildly. "I was promoted for taking such good care of you."

"Taking such good care of . . ." Alania pulled her hand free from Danyl's and stepped toward Beruthi. "You never showed me affection. And you spied on me. My whole life! There were cameras in my room! Guardian? More like a *warden*."

"Kranz insisted on the cameras," Beruthi said. "I had no choice. And I could not show you affection, because it would have raised suspicion, and I couldn't afford that. My position was too important for us to risk."

"Us?" Danyl said sharply.

"The Free Citizens. The organization dedicated to overthrowing the tyranny of the Officers forever."

Alania gaped at him. "You're saying *you're* part of the revolution?"

"A rather important part," Beruthi said. "They call me Prime."

Danyl blinked. Alania, after a moment's shocked silence, whispered, "You're lying."

"No," Beruthi said. "I'm not."

"Can you prove it?" Danyl asked.

"Other than the fact you followed the instructions Erl

was given by Prime to take you to Prime, and here I am, I don't suppose I can," Beruthi said. "It's not like I keep a special ID badge lying around that says, 'Hello, my name is Ipsil, and I'll be your revolutionary leader today.'" He smiled. "But if you will come into the house, I can at least offer *evidence* I speak truth." The smile faded as he looked from Danyl to Alania and back again. "And I can tell you what this is all about: why you were born, why Yvelle did what she did, what Kranz wants Alania for, why the Provosts have been sent to kill and die to get you back. I can tell you all of that, if you'll trust me."

"What if we say no?" Danyl asked.

"Don't say no," Beruthi said.

"That's not an answer."

"I rather think it is."

Danyl frowned; then he realized what Beruthi's response must mean. He looked past the Lieutenant Commander to the sentry robots.

"They won't kill you," Beruthi said. "No one wants you dead, myself least of all. But if you try to draw your weapon, they will incapacitate you, temporarily but quite painfully."

"And if we refuse to accompany you?" Danyl asked.

"The same result. Then they will carry you into the house, and we will continue this discussion once you have recovered. That would delay our talk by a good hour, though, and, frankly, I need to get back to the City as soon as possible to help obfuscate the Provosts' search for you."

"They don't think we're dead?" Alania asked.

"Apparently not," Beruthi said. "All owners of Estates near the City have received orders from Kranz to keep our eyes peeled for two young but dangerous renegades who must be detained and returned to the City at all costs. There's a considerable reward attached to you, albeit with stern warnings that if you cannot be captured safely, you should simply be reported so the Provosts can arrest you. You are not to be harmed."

Danyl looked at Alania. "Your call," he said. "You know him."

"Apparently not," Alania muttered. She looked at the security robots, then back at Beruthi. "All right," she said. "We'll come with you."

"But I'm not giving up my weapon," Danyl said.

"As I've already indicated," Beruthi said, "I can live with that." His mouth twitched. "At least, I hope so. this way."

He turned and started toward the house. Danyl glanced at Alania. She still looked pale, but she stepped forward, and side by side they followed the Lieutenant Commander.

Once out of the transport, Danyl could see more of the house's surroundings. Two ridges of the mountain behind it embraced it like arms so that it nestled comfortably in a sheltered hollow. *Does Beruthi have servants with him here?* he wondered. He doubted it—Alania had told him she'd grown up surrounded by robots, and why would Beruthi, whose family had built robots since the founding of the City, risk allowing anyone living to see or hear something that might betray him? No, he thought, Beruthi had almost certainly waited alone for their arrival.

Something to remember, should things go badly, Danyl thought. Then his gaze slid to the robot sentries they were passing between. Things would have to go very badly indeed before he would risk facing armed robots. Occasionally a robot from the City would descend into the Middens on a scavenging mission. No one ever knew who sent them or what they were looking for, but Erl had impressed on Danyl from childhood that the technical term for attacking an armed robot, barring its instant destruction with more firepower than anyone in the

Middens possessed, was "suicide." That warning had been in the back of his mind during their adventure on the Rim, and seeing the Guardians in action against the Provosts' helicopter had reinforced it mightily.

Since the only weapon he had was a slugthrower that probably wouldn't even dent their armored hides, "instant destruction" seemed unlikely. Which left the "suicide" part.

They climbed the stone steps and passed through the open door into the interior of the house: a large open space three stories tall with the underside of the roof forming a steeply pitched canopy of golden wood high overhead. Directly in front of them, a stairway led up to an overlooking balcony with doors at either end and two in the middle leading into the back of the house.

On their own level, four archways led out of the big living space: one on either side of the stairs, the others to the right and left. Ahead and to the right, Danyl glimpsed gleaming pots and an oven: the kitchen. The room ahead and to the left he guessed might therefore be the dining room. To their right, the archway led into a comfortable-looking room with chairs and couches covered with dark-red synthileather (or more likely, *real* leather) and a massive fireplace, flames leaping within it to ward off the chill of the mountain air. The room to their left contained multiple video screens, looking strangely out of place in the otherwise rustic dwelling and surrounding a stone-topped desk whose base appeared to have been made from a single massive tree trunk. The archway into that room was the only one with a door.

A deep silence hung over everything, broken only by the crackle of the fire in the room to their right, where Beruthi led them now. The south wall boasted a giant window. The view beyond was so breathtaking that Danyl forgot all about Beruthi for a moment, instead moving to the window as though drawn by a magnet, Alania beside him.

They had climbed a long, long way. Below the plateau where Beruthi's house stood, wooded hills rolled away, the road winding through them and down to the forests and farms and valleys and villages of the Heartland. Off to their left a ravine emerged from the mountains, growing ever-deeper as it curved its way across the Heartland: the Canyon. Danyl followed its long zigzagging scar into the misty blue distance, and there, just at the edge of his vision before the horizon fell away, saw a glint of light, a tiny egg shape: the City. He stared at it. It seemed incredible that that barely visible structure could contain tens of thousands of people, the Captain, the Officers, the Provosts. It looked completely insignificant, and yet it loomed larger in his mind and his life than ever before.

He tore his gaze from it and looked east and west. The Iron Ring curved toward the south in both directions, encircling the Heartland below: a vast, vast space, and yet that tiny speck in the distance ruled it all. The checkered fields, the distant villages, the forests—all of it belonged to the Officers, who ruled with absolute authority. And still, competition for the jobs and accompanying living space in those tightly controlled communities was fierce, for who wouldn't rather live in the country—even in indentured servitude—than in the squalor of the lower Tiers?

The Officers have everything, and most people have next to nothing, Danyl thought. *That's not right.*

But *this* Officer claimed he wanted to change that.

Danyl was reserving judgment.

He turned away from the window and looked at Beruthi, who stood beside the fireplace. Above it and to either side hung paintings of mountain scenery. Though they weren't bad, they had a certain amateurish quality to them that made Danyl suspect Beruthi had painted them himself. *Unless he has a robot do it for him.*

As Alania, too, tore herself away from the view, Beruthi

indicated one of the two hide-covered couches. "Please, sit," he said.

Danyl glanced at Alania, who shrugged. Together they crossed to the couch. Alania sat down first; Danyl took a second to slip his arms out of the straps of his backpack and place it on the floor at his feet. Then he sat beside Alania, though he didn't sit comfortably, holding himself as close to the edge as he could so he could still reach the slugthrower on his hip if need be. He sensed similar tension in Alania, whose hip touched his.

Beruthi sat on the couch opposite them across a low, stone-topped table. He studied them for a long moment. "Before I begin," he said at last, "I need to know: what has Erl told you?"

"Not much," Danyl said. He didn't try to keep the bitterness out of his voice. "I didn't even know he used to be an Officer until the day before yesterday." He bent down and opened the backpack, reaching inside to pull out the data crystal. The leaping flames in the fireplace cast red-blue sparks off its faceted sides as he held it up. "He gave me this and a reader, but the reader got wrecked before I could use it. We were a little too busy running for our lives."

"Ah." Beruthi got up from the couch. "I have a reader in my office across the hall. One moment."

He went out. Danyl looked at Alania. "All right?" he asked softly.

She shook her head. "Not really," she replied, her voice barely audible. "It's a lot to process. Of all the people for Prime to be . . . How can I trust him now after . . ." Her words faded into silence, and her gaze dropped.

Danyl put a hand on her knee, and she looked up at him, eyes bright with unshed tears. "I can't really understand, I know," he said, keeping his voice low. "But we've both had a lot of shocks the past couple of days. One thing I *do* know: we're family. Whatever we decide to do from here on out, we decide it together. Agreed, sister?"

A smile played across her lips—a small smile, but he felt as if he'd won a prize. She put her hand on his and gave it a small squeeze. "Agreed, brother."

"Here we are," Beruthi said, coming back into the room. He carried a reader identical to the one Erl had provided. He put it on the low table and pressed a button, and a screen unfolded. Below it, a hexagonal opening just the right size to accept the crystal glowed green. "Listen to what Erl has to tell you," Beruthi said. "I'm going back to my office, where I won't be able to hear. Once you've listened to him, come talk to me. Ask me any questions you want. That way you'll know I'm not just parroting Erl."

He turned and went out again, crossing to his office and closing the door behind him.

Danyl reached forward and slid the blue crystal into the receptacle.

The screen lit, and Erl looked out at them. Danyl recognized the background as Erl's bedroom. He looked slightly younger than he had the last time Danyl had seen him.

I'll see him again, he thought fiercely. *He's still alive. He has to be.*

"Danyl," Erl said. "If you are viewing this, then something has gone wrong, you are on the run, and I am not with you. I am recording this on your sixteenth birthday, and I hope you never see it. It is encrypted with an algorithm that only a select few have access to, which should prevent it from being read by anyone except you. I will unencrypt it before I give it to you. But in case it has fallen into the wrong hands, I will be vague about some details in what follows.

"To begin with: I am not your father. You know this. You are, literally, a son of the City. You are the Cityborn."

Danyl didn't have a clue what he meant.

"It's a term you've never heard, I know," Erl said, as

if he had read Danyl's mind across the years. "It's a term almost no one has heard. I had not heard of it until the day almost two decades ago when the person I will refer to as Prime asked me if I would take on a special mission for the Free Citizens, a revolutionary organization dedicated to a complete change in the way this City is governed.

"I was recruited into the Free Citizens—the Free, for short—as a young man, after my father, Ensign Hanikin Orillia, evicted a family from their quarters in Fourth Tier simply because he wanted more space for one of his illegal drug factories. I was never close to my father, and my words with him on that occasion ruptured our relationship completely. Nevertheless, I was his sole son and heir, and when he died shortly thereafter, I assumed the Ensignship. I promptly closed the drug factories, at great cost to the family fortune, but I was unmarried and childless and had no one to answer to except myself.

"And then I was contacted by Prime, a man who had been a friend all my life but whose revolutionary leanings I had never even guessed at. He told me about the Free Citizens and what he hoped to accomplish, and I leaped at the opportunity to help him.

"Originally, my role within the Free was simply to report on what I learned as I performed my duties as an Officer. My family was low in the hierarchy to begin with and lower still after I closed the drug factories and thus cut ties with some of the higher-ranking Officers, so I had little to report. I managed Third- and Fourth-Tier sanitation, as my father had before me, and though I tried to do a better job of it than he had, the resources I needed were never forthcoming, as they never are within the lower Tiers. Money and materials went to the Officers first; in particular, the raw materials needed to repair and renovate were largely siphoned off to the Officers' vast Estates."

Danyl raised his eyes from the screen for a moment

to look around the grand room, then lowered his gaze again.

"Prime, however, for . . . a number of reasons, had the confidence of First Officer Kranz, and he cultivated it carefully. And so he became one of the few to know of an impending event of City-shaking impact, and he called on me to take on a very special mission—one, he explained, that had to be undertaken by an Officer so far down in the ranks that his disappearance would cause little consternation. I had cut so many ties by shutting down my father's shadier operations that my fellow Officers would certainly say nothing more than 'good riddance' once I disappeared. Quarters Orillia on Eleventh Tier were remarkably large and well-appointed for a family with only the rank of Ensign, thanks to my father's ill-gotten gains; that would make my disappearance all the more popular, since my neighbors could then maneuver to claim them.

"I can't tell you everything Prime told me. I can't risk committing that to a recording, even one as well encrypted as this one. But I can tell you this: you were born on Twelfth Tier, and you were intended to be raised there as a tool of First Officer Kranz, to be used to cement the Kranz family's power over the City for generations to come. As part of an effort to subvert Kranz's plan, you were abducted from Twelfth Tier and delivered to me. My daunting task: to disappear with you and make it appear that both of us had fled far, far away, most likely to our deaths.

"Prime and I discussed how that might be accomplished, and in the end we settled on a fictitious flight to the Iron Ring, making it appear as if I had taken you and disappeared into the wilderness. We discussed the comments I should make in front of other Officers to indicate my longing for a child and other steps I should take to make our cover story believable. It took us months to set the stage and make the other necessary preparations.

"On the appointed night, a Free Citizens operative successfully infiltrated the hospital, abducted you, and delivered you into my care. My aircar had been programmed to launch itself, and its autopilot was set to fly it to the Iron Ring and land there, but before its flight even began, I was already descending with you to the Middens.

"Preparations had been made there, too. The quarters in which we live were secretly excavated for us by robots before you were born. The hovel that was our putative home was built by another operative, who lived there and then conveniently 'vanished' when it was time for us to move in.

"So began the only life you've ever known. My mission is a long one, but it has an end date: your twentieth birthday. After that, something else will happen. I cannot tell you what, but I can tell you that you are the sole hope for the ushering in of a new era."

On the screen, Erl looked suddenly to the left. "You've just come in." He turned back to the camera. "There is one other thing you should know. While I have watched over you carefully your whole life, even when you were not aware of it, you have had other protection, too: powerful protection. You have been hurt many times while living in the Middens, but your life has never been in danger, and that gives me hope that even if you are viewing this and all our plans have fallen apart, you are still alive and well. Stay that way. Be safe. Be strong. Be free." He turned his head to the left again. "Coming!" he shouted.

The screen blanked.

Danyl blinked hard and swallowed harder.

"Nothing about me," Alania said.

"He said he didn't know you existed until he was warned you were about to fall out of the City," Danyl said. "Prime—Beruthi—must have messaged him. But you must be a . . . a Cityborn, too. Whatever that means."

He shook his head. "Twenty years of hiding me in plain sight in the Middens . . . but for what? What is a City-born? How can I—how can *we*—possibly be key to 'ushering in a new era'?"

"I don't know," Alania said. She got to her feet. "But I know who does."

TWENTY-TWO

THE MAN ALANIA had always thought of as cold and distant (but whom she was now apparently expected to trust completely) stood at the window, staring out at the vast panorama of the Heartland. He spoke without turning around as Alania led Danyl through the door. "So. What did Erl tell you?"

"That's not how this works," Alania said. "You tell us what you were going to tell us, and we'll see if it matches up with what Erl said." Erl had said nothing about *her*. As Danyl had pointed out, he hadn't even known she existed—or at least he'd claimed he hadn't. But Beruthi—Prime—had. From the very beginning, Beruthi had.

"Very well." Beruthi turned. "Let's go back into the other room. It's more comfortable."

"Let's stay here," Alania said. It was silly, but she took perverse pleasure in not doing anything Beruthi told her to do. *He's not my guardian anymore. He never was. He was always something else.*

Beruthi sighed. "Have it your way." He turned to them, the light from the window casting one side of his thin, tanned face into shadow. "You are—both of you—something Kranz dubbed the Cityborn. You are also brother and sister."

So it's true. She glanced at Danyl, who gave her a small smile. *We're family.* She looked back at Beruthi. "Who were our parents?"

"Your father," Beruthi said, "is Staydmore Kranz."

"No!" The word burst out of her in revulsion.

"I'm afraid so."

"And our mother?" Danyl asked. From the tightness of his voice, Alania could tell he didn't like Beruthi's revelation any more than she did.

Beruthi's gaze didn't waver. "The Captain."

Alania's mouth fell open. Danyl gasped, then burst out, "That's impossible! The Captain has to have been dead for *centuries*. Erl told me she's just a mythical figurehead the Officers use to prop up their rule."

"Erl told you what you needed to believe," Beruthi said. "But he knows the truth, although he is one of the few who does, even among the Free Citizens. Only I know *everything* about the Cityborn, the City . . . and Staydmore Kranz." He paused. "You both look a little pale. Are you sure you don't want to sit down?"

Alania folded her arms. "We're fine," she said tightly. "Go on. I'm dying to hear how we can possibly be children of a myth . . . and a monster."

"The Captain is not a myth," Beruthi said. Alania noted he didn't deny that Kranz was a monster. "She still lives, and her continued life is vital to both the operation and control of the City."

"She's actually giving orders?" Danyl put in.

"Nothing so simple," Beruthi said. "She has no political control. Kranz does what he wants, as the Kranz dynasty has since First Officer Thomas Kranz seized control at the founding of the City."

"What?" Alania had never heard *that*.

"There's more," Beruthi said. "Staydmore Kranz is not really Staydmore Kranz. He's a clone, body and mind, of Thomas Kranz."

"A clone!" Alania blinked. "But . . . cloning technology doesn't exist anymore. It was used to rapidly multiply livestock and crops right after the Awakening, but then it was outlawed. The equipment was destroyed."

"You learned your lessons well," Beruthi said. A small smile flickered across his face. "Your adventure on Fifth focused your mind, as I intended." The smile vanished. "But in truth, one cloning unit has remained operational— one that is used every generation to create the replacement for the current First Officer."

"You said a clone, body *and* mind," Danyl said sharply. "Erl made sure I learned *my* lessons well, too. Cloning produces a genetic copy, an identical twin. It doesn't copy the mind. How could it?"

"It can't," Beruthi agreed. "But cloning is not the only ancient and outlawed technology at work here. The other is one you will not have read about, because it has always been kept secret: nanobots."

Alania cocked her head to one side. "Nano means microscopic. Microscopic robots?"

Beruthi inclined his head. Alania glanced at Danyl, who looked as bewildered as she felt. She turned to Beruthi. "What do they do?"

"There are a lot of things they *could* do, some of them quite destructive," Beruthi said. "But the ones I'm speaking of are injected into human beings."

"What?" Alania said, horrified. "Robots *inside* a person?"

"Yes," Beruthi said. "They can protect that person from disease, speed the healing of injuries, extend life ... and some of them, some very special ones, can go to work inside the brain, rewriting memories, altering personalities. Nanobots, in other words, are a way to program a human being just like you would program a robot."

"And Kranz has these things inside him?" Danyl said.

Beruthi nodded. "He does. And Thomas Kranz, the original Kranz, carried nanobots of his own: nanobots that recorded selected memories and elements of his mind. Thomas injected a colony of his nanobots into his clone when the clone was an infant. During childhood and adolescence, the nanobots remained only partially active, providing some physical protection but not affecting the clone's mind. When he was old enough, his nanobots were fully activated. The already extant physical protection was further enhanced, but more importantly, the nanobots rewrote the clone's brain. Thomas Kranz's memories and motivations have been handed down from clone to clone in that fashion ever since. Our First Officer Kranz, the seventh successive clone of Thomas Kranz, doesn't just *know* the truth about the founding of the City . . . he *remembers* it. Or at least he remembers what Thomas Kranz wanted him to remember."

Alania drew in a deep breath. "That's . . . mind-boggling."

"Literally," Beruthi said.

"But all of this must be Kranz's deepest, darkest secret," Danyl said sharply. "How do *you* know about it?"

"Because of my own family history," Beruthi said. "Since the Awakening, the Beruthis have had a monopoly on the construction of high-level robotic technology. Among the items my factory manufactures are special devices for both the maintenance of the Kranz nanobots—something which must be done every few months—and their activation. Not that my ancestors, who did *not* inherit the memories of the first Beruthi, knew what those devices were for. The manufacturing process is entirely automated and takes place in a sealed room solely on the First Officer's orders."

"But you found out," Alania said.

Beruthi nodded. "Yes. Because nothing lasts forever. The Science Officer is responsible for injecting and activating the nanobots in each Kranz clone when the time is right. Another secret duty handed down from generation to generation—the City seems to be rife with such things. The nanobots are self-assembling: a few are withdrawn from the blood of the progenitor clone and provided with a 'stew' of raw materials, allowing them to replicate. But as Science Officer Prentis prepared the replicated nanobots for injection into Kranz's clone, Falkin, she found that an unacceptable number of them were inert—they had been assembled incorrectly. Others showed signs of less fatal faults. She began to wonder what state *Kranz's* nanobots were in. Rather bravely, she broached the subject with Kranz, who allowed her to test his nanobots' programming by comparing his recollection of certain events against accounts left by previous First Officers. She found that our Kranz has both missing memories and false memories, an indication that this problem has been growing generation by generation. How it has affected Kranz, we can't be certain, but we do know how the copies of *his* nanobots affected his clone."

"Falkin," Alania said. "The one who died in an aircar crash."

Beruthi nodded.

"I saw that crash!" Danyl said. "I was in the Last Chance Market. The aircar flew straight into the ground."

"It was suicide," Beruthi said. "When Falkin's nanobots were activated, they rewrote his brain, as they had for every Kranz clone before him—but this time the result was utter paranoia, to the point where he saw death as his only escape."

"But if he was that paranoid, and Kranz's nanobots are also faulty . . ." Alania said slowly.

"Then Kranz could be tending toward paranoia himself," Beruthi finished. "Which is one reason his rule must be overthrown."

"Why did Prentis tell you all this?" Danyl demanded.

Beruthi raised an eyebrow. "You sound a little paranoid yourself."

"I think I've earned it," Danyl growled, and Alania couldn't disagree.

"Prentis *didn't* tell me this," Beruthi said. "I don't think she knows that I know. Kranz himself came to me and told me about her concerns and . . . several other things, including the truth about what is manufactured in that secret space in my factory."

"Why would he trust you with that?" Alania heard the anger in her voice but didn't care. Her patience was wearing thin. "And what has any of this to do with us? Or with the Captain? You said she was our mother, but you haven't explained how that's even possible!"

"Kranz chose to trust me because he was—he *is*—desperate," Beruthi said quietly. "For two reasons." He turned and looked out over the Heartland again. The setting sun had almost reached the peaks of the western Iron Ring, and far, far away, the City glinted gold, like a nugget of precious metal in the Heartland's green fields. "The first reason was very personal. Falkin was the only viable embryo created by the aging cloning equipment, and he was the last that will *ever* be created. Like so much else in the City, that cloning unit is now junk, and we no longer have the knowledge, tools, or materials to repair it. Even before Falkin's nanobot activation failed so spectacularly, Kranz knew the Kranz line was coming to an end."

"And the second reason?" Alania asked.

Beruthi faced them again. "The second reason is that the Captain is dying."

"You still haven't explained how she can even be alive," Danyl said.

"Technology, of course," Beruthi said impatiently. "Technology from the founding of the City that we could not replicate today but that continues to function. Including, of course, nanobots: her body is swarming with them." He spread his hands. "But even founding-era technology has its limitations, and those limitations have now been reached. Yes, the Captain is still alive . . . but she won't be much longer."

"Most people already think she's dead," Danyl said. "How could it matter if she died for real?"

"I'll get to that," Beruthi said. "For the moment, just

accept that it would be a very bad thing if the Captain died . . . bad for everyone. There must be a Captain, and therefore there must be a replacement Captain. And because of . . . what the Captain does, that replacement must carry certain genetic tags.

"The failure of the cloning unit not only meant no more Kranzes could be produced, it meant no clone of the Captain could be produced. But in his desperation, Kranz saw an opportunity: an opportunity to combine the special qualities of the Captain with the Kranzes' ancient memories and sense of duty to renew the City and Heartland. To make it happen, he needed help—my help. And so, shortly after Falkin's birth, almost four years before the two of you were born, he told me of his plan to create children who would be heirs of both the Captain and the First Officer. He called them the Cityborn, conceived in vitro by the union of the Captain's preserved eggs and his donated sperm."

Alania shuddered. "Ew." Learning that she was Kranz's biological daughter was the most horrifying thing that had happened to her in two horrifying days.

Beruthi smiled a little ruefully. "Yes. But remember, none of us can choose our parents. My own father . . . was not exactly a wonderful human being." He shook his head. "Never mind. One of these Cityborn, Kranz said, would ascend to the Captaincy once fully mature. All of them—at least, any who had the necessary genetic tags—had to be protected until then so that there would be . . . spares."

"By you?" Alania said. "Is that why you were my 'guardian'?"

"Partly," Beruthi said. "But your true protection, you have had since birth." He glanced at Danyl. "Both of you."

Alania remembered Erl's recorded words: *While I have watched over you carefully your whole life, even when you were not aware of it, you have had other protection, too: powerful protection. You have been hurt many times while living in the Middens, but your life has never been in danger.*

Danyl must have been remembering that, too. "Some protection," he said. "Considering how many scars I've got."

"Yes, you've been hurt, but you've always healed quickly and without infection," Beruthi said. "Alania, living a much more sheltered life, would have been less aware of it, but it's the same for both of you. Alania, I see you've suffered minor wounds since I saw you at your birthday party, but they're already fully healed."

Alania's hand went to her forehead. It was true—all that remained of the cut there and the one on her cheek was a slight tenderness. The skin was smooth, and the last synthiskin patch—the one Chrima had put on her—was gone; she didn't even know when it had fallen off. She had a sudden, horrible feeling she knew where this was going, and an instant later, Beruthi confirmed it.

"When you were born," he said, "each of you was injected with your own colony of nanobots. But not drawn from Kranz. Yours come from—"

"The Captain," Alania breathed.

"The Captain," Beruthi said.

Out the window, over Beruthi's shoulder, Alania saw a guard robot roll past. The thought that her own blood-stream contained robots . . . she swallowed. Maybe finding out she was Kranz's daughter *wasn't* the most horrible thing to happen to her in the past two days.

"They're not fully activated yet," Beruthi went on, "but they are still capable of protecting you from infection, autoimmune diseases, and cancer, as well as reducing bleeding and rebuilding nerves and connective tissue in the event of an injury." He spread his hands. "They would not have protected you from, say, brain-destroying head trauma or disembowelment, but fortunately the risk of such things is low, at least on Twelfth Tier." He glanced at Danyl. "Somewhat higher in the Middens."

"Somewhat," Danyl said quietly.

"Why weren't they fully activated?" Alania demanded.

"Because your bodies were still developing. If fully activated, the nanobots would have greatly slowed that—you'd both still be prepubescent. Erl did increase the effectiveness of yours temporarily a couple of times, Danyl, when you managed to get yourself seriously injured. And both of you, of course, have had your nanobots carefully monitored and tuned as required, as your bodies changed."

"Tuned?" Danyl frowned. Then his eyes widened. "Oh. The docbot!"

Beruthi nodded. "An archaic model, should anyone ever see it who shouldn't, but heavily modified." He glanced at Alania. "It was far easier in Alania's case, since she lived in my house and underwent regular medical checkups."

Alania looked at her hands. *Robots. Inside me.* She felt violated all over again, as she had when she'd discovered the cameras in her room. The ones Beruthi insisted had not been his idea, but by order of First Officer Kranz . . . her father.

Not that that made her feel any better.

"And what part of all this required you to be so cold and distant?" she demanded. "Yes, I lived in your house. But you may as well have been a robot yourself for all the warmth you showed me." She felt alarmingly close to tears. "I kept wanting that, you know. As a little girl, at all those birthday parties, I'd see other girls' families, other girls' parents. I wanted a daddy like the ones my friends had, and instead I got you: an Officer. Always an Officer. Never a human. Never a father . . . or even a father figure."

Beruthi looked down, rubbing the ring finger of his left hand. "I'm so sorry about that, Alania," he said softly. "Kranz gave me strict orders not to get too close to you. He didn't want anything to interfere with his plans, wanted me to be willing to hand you over to him when the time came. You don't know how many times I wanted to pick you up when you were little, cuddle you, read to you, hold you tight . . . but I couldn't. I couldn't jeopardize everything that way. Erl could, with Danyl, and I envied him that, too."

Alania's throat felt tight. She wanted both to believe Beruthi and to scream at him, call him a liar, because it was almost easier to think that he had never wanted to give her love and affection than to think he had wanted to but hadn't because he was following orders. In the end, she said nothing.

"What happens when these nanobots are *fully* activated?" Danyl asked.

"First," Beruthi said, "they will work much more aggressively to prevent harm to your body."

"And second?"

"Second, the Captain's nanobots will allow you to control most of your bodily functions *consciously*." He looked from Alania to Danyl and back again. "They have to give you that ability because it is the combination of nanobots and unique genetic characteristics that allows the Captain to *become* the City."

"Become . . ." Alania blinked. "I don't understand."

"Danyl asked if the Captain is giving orders. She's not, in the traditional sense . . . but in another way, she is. The nanobots and the genetic modifications allow the Captain to interface with the City as if it were her own body.

"In essence, the City is a living organism with the Captain as its brain and nervous system. She can control its power and water and ventilation, maintenance robots, everything that is plugged into the City's computer network, merely by thought. Or without thought—as her brain regulates her body's functions, it also regulates the City's."

"But the City is falling apart," Danyl said.

"Because the Captain is dying. After all these centuries. Which is why she needs an heir." He looked from one to the other of them. "The Cityborn."

"Why are there two of us, then?" Danyl demanded. "Why me in the Middens and Alania on Twelfth Tier? Surely there can be only one heir to the Captain."

"There can," Beruthi said. "And our plan has always been that it would be you, Danyl."

Alania blinked at him. "But then why . . ."

"*Your* purpose was to keep Kranz happy. As long as he had you, and you seemed safely tucked away, he wouldn't be keeping an eye out for the mysteriously vanished Danyl. But we never intended for you to become Captain. In fact, four years ago, after his clone died, I had to talk Kranz out of making you Captain right away."

"I overheard part of that conversation," Alania said, and she had the satisfaction of seeing Beruthi's eyes widen in surprise, though he schooled his expression again quickly before he continued.

"Fortunately, I had the perfect excuse for why that couldn't be done—perfect, because it happened to be true. I reminded him of what I just told you: that your brain and body were still not sufficiently developed. I promised Kranz I would keep you safe until you turned twenty, and then he could have you. Knowing he would insist you be sent to him the day after your birthday, I made plans to have you kidnapped before you could get to Quarters Kranz." He grimaced. "And what a fuckup *that* turned out to be."

Alania looked at him, and a gaping void opened inside her as a dark fact she had pushed deep down in her thoughts came bobbing back to the surface. "What did you intend to do to me after you kidnapped me to keep me out of Kranz's clutches?" she asked softly. "The same thing Yvelle did to the third baby who tested positive for the Captain's genes?"

Beruthi shook his head violently. "No! Alania, you

wouldn't have been harmed. If the kidnapping had gone as planned—if those extra Provosts hadn't been in the wrong place at the wrong time—you would simply have vanished. I would have smuggled you out of the City, and you'd have lived *here*, safely tucked away. As Kranz poured all his efforts into finding you, we—the Free—would have taken Danyl to the Thirteenth Tier, installed *him* as Captain, and seized control of the City. And then you would have been free to return to your old home . . . our home . . . on Twelfth. Or go wherever else you wished."

"So why did that baby have to die?" Alania demanded. "Why did you make Yvelle do that?"

Beruthi set his jaw. "A third Cityborn was too difficult to deal with. I identified you as Cityborn long before Yvelle arrived and had one of the caregiver robots remove you from the ward until Yvelle had come and gone so that Kranz would have one Cityborn to focus his attention on while we raised *our* Cityborn in secret. Yvelle's orders were to take the first baby she found who tested positive to Erl. Any who did not test positive, she was to leave alone. But any that did . . . had to be eliminated." His met Alania's eyes steadily. "This is a revolution, Alania. There are always casualties in revolutions."

"How can you be so callous?" For the first time, Alania was *glad* her guardian had never shown her affection, because what she was learning about him now would have been devastating if she had ever begun to think of him as her father.

"There's callousness enough on Kranz's side. We must be as hard as he is if we are to defeat him. Those babies who didn't have the genetic tags, the ones I told Yvelle to leave alone? Kranz had them all killed."

Alania gasped. *Our brothers and sisters . . .*

"There's something I still don't understand," Danyl said. "You said Kranz wants a Captain who is also an heir of the Kranzes. But the only nanobots we carry are the Captain's—we don't carry the nanobots that bear Kranz's memories. So how ... ?"

"That's also where I came in," Beruthi said. For some reason, he looked only at Alania as he explained. "Once Kranz gave me access to the secret manufactory for the nanobot maintenance and programming equipment, I learned how to modify the Captain's nanobots—far less degraded than Kranz's—to accept programming from the Kranz ones. Kranz's plan was for me to turn the Captain's nanobots, over time, into modified versions of his own. That way they would do everything for the Cityborn candidate that the Captain's nanobots do but also rewrite the Cityborn's mind with the memories of Thomas Kranz."

Alania thought she might throw up. "So when my nanobots were being 'tuned' during those regular check-ups, when I was lying in the docbot ..."

"You were being prepared to be exactly what Kranz wants: a copy of himself with the power of the Captain," Beruthi said. "Which is why we had to make certain you never made it to his Quarters."

"And me?" Danyl demanded.

Beruthi looked at him at last. "Your nanobots were *not* programmed with Thomas Kranz's memories. When you become Captain, you will be free to act in the best interest of the people of the City rather than Kranz and his Officers."

"You sound awfully certain," Alania said. "As certain as you were that you could safely kidnap me off the streets of Twelfth Tier before I got to Quarters Kranz. And look how that turned out." As the shock and horror of what they'd been told fell away, fury boiled up to take its place. "You expect us to trust you. You expect us to leap at the chance to help the Free. But answer me this: do other people join you of their own free will?"

"Yes, of course."

"Knowing the risks?"

"Of course. They know what happens on Tenth as well as anyone."

"So *they* join freely. But we *didn't*. We're nothing but pawns to you." She took a step toward him. "That baby that Yvelle killed was one of us, a Cityborn, our sister. Did *she* volunteer, knowing the risks? Of course not. She didn't know anything. She was our *sister*, and you had her killed without remorse. And then Kranz killed the ones who were left, *also* our brothers and sisters, babies *you could have rescued*." The words rushed out of her, borne on the hot wind of her anger. "So why should I believe you when you say you felt affection for me? Why should I believe you when you say you would have simply hidden me away somewhere and not killed me? Why should I believe *anything* you say? And why should I help the kind of people who could order the murder of a baby *to take control of the City*?"

Beruthi looked almost shocked. "Alania, we're not . . ."

"What?" Alania said. "As bad as Kranz? You could have fooled me." She took another step toward him, eyes locked on his face. "It's not just that baby, either. How many River People died yesterday? Except for Yvelle, *they* didn't volunteer or know the risks. They died because Erl—*you*, ultimately—sent us to them. You've made Danyl and me *accessories* to your murders!" Her anger swelled so much then that it choked her to silence at last.

Beruthi took a deep breath, straightened his back, and met her gaze squarely. "I did what I thought was best, Alania. I did it because it seems to me that the end we are trying to reach more than justifies the unsavory means we've had to use to get there." Behind him, the sun still lit the distant City, but it was more red than gold now, a tiny sliver of scarlet like a shard of bloodstained glass.

Danyl stepped forward to stand at her left shoulder, and she could almost feel the heat of his anger radiating from him. "And what end *is* that, exactly?" he snarled. "To make me Captain? What would that mean? What would it mean to *me*?"

"It would mean we'd finally have a Captain who understood what life was like for those who were not Officers, someone who wouldn't just be a figurehead exploited by the First Officer," Beruthi began. "It would—"

"Not enough," Danyl snapped, cutting him off.

"No?" Beruthi glared at him. "Then how about this? It would mean the City would not collapse into utter chaos."

"Explain."

"I *told* you—the Captain is dying. She's been dying for a very long time, but the process is accelerating. If she dies without being replaced, the City's infrastructure will completely shut down. No power on any of the Tiers. Elevators inoperable. Doors sealed shut. No water flowing. No air circulating. No way to get food in or to get anyone out except by aircar, and do you really think the Officers would gladly ferry lower-Tier denizens out to their Estates and Retreats?

"There *has* to be a Captain, or the City dies, and thousands of people die with it. And only one of you can take her place. Only you two carry the Captain's genetic modifications encoded in your genomes. Only you two have her specialized nanobots. Alania is compromised, because Kranz has programmed her nanobots to overwrite her memories at his command. That leaves you.

"Danyl, this is our last—our only!—opportunity to make things better, to fix things. We've worked for twenty years to seize this moment, to put in place a new Captain who is not under Kranz's control."

Danyl was silent for a moment. "How would it work?" he said at last.

"The mechanism is automated," Beruthi said. "It's just like plugging any standard component into any other system. You unplug the current Captain, remove her from the system, and plug yourself in."

"And the Captain has been 'plugged in' for centuries?" Alania said in horror. "No wonder she's 'failing.' She must be insane!"

"She may be," Beruthi said. "Or she may have no human consciousness left at all. Kranz didn't tell me everything he knows about her. In particular, he didn't tell me how she has been kept under the control of the First Officers all this time. He claims Thomas Kranz seized control from her to save the City from disaster. That's what his memories tell him."

"You keep talking about her genetic modifications," Alania said. "But . . . who did those? Who created the Captain? City history begins with the City fully operational, the Captain sequestered on Thirteenth, the First Officer in charge, and the Awakening of the First Citizens, who had no memories of what came before. Do *you* know anything about what came before?"

Did Beruthi hesitate before answering? If so, it was only an instant. "No," he said. "I don't. I have no more knowledge of the Great Mystery than anyone else."

I don't believe you, Alania thought.

"However we got here," Beruthi rushed on, "if we're going to improve things, we need a new Captain, a young Captain with the will and the wherewithal to wrest control of the City from Kranz."

"And give it to who?" Danyl demanded. "You?"

"You would be Captain. Not I."

"Removing the Officers from power sounds like a recipe for anarchy. How would that be an improvement?"

"At least anarchy provides space for something better to take root," Beruthi snapped. Then he took another deep breath and softened his tone. "But anarchy is not our goal. The Free Citizens have had more than twenty years to draw up plans for seizing control of the City the moment a new Captain takes command. Shut down access to Twelfth and Eleventh Tiers, open the cells on Tenth, and there *is* no Officer presence to speak of. Some

Provosts will likely attempt to preserve the old order, but we count several Provosts among the Free—many Provosts are recruited from the lower Tiers, after all. The Free will be alerted to the imminent changeover. Once you take control, they'll act."

"And why will this new world be better than the current one?" Alania demanded.

"It will have a properly functioning City, to begin with. But the Free want far more than that. They want a more equitable distribution of resources, freedom for people to live their own lives, freedom for anyone to move out into the Heartland and settle and farm and build new towns and start new businesses."

"So," Danyl said. "It all comes down to me agreeing to do this." He paused. "Let me ask you this. *What if I refuse?*"

Beruthi said nothing.

Alania's eyes narrowed. "No," she said. Anger boiled up in her again. "No, it *doesn't* come down to him agreeing, does it? You've—*we've*—made it so that there's no choice left." She rounded on Danyl. "We've made ourselves prisoners, coming here! I've ended up right where the kidnappers would have brought me. Beruthi will imprison me here, just like he always intended, guarded by more of his damn robots, and robots will drag *you* off to the City to be 'plugged in' as Captain whether you like it or not!"

"Alania," Beruthi said, his tone pleading, "you don't understand how vital this all is. How could you? You've lived a pampered life. You don't know what life is like below Twelfth Tier—"

"Don't I?" Alania snapped, rounding on him. "You made a point of letting me 'escape' to Fifth and be threatened by a gang . . . although that was just a way to make sure I never made a serious attempt to escape again, wasn't it? But it still made an impression. And in the last two days, I've seen the Middens, been threatened by the

Rustbloods, fought Provosts, met the River People. I understand that the world could be better. But I keep coming back to one question: do you really begin making a better world by treating people like robots? *Making* them robots, in our case? *Or by murdering babies?*"

"Alania," Danyl said. His voice was soft, but there was a note in it that made her turn to look at him. "I'll do it."

Alania felt like he'd driven his fist into her gut. "Danyl! Become Captain? Give up your life for some nightmarish existence as a glorified circuit board? *Why?*"

"Because Erl believed in this cause," Danyl said simply. "Because things have to change. Because no one else can do it."

I can, Alania almost said, but she didn't. There was no way *she* would allow herself to be plugged into the City, to become Captain—if Beruthi were telling the truth, to become *Kranz*. Nobody should be sentenced to that. And the thought that Danyl might be . . .

Danyl turned to Beruthi. "How do we make this happen?"

Beruthi let out a gust of air, as though he'd been holding his breath. Then he reached into his pocket. "The first thing is to give you this." He pulled out a golden rod about ten centimeters long and a centimeter in diameter. Alania recognized it instantly, and she gasped.

Danyl glanced at her. "What is it?"

"A high-level City access key," she said. "Most of the Officers carry one. They open a lot of doors and give elevator access."

"But only some doors and limited elevator access," Beruthi said. "This one . . ." He held the key up. Twilight was falling outside, and the City had vanished in the gathering gloom, but the office lights glinted off the key's golden length. "*This* one opens all doors, public *or* private, and allows access to *all* Tiers . . . including Thirteenth." He lowered the key and held it out to Danyl. "To the Captain."

Alania stared at the rod as Danyl took it, a little gingerly. "How is that possible?" she breathed.

"Because it tells all security systems that the person wielding it *is* the Captain," Beruthi said. "It's keyed to your Captain-specific genetic traits and the Captain's nanobots in your bloodstreams, which means it will only work for Danyl or you. For anyone else, it not only won't open a thing, it will set off alarms that will bring a horde of Provosts running."

"How did you make something like this?" Danyl said.

Beruthi shrugged. "Once I had access to the nanobot equipment, it was easy. Well, maybe not easy, but at least possible."

"Wow," Danyl said. He tucked the key very carefully into his left pants pocket, then patted it as if to reassure himself it was there. "Wow," he said again. "And three days ago, all I wanted was an ordinary City Pass."

"You won't need one of those," Beruthi assured him. "You will be smuggled into the City aboard the same transport that brought you here and let off in First Tier. There's a secure haven there, a place called Bertel's Bar. You'll be expected. The owner is a friend. She'll tuck you away until I can join you. Then I'll take you to Twelfth and get you to the elevator to Thirteenth—and we'll do what must be done."

Danyl nodded. "Bertel's Bar," he repeated.

"Kranz is looking for us," Alania said. "There'll be cameras . . ."

"Cameras," Beruthi said, "do not survive long in First Tier. And the few that are operational will suffer a minor malfunction for an hour or so after your transport arrives. No one will see you." His lips quirked again. "In any event, the last place Kranz will expect you to show up is the City."

Danyl nodded. Alania couldn't believe he was taking all of this so calmly, considering he was planning to *take the place of the Captain*. "When do I leave?" he asked.

"My robots are already preparing the transport. It was one thing to bring you here in an empty one, but it needs to be loaded to hide you from cursory inspection before you use it to enter the City. It should be ready within an hour or two, but I was thinking you must both need baths, a decent dinner, and a good night's sleep. How about first thing in the morning?"

How about never? Alania thought, but Danyl said, "That sounds great."

"In that case," Beruthi said, "if you'll come with me, I'll—"

An urgent chime from his desk cut him off.

TWENTY-THREE

BERUTHI'S HEAD JERKED around. He crossed to his desk in two strides, rounded it, and swept his hand over its surface. He stared down at a glowing screen, frowning. "Provosts," he said. "At the gate to my Estate."

"They know we went there to catch the transport?" Danyl asked.

Beruthi shook his head. "No. They can't. They're probably conducting a routine Estate-to-Estate search. They'll see my security is intact and be on their—"

A new alarm sounded. Beruthi's eyes widened, and he suddenly went pale. "They just blew the gate. They're storming the house." He spun toward Danyl and Alania. "That means they're already on their way *here*. You have to go. Now. I can talk my way out of whatever has brought this on, but not if they actually find you on my property."

Danyl stared at him. "Go *where*? How? If they've linked you to all this, the transport I'm taking will be intercepted before we can get anywhere near the City!" *It's all falling apart,* a part of him whispered with shameful relief. *You won't have to be Captain. You won't have to plug yourself into the City . . .*

"There's another option. Come with me." Beruthi almost ran to the front door. Danyl exchanged one glance with Alania, and then they hurried after him together.

It wasn't as dark outside as it had seemed when they

were looking out from the bright office; the west still glowed pink, though a few stars were beginning to prick the sky. Beruthi strode swiftly across the stones of the compound to a side gate in the wall, made of the same golden wood as the beams of the house bound in black iron. He slapped his palm against a plate in the rock, and the gate swung open. A dirt path stretched away beyond it. "Follow that path," he said. "To the River."

"The River?" Danyl said. He blinked. "You mean, *the* River?" Considering that their last experience on the River had involved being swept over a waterfall and netted like fish, he didn't like the sound of that.

"There's a boat. A contingency vessel, in case I ever had to flee the Retreat and make my way to the City by a more secretive route. It will take you down to the Middens. You know your way around down there. Get up into the City however you can. If I had more time, I could arrange safe passage, but ... you'll have to manage it on your own. Find an access port in the Undercity; the key will get you through it. Get up to First and go to Bertel's as planned. I'll meet you there once I've smoothed everything out."

"What if you can't?" Alania demanded.

"I can," Beruthi said, and if he felt any doubt, he didn't let it into his voice. "Kranz trusts me completely. There's no way he ordered this. I'll go back to the City with the Provosts when they arrive and straighten it out once I'm there, then find you at Bertel's. Now hurry up—they'll be sending 'copters, and that means we don't have much time."

He twisted around to look out over the Heartland. "It's almost dark. There's no reason for them to go to the River, but even if they do, they won't be able to see you. The Canyon isn't very deep this far north, but it's deep enough, and the boat is designed to be hard to see—and stealthed against radar and infrared sensors. But you have to go *now*."

With that, he shoved them both through the gate with such sudden force that Danyl had no time to react. He spun, only to see the gate slam shut. He tried the latch, but the gate wouldn't budge, and it ignored his palm against the lockplate.

"Another boat?" Alania said from behind him. "The last one almost killed us."

"At least the water should be clean on this side of the City," Danyl said. He stepped back from the gate and looked up at the towering peaks, now just black silhouettes against the brightening stars, remembering the glaciers that topped them. "And very, very cold. But what choice do we have?"

His head jerked to the left as he heard the sound of rotors, far off in the distance but rapidly growing closer.

"That answers that," Alania said.

They hurried along the trail, which at first climbed up into the woods on the arm of the mountain embracing the house to the east. At the top of the ridge, breathing hard, Alania panting beside him, Danyl turned and looked back, just as the helicopters thundering toward Retreat Beruthi turned on their nose lights. A harsh white glare pinned the house and its fenced compound to the mountainside.

Beruthi stood in the open, hands behind his back, clearly nonthreatening. Danyl glanced around the compound. No sentry robots were in sight. *He's doing his best to defuse the situation.* "He seems awfully confident he can talk his way out of being arrested," he said out loud.

"He probably can," Alania said. "A friend of Kranz's, recently promoted to Lieutenant Commander? He's got every reason to be confident." She shook her head. "I've never met any Officer who wasn't supremely self-confident. You might even say arrogant."

Danyl glanced at his . . . sister? The word seemed as unreal as everything else that was happening.

We're Cityborn. Not even fully human. Special genetic

*makeup ... nanobots ... literally bred to be what we are,
like prize cattle.*

But still. She was his *sister*, and he felt a surge of protectiveness as he looked at her. Erl had been the only member of his family, and he was ... missing. Now he had another, and he vowed there and then that he wouldn't lose her, too. If the only way to keep her safe was to become Captain, he would do it. No matter what it meant for him. No matter how terrifying it might be ... and it sounded supremely terrifying.

"We should push on toward the River," Alania said. "If things go badly, we need to be as far away from here as possible." But she made no move to follow her own advice. Instead she waited, like Danyl, to see what would happen next.

Kranz barely slept the night after the raid on the River People; he sat up anxiously and waited for word—which never came—of Alania's and Danyl's recapture. Earlier than usual the following morning, he plunged back into routine work.

How did it come to this? he thought as he slogged through yet another report of failing infrastructure. How had the life of the City—the City the Kranzes had devoted their lives to since before it was a City, the City they had given everything over almost five centuries of selfless service—come to depend on two young people on the run?

He blamed his predecessors. Had his grandclone done his duty a century ago, when the replacement *should* have taken place, long before the cloning unit finally broke down, there would have been no need for his desperate Cityborn Project. Even if cloning the Captain had failed and his forerunner had hit upon the same scheme he had, there would have been many more viable eggs remaining, frozen when the Captain became the Captain, long before the founding of the City. There would've been more opportunities to get things right, more redundancy in case things went wrong.

But the uncertainty of the replacement process, which had never been attempted, had stayed his grandclone's hand and Kranz's own "father's." And the Captain's decline had been slow at first, almost imperceptible. The signals of it—temperature controls run amok, ventilation failures, computer malfunctions, blackouts, other breakdowns, too many to enumerate—were impossible to untangle from the general decline of the City, which, after all, had never been intended to remain intact this long. Every First Officer Kranz knew that the Captain would eventually wear out and have to be replaced, because Thomas Kranz himself had known it. It was the great doom hanging over them all, passed down from Kranz to Kranz. Cloning the Captain, with her peculiar genetic makeup and even more advanced nanobots, had seemed a different order of magnitude from simply cloning another Kranz. None of them had wanted to act. The uncertainties were too great, the risks almost unthinkable.

Yet procrastination could go on only so long, and it had been Kranz's misfortune to be the First Officer who could procrastinate no longer. When the cloning unit had finally and irreparably failed after Falkin's creation, he had realized that he could not carry out the long-planned procedure for replacing the Captain, the one crystal-clear in the memories he carried from Thomas Kranz. He could not clone the Captain.

Making the blow even more devastating, he knew that with the failure of the cloning unit, Falkin would be the last First Officer Kranz. And he knew that would have been true even if the cloning unit hadn't failed, because the nanobots that turned each generation's clone into a new First Officer Kranz were also failing. Science Officer

Prentis had made that clear. Kranz had been forced to accept that his Thomas Kranz memories were faulty because his nanobots had been degraded by too much copying.

It would be years before Falkin's nanobots were fully activated and Kranz would learn just how faulty they were. But the moment Prentis had proven to him that the line of First Officer Kranzes would end with them, he had set his mind to figure out how to salvage the situation, how to ensure that both the Kranz memories and the Captain's unique ability to become the brain and nervous system of the City were preserved.

And that had led to the Cityborn. He had decided that the only hope was to merge Captain and First Officer into one person, to create a Captain who would be conscious and aware, able to both control the City and to govern it the way the Kranzes had always governed it.

That had, after all, been the original intention for the Captain. She was supposed to have been conscious and aware. But Thomas Kranz had discovered that it could not work; the Captain had been unstable, and the City had been fatally damaged because of her instability. He had made the difficult but necessary choice to keep the Captain less than fully functional while taking operational control himself. Kranz remembered that choice as clearly as if he had made it himself, which in some ways he had. That memory of the Captain's instability was another reason his ancestors had put off the replacement process too long. If that instability were somehow inherent in the Captain's genetic makeup, then the new Captain might endanger the City all over again, just like the original had.

His more recent choice had been no less difficult than his original's, but also no less necessary. And so he had donated his sperm to fertilize the Captain's eggs, the embryos were implanted into the artificial wombs, and at the appropriate time, the Cityborn had come into the world: seven babies with the potential to save the City from collapse.

The genetics had been hit or miss, as he had feared. The initial tests showed that only three of the seven children had the genes both to become Captain and accept the Kranz memories. Three infants on whose tiny shoulders rested the future of everything.

Then . . . *that night.* Kranz's teeth clenched as he thought about it. The supposedly secure Twelfth Tier had been infiltrated. One of the precious Cityborn had been killed as she lay in her crib. Another—Danyl, he knew now—had been spirited away by the thrice-damned Ensign Erlkin Orillia, who was now lying in that same hospital, critically wounded and unconscious but heavily guarded all the same. Only the fact Alania had been taken out of the ward by one of the carebots because of a slight fever, placing her safely out of reach of the child-murderer, had prevented total disaster.

Yet now total disaster might have come upon Kranz anyway. Danyl and Alania had spent a night in the open. They might have been seriously injured when the helicopter had crashed. The nanobots Alania had been injected with at birth *should* have protected her, since they had been carefully programmed (oh, so carefully programmed!) and maintained throughout her life. Danyl's had surely deteriorated to uselessness by now, since he'd been living in the Middens without access to proper care. But in truth, Kranz couldn't even be sure Alania was safe. Her nanobots were not fully activated yet, and they could be overwhelmed by severe enough trauma.

Just after lunch, which he took at his desk, he at last heard a chime. His heart jumped. He glanced at the comm panel and felt a flicker of annoyance that it wasn't the call he was waiting for from Commander Havelin. He touched the Accept button. "Yes, Science Officer Prentis?" he said, trying not to sound peevish and almost succeeding.

The rotund, apple-cheeked, gray-haired woman on the screen was the very image of a cheerful grandmother—and one of the brightest minds in the City. "We found something strange among Erlkin Orillia's effects, sir," she said. Her voice had a cold note that belied her appearance. Her image vanished, replaced by that of a metallic sphere on three spindly legs. Kranz recognized it at once as a docbot, though it was practically an antique; there'd been one like it at Retreat Kranz when he and his late "brothers" had been children. It had always terrified him. More recent models were egg-shaped and had four legs instead of three. They also tended to be white or pale blue or green instead of shining chrome. The one at Retreat Kranz had been special, of course, designed to check on and maintain the nanobots that would eventually. . . .

Wait. Is it possible . . . ?

"It's an old docbot," Kranz said. He wouldn't jump to conclusions—let Prentis tell him what she had found. "Not surprising that Orillia would have an obsolete model, if he scavenged it from—"

Prentis's face reappeared. "This wasn't scavenged, sir," she said.

That alone told him that what he suspected was true, as did the fact she had dared to interrupt him, so rather than bite her head off for the breach of protocol, he leaned back and said, "Explain."

"It looks old, but both its hardware and software have been extensively upgraded." Her face was replaced by the docbot again, this time exploded so that its interior could be seen. A green arrow appeared, pointing to a trio of gleaming hair-like needles folded up inside a small compartment. "These are nanoprobes, sir. They're used to remove, program, and reinject nanobots."

Kranz already knew that, of course. He stared at the probes. So much for his assumption that Danyl's nanobots would have failed by now. On the one hand, the fact that Danyl's nanobots had been maintained made it somewhat more likely that the boy had survived whatever had happened on the Rim. But on the other hand . . .

He felt like gears were engaging in his head, clicking into place, making connections. But he didn't like the connections they made. "All docbots are manufactured by Beruthi Enterprises, are they not?" Kranz asked slowly.

The Science Officer nodded. "Yes, sir."

"Including this one."

"Yes, sir."

"And how easy are they to modify?" he asked, even though he already knew.

"That's just it, sir," Prentis said. "They *can't* be modified unless you have the correct encryption codes. Any maintenance work on a docbot *must* be done by a Beruthi Enterprises technician. And even they couldn't go out and *modify* one. That would have to be authorized by someone at the highest levels of the company, and it would have to be done right in the Beruthi Enterprises factory."

A bubble of anger rose inside Kranz, hot as lava. "Beruthi."

Prentis said nothing.

"Thank you, Science Officer. You've been . . . most helpful."

"My pleasure, sir." The screen blanked.

Science Officer Prentis had no doubt been *very* pleased to be able to attach Lieutenant Commander Beruthi's name to the modified docbot. Her own family had a robot manufactory as well, but *their* bots were limited to streetsweeping and window-washing. Acquiring Beruthi Enterprises after its owner's arrest for treason would be of huge benefit to the Prentis clan. But even allowing for that personal animus and ambition—something Kranz was used to, since personal animus and ambition drove every aspect of Officer interaction, each Officer eager to increase his or her own standing in the centuries-old hierarchy—

Kranz did not doubt Prentis's claim. It was too specific and too easy to check to be a lie.

Someone at Beruthi Enterprises had had a hand in the abduction of Danyl and the murder of the other Cityborn twenty years before. Add that to the mysterious knowledge Alania's would-be kidnappers had had of her movements when she was being escorted to Quarters Kranz, and Kranz suddenly had no doubt at all who the traitor among the Officers was, despite the years of Kranz memories within him telling him the Beruthis were the most loyal of all.

"I trusted the bastard," he snarled out loud. "Hell, I *promoted* him."

He called up a map. Estate Beruthi was just a few kilometers from the City—easily accessible on foot from the very spot where the helicopter had crashed on the Rim.

But that wasn't Beruthi's *only* property. Like Kranz himself, like many of the wealthier Officers, the Lieutenant—Lieutenant *Commander*, Kranz thought with another surge of anger—maintained a Retreat. His was located in the northern foothills of the Iron Ring. Kranz's eyes traced the transport roads: Estate Beruthi and Retreat Beruthi were directly linked. He frowned. It was unlikely Beruthi would have taken them up there when his Estate was so close, but just to be sure ...

He activated the communicator panel again and issued orders.

This ends tonight, he thought with grim satisfaction as he sat back in his chair. And then his eyes strayed to that *other* display.

The Captain's vital signs had continued to deteriorate. More green symbols had slipped to yellow. A couple of yellow ones had turned red. The Captain's ancient heart still beat, but slowly ... so slowly ... and unsteadily, too.

Kranz's satisfaction ebbed. *This has cost me too much time. If Alania had come to me when she was supposed to, we would* already *have a new Captain, and together she and I would be working to save the City.*

The *minute* the girl was back in his possession, he would take her to Thirteenth Tier. He shifted his gaze to the Elevator. The City *would* have a new Captain, and new life.

And so would he.

TWENTY-FOUR

ALANIA WATCHED THE HELICOPTERS settle into the compound, the blast from their rotors making Beruthi stagger. Her emotions swirled as wildly within her as the air buffeting the distant figure of her erstwhile guardian. She didn't know how to process what she and Danyl had been told, didn't know what to think of the man in whose house she had grown up, the man from whom she had longed for affection as a child but who had always remained a cold, distant figure, right up until the moment he had handed her over to Kranz—and then, apparently, had attempted to kidnap her right back. He had sentenced her to twenty years of what was essentially house arrest merely to keep Kranz from looking for Danyl down in the Middens. What kind of man could devote two decades of his life to a scheme like that? What kind of man could turn away from the smile of a little girl at every birthday party?

Not that she'd been smiling at him at birthdays for years.

As for the rest . . . genetic modification? Nanobots? She glanced at Danyl. Her brother. *And he's not just my brother. He's supposed to be the new Captain.*

Although it seemed *she* could have been the Captain instead. Even thinking it seemed absurd, but it was hardly the only absurd thing she was expected to believe. According to Beruthi, she and Danyl were literally offspring

of the Captain, a figure of such myth that they might as
well have been told they were demigods.

And First Officer Kranz was their father. That was
just . . . disgusting. Especially if he'd been watching her
over the years through that camera in her bedroom . . .

Beruthi could be lying, she thought. *There could be
something else happening here.*

There could be. But she couldn't imagine what.

The rotors slowed, though they kept moving, the 'copters ready to take off again at a moment's notice. An
amplified voice rang out, carrying clearly up to the ridge
where Alania and Danyl waited. "Lieutenant Commander Ipsil Beruthi, you are under arrest on suspicion
of mutiny. Raise your hands and keep them above your
head."

"They don't intend to kill him," Alania said, feeling an
unexpected surge of relief.

"No," Danyl said. "They want to question him."

Beruthi raised his hands above his head as ordered.
Provosts emerged cautiously from the 'copters, weapons
ready. One of them, clearly the Commander, strode
toward Beruthi.

"There's no need for this," Beruthi said. Even without
amplification, they could hear his words—the courtyard
of the house and the enveloping mountain ridges forming a natural amphitheater. "I'll come quietly. I can explain everything."

"Save it for the First Officer," the Mission Commander
growled.

At that moment, a robot trundled into the open.

It wasn't one of the security robots, which had clearly
been ordered to stay out of sight. It looked, in fact, exactly like the gardening robot Alania had glimpsed
through the gate of Estate Beruthi, brushes and clippers
attached to its arms. Harmless. But it clearly startled Beruthi, who jerked toward it, half lowering his arms . . .

One of the Provosts must have been nervous. You

could hardly blame him, Alania thought later; three helicopters full of Provosts had been blown up just the day before, and the man they were arresting might have been behind it all. They must have been under orders to take him alive, but ...

But.

There was a flash of flame from one of the helicopters. The sound of the shot reached Alania's ears a moment later as Beruthi, felled by a bullet to the head, toppled backward in a spray of blood and brains and bone.

An instant later, the house exploded.

The windows burst outward in showers of glass riding gouts of orange flame, the blast bowling over the Provosts in the courtyard. The roof lifted as a whole, then collapsed back into the inferno suddenly engulfing the structure. The fallen Provosts were just starting to scramble to their feet when the missiles struck, streaking from wherever a security robot had taken up station around the compound.

The missiles slammed into the 'copters. The resulting explosions knocked Alania and Danyl from their feet, slamming them onto their backs. Groggily, Alania rose on her elbows and stared down in horror at a lake of fire, a burning sea through which trundled the black shapes of the security robots. One stopped by a writhing, burning figure on the ground and put a slug through its head. The writhing stopped instantly.

"Captain!" Alania whispered, the oath coming to her lips despite everything they had just learned.

Danyl staggered to his feet. "Let's get out of here. Kranz must be watching. More 'copters will be coming. With luck they'll waste time searching for our bodies down there ... but not if they see us. We've got to find that boat." He held out his hand; Alania took it and let him pull her to her feet.

They stumbled along the path and down the other side of the ridge, the sky behind them filled with flame-tinged smoke. Nothing moved among the spiky trees; if any wild-life lurked nearby, it had been terrified into cowering silence. For much the same reason, Alania and Danyl said nothing as they hurried through the forest.

Once again horrible questions ran through her brain. How many people had died because of what she and Danyl were? How many *more* would die?

They could not move swiftly, not with only the stars providing light, though at least the sky was full of them, so they could sort of see the path by their silvery glow. They heard the River before they saw it and slowed; even so, the light was so dim that Danyl had to catch Alania's arm and hold her back from taking one step too many and tumbling off the edge of a cliff. The path had turned, leading to a wooden platform, which proved to the be top landing of a staircase down into a canyon below—the Canyon, presumably, though they descended only fifty or sixty meters before they reached the bottom, where a wooden pier thrust into the rushing, tumbling water. The River's surface glittered in the starlight, twisting streaks and swirls of white marking rocks beneath the surface.

"We're supposed to take a boat on *that*?" said Alania.

"I guess," Danyl said. He sounded as uncertain as she felt. "Let's find it and see what's what."

He walked out onto the pier, Alania following close behind. Together they stood looking down into the swiftly flowing water.

How swift? she wondered. They were a long way from the City, and even a fast river must flow a lot slower than a transport moved. It could take them days to drift down to the—

A dim green light suddenly sprang to life in front of them, *under* the water. Alania grabbed Danyl's arm and took an involuntary step back, then watched in fascination as the light moved toward the surface and broke it.

No brighter than the worn-out eternals by the light of which they seemed to be forever negotiating ancient stairwells, it lit the water streaming from the metal sides of the dark bulk on which it rode: presumably their boat. Somehow the craft remained stationary against the current, and in fact it moved toward them, closer and closer, until at last it bumped gently against the pier.

A hatch opened in its side. Bluish light streamed out. Though it was almost painfully bright to Alania's eyes after so long in the dark, it revealed little of the vessel's interior.

Clearly they were supposed to get on board. Somehow the boat had sensed their presence.

Danyl glanced at Alania. "Well?" he said.

"What choice do we have?" Alania said with a surge of bitterness. How many times had she thought that over the past few days?

But what choice *did* they have? What choice had they *ever* had? Beruthi was dead, but he was *still* manipulating them. The boat was clearly just another of his robots, and while that meant it would presumably take them safely down the river, it also meant that they remained under his thumb, where Alania had lived her whole life. They were still blindly following the path he had set them on before they were even born, the path that ended with Danyl becoming Captain.

They could refuse to board, walk away from the River, but to what end? They couldn't live in the wilderness. They'd starve or freeze within days, even if they evaded the additional Provosts who would soon be arriving to try to figure out what had happened at Retreat Beruthi . . . and search for them or their bodies.

Almost angrily, Alania brushed past Danyl and stepped onto the boat, which listed a little under her weight. Ducking, she entered the hatch, finding two steps leading down into a kind of padded cocoon. There was a blank vidscreen at the front—the bow, wasn't that what it was called on a boat?—and a hatch at the . . . stern? Two narrow cots ran along the sides with latched cabinets beneath them.

Danyl climbed in behind her. As she turned to look at him, the hatch hissed closed, then sealed with finality. The moment it had done so, the boat thrummed and jerked sideways so suddenly she grabbed Danyl for support. "Steady," he murmured.

The interior lights dimmed slightly. Then the vidscreen at the bow flicked on.

Alania half expected a recorded message from Beruthi, but all she saw was a map showing their location, the twists and turns of the River, and the City . . . almost two hundred kilometers away.

The thrum of the engines deepened. They were moving.

Danyl knelt to look in the cabinets under the cots. "Food and water," he reported. He went to the back of the cabin, opened the stern hatch, and stuck his head through. "Toilet."

"I think they call it a head," Alania said.

He turned back to her. "What?"

"The toilet. On boats, they call it a head."

"They call it ahead? You have to schedule a time to go?"

"No, I mean, the name for a toilet on a boat is 'head.' So that's the head."

"I thought the head of a boat is the bow."

"No, that's the front."

Danyl frowned. "Don't make me be stern with you."

It took Alania a second to react; then she laughed. It felt good.

Danyl grinned at her, then closed the hatch. "How do you know what things are called on a boat, anyway?" he asked as he returned to her.

"I had a lot of time to read growing up," Alania said. "What with being Beruthi's prisoner and all."

"I read, too," Danyl said. "Stuff Erl gave me. Technical

books, mostly. Although he also made me read a lot of Earthmyth."

Alania's eyes widened. "I *love* Earthmyth stories."

"They're okay," Danyl said. "Erl kept telling me they were full of valuable lessons. But I never understood how knowing the ways fictional rulers in a made-up world dealt with things like revolutions and famines and wars and poverty is supposed to help us in the real world. I don't care how elaborate the made-up world is. And anyway, so much of it is unbelievable: a whole world filled with people, multiple . . . what did they call them? Countries? A bunch of different languages, a bunch of different . . . what's that word . . . religions? It's just children's nonsense."

"But that's what I loved about it," Alania said. "I knew 'Earth' was a made-up place. But it was a different world from the one I was stuck in. And the stories were so exciting!"

"I had enough excitement in the Middens just staying alive." Danyl looked around the cabin. "You've had rather a lot of excitement yourself these past three days. Still like it?"

Alania chewed on her lip for a minute, thinking. "Yes," she said slowly, to her own surprise. "Yes." She met Danyl's blue eyes, the same shade of blue as her own—and now she knew why. "Or . . . I don't *like* it, exactly but . . . it all *matters*. It matters like nothing else I've ever done. That's uncomfortable, in a way . . . but it's better than being a prisoner. Truth is, I wouldn't change it." She smiled a little. "Would you?"

"Not on your life," Danyl said. His expression hardened. "And if what we've been told is true and I really am going to become the new Captain . . . well, then, there are going to be a lot of changes made, and Kranz and the rest of the Officers aren't going to like them one bit." He looked down at his hands, which had clenched into fists, and relaxed them. He took a deep breath, looked back up at her, and smiled. "Now," he said. "I'm hungry. What about you?"

"Starved," Alania said.

"Then let's see what we have." He knelt on the floor and began rummaging through the cabinets beneath the beds.

TWENTY-FIVE

KRANZ SAT in his darkened office, his heart laboring in his chest, his breath coming in ragged gasps. He had never felt so helpless, so panicked. The flames of the inferno that had engulfed Retreat Beruthi still flickered on one of the screens on his desk. More helicopters were screaming that way, but he knew they would find no survivors.

Estate Beruthi had been empty. Retreat Beruthi had not. But some fool of a Provost had overreacted, and Beruthi had clearly programmed his damnable robots to attack if anything happened to him ... and to destroy any evidence in the bargain. Kranz had a horrible feeling that destroying the evidence had also meant destroying Alania and Danyl on the theory that it was better for the Captain and all her heirs to die, better for chaos to descend on the City than for Kranz to install Alania and carry out his plans ... plans of which Beruthi had known every detail.

Selfish bastard, Kranz thought savagely. *Does he know what will happen when the Captain dies?*

No, he thought then. *Because you don't either. Not really. All you know is it will be very, very bad.*

His eyes flicked to the monitor on the wall. The nanobots in the Captain's body could no longer stay ahead of the cascading cellular damage, some of it at the molecular level where even nanobots could not function. No one had ever lived as long as the Captain. When she had been . . . installed in her current position, the thinking had been that the nanobots would make her functionally immortal.

But functionally immortal was a long way from *actually* immortal.

The nanobots Alania and Danyl carried, had they been fully activated, might have protected them from the destruction of Retreat Beruthi. But they were *not* fully activated.

Kranz's only hope—and it was a slim one—was that the two had been sheltered from the explosion, perhaps in the basement, perhaps in the surrounding woods. If they were in the basement, they might be horribly injured and probably trapped but possibly—just possibly—still alive. If they were in the woods, the nanobots could keep them from dying of exposure, but they could do nothing about the effects of thirst and hunger. Alania and Danyl would find no food in the foothills of the Iron Ring, where no edible vegetation grew; in all of the Heartland, only the plants grown and tended on the Estates could be eaten. Alania and Danyl wouldn't be edible to the wildlife in the Iron Ring, either, but that wouldn't stop the wildlife from trying to kill them. The nanobots couldn't save them if they stumbled on something really dangerous, like a dragonbear or spidercat, and were disemboweled or torn limb from limb.

The original First Officer Kranz had not been a religious man. He had believed only in himself, in his own power of reason, and in the righteousness of his actions. Kranz had inherited those attitudes along with his nanobots, and thus he had no god he could pray to. The ordinary citizens of the lower Tiers had been known to pray to the Captain, but Kranz knew better than anyone else just how futile that would be.

All the same, he offered a silent appeal to the uncaring universe. *Let them be alive*, he thought. *Let them be alive, for all our sakes.*

His eyes flicked back to the Captain's medical monitor. Another of the few green lights on it had just turned to blinking yellow.

Danyl had no idea if the strange craft they had boarded was traveling underwater or above the water. Probably, he thought, a bit of both—while underwater travel would reduce the chance of detection, he doubted the River was always deep enough to enable it.

Nor did he have any idea how fast they might be moving or how long it would take to reach the City. If they had simply been drifting with the current, it would surely have taken at least a couple of days, but from the thrum of the boat and the way it resisted being swirled around, it was clearly powered and under computer control.

Despite that, it had lurched or bucked hard enough to toss them around several times, which was why both Alania and Danyl now kept their rears firmly planted on the cots as they ate the self-heating, prepackaged stew—though "slop" might have been more accurate—they had found in the storage lockers. To drink, there was bottled water.

Danyl touched the left pocket of his pants, where the precious access key rested. Just . . . what, three days ago? . . . he'd hoped to trade Alania at the Last Chance Market for a mere City Pass. Now he had the means to ascend all the way to Thirteenth . . .

. . . where he was expected to become the new Captain.

The idea was mind-boggling, yet he felt a fierce excitement at the same time. He had no idea what it would mean to "plug" himself into the City in place of the dying shell of the previous Captain. But clearly Beruthi expected that he would retain free will and could seize control of the City from Kranz and the Officers. Whatever happened after that would have to be better than the stultified hierarchical tyranny that now ruled the City and Heartland.

Wouldn't it?

It wasn't like he had any better options. He could no longer doubt the outlandish truth of his origins, not with people dying in droves as Kranz desperately sought to capture him and Alania. That being the case, they literally had nowhere else to go. The Heartland stretched two to three hundred kilometers in every direction from the City, but there was nowhere to hide in all that space. They might evade capture for a while, but not for long, and if they were taken prisoner by Kranz, all hope of achieving the goals of the Free Citizens would be lost. Kranz would install Alania as Captain, and her nanobots were programmed to override her own will and memories and personality, turning her into yet another copy of the first First Officer, Thomas Kranz.

Their only hope, slim though it was, was to reach the Thirteenth Tier undetected and for Danyl to take over as Captain . . . without the late Beruthi's help or guidance.

There could be no planning beyond that.

One step at a time, he thought, not for the first time. *First, get to the City.*

He took another bite of the "stew," the need for sustenance overcoming his distaste. *No*, he amended his previous thought. *First, we have to get through the Middens.*

His old stomping grounds, of course, but not *this* side—this side belonged to the Greenskulls. Unless the Provosts had finally destroyed them, as they had certainly destroyed the Rustbloods by now, in which case this side belonged to the Provosts.

The boat lurched again, and this time it kept on lurching and bucking. Danyl gripped the edge of the cot with one hand. "Hope you're not prone to motion sickness," he said to Alania.

"How would I know?" Alania said, holding on to her own cot. "Not a lot of movement on Twelfth Tier." She grinned at him. "Besides, if I am, you probably are, too . . . brother."

Does it run in families? he wondered, and realized he didn't know. But he couldn't deny that his insides did feel a little ... not exactly nauseated, but certainly unsettled. Although that might have been just a reaction to the stew. "You'd think someone with Beruthi's resources could have stocked this thing with better food," he muttered.

"He probably stocked it with whatever he could get that could go missing without anyone noticing," Alania said. The boat lurched again, and her hands tightened on the cot. Danyl thought she looked a little green. "He must have built this thing recently. He couldn't have known when all this started that he'd be bringing us up here."

"He said this was for his own use in an emergency," Danyl said. "A way to get back to the City without being seen." A particularly violent lurch threw him back against the wall, and he decided he'd just lie down. Alania clearly thought that was a good idea; she stretched out on her own cot. "It could have been built years ago."

"Maybe," Alania said a little weakly as the turbulence intensified, "he built it for fun."

Danyl closed his eyes and swallowed hard. "If he did," he groaned, "he had a very twisted idea of fun."

After that, he was too busy trying not to throw up to talk.

An interminable time later, the bucking and bouncing eased. Danyl hadn't quite thrown up, and he hadn't heard Alania throw up, either, which was a good thing, since he was pretty sure the sound and smell in the small cabin would have pushed him over the edge of regurgitation himself. As his insides settled, his eyelids closed, and he slept.

He woke to a grating noise beneath him, a sudden slowing. There was a crunch, a thud, a tearing screech ... and then the storage lockers beneath Alania's bed burst open. Water gushed into the interior of the boat, carrying with it more packages of stew, bottles of water, and other supplies. Danyl jerked upward, meeting Alania's wide eyes across the way. "We've got to get out of here!" he shouted. He swung his feet over the edge of the cot and stood up in the cold, swirling water, already up to his calves and rising fast. He waded to the hatch and pounded on it. It remained stubbornly closed.

Alania joined him, ran her fingers around the edge, and found the hidden panel he'd missed. It popped open at her touch, revealing two buttons, helpfully labeled CLOSE and OPEN. Alania punched the OPEN button. It flashed red, and a woman's voice said, "Main hatch is underwater. OPEN command denied."

Alania shot Danyl a horror-filled glance. He turned back into the interior as the water reached his thighs. There was no way out through the head. But surely there was more than one exit . . .

There! A square in the ceiling, offset from the central band of illumination. He scrambled up onto Alania's cot, already underwater and squishy underfoot, ran his fingers around the edges as Alania had done with the main hatch, and found another small panel that also concealed two buttons. He punched OPEN. The small hatch slid aside, letting in cool air—and more water, though this was in the form of drenching, ice-cold rain.

"Hurry up!" Alania cried.

Danyl fumbled around on the outside of the boat and found what felt like a ladder rung: he pulled on it, and a chain ladder promptly fell onto his head and then down, splashing into the water at his feet. He scrambled up it and onto the hull of the boat, then turned and helped Alania out. The boat listed alarmingly beneath them, and Danyl looked frantically around. The heavy rain and thick mist obscured their surroundings, but he could make out a rocky beach off to their right, and behind it a wall of familiar reddish stone.

The boat tilted again . . . and kept on tilting, beginning a roll toward that red cliff. "Jump!" Danyl yelled and leaped into the water. He hit it awkwardly with an almighty belly flop and struggled to get his feet under him, terrified he wouldn't find bottom ... but there it was. He turned, expecting to see Alania floundering in the water, only to see her swim a few strokes past him before standing in much shallower water and wading ashore. He waded after her, and in a moment they both stood shivering on the beach. The lightless boat, now just a black lump in the water, had rolled hatch-down. If they hadn't gotten out when they had ...

"Shit! My backpack was in there." At least he still had the slugthrower; he'd fallen asleep with it holstered at his side. He looked at Alania, her face a pale blotch in the dim rainy twilight. "You know how to swim!" he said almost accusingly.

"Quarters Beruthi has a pool," she said, sounding a little embarrassed. "Sala—my servant—taught me as a child."

"Well, that explains it," Danyl said. "Somehow my servant never got around to it. It's so hard to get good help in the Middens."

Alania laughed a little shakily. She stared at the capsized boat. "Now what? Where are we?"

Danyl looked downstream. "I don't ..." He paused. "Do you see a light?"

Alania stepped up beside him and followed his gaze. "Barely," she said. "Down low."

"Come on." Danyl led the way downstream, picking his way carefully through the loose rocks. As they approached the dim yellow glow, he realized that the river was making a new sound, a deep grumbling, and that the gray mist ahead of them was darkening, not growing lighter, even though the light all around them was slowly waxing. They'd traveled all night, and dawn was coming.

Then, suddenly, he realized what he was seeing, and he stopped, holding out his arm to halt Alania. "We're here," he said.

"Where?"

"The north side of the Middens. Wait."

The light continued to grow, and the vague dark bulk in front of them slowly became clear: a wall of rubbish rising up and up until it vanished into the fog. Danyl didn't need to see all the way to the top of that pile of refuse to know what squatted above it: the City.

He'd never been to this side of the Middens, but he'd known it rose more steeply from the Canyon floor than the other side and was not as deep. He'd learned from his studies that the City perched above a place where the Canyon depth abruptly plunged from "only" three hundred meters deep to the full half a kilometer their aching legs had climbed to the Rim Guardians' nest. At one time there must have been a spectacular cascade here. The Middens had swallowed it long ago, of course.

"Shouldn't we be climbing it?" Alania said, staring up into the rain at the mountain of trash.

"Wait," Danyl said again. He kept his own gaze on the yellow glow. If he was right . . .

The spark of illumination vanished for an instant, reappeared . . . and then brightened and grew larger: a door had opened. A dark figure half obscured the opening—

—and then a bright white light speared through the rain, pinning Danyl and Alania where they stood. "Move a muscle and die," a woman shouted. And then, to someone else, "Spika here. We've got strangers at the River. Send reinforcements."

TWENTY-SIX

ALANIA TURNED HER HEAD away from the painfully bright glare of the light and looked at Danyl instead.

"Call her over," he whispered, and then, with a groan, he fell to his knees and onto his side.

Alania gaped for only an instant, then understood. "My brother is injured!" she cried. "Please, come help!"

The woman—Spika—hesitated, then approached, lowering the light to illuminate Danyl's apparently senseless body. In the process, she revealed that the light was attached to a battered-looking but undoubtedly still deadly automatic rifle and that she was a dark-skinned woman in her thirties or early forties with short, curly black hair, wearing a too-large black synthileather jacket over greasy green overalls. Alania dropped to her knees beside Danyl, both to continue the charade and to avoid doing anything Spika might interpret as threatening. She didn't know exactly what Danyl had in mind, but she assumed he planned to try to disarm the woman once she got close enough.

But Spika didn't get close enough. She stopped well out of reach. "I don't see any injuries," she snarled.

Danyl opened his eyes. "There aren't any," he said in a low voice. "But I figure out here I can talk to you without anyone else listening in, like I assume they could do back there at your post."

The woman stiffened. "What are you up to? There'll be two more Greenskulls here in ten minutes."

"Call them off."

"Why would I do that?"

"Because they'll take this away from me . . . and then you won't get into the City." Very slowly, Danyl moved his hand to the breast pocket of his jacket, unbuttoned it, and showed just the top of the golden key Beruthi had given him.

The effect was instantaneous—Spika gasped. "Is that . . ."

"It's exactly what it looks like. A high-level City access key. It'll get us into the Bowels and from the Bowels to the First Tier."

The rifle came up. "Then I'll kill you and take it."

"No, you won't," Danyl said. "It's biolocked to me. I'm the only one who can use it. The key alone can't get you into the City, but with it, I *can*. And I will . . . if you'll call off the others."

"The only way I know into the City is through the main gate," Spika said. "That thing is useless there. You need a City Pass."

"I know an entrance," Danyl said. "But we need your help to get there."

Spika hesitated.

"You'll never have a chance like this again. And you know it."

An agonizingly long pause. Alania stayed where she was, knees pressed painfully to the stones, and stared at the Greenskull woman. Then, almost spasmodically, Spika lowered her weapon and the blinding light and raised her arm, speaking into her wrist. "False alarm," she said. "Just shadows. Cancel backup."

"You sure?" a voice crackled back.

"Yeah, I'm sure. Damn rain is playing tricks."

"All right."

"Spika clear and out." The woman lowered her wrist

and raised the rifle again. "Talk fast. I could still shoot you."

Danyl carefully got to his feet in a nonthreatening fashion, and Alania just as carefully got up to stand beside him. "I grew up in the Middens," he said. "South side."

"Rustblood?" Spika snapped.

"No," Danyl said. "Independent. You ever heard of Erl?"

"'Course I've heard of Erl. Everyone in the Middens has heard of Erl." Spika squinted at him. "Wait a minute. You're that kid of his?"

Danyl nodded.

"Then who the hell is she?" She jerked her head in Alania's direction. "She called you her brother."

"I had to call him something," Alania said.

"Just someone else who fell out of the City," Danyl said. "Like I did as a baby. Like you did once upon a time."

Spika barked a laugh. "Once upon a time? Don't make it sound like some Earthmyth tale. I ended up down here because I thought nothing could be worse than up there."

"Yet you want to go back?" Alania said.

"I was wrong," Spika said. "Turns out it *is* worse down here." She smiled without humor. "Besides, I've learned a few ... skills ... down here. Maybe the bastard I ran away from is still alive up there, and maybe he isn't. All I know is, after what I've seen and done in the Middens, he doesn't scare me anymore." She turned her gaze back to Danyl. "So what's your way into the City?"

"Hazardous Waste Holding Tank, near the southeastern strut," he said. "You know it?"

Spika nodded. "I know it. Never been too close to it, though. Not healthy."

"I have," Danyl said. He glanced at Alania. "*We* have. There's a maintenance hatch into the Bowels. This key will open it."

Spika chewed on her lip. "Not easy getting from here to there in one piece."

"I know," Danyl said. "But that's Greenskull territory if it's anyone's. There must be safe paths."

"Safe might be a little strong," Spika said. "I think I'd go with likely—no, make that *possibly*—survivable."

"Good enough. Do we have a deal?"

"Show me that key again," Spika said. "No teasing this time. The whole thing."

"Sure." Danyl drew out the key. Even in the gray, rain-dampened light, it gleamed.

Spika blew out a breath through pursed lips. "That's the real deal, all right. When I lived up top, I saw an Officer use one once to open a hatch I didn't even know was a hatch." Her eyes narrowed. "How'd *you* get it?"

"Traded salvage for it," Danyl said. "That's all you need to know."

Spika grunted. She looked back at the doorway in the wall of trash, then pointed right. "Over there. A path all the way to the top."

"Watched?" Danyl said.

"Yeah. But mainly by me. Come on."

She led them a short distance along the rocks of the riverbank to where the rubbish began. As always, Alania couldn't believe how much of it there was. But tens of thousands of people lived in the giant City somewhere out of sight in the mists above, and they had lived there for centuries. All their trash had to go somewhere, and for most of the City's existence, that somewhere had been the Canyon. The settlements in the Heartland carted their rubbish here, too. *At least this way all the pollution is centralized*, she thought. *Very efficient, when you think about it.*

Down here, as at the bottom of the Middens to the south where they'd seen the mine shafts the River People had excavated, the weight of years had compressed the trash into a kind of conglomerate, hard as rock in some places and soft and porous in others. Sharp bits of glass and metal and plastic and wood pushed through the oozing black surface down which the rain ran in rivulets that seemed to darken the moment they touched it.

Spika paused to pull on heavy gloves. "Don't want to get cut," she commented. "Nasty bugs live in the Middens. Goes with the nasty people."

Alania looked down at herself. She still wore the baggy blue shirt and rolled-up pants the River People had provided, soaked and thin. The canvas shoes she'd put on after the decontamination shower in the Whitewater Resort squelched with every step. She felt almost numb with cold. At least climbing would warm her up.

She wasn't worried about cuts. Not anymore. *The tiny robots living in my bloodstream will take care of that*, she thought, and she shivered with more than the cold.

"Path is pretty clear, just steep," Spika said. "We've stuck in some handholds. Use them. First challenge will be at the top. There's another watch hole there. Might or might not be anyone in it; there's supposed to be, but Greenskulls aren't all that great at following orders. If we're lucky, the sentry's gone back to bed because it's raining."

"And if we're unlucky?" Alania asked.

"Then we deal with him. Or her."

"Could be a friend of yours," Alania said.

Spika snorted. "I don't have 'friends' down here. Nobody does." She looked up into the rain. "Let's climb."

At first the going was easy, a not-too-steep ascent diagonally across the trash. Somewhere far beneath it, the clear mountain stream they had entered in the Iron Ring was being transformed into the vile black current scavenged by the River People. The light grew, but only a little—the thick clouds and mist and continuing rain saw to that. Alania's hope that climbing would warm her up proved false; she felt every bit as miserably cold and wet twenty minutes into their long upward hike as she had when they'd set out.

When at last the path switchbacked the other way, it also grew steeper. The mass of rotted wood, compacted paper, chunks of plastic, bits of cloth, strips of metal and broken glass they traversed changed, too; it was no longer as tightly compressed and was far more likely to shift underfoot without warning. Climbing that mountain without a path would have been more than a nightmare; it would have been impossible. But the Greenskulls had obviously put a lot of effort into making their territory traversable. As the trash mountain became looser and more precarious with height, they moved from walking directly on it to a rough boardwalk, though not every "board" in it was made of wood—some were stone, others metal, others plastic. Even when it moved underfoot— and it often did—it still provided better purchase than the garbage itself.

As they approached the middle of the mountain again, Spika held up a hand. "Watch hole is just ahead," she said. "Wait here." She moved forward. The downpour that had greeted Danyl and Alania when they'd opened the boat's escape hatch had lessened to a miserable drizzle, but visibility remained poor, and after just a few steps, Spika faded into a vague gray shape.

"How are you doing?" Danyl asked.

Alania looked at him. With his hair plastered to his head and his red shirt plastered to his body, he looked like a drowned rat. She shoved a stray lank strand away from her own face, knowing she didn't look any better. "I'm cold, I'm wet, I'm terrified, and if I survive climbing the Middens, I figure I've still got several excellent chances of being dead before the day is half over," she said. "How about you?"

He stared at her, then laughed. "The same, I guess."

Alania looked after Spika again. "Do you think we can trust her?"

"I think we can trust her to get us to the Hazardous Waste Holding Tank and the access hatch," Danyl said.

"But what happens after that?"

"One thing at a time," Danyl said. His eyes narrowed as he peered through the drizzle. "Damn. Looks like someone *is* home."

Alania squinted. Sure enough, there were two figures visible now. She couldn't tell them apart. She heard shouting, though she couldn't understand it. The figures suddenly clinched, struggled. Light flashed, and the sharp report of a firearm rang through the rain. One of the figures crumpled to the ground. The other kicked the body hard in the side. It tumbled over the edge of the path and down the trash mountain, rolling in a loose welter of garbage to a sharp drop-off and then out of sight. Alania thought she heard it hit somewhere below them with a wet thud, but that might have been her imagination.

The remaining figure turned and came back toward them. "Is that Spika?" Alania whispered.

"Can't tell." Danyl drew his slugthrower and aimed it at the approaching figure.

"You shoot me, you'll never get where you're going," Spika's voice came through the drizzle, and Danyl took a deep breath and put the gun away.

"Couldn't be sure it was you," he said. "What happened?"

Spika's lip was bleeding; she licked it and said, "Jameson Harker. Damn fool. Told him he could come with us, but turned out he is—was—actually *loyal* to Shanky. Had to kill him." A tremor in her voice belied her calm words.

"Shanky?" Alania asked.

"Head Greenskull," Danyl said. "Makes the late, unlamented Cark of the Rustbloods look like a Twelfth-Tier socialite." He paused. "Um, no offense."

"None taken," Alania said.

"No going back for me now," Spika said. "And someone may have heard that shot. Let's get moving."

A minute later they passed the watch hole Harker had been manning. Alania glanced inside. At the back of a small chamber excavated in the trash and shored up with plastic panels, a similarly braced tunnel continued into the mountain, lit (of course) by dim eternals. After a few meters, it turned sharply right. As the three of them pressed on, Alania pictured gang members pouring out of that hole at their backs and wished Spika would climb even faster.

They finished that traverse of the mountain and paused on a broad wooden platform. The drizzling rain continued. Alania doubled over, puffing. Danyl and Spika were barely breathing hard. "One more time across," Spika said. "No watch holes on this part of the path. Guard post at the other end, but we won't get that far. There's a shortcut up to the Undercity—well, there used to be one. Might have collapsed or been swallowed by a trashslide since the last time I used it."

"And if it has?" Danyl said.

"Then we'll need that slugthrower of yours, and you'd better be a damn good shot with it," Spika said. "There'll be at least two at the guard post, and if we have to go that way, we'll need to get them both at once to stop them sounding an alarm."

Danyl nodded. Alania wondered how good a shot he could possibly be, since from what he'd said, he and Erl had never had any firearms. Simulations were one thing, but . . .

Fortunately, they didn't have to find out. Three-quarters of the way back across the mountain, they reached a kind of ravine slashing across the path, spanned by a rope-and-trestle bridge that Alania didn't like the looks of. But Spika didn't cross it. Instead, she swung down off the path onto the slope of the ravine, and when Alania followed, she found herself standing with Spika on top of an old dining room table, its thick black wood split down the middle. It shifted a little as Danyl stepped onto it behind them, and she tensed. "Is this secure?"

"Who knows?" Spika pointed up the ravine. "There's a whole tangle of old furniture up there. All locked together, more or less. It's tough going, but after about a hundred meters there's a rope ladder that will take us the rest of the way . . . or there used to be."

"Tough going" was one way to put it, Alania thought a few minutes later. "Nightmarish" would have been more accurate.

At some point, it seemed a warehouse full of wooden tables and chairs had been dumped into the Canyon. Out of style? Wood rot? Bankruptcy? She couldn't understand why the furniture hadn't been salvaged, or recycled, or at least burned for warmth in some underpowered corner of First or in a last-ditch squatter's hole in the Bowels or in the depths of the Greenskulls' hideaway. Whatever the reason, here it was, and Alania picked her way through the tangled table and chair legs, trying to avoid the splintery bits, feeling the whole framework shift with every move she, Danyl, and Spika made. She had no trouble at all imagining the whole thing collapsing, either impaling them all on wooden stakes or sending them sliding down the steep ravine to the same drop-off the unfortunate Harker's body had fallen from, hitting somewhere far below with the same wet, crunching thud . . .

Her arms and legs trembled, and her heart was racing even more than the climb could account for by the time they arrived, wet and exhausted, at a relatively flat spot in the trash wall. "It's here," Spika said as she stepped onto that sanctuary. Alania looked up and saw that the slope above them was even steeper than the one behind them . . . but there was indeed a rope ladder with rungs made of random materials stretching up out of sight. The sky was much darker here, and for a minute she thought it must be about to rain harder. Then she realized the darkness above the mist wasn't cloud but the vast bulk of the City.

Rain still fell on them, so they weren't quite under it yet, but they would be soon. "What's at the top of the ladder?" Danyl asked as Spika took hold of the lowest rungs.

"A path. I hope."

"You hope?"

Spika shrugged. "Things change, and I haven't been up here for weeks. Last time there was a path." She looked at him. "Does it matter? Got a better option?"

"I suppose not," Danyl said. He glanced back at Alania and gave her a wet, crooked smile. "All right?"

"Never better," Alania lied. She wanted to rest. She wanted to be warm. She wanted to be dry. She wanted to be clean. But none of those things were possible, so instead she said, "What are we waiting for?" She was rewarded by another quick smile from her brother, then followed him and Spika up the ladder and deeper into the looming shadow of the City.

TWENTY-SEVEN

DANYL WAS ONLY FAMILIAR with the southern fringes of the Undercity. Despite having grown up in the Middens, he wasn't prepared for what he saw when they reached the top of the rope ladder, passing out from beneath the miserable drizzling sky as they did so.

He'd been aware for some time of the sound of falling liquid, as though they were approaching a waterfall. Now, as he straightened, a gust of warm wind blew an incredible stench toward him. He gagged.

"What *is* that?" Alania choked out as she climbed up beside him.

He shot her a quick look. She looked pale and was as soaked to the skin and streaked with nameless grime as he was. Her eyes were wide and white, her mouth half open, her nose wrinkled in a look of almost comical disgust.

"Sewers," Spika said. "Ruptured pipes." She pointed off to the right, and Danyl saw the source of both the waterfall sound and the stench: a torrent of brown liquid falling from high above, turning into a noxious mist as it hit the trash heap.

"Why don't they fix them?" Alania cried.

"Been that way ten years, I've been told," Spika said. "No doubt 'they' will get around to it any day now."

"We're not going that way," Danyl said. He supposed it was a question, but he hoped it came off as a command.

"No," Spika said. She turned in a slow circle, staring

up at the vast black underside of the City, then down at the mounds of trash all around them: more recent stuff, mostly paper and plastic. Lights flashed here and there among the tangled pipes and conduits on the City's belly. In the distance, Danyl could see the vast empty hole in the middle of the Bowels, which stretched up to the underside of First Tier. "Everything still looks the same," Spika said. "Maybe we're lucky."

She turned to stare back down the slope they'd just climbed, down into the ravine and its tangle of old furniture, and then out into the mist that hid the Canyon. She stood there for a long moment, then turned abruptly. "This way."

To Danyl's great relief, her chosen path did indeed take them away from that torrent of raw sewage. They wound their way through the mounds of rubbish, dark and gloomy beneath the City's shadowing mass. The uncertain footing made the going very slow. Spika kept looking up, and Danyl realized she was using the City's underside as a map, judging their location by landmarks high above.

The "path" seemed aimless, winding and sometimes doubling back, and two hours later, they were only halfway across the City's underside, by his estimation. They stopped to rest on a slab of slightly tilted sheet metal. Alania sat down and pulled her knees to her chest. Danyl remained standing. "How much farther?" he asked. He followed Spika's upward gaze, but he still didn't recognize anything.

"Just a few hundred meters," Spika said. "This has gone a lot better than I feared. The path hasn't changed. All the Drops since the last time I was up here must have been in other sectors."

Danyl nodded. *A few hundred meters,* he thought. The key in his pocket seemed to burn against his thigh. *Just a few hundred meters, and then into the City at last.* He glanced at Alania. *Home for her. Terra incognita for me.*

Although he doubted Alania's sheltered upbringing as ward/prisoner of Beruthi on Twelfth Tier would give her much advantage over him when it came to finding their way to Bertel's Bar on First. She'd only studied the lower Tiers virtually, same as him.

Spika might be able to help, but he had no intention whatsoever of telling Spika where they were really going. Once *she* was in the City, she'd be on home territory, and she'd already proven she'd betray her companions in a heartbeat if she could benefit from it. Poor dead Harker was proof. *But maybe we can use that* . . .

"Any City security systems to worry about?" he asked.

"Not here," Spika said. "What about at this hazardous waste tank?"

"Never seen any," Danyl said.

"Well then," Spika said. "We're practically home free."

"Practically," Danyl said.

Half an hour later, the Hazardous Waste Holding Tank came into sight, and he realized just how wrong he had been.

The tank rose out of the sea of trash all around it. Here under the City, the rubbish had not piled right up to the top of the concrete wall as it had on the other side, where he and Alania had climbed the morning she had dropped so unexpectedly into his life. *That was just the day before yesterday. Seems more like the century before last.* Danyl had planned to circle around the tank to his old stomping grounds and get inside the same way he and Alania had when they were fleeing the Rustbloods. But that plan shattered when he caught a flicker of movement atop the wall. It took him only an instant to realize what it was.

"Provosts!" he half cried, half gasped. "Down!"

He suited actions to words, flinging himself behind the nearest trash heap, out of sight of the watchers on the wall.

Spika and Alania crashed down beside him. "How many did you see?" Spika asked. "I only saw one."

"Two," Danyl said.

"Three," Alania said. "Two directly ahead, one rounding the corner to our left."

"Could be ten for all we can tell from here," Spika muttered. "What the hell are they doing up there? I thought they'd mostly cleared out after they took out the Rustbloods." She shot Danyl a look filled with suspicion and anger. "Waiting for you two?"

"I don't think so," Danyl said, but he thought, *if they are, we've already failed.* "Maybe they're planning to move on the Greenskulls?"

Spika shook her head. "Greenskulls are smarter than Rustbloods. We *pay* to be left alone."

"Bribes?" Alania sounded shocked.

Spika snorted. "Yeah," she said. "Bribes. If you can imagine."

Danyl chewed his lip. "My best guess is that they're up there because it gives them a view over the tops of the trash piles. So if something happened to draw their attention . . . we might be able to get by them."

"A distraction," Spika said.

"Exactly. Any ideas?"

"Yeah," she said. "Maybe." She sat up and, after a quick glance to be sure her head remained out of sight of the Provosts atop the walls of the waste-holding tank, peered off into the distance. She pointed. "You see that?"

Danyl followed her finger. "That upside-down dome?"

She nodded. "AWS."

Danyl whistled. "And it still works?"

"Yeah. We steer clear of it."

"Can't imagine why."

"AWS," Alania said. "Wait, I know this . . ." She frowned, and then her face cleared. "I remember. Automated Weapons System. There should be . . . let me think . . . twenty of them down here?"

Danyl glanced at her, impressed. "Yeah," he said. "The

City designers, whoever they were, figured the belly of the City was its most vulnerable part, just like the belly of an animal." He looked at Spika. "I know about them, but I've never seen one. Erl told me they'd all been ripped apart a long time ago, scavenged for weapons."

"This is the only one that's still active, as far as we know," Spika said. "It's a big Greenskull secret."

"Why?" Alania asked.

Spika gave her an unsmiling look. "Last Greenskull-Rustblood war, Greenskulls took out half a dozen Rustbloods by luring them under that one there. Thing used up a lot of ammo that day. Hope it still has some left."

"What do you intend?" Danyl asked.

"You saw that red barrel we passed a couple hundred meters back?"

Danyl nodded.

"The label on the side said 'Flammable waste. Do not puncture or expose to heat.'"

"Oh," Danyl said, suddenly understanding. "Yeah, that should prove a diversion."

"You're going to get the AWS to blow up that barrel?" Alania said.

Quick as always, Danyl thought. *It's like she's just as smart as I am.* His mouth quirked. *Guess that's understandable. Kind of annoying, but understandable.*

"Yeah," he said to Alania. Then, to Spika, "How do we rig it?"

"Roll it up to the top of a heap of rubbish, let it roll down into the kill zone. Run like hell. Even if it doesn't explode or burn, the fact that the AWS is firing should draw serious attention." She cocked her head at him. "Unless you've got a better idea?"

"It'll take two to handle the barrel," Alania pointed out. "The third should get to the Hazardous Waste Holding Tank and make sure nobody stays behind."

"Good thinking," Danyl said, impressed anew, not

only because she'd thought of something he hadn't, but also that she could be so matter-of-fact about what that could mean . . .

"That could mean shooting," Spika said, vocalizing his thoughts. She hefted her rifle. "Not letting either of you take this, and that slugthrower's no good for long-range work, so that means me." She looked at Alania doubtfully. "Sure you two are strong enough to move the barrel?"

"Let's find out first," Danyl said.

Keeping their heads down, they made their cautious way back to the barrel. It wasn't, fortunately, a particularly large barrel; it had probably been part of a waste-collection system in a workshop or factory, probably intended to be hauled away, emptied, and reattached to some piece of machinery. But instead it had simply been discarded and ended up down here. It was heavy but manageable for two people, though probably not for one.

"We can do it," Danyl said. He looked at Spika again. "Just one question. How do we recognize the kill zone?"

"Remember I told you it took out a bunch of Rust-bloods?" Spika said.

"Yeah . . ."

"Look for bits of Rustbloods."

Danyl grimaced. "Oh."

"Don't worry," Spika said. "It was a few months ago. The smell is probably mostly gone by now." She gave him a grim grin, teeth flashing white against her dark-skinned face. "I'm heading back to where we were. I'll wait there for an explosion or something."

She set off, disappearing between mounds of trash a moment later.

Danyl turned back to the barrel. Alania was staring past him, after Spika. "What if she decides to turn us in to the Provosts for a reward?"

The same thought had crossed Danyl's mind. "I don't think she'd risk it," he said after a moment. "Not down here. They could just throw her back into the Middens, and if the Greenskulls haven't figured out what she's done already, they will soon enough. She doesn't just *want* access to the City now; she absolutely *needs* it, same as us. Until we're inside, I think she'll stick to the plan. After that ... well, we'll worry about that when we get there." He bent down and put his hands under his end of the barrel. "Let's get moving."

Walking over the loose surface of the trash heap had never been easy; it was doubly difficult with the barrel. They sidled their way along winding paths, Danyl uneasily aware the entire time that if they were attacked, he couldn't do a thing about it. One shot into the barrel could flambé them both if its contents really were flammable.

But no one attacked them, and eventually, panting with the effort, they drew close enough to the dome of the AWS that he called a halt. "I've got to figure out where the kill zone is," he said. "Stay here."

"No," Alania said. "I need to know, too."

Danyl hesitated, then nodded. They climbed cautiously up a particularly large heap of tangled, half-melted plastic toward the AWS, and a moment later they peeked over the mound's top.

"Oh," Alania said in a small voice. "The kill zone."

Spika had told him what to expect, but he still felt his gorge rising at the carnage below ... and the smell of decay rising from it, not anywhere near gone. He counted six bodies, little more than skin and hair clinging to shattered bones: skulls, femurs, rib cages. The AWS had pulverized the men and women below, and the deadly threat it posed was best proven by the fact that several highly salvageable objects glinted among the remains: knives, chains, even something that looked 'tronic—a mapping unit, maybe. No one had dared go down there after them.

The slope below them looked both steep and reasonably solid: the perfect location for their ruse.

"What did they have to fight about?" Alania asked as they scuttled back down to where they had left the barrel.

"Who?"

"The Greenskulls and the Rustbloods."

"Prime scavenging grounds," Danyl said. "There are places where Drops happen regularly. The Rustbloods wanted to expand their territory; the Greenskulls fought back. The Rustbloods have never had any luck trying to take on the Greenskulls. They probably don't even *exist* now, with the Provosts all over the South Middens. The Greenskulls have always controlled the best Drop zones. If they have a deal with the Provosts, they probably control all of them now."

"Fighting over trash?" Alania said.

"People down here survive on trash," Danyl snapped more harshly than he intended, but her disbelieving tone had stung. "Scavenge, then barter what you scavenge at the Last Chance Market for food and whatever else you need. People will do what they have to to survive."

Alania didn't reply, but she looked thoughtful.

They took hold of the barrel and, grunting, hauled it up the slope. "The minute we let it go, we jump down this side again," Danyl said as they neared the top. "We don't know how wide its firing range is. Also, if this really goes up with a bang . . ."

"We don't want to go up with it," Alania said. "Got it."

They eased the barrel up onto a plastic crate half buried in paper. The crate sloped toward the AWS; all they had to do was release the barrel, and gravity would do the rest.

"Ready?" Danyl asked Alania.

"Ready," Alania replied.

"On three. One . . . two . . . three!"

They let go, and the red barrel started to roll, faster and faster, toward the kill zone below.

TWENTY-EIGHT

KRANZ'S DESPAIR LIFTED slightly when the second team of Provosts sent to Retreat Beruthi reported that their tracker had found signs that two people had fled before the explosion. It lifted more when the Provosts reported that the tracks led to wooden stairs down to a pier in the River. *There must have been a boat*, Kranz thought.

The likelihood of a boat capsizing and drowning all aboard in the white water of the upper Canyon seemed high, but Kranz refused to consider that possibility seriously; the abyss waiting on the other side of Alania's and Danyl's demise was too deep and dark to contemplate for long. It was an abyss into which he might fling himself headlong, like Falkin flying his aircar into the ground.

The River led eventually to the City, of course, but it seemed unlikely that a boat would take the duo all the way there. Delivering Alania and Danyl to the gangs in the Middens couldn't have been Beruthi's plan, and the Greenskulls who ran the northern side of the trash mountain would report anyone who came their way to the Provosts, as per the "arrangement" the Greenskulls—and the Provosts—thought Kranz didn't know about. A foolish thought. He hadn't done anything about the bribery because it kept the peace in the Middens. Not that he'd ever thought anything that happened in the Middens could threaten the City—at least not until three days ago—but having hooks into one of the gangs that ruled it seemed an excellent way to exert some kind of control down there.

A similar arrangement had never been managed with the Rustbloods, because they kept changing leaders: all brutal, none very bright. Now, of course, there was nobody left in the southern Middens, not after the Provosts' vicious sweep of the trash heap in the wake of their embarrassing loss of Danyl and their near-Pyrrhic "victory" over the River People. Three helicopters lost, two of them to a *crossbow*? They'd wanted revenge on someone, and while they'd taken a great deal of revenge on the River People themselves, very few of whom had emerged from the Whitewater Resort intact and ready for incarceration in Tenth Tier, blowing off a few Rustblood heads had apparently helped ease their shame as well.

Commander Havelin had delegated the Middens Expeditionary Force to a Sergeant Paskal. Kranz woke the Sergeant and told him to check in with his Greenskull contacts at first light to see if anything or anyone had washed up in their territory. He had also made it very, very clear that if anyone did, they were to be captured alive, disarmed, and turned over to the Provosts immediately. Paskal didn't turn on his video—Kranz couldn't blame him at 0200—but he suspected the Sergeant was blanching at the realization that the First Officer knew all about the Provosts' arrangement with the Greenskulls.

Not that Kranz cared.

"Send out drones along the Canyon at first light as well," he continued. "You're looking for a boat and possibly a camp on the shore. Circulate the photo of Alania to the Gate guards and any informants you have in the Bowels. I want her arrested the moment she makes an appearance."

"Yes, sir." Sergeant Paskal sounded very much like he was trying hard to stifle a yawn he was worried might offend Kranz.

"Sorry to have woken you, Sergeant," Kranz lied. "Get some sleep. But I want those orders issued before dawn."

"Yes, sir," Paskal said again.

"Dismissed." Kranz cut the connection.

He supposed he should follow his own advice and get some sleep, so he left his office and went down the hall to his bedroom. He stripped out of his uniform and got into bed, but sleep, as he had expected, proved elusive.

Morning would tell the tale. Either Danyl and Alania lived, or . . .

He dozed at last, falling into a fitful sleep punctuated by nightmares in which the red lights of the Captain's medical panel turned into the aiming lasers of beamer rifles tracking him as he fled through a maze of darkened hallways.

Alania had never heard—had never even *imagined*—a sound like the thunder of the Automated Weapons System firing at the barrel of waste they had rolled into its kill zone. However ancient the turret might be, its targeting systems clearly still worked perfectly. The barrel exploded just as they'd hoped, a splash of orange flame rising above the crest of the hill of plastic, followed by a mushroom of black smoke that reached all the way to the City's underside, spreading out into a rolling cloud.

"That'll bring 'em running," Danyl panted. "Come on."

They hurried as quickly as they could back down the path along which they'd lugged the red barrel just moments before, and a few minutes later, they were looking at the stained concrete walls of the Hazardous Waste Holding Tank once again. "Dammit," Danyl muttered. "There's still one up there."

Alania had already spotted the Provost at the northwest corner of the tank, looking through binoculars in the direction of the AWS, which continued to fire intermittently—at what, Alania wasn't sure, unless the black smoke was triggering its motion sensors. "Where's Spika?" she whispered.

"I don't—"

The AWS fired another brief burst, and at the same moment, a single sharp report rang out from off to the left, much closer to the hazwaste tank. It was almost lost in the AWS's thunder. The Provost arched his back and dropped out of sight. Alania imagined the body falling into the poisonous pond inside and hoped the man was dead before he hit it.

Danyl scrambled up and dashed for the hazwaste tank. Alania stumbled after him, shooting a look over her shoulder in the direction of the AWS and the still-billowing smoke. The guns spoke again. The Provosts wouldn't be able to get close to the turret unless they figured out some way to disable it, and all their attention was almost certainly focused on it.

It had to be, because if they were wrong about that . . .

They reached the pitted wall of the tank and moved along it to the northeast corner, where they found Spika tucked away just out of sight. "Worked," she said laconically. "Now what?"

"There's a ladder. South side. Come on." Danyl led the way through the drifted trash, and a few moments later Alania found herself looking at the very spot where she had fallen from the City just . . . the day before yesterday? *Is that all?*

They hurried to the same ladder Danyl had taken her up when the Rustbloods had been chasing them, and soon after that they stood on the ledge from which one of the twins had fallen to her death. The fumes rising from the liquid below both choked and burned them, much worse than the last time Alania had been at the tank. "We can't . . . stay here . . ." Spika gasped out.

"Won't," Danyl spat back. He hurried along the ledge.

The last time, Alania had barely registered the door at the end of the ledge. Holding her arm over her nose, she stumbled in her brother's wake to where the eternal gleamed above the smoothly sealed hatch. Danyl pulled out the golden key and slipped it into the port in the lockplate to the right of the doorframe.

With an ear-splitting groan, the hatch slid half open, fortunately just wide enough to admit entrance ... and stopped.. One by one they squeezed through into a short corridor ending in an elevator. Danyl closed the hatch behind them, shutting out the choking fumes, then inserted the key into the elevator's call panel. The door opened at once, though it shuddered as it did so. White lights flickered to life, and they crammed into a chrome-walled car. There were only two buttons: up and down. Danyl pushed the up button. The door slid closed.

Coughing, Alania lowered her arm and wiped her streaming eyes. Danyl blinked at her, his own eyes bloodshot. Spika's nose had dribbled blood; she swiped her hand across it, registered the red streak, then ignored it. "Where will this take us?" she demanded.

"I have no idea," Danyl said, but Alania knew that wasn't true. He'd studied the City as thoroughly as she had. *He just doesn't want Spika to know it.*

He drew his slugthrower. Spika raised her rifle to her shoulder.

The car stopped. The door opened. Alania tensed, but no Provosts waited to arrest them. White lights flickered to life but kept flickering, never steadying. They stepped into what she knew from her own studies was the haz-waste tank's control room, though the display screens and control panels were dark and covered with dust. Clearly no one had been there in years ... which rather explained the state of the tank.

Living on Twelfth Tier, she had never realized just how badly the City had deteriorated. In the plans she had studied, it was pristine. But down here was raw sewage flowing from broken pipes, a mountain of trash, the oozing Black River downstream, security systems that were mostly broken, dark and dusty control rooms . . . how had it come to this?

The dying Captain, Beruthi had claimed, but surely some—maybe most—of the fault rested with the Officers, who kept *their* Tiers functioning without regard to those below them. They escaped the City at every opportunity to live in the pristine countryside, *kept* pristine by dumping all the waste generated by their Estates and workers' villages into the Canyon.

And the leader of the Officers, ruling with an iron fist, was First Officer Kranz. The man who had spied on her her entire life, watching, waiting until she was old enough to plug into the City and ensure his rule continued.

Alania felt a surge of loathing, of hatred, that surprised her. In four days she had gone from fearing but respecting Kranz to detesting and despising him. So many people had died because of him. So many people had suffered—*were* suffering—because of him and the Officers he led. It was time to put an end to it, whatever that took. Even if it brought the whole City down in chaos, it would be worth it if it meant the end of Officer rule; whatever came afterward would *have* to be better. The people would never go back to this broken, stultified system once they were free to make their own choices.

For the first time, she understood why Danyl had agreed to allow himself to become Captain.

Spika shouldered her weapon and went to a station in the corner, a standard information terminal connected to the public network. It flickered to life at Spika's touch, rather to Alania's surprise. "Location," Spika demanded.

"You are here," said a female voice, the familiar voice of the City that Alania had heard every day of her life until the last three days. Danyl and Alania joined Spika at the terminal.

"Got it," Spika said, staring down at a map, where a blinking green light marked their location. "Maintenance Block 12."

"Staffed?" Danyl asked, and Alania knew why he asked; if the City were operating as it was supposed to, it would have been.

Spika snorted. "If it were, the Bowels wouldn't be the Bowels. I squatted down here for a while before I went on to the Middens. In three months I saw maybe two maintenance people and twice that many robots."

Danyl nodded. He studied the map, tracing his finger along it to the central elevators. Spika's eyes followed the movement like a bird of prey tracking something small and edible in long grass. "Heading up?" she said.

Danyl grunted. "Tenth."

"Prison break? Bold. You got a plan?"

"I've got a plan. But you're not coming with us, so . . ."

Spika shrugged. "Just curious."

Alania stared at Danyl. *Tenth?* Then she understood and approved. *He doesn't trust her.* "Where are *you* going?" she asked Spika.

"I've got a friend'll take me in," Spika said. "After that . . . I've got my own plans."

"Which are?" Danyl said.

"You're not coming with me, either," Spika said.

Danyl laughed. "Fair enough." He zoomed in the map. "There's a stair up to First not far away. We'll stick together that far, then split up. Okay?"

"Works for me."

The door opened at their approach, letting them into a corridor whose lights flickered exactly once, then went out with a sense of finality, leaving them to navigate by the dim green glow of emergency eternals once again. But they didn't have far to go before they found an exit, and it, too, slid open at their approach.

They stepped into a stairwell and climbed half a dozen flights to a door. Though it might have been locked from the other side, it wasn't from theirs, and they pushed it open and stepped out into a dark alley. Faint illumination came from around a corner to their left; to their right there was only darkness. The exit closed behind them and vanished into smooth metal.

The alley was roofed with corrugated steel maybe two meters over their heads, and across from them the dim light revealed a wall made of rough brick. Alania stared from one to the other. She'd known the original City plans she'd studied wouldn't match what the City was like now, but she hadn't expected anything so blatantly out of place.

"City maps like the one we just accessed don't count for much down here," Spika said. "Not much left of the original walls and structures. It's mostly a maze built from whatever workers can smuggle in or grab from the trash before it hit the Drops." She rapped the far wall. "Brick's kind of unusual. Lots of old metal like the ceiling over our heads. Lots of old plastic wall panels. Sometimes you'll see plastic sheeting or even cardboard or paper." She flashed them a grim smile in the gloom. "Watch yourselves down here. Provosts don't pay much more attention to what happens on First than they do in the Middens. Thanks for the access. I'm out of here." Then she turned and loped away, disappearing around the corner of the alley.

Alania heard footsteps running toward them on the other side of the corrugated-steel ceiling and looked up as they rattled overhead, afraid for a moment the whole thing would collapse on their heads . . . but it held. The footsteps hurried on.

She glanced at Danyl. "You lied about where we're going because you think she'll betray us."

Danyl nodded. "At the first opportunity. We were her ticket into the City, but now we're just salvage—something she can sell. And she's desperate, or she will be soon enough. The Greenskulls have tentacles in First and Second, I've heard. If they figure out she got up here . . ."

"If they do, they'll be looking for us, too," Alania said.

"Yeah," Danyl said. He drew his slugthrower. "So let's find this Bertel's Bar. It's supposed to be safe. Then we can figure out how to get up to Thirteenth."

"Without Beruthi?"

"He's dead. If this is going to happen, we have to do it ourselves." Danyl sounded angry. "What else can we do? If Kranz gets us, you're going to be made Captain, and nothing will change. If I can make *myself* Captain, then maybe I can *make* them change."

"You hope."

"Of course I *hope*. I'm not sure about anything. But Beruthi said this key can get us anywhere, even to Thirteenth. And he said the process of becoming Captain is automated. If we get there, maybe we can figure it out. At least we have to *try*."

Alania wished she could disagree . . . but she couldn't. They were on their own, but they still weren't free from the machinations they'd been part of since before they were born. "Maybe this Bertel will know something that can help us. But how do we find her?"

"I hate to say it, but we're going to have to ask for directions." Danyl looked after Spika, then turned in the opposite direction. "Pretty sure we don't want to follow her. This way."

Of course, since Spika had headed for the light, "this way" moved them deeper and deeper into darkness. It was daytime, so presumably the City's normal daylight illumination beamed down on the Tier from the ceiling, but if so, none if it penetrated to where they were. The only light came from the far end of the alley, where Spika had fled, until they came to a sharp left turn. Once they rounded it they were in utter darkness, navigating by feel, but after a few steps the corridor turned right again, and they saw more light—just a crack of it, fitful and

flickering, outlining a makeshift door made of corrugated metal like the ceiling.

The door had a wire handle and swung in their direction. Danyl cautiously pulled it open, and they found
themselves peering into a courtyard. Though two stories high, it still wasn't open to the Tier ceiling lights;
again, there was a ceiling of corrugated metal. A single
flickering light fixture hung up there. The corridor they
had been in was a lean-to attached to the brick structure that had surprised Alania when they'd entered the
Tier. The brick continued to their left.

To their right stretched the metal wall in which their
exit was located. Someone had scrawled the word POI-
SONERS across it in green paint.

"Well, that's comforting," Alania said.

"Gang sign," Danyl said. "Probably." He kept his
hand on his holstered slugthrower as he slowly turned to
take in the rest of the courtyard.

Across from them rose a wooden wall with multiple
windows shuttered with metal. To their left, the gap between the brick building behind them and the wooden
building in front of them had been sealed with a sheet of
black plastic. The only exit from the courtyard appeared
to be a door into the wooden building directly across
from them. It stood slightly ajar, and brighter light
gleamed through the opening.

"That," Alania said, "looks like a trap."

"Everything in this place looks like a trap," Danyl
said. He glanced over his shoulder. "We could go back
the way Spika went, but if her first order of business is to
sell us out . . ."

Alania looked at that too-inviting door. Then she
looked at the plastic sheeting to the left. "Got a knife?"
she asked.

Danyl followed her gaze. "I like the way you think, sis."

"Thanks," Alania said. "And don't call me sis, or I'll
have to call you bro."

Danyl grimaced. "I see your point." He shifted the slugthrower to his left hand, drew his belt knife with his right, and handed it to Alania. Then he took the slugthrower in his right again. "You do the honors. Probably a good idea to be ready with this, just in case."

Alania nodded and walked over to the sheet of plastic. Embossed letters on the metal plating of the floor read "London Lane"—the names of the streets on Twelfth were marked the same way. London was a city that figured prominently in many Earthmyth stories—those old tales had provided a lot of the City's street names. Alania had always wondered why.

The plastic sheeting glistened with condensation. *The air must be cooler on the other side.* She put her ear to the damp plastic, listening for voices or movement. She heard neither. She glanced at Danyl, who raised the slugthrower. "Go ahead."

She lifted the blade he had given her and stabbed it through the black membrane. It slid in easily, and she swept the knife down, opening a long gash. No one shouted or shot at them, but she stepped aside to let Danyl and his weapon go first. He pushed the opening wider. "Looks clear." He stepped through and disappeared.

Alania followed and found herself at last in a proper Tier street—or a segment of one, anyway—with Tierlight glowing down from four stories above, brighter and bluer than Twelfth's. To their left, the blank wall of the brick building, two stories high, ran down to the street into which Spika must have exited, while the wooden building ran the other way. The wall across from them was the pitted metal of some original Tier structure, its windows spray-painted black.

A cold breeze blew through the street, swirling dust along with it, and Alania shivered, her clothes still damp from the rain they had slogged through as they climbed the trash mountain and the dunking in the River before that. An old man hurried by, eyeing them warily and altering his path so that he stayed well out of their reach. Alania realized she was still holding the knife and passed it back to Danyl, who sheathed it. He'd already holstered his slugthrower.

"It's cold," she said. "Environmental controls must be screwed up along with everything else."

"I wouldn't know," Danyl said. "First time in the City, remember?" He looked up at the ceiling. "That's the only thing that looks the same as the virtual City I explored in our simulator."

"None of these weird buildings were in mine, either," Alania admitted. She pointed down the street. "Let's see what's at the other end of this wooden one."

They walked down the narrow lane. Alania heard voices ahead of them, and without a word, she and Danyl slowed, stopping at the corner of the building to peer into another courtyard. Just past this end of the wooden building was a space crammed with . . . well, *hovels* was the only word Alania could think of that seemed appropriate. The small shelters made of scraps of lumber, plastic, metal, and cloth clung to the base of the wooden building. There was a building made of plastic wall panels across from it, and the metal Tier wall rose off to their right. Alania gave it a close look in case it had security cameras on it, but there were only a few broken supports where cameras or other equipment might once have been perched. Wary eyes watched them from the shadows of the rickety shelters. The few people in the open turned to stare at them, faces closed and unfriendly.

"They don't look like they're likely to give us directions," Alania said. She looked up the side of the building across from them, a weird structure with balconies and stairs jutting out at odd angles. Her eyes briefly met those of a small girl staring down at them. The girl squeaked and disappeared.

What kind of life does she have to look forward to?

Alania thought, and then, guiltily, *Bet it doesn't include lavish birthday parties.*

The street continued to the left, so they did, too. They crossed a new street sign: Bombay Boulevard. The hovels continued as well, choking the boulevard to a narrow lane. In places, the metal was covered with trash and liquids Alania did her best to step over or around, not through. Not everyone hid from them, but everyone's eyes followed them. "I don't like this," she muttered to Danyl.

"The street up ahead looks busier," Danyl said. His eyes flicked from side to side as they walked, and his hand rested on his slugthrower, but nobody approached or spoke to them.

A few moments later they emerged onto Singapore Street. For a block in either direction, First Tier looked almost like the more utilitarian parts of Twelfth Tier—as long as Alania ignored the garbage blowing along the streets, the precarious-looking balconies, and the pungent blue liquid dripping from somewhere high above, which formed a steaming puddle flowing sluggishly down a crude drain that had apparently been cut in the floor with a hacksaw . . .

Actually, it didn't look like Twelfth Tier at all.

A few shabbily dressed people hurried along the street, heads down, not meeting *anyone's* eyes. There were shops of a sort, selling—or more likely bartering— used clothes and housewares, and there was one food store that seemed to traffic entirely in mealpaks like the ones they'd unenthusiastically consumed on Beruthi's boat. The shop structures were only slightly sturdier than the hovels in the street they'd left behind.

A woman approached from their left. Danyl placed himself in front of her, and she pulled up short. She wore a shapeless black dress, her hair tucked up under a white scarf. "Hi," Danyl said. "Can you help us?"

The woman's eyes flicked left and right. "Don't hurt me," she whispered.

Alania stepped to Danyl's side. "We're not going to hurt you. We just need directions."

"City map," the woman mumbled. "Information station. Next block." She stepped to one side to go around them, but Alania moved in front of her again.

"We've seen a City map," she said, keeping her voice as friendly and nonthreatening as she could. "It wasn't much help. We're looking for Bertel's Bar."

For a moment it looked like the woman would answer, but then her gaze flicked right and her eyes widened. "Ask *him*," she hissed, then darted past before Alania could block her path again.

Danyl stared after her. "Ask *who*?"

"Me," said a voice from behind them. Alania's heart skipped two beats and then started racing. She whirled, as did Danyl, to find a young man looking at them from an open door that had been closed seconds before. "I can take you there." He smiled. His incisors had been sharpened to points, turning his grin feral. "For a price, of course."

Danyl's hand had flown to the slugthrower; he kept it there. "What price?" he snarled.

"That nice little piece you've got on your belt," the young man said.

Danyl's hand gripped tighter. "Why would I give it to you?"

"Because if you don't, I'll burn you down where you stand," said another voice behind them.

Alania whirled again.

A teenaged girl stared calmly at them, a beamer in her hand.

TWENTY-NINE

DANYL WAS A hair's-breadth away from drawing his slugthrower when the boy spoke—and therefore probably a hair's-breadth away from dying, since the girl with the beamer would have sliced him down before his own weapon cleared the holster. The young man—who looked to be a couple of years younger than Danyl and Alania—came around in front of them and allowed his pointy-toothed smile to grow even wider. "This is my little sister," he said. "She has a beamer. All I've got is a knife. So you see, I need your slugthrower to make us equal. Sibling rivalry and all that."

Danyl very carefully removed his hand from the slugthrower's grip.

Alania was looking from one to the other. "I can see the family resemblance," she said slowly, and Danyl could see it now, too. Although the younger girl didn't have the boy's sharpened incisors, the rest of her face was just as lean and predatory . . . and both, though he couldn't say exactly how, seemed strangely familiar to him.

"Look who's talking," the boy said. "You two twins?"

"Um . . . kind of," said Alania. She looked at the girl's beamer. "If you want the slugthrower, why not just shoot us and rob us?"

Don't give them ideas, Danyl thought, but like Alania, he knew something else was going on besides ordinary robbery.

"We don't steal," snapped the girl with the beamer. "We barter."

"Right," the boy said cheerfully. "I'm offering you a business transaction. I show you the way to Bertel's Bar, you give me the slugthrower in exchange. Deal?"

"What if I turn it down?" Danyl said.

The boy shrugged. "Then I offer a different deal. You give me the slugthrower, my sister doesn't shoot you. Still a business transaction."

"How is that different from robbing?" Alania demanded.

"If we were robbers," the girl said, as if explaining something to a very dim child, "I would have shot you two blocks ago, when we first started trailing you."

"If we were robbers," the boy said in the same tone of voice, "this encounter would end with you dead and stripped and us alive and richer."

"That's still one possible outcome," Alania said.

"Yes," the girl agreed. "But only one. Since we are barterers, *not* robbers, we are offering you an alternative outcome—one in which you do *not* end up dead."

Danyl sighed. "I'll take it."

"I thought you would," the boy said. He held out his hand. Danyl unbuckled his belt, slipped off the holstered slugthrower, and handed it to the boy, who attached the holster to his own belt. "Any more ammo?" he said.

"No," Danyl said shortly. "It's at the bottom of the River. Now take us to Bertel's."

"Follow me," the boy said. He turned around and led them back down Singapore Street and across the mouth of Bombay Boulevard. Men who had watched them suspiciously before quickly turned away this time. The boy led them to another ramshackle wooden structure and through a door Danyl doubted he would have spotted on his own. "Almost there. It's straight down the hall, up the stairs, third floor." The boy smiled again, sharp teeth gleaming against his upper lip, and patted the slug-thrower. "Thanks for this."

Danyl felt a strong desire to shove those sharp teeth down the boy's throat, but the girl still held her beamer ready, and she wasn't smiling.

"If it's any consolation," the boy said, "Bertel's has a strict no-weapons policy. We would have confiscated your weapon anyway."

"We?"

"Bertel's our mother," the boy said. "We're the bouncers. And we've been expecting you. Prime told us you'd be coming."

"What?" Alania said.

Danyl's fists clenched. "If you were going to bring us here anyway, why go through this charade?"

"For fun." The boy grinned. "This way." He led them down the hallway to a narrow staircase and up it two floors to a wooden door that opened to a push. Danyl, with Alania behind him and the beamer-armed girl behind her, followed him down a dark corridor with walls made of wooden planks roughly nailed together. At the end of the hall, a beaded curtain hung across an archway through which came the smell of baking bread. Danyl's mouth watered, and he heard Alania's stomach rumble; he glanced at her with a raised eyebrow, and she gave him an embarrassed smile.

"Sorry," she said. "Long time since we ate. And that stew on the boat . . . blech."

"Blech," Danyl agreed. Since that sad meal on the boat, they'd capsized, waded ashore, climbed a mountain of trash, distracted Provosts, sneaked into the Bowels of the City, made their way to First Tier . . . and been easily taken prisoner by two teenagers. Which was way more embarrassing than Alania's growling stomach.

Danyl had pictured Bertel's Bar as a filthy hole-in-the-wall where the down-and-out came to drink away their troubles. But what they found on the other side of the dangling beads was a small but clean room with four round tables and a bar of polished wood, glowing in the light of yellow lamps. Danyl stared around. "I don't get it. How can this place have a clientele?"

"Our clientele is . . . select," said the girl.

"What my daughter means," said a woman, coming into sight behind the bar through another beaded curtain, "is that Bertel's Bar is open by invitation only."

Danyl studied her with interest. Thin, almost gaunt, with sharp features Danyl could absolutely see echoed in the faces of her children, she had the largest, strongest-looking hands he had ever seen on a woman. Her red hair, just beginning to show gray, was piled carelessly atop her head. She wore a clean white apron over a worn green dress . . . and over both, a belt bearing a holstered slugthrower, twin of the one he had been forced to hand over to her son. *Probably* is *its twin*, he thought. *Erl was one of the Free, and she must be, too. How many sources of weapons can they have?*

"My name is Elissa Bertel," the woman said. "Prime told me you would be coming and to hide you until he arrives."

Danyl shook his head. "He's not coming. He's dead."

He didn't expect the reaction he got. The woman went pale and clutched at the bar. "No . . ." Behind them, the teenagers gasped.

"It's a lie!" the boy shouted.

"It's true," Alania said, turning to them. "We saw him die."

The girl sobbed. Danyl glanced back to see her head buried in her brother's shoulder, her beamer hanging loose at her side. The boy's face had gone as white as Bertel's. *What's going on?*

Alania put two and two together faster than he did. "He was your father, wasn't he?" she said softly to the young-sters, then turned back to Bertel. "And your husband."

"Not husband." Bertel's mouth twisted. Tears glistened on her cheeks. "How could he be? He was an Officer. But we loved each other."

The girl continued to sob.

Danyl felt an unfamiliar pang of shame. "I'm sorry," he said awkwardly. "I shouldn't have been so blunt."

"You had no way of knowing," Bertel said. "And even if you had, there's no soft way to break such news." With visible effort, she straightened. "How did he die?"

"Provosts came for him at his Retreat," Danyl said. "He planned to give himself up, sure he could talk his way out of any charges. He surrendered, but something went wrong. A Provost shot him, and then his security robots . . . blew up everything. There's nothing left."

The girl's sobs cut off, and she stormed around in front of him and Alania. "And who the hell are *you*?" she snarled through her tears. She pointed the beamer at his face. "Who the hell are you that my father should die for you?"

"Stand down, Pertha," Bertel snapped. "You know Ipsil told me they were coming."

Danyl met the girl's eyes steadily. "Your father worked for twenty years to get me right where I am now," he said softly.

Pertha glared at him a moment longer, then her eyes flooded with tears again, and she lowered the beamer and moved to one of the tables, where she sat down heavily. Her brother, dry-eyed but grim-faced, went to her and draped his arms protectively over her shoulders.

"We don't know what Ipsil intended," Bertel said. "Do you?"

Danyl hesitated, not sure what he should tell her. He settled on, "Not exactly," which was certainly the truth.

"There must be a second-in-command," Alania interrupted, and Danyl shot her a look of gratitude. "Someone who will take over as Prime?"

Bertel shook her head. "Not inside the City. Second

to Ipsil was Erl. If you could get back in touch with him ..."

Danyl shook his head. "Erl might be dead, too."

Bertel's shoulders sagged. "Then the Free Citizens has been decapitated."

Alania looked at Danyl. "What do we do?"

"I don't know," Danyl said. Anger bubbled up in him. "How the hell am I supposed to know? Until three days ago, I didn't know anything about the Cityborn, or the Free Citizens, or Beruthi, or—" His voice choked off.

"Do you know anything about what he intended?" Bertel asked quietly.

Danyl took a deep breath. "Only in broad strokes. I know I have to get to Thirteenth Tier. After that ..." *After that, I don't have a fucking clue. Except that I'm supposed to become Captain. Whatever that means.*

"Thirteenth?" said the boy, staring at him. "That's impossible."

"Not according to your father," Danyl said.

"But ... why?" Bertel asked. "To kill the Captain?"

Alania, to his relief, stepped in again. "What did Beruthi tell you about us?"

"Very little," Bertel said. "But ..." Her eyes flicked past them, at her children. "I know you were his ward on Twelfth Tier, while you"—she nodded to Danyl—"were raised by Erl in the Middens. I know you are called Cityborn. I know the future of the City hinges on you. But how that can be true ..." She shook her head. "I don't have the slightest idea."

Then we can't tell you, Danyl thought. *For your protection ... and ours.* "Can you get us to an elevator that will take us to Thirteenth Tier?"

"No," Bertel said.

Danyl's anger rose again. He felt his fists clench ... and then a soft touch on his arm. Alania gave him a warning look and shook her head slightly. "Why not?" she asked, and her tone was far softer and more sympathetic than he could have managed. All *he* could think of were the Provosts who might be closing in on them even now.

"No elevators go to Thirteenth from the lower Tiers," Bertel said. "As far as I know, nobody knows how to get to Thirteenth Tier except the First Officer."

Alania gasped. "Oh . . ." she said. She gave Danyl a wide-eyed look. "It's in his house! Quarters Kranz. Where I was being taken when this all started. That's the only access to Thirteenth. It has to be."

Danyl snorted. "So all we have to do is to get to Twelfth, break into Kranz's quarters, find this special elevator, and somehow make it to Thirteenth . . . *without Kranz noticing?*" He rolled his eyes. "*Per*fect."

"You can't even get to Twelfth," Bertel said flatly. "Not unless you . . ." Her voice trailed off. "Oh," she said after a moment, much more softly. "He gave you a key, didn't he?"

"An access key?" The boy suddenly released his sister and rounded the table to face them. "You have a high-level *City access key*?" He spun to his mother. "Mom, with a key like that, we could get out of First. Up as many Tiers as we want. You have money. You could set up the restaurant you've always wanted on Fifth or Sixth, even Seventh, maybe even Eighth. You wouldn't have to—"

The key won't do you any good unless you have the Captain's genetic tags, Danyl thought, but he couldn't tell them that—and he didn't have to.

Bertel silenced her son with a sharp, "No! *No*, Kreska. Your father believed these two could free the City. We have to do everything we can to make that happen."

"These two?" Kreska glared at Danyl and Alania. "They can't even find their way around First. They don't have a fucking clue what they're doing." His contemptuous assessment so closely echoed Danyl's own thoughts that it stung. "How are *they* supposed to free the City?"

"I don't know," Bertel said. "But your father did. He

believed they could do it, and he gave his life so they could make the attempt. That's good enough for me." Her lips tightened. "Is it good enough for you?"

The boy stared at her. Then he turned to Danyl and Alania again. And then he . . . wilted. "Yes," he said. "Of course."

"Good." Bertel stood as straight as ever, though her face was slick with sweat, and her hands still clutched the edge of the table. Danyl knew she must want to retreat and weep and rage—but she didn't. "Then you will guide them to the elevator in Sector One."

"They can't—" Kreska began, but then he subsided. "Of course they can. If Father gave them a key."

"Exactly." Bertel looked at Alania and Danyl. "Your key will operate all elevators, but the public elevators are of no use to you. They are closely monitored, and the Provosts will spot you the minute you enter one. Even the segregated Officer elevators in the Core are no better."

"But this Sector One elevator is different?" Alania asked. She frowned, and Danyl thought he knew why— like him, she must be running over her knowledge of the City's construction. *Sector One elevator . . . oh!* He looked at her, and they said, "Maintenance elevator!" together.

Danyl turned back to Bertel. "But those were shut down ages ago by the Officers for security reasons. Most of the shafts have been cut through."

"Not this one," Alania said. She looked bemused.

Bertel nodded. "In Ipsil's father's day, it only went as far down as Fifth, where the Beruthi factories are. But Ipsil discovered that the shaft was intact below that. As Prime, he thought he could make good use of a private elevator from Twelfth to First, and of course, once we met . . ." She colored slightly, and Danyl knew exactly what kind of "good use" Beruthi had put the elevator to. "He had it secured so he was the only one who could use it."

"Except once," Alania murmured.

Bertel glanced at her with a puzzled expression.

"But with this key, we can use it, too," Danyl said.

Bertel nodded. "Almost certainly."

"Where will it take us?" Danyl asked.

But this time, it was Alania who answered. "Quarters Beruthi," she said. "Where I grew up."

THIRTY

PERTHA LEAPED to her feet, her chair toppling backward to crash against the wooden floor. Anger had wiped the grief from her face, though tears still glistened on her cheeks—anger that was focused, beamer-like, on Alania, as was the actual beamer. "You lived with my father every day of your life! I only saw him once every couple of weeks . . . or *months*. And now we're sending *you* back to the home you shared with him? The home where he spent all the time with you that you stole from us?"

"Not home." Anger and grief rose inside Alania, too. "*Not* home. It was *never* home. It was where I lived, but I got no love from your father. At least you had that!"

"At least you had *him*!"

"I would have traded what I had for what you enjoyed."

"Wealth? Comfort? Everything your heart desired? Don't lie to me."

"*Everything my heart desired* was a father or mother!"

Pertha opened her mouth to say something else, but her mother's voice cut her off. "Enough! Your father wanted us to help the Cityborn. He died so we could help them. *We will honor his wishes.*"

Pertha spun to face her. "Why? You're right, he's dead. But they have a City access key. With a key, we could have a new life. A better life."

"A short life," Danyl said harshly, while Alania was

still trying to figure out how to tell Pertha the key wouldn't work for anyone but her and Danyl, without telling her more about the Cityborn than it was safe for her or her family to know. "I don't understand everything that I—that *we* are, but if we don't succeed, if we don't get to Thirteenth Tier . . . I think things are going to go very badly in the City very soon."

Pertha twisted around again. "It couldn't be worse than it is now," she snarled.

"Yes, it could," Alania said softly. "You could lose what you already have. A home. A brother. A mother. A family."

"Pertha," Bertel said, speaking now in a pleading whisper. "Please."

For a moment Pertha kept the beamer pointed at Danyl and Alania; then she jerked it down. "Fine!" She glared at them. "But not for you. Not for the Free. Not for some stupid revolution that will never change a thing. Only because of Father. Because I loved my . . ." Her voice broke. She turned to Kreska. "You take them. I can't . . ."

Kreska nodded mutely.

"Kreska, give Danyl back his slugthrower," Bertel said.

Kreska silently complied. Danyl slipped the holster back onto his belt without a word.

"There's a path to the Sector One elevator through the service level," Bertel said. "It's still secure."

"You're sure?" Danyl said.

"It has its own security system," Bertel said. "And it hasn't been triggered."

Danyl nodded. "Good. Then let's get going."

"Wait a minute," Alania said.

Danyl shot her a look. "Why?"

She ignored him, going instead to Bertel. She took the older woman's hands. "I'm so sorry for your loss," she murmured. "So sorry you didn't have more time to spend with Beru—with Ipsil. So sorry I saw him every day, even

if we weren't close, and you hardly saw him at all. If
everything had gone as he'd hoped . . ."

"In my experience," Bertel said, her face bleak,
"nothing *ever* goes as we hope." But then her expression
softened. "All the same . . . thank you."

Alania nodded, then surprised herself—and certainly
Bertel—by giving the woman a hug. She stepped back
and turned to face Bertel's children and Danyl. Danyl's
expression was unreadable; Kreska and Pertha looked
grim. New tears tracked down Pertha's face.

"All right," Alania said to Kreska. "Now we can go."

Kreska took a deep breath. "This way."

He didn't lead them back the way they had come but
through the beaded curtain behind the bar into the
kitchen. A door there opened into a pantry, just a small
room with very little on the shelves—a few sacks of flour,
some canned goods, salt, a few spices. At Kreska's touch,
the shelves at the back swung aside, revealing a staircase
spiralling down, lit by—Alania sighed—the dim green
glow of eternals.

"How was this done?" Danyl asked, staring down.

"Beruthi Enterprise robots built the whole path without anyone up above being the wiser," Kreska said.
"They were supposed to be doing ordinary maintenance
on the sewer pipes and ventilation ducts—which should
have raised suspicions right there, if you ask me, considering how rarely we *see* maintenance done on First. A lot
of the way, it's just a narrow corridor carved out of exist-
ing corridors that are now a meter skinnier than they
used to be. But in a few places the robots had to get
more . . . creative. As you'll see. Wait a second." He
turned to the right and placed his hand on a glass plate
in the wall.

"Kreska recognized and approved," said the familiar
voice of every computer in the City.

"Two approved guests," Kreska said.

"Please have guests present palm prints for scanning."

Kreska nodded at Alania, who put her palm to the plate. "Alania Beruthi," the voice said. "Recognized and approved."

Alania felt a chill that the system knew who she was. But even if this was Beruthi's own private system, it undoubtedly had access to the City's central databases, and she had lived openly in the City—well, as openly as her guardian/captor had allowed—for twenty years.

Danyl stepped forward and presented his palm to the plate. "Unknown male," the voice said. "Kreska, please confirm approval."

"Approval confirmed," Kreska said, though from his tone, he wished he hadn't had to.

"Unknown male approved," the computer said.

Kreska pushed by Danyl and led the way onto the stairs. The door to the pantry closed behind them.

They spiraled tightly down to street level and two levels lower, almost as low as the Bowels. For the first hundred meters or so, Beruthi's "secret path" was much like any other City corridor, though narrower—except, of course, that it was lit by damnable eternals. But then they had to crawl on their hands and knees for twenty meters beneath an insulated pipe through which Alania heard the rush of liquid. The next stretch of the path was so narrow they had to turn sideways, and one wall was alarmingly warm. Strange noises accompanied them: clattering, roaring, pounding.

After several twists and turns and stairs up and ladders down, Alania had no concept of where they were in relation to where they had started, but at last they reached a small room with a single elevator door and a standard lockplate in the wall next to it. Kreska indicated it. "I can't open it," he said. "Try your key."

Danyl nodded. He pulled the golden rod from his pocket and inserted it into the lockplate. A light flashed green. "Elevator access granted," said the familiar City-computer voice, and the door opened as Danyl removed the key from the plate. He blinked at the interior of the elevator. "What the . . . ?"

A quiescent cleaning robot took up about half of the space, and its various attachments hung from the walls.

"It's the broom closet from the hallway outside my room," Alania said. "Believe it or not." She felt a strange pang at the sight of the familiar space. She couldn't really be homesick for Quarters Beruthi . . . could she?

"Father was clever," Kreska said, his voice tight. He looked from Alania to Danyl. "I guess this is where I'm supposed to wish you luck. So . . . I hope you succeed at whatever it is you have to do, for Father's sake. For Mom's sake." He paused as if he were going to say something else, then abruptly turned and strode down the hidden passage without looking back.

Alania turned back to the elevator. "I know how to get from Quarters Beruthi to Quarters Kranz," she told Danyl. "But as for how we'll get *into* it . . ."

"First we have to get *out* of Beruthi's house," Danyl pointed out. "Kranz must have searched it—might *still* be searching it. We may not be alone when we get there. Even if he's done with the search, he may have Provosts stationed there to see who comes calling."

"Quarters Beruthi is a big place, and I know every centimeter of it," Alania said. "If we're cautious . . ."

"We'll still be left with the problem of how to get into Quarters Kranz." Danyl sighed. "Well, one thing at a time." He indicated the cleaning closet/elevator. "After you, sis."

"I told you not to call me that, bro," Alania said as she entered. Danyl crowded in behind her.

The door closed, and they began their ascent.

I'm going home, Alania thought.

But as she'd told Pertha, it didn't feel that way.

They're alive.

The flood of relief Kranz felt as Sergeant Paskal reported what had happened in the northern Middens the morning after Beruthi's spectacular unplanned demise blotted out many of the details the Sergeant insisted on providing.

"...patrols turned up a capsized submarine... Greenskull contacts told me a sentry reported seeing someone, then claimed she didn't...killed another sentry...diversionary explosion...Provost killed at the Hazardous Waste Holding Tank...gained access to the City through the..."

"That's enough, Sergeant," Kranz said, cutting off the flow of words. The Provost was clearly flustered to be reporting what he must have assumed Kranz would take as bad news, especially since he knew Commander Havelin was listening in, his face side by side with the Sergeant's in Kranz's desktop display. Someone would have to be punished, of course, but that could wait until later. For now, the important thing was that the Cityborn had survived the explosion at Retreat Beruthi and had very kindly delivered themselves back to the City, right where he needed them to be. Now it was only a matter of time before he recaptured them.

Kranz shot a reflexive glance at the Captain's medical monitor. *Hopefully not very much time.* "Thank you, Sergeant," he said, turning his attention back to the screen. "You're dismissed."

He killed the connection before the Sergeant could finish his salute and turned his undivided attention to Commander Havelin. "Do you have a name for this missing Greenskull sentry, Commander?"

Havelin nodded. "Spika Constant, sir. We're already searching for her on First. She lived there for many years, so we're monitoring known contacts and haunts. We should have her soon. The other two may well be with her—"

"No, I doubt that," Kranz said. "They'll try to lose themselves in the general population. I know our security camera coverage is . . . spotty on First Tier, so we'll need more boots on the floor. I want a thorough search of the Tier and Provosts stationed in all public spaces, *especially* around the Core. Arrest them on sight, but carefully—it's vital that they're captured unharmed." He sharpened his voice. "You hear that, Commander Havelin? *They must not be harmed.* I don't want a repeat of what happened to Beruthi."

"Understood," the Commander said.

"Keep me apprised," Kranz said. "First Officer out."

The screen blanked. Kranz leaned back in his chair, thinking hard.

He was glad Beruthi had sent the two Cityborn back to the City, but why had he done it? Why put Alania back within easy reach of Kranz?

Of course, he'd expected to still be operating in the clear as Lieutenant Commander Beruthi. Which meant his original plan must have involved smuggling the two of them into his own quarters. But from there . . . what?

There could be only one explanation. Beruthi intended to replace the old Captain not with Alania, but with Danyl. Danyl, whose nanobots had been programmed for years by the docbot Beruthi had modified. Kranz had programmed Alania's nanobots to rewrite her memories and personality once they were fully activated, turning her into a new Kranz. Beruthi must have similarly primed Danyl, but his goal must have been to keep the boy as quiescent as the old Captain, allowing him to seize control as the new First Officer.

Kranz knew well enough how hated he was in certain circles of the City, and even among the Officers: hated because of his methods, hated because of the power his family had wielded for generations, hated for his wealth. He didn't mind that hatred; he preferred to think of it as respect. Even the Officers did not know what every

Kranz knew, the truth burned into them by the nanobots carrying the memories of the first First Officer Kranz. They did not know that only the strong and steady hand of the First Officer and the armed power of the Provosts kept the City and the Heartland from collapsing into chaos. They didn't know just how narrow was the knife's edge on which their very existences balanced. Only the Kranzes knew the truth. Only the Kranzes knew how heroically and selflessly Thomas Kranz had acted when he overthrew the Captain and set himself up as the City's ruler. It hadn't been because he sought power but because he sought safety, security, and stability for the City's then-sleeping citizens. He had allowed them to Awaken into a world that worked rather than into chaos and uncertainty.

Once Alania became Captain and she received the Kranz programming, she too would know the truth, would know how important it was to keep tight control over the fragile society humanity had established in the City and Heartland. With her as Captain and First Officer rolled into one, stability would be ensured for another five hundred years. Even the resentment directed at the Officers would ease once the City was restored to full working condition.

But if the Captain died before she could be replaced . . .

Old nightmares ran through Kranz's head, nightmares passed down from Thomas Kranz, nightmares from before the City stood in the Heartland: fighting, blood, fire, memories of the revolution the original Kranz had led to save all the then-sleeping inhabitants from certain disaster, fears of what would happen if the revolution failed. Thomas Kranz, with regret but without hesitation, had killed his best friend during the fighting. That fierce sense of duty, that determination to let nothing stop him from doing what he knew to be necessary, flowed through Kranz's veins, too—as it would soon flow through Alania's.

Beruthi had known about the Kranz nanobots, but of course he did not share the Kranz memories. Clearly he hadn't understood, as Kranz had foolishly hoped he would. Beruthi must have seen Kranz as nothing but a dictator weakened by the death of Falkin, the failure of the cloning unit, and the degradation of the Kranz nanobots—ripe for overthrow. And so he'd had Danyl abducted and raised by Erl and made sure the third usable Cityborn baby was killed. And then—the cold-blooded rationality of it was something Kranz could almost admire—he had raised Alania for Kranz himself, always planning to have her removed from the equation before Kranz could make use of her, clearing the way for Beruthi to install Danyl as his pet Captain.

Kranz had probably surprised him, coming for Alania on the very day of her twentieth birthday; he hadn't warned Beruthi about that. Perhaps Beruthi had had a cleverer plan for Alania's abduction that hadn't yet been ready, so he had fallen back on the ragtag collection of street thugs from the lower Tiers who had failed so miserably. Or perhaps their failure had just been bad luck. Either way, Beruthi had clearly seen a chance long ago and thrown the dice, hoping to win the jackpot. Now he was dead, but the dice were still rolling. And if something happened to Alania and Danyl . . .

Without Beruthi, they're just two young people trying to avoid arrest, Kranz reassured himself. *Even if they know Beruthi's intention, they can't act on it. They can't get to the Captain. And without Beruthi's encouragement, why would they even try? Unless . . .*

Kranz frowned. Perhaps Beruthi, hoping to seize control, had very carefully *not* told Alania and Danyl what it would really mean to become Captain, and they thought it entailed nothing more than ordering people around. In that case, they might try something spectacularly foolish . . .

He'd been chasing events for too long. Perhaps he could get in front of them at last.

He touched the communicator screen, calling up Lieutenant Commander Shaloma Trishel, his Head of Household Security. "Seal the house," he ordered when the woman's angular face appeared. "It's possible two fugitives may try to enter it."

"Fugitives?" Trishel said, left eyebrow lifting.

"Alania Beruthi and a young man. If you see them, apprehend them—gently. *Do not harm them.* Hold them until I get there."

Trishel nodded once. "Yes, sir."

"First Officer out." Kranz killed the connection. He rubbed the back of his neck. *There's only one person who might know Beruthi's entire plan,* he thought. His last attempt to question that individual had been unsatisfactory, but the doctor had held out hope . . .

He rolled his chair back from his desk. Time to pay a visit to the hospital.

The journey to Quarters Beruthi took ten minutes, but it seemed to last ten years. Alania knew they were rising through the Tiers, but after the initial upward acceleration, they could have simply been standing in a stationary broom closet. She stared around at the familiar cleaning equipment, remembering that long-ago adventure to Fifth Tier. She'd noticed way back then that the elevator's only other stop besides Fifth was First, but she'd never imagined the reason why. She had never even considered the possibility that Lieutenant Beruthi, the famously single Officer who seemed to prefer the company of robots to people, might have a lover and two children on the lowest Tier of all.

She wondered when and how he had met Bertel. How

much of Beruthi's desire to overthrow the First Officer came from his firsthand knowledge of how difficult life was in the lower Tiers?

And yet . . .

Alania remembered the other candidate baby, a sister to herself and Danyl, who had been "eliminated." How could the man Bertel, Pertha, and Kreska had so obviously loved have ordered such a draconian action? How could one reconcile the two sides of such a person?

His own children hadn't been born yet. Maybe that would have made a difference.

Maybe. But maybe not. If there was one thing Alania had learned in the past three days, it was that people were complicated.

She looked at Danyl, who held his slugthrower in both hands, pointed at the floor. She read his tension in the way the muscles in his neck stood out. "We're going to come out in a third-floor hallway," she told him. "There's unlikely to be anyone there."

"Unlikely isn't the same as impossible," Danyl returned shortly, which of course Alania couldn't argue with, since it was true.

Finally she felt a change—they were slowing. Danyl aimed the slugthrower at the door.

They stopped.

The door opened.

Nobody shot or even shouted at them.

Danyl took a quick look into the hall, left-right, then stepped back into the closet/elevator. "Clear," he said. "And wow. I had no idea people lived like this."

"Like what?" Alania squeezed past him into the hallway. It hadn't changed in the slightest. *Well, why would it? You were still living here just four days ago.* Which was objectively true but subjectively hard to believe.

Beruthi had always favored a very conservative decor; the hallway was almost oppressive, with its dark wood paneling and thick red carpet. Golden chandeliers provided ceiling light, while paintings and sculptures were set into softly lit niches in the walls between the doors. There were thirteen doors in all, as Alania knew well: eight to their left, four to their right, and the hidden one at the end of the hallway, which opened into the servants' stair where she had hidden from the watchbot with Lissa and Sandi.

Alania had never understood why Beruthi needed so many rooms, why *any* of the senior Officers needed the vast quarters they occupied. There was never a need to stay over at some other senior Officer's house, since they all lived on the same Tier. Perhaps out in the country at the Retreats and Estates it made sense, but why here?

Of course, Beruthi hadn't built this house. He had inherited it, and the only reason he rated such a massive amount of space was how integral to the operation of the City his family had been over the decades with their near monopoly on robotic and computer technology.

Alania wondered to whom the house would go now Beruthi was dead and disgraced. *It* should *go to Bertel and Kreska and Pertha*, she thought, but of course that was impossible. No, it would go to some other Officer, and the infighting to claim it would be intense.

Or would it? If they succeeded . . .

Suddenly she heard voices from somewhere downstairs. They weren't alone.

"Damn!" Danyl raised the slugthrower.

Alania pushed it down again. "That's coming from the main floor," she whispered. She tugged at his hand and pulled him toward the stairs.

He resisted. "We can't go down there!"

"We're not going down the main stairs," Alania said impatiently. "There's a door you can't see." Danyl relented, and she led him toward the hidden servants' stair, their footsteps muffled by the carpet's thick weave. They passed the door to her old room, but she resisted the urge to look inside it, not only because of the cameras but because she never wanted to see it again. It belonged to a part of her life as dead and gone as the man who had been her guardian.

As they reached the end of the hall, Alania slowed. She took a quick look around the corner. The stairs to the main floor were deserted, and no one was in sight. She stepped across to the hidden door and reached for the latch, disguised as a part of the molding, but before she could touch it, the door swung outward.

She stumbled backward, shocked. Danyl jerked up the gun. But again Alania pushed it down as she found herself staring into the wide-eyed, terrified face of her lifelong maid and confidante, Sala.

"Alania?" Sala whispered. "What are you doing here?"

"What are *you* doing here?" Alania countered.

"I can't . . ." Sala shot a frightened glance toward the stairs. "We can't talk here. There are Provosts in the dining room. Inside, quickly." She stepped back through the hidden door. Alania and Danyl crowded in after her, and she shut the door behind them.

Unlike the rest of Quarters Beruthi, the servants' stairs did not attempt to pretend they belonged to a house in the countryside. Both the walls and the steps were metal, the lights bright and industrial.

"Who is this?" Danyl demanded. At least he kept the slugthrower lowered.

"Sala," Alania said. "My servant."

"The one who taught you to swim?"

Alania smiled briefly. "Among other things." She turned to Sala. "Sal, you were fired!"

"I told you I'd be all right. I just couldn't tell you why. Lieutenant—Lieutenant Commander—Beruthi only *publicly* fired me. Privately, he found me a new job in Quarters Praterus."

"*Sandi*'s house?"

Sala nodded. "The Lieutenant Commander is very kind," she said. "I know he's always seemed cold to you,

Alania, and I don't know why, but to me ... to me, he's been Captain-sent."

Danyl stirred, but Alania shot him a warning look. Sala clearly didn't know Beruthi was dead, and Alania didn't want to tell her until she had to. Danyl frowned but said nothing.

"But what are you doing back in the house?" Alania asked, returning her attention to Sala. "How did you get in here without the Provosts downstairs knowing about it?"

"I could ask you the same thing," Sala said.

"There's a ... a secret way in," Alania said carefully. "One Beruthi told me about."

Sala laughed a little. "Funny," she said. "That's exactly what I was going to say."

Alania looked down the servants' stairs. "Don't these just lead to the kitchen and servants' quarters on the main floor?"

"Sure," Sala said. "And then lower."

Alania felt like an idiot. "Of course. The service level." Even without her intensive study of the City over the years, she should have thought of that. Deliveries to Officers' Quarters and the comings and goings of staff couldn't take place through the front door: too gauche. There was a network of passages—underground streets, really—one level down. Below that lay the infrastructure level, like the one they had traversed on First from Bertel's Bar to the elevator, where the pipes and shafts and cables and things ran. She frowned. "But aren't the doors into the Quarters from the service level even more secure than the doors at floor level? And isn't there a lot of traffic down there, not to mention Provost patrols? They're not where you'd want to go if you were sneaking around."

"You're right," Sala said. "So I didn't use them."

Alania shook her head. "I don't understand."

Sala looked down for a moment. "I don't suppose it

matters if you know now," she said, almost as if to herself. She raised her head. "For many years while I was your maid, I had a lover. The third son of an Officer. A low-ranked Officer, a mere Ensign, but still way above my station. We had to meet in secret and needed some way to move around unseen. The Lieutenant found out about it; I don't know how. He confronted me, but rather than dismiss me or expose me, he showed me how to get even lower than the service level, onto the infrastructure level. Only robots ever go down there—*his* robots. He charted a path to my lover's house for me." Her voice grew wistful.

"And this lover," Danyl said. "What happened to him?"

Sala's face snapped closed like shutters on a window. "None of *your* damn business. I don't even know who *you* are."

"He's a . . . a friend," Alania said hastily. "Brother" would have been impossible to explain. "Danyl, be kind."

He blinked. "I didn't know I was being unkind."

Alania sighed. "Forgive him, Sal. He grew up in the Middens."

"The . . ." Her eyes widened. "What's going on, Alania? You're supposed to be in Quarters Kranz!"

"I can't tell you," Alania said. She held up a hand. "Not because I don't want to, but because it would be dangerous for you. The Provosts are after us."

"That's why they're watching the house? Why they're *in* the house?"

"Part of the reason," Alania said. "Also . . ." She hesitated but decided there would never be a better time to break the news. "Also, Sal, I'm . . . I'm so sorry, but . . . Lieutenant Commander Beruthi is dead."

Sala's hand flew to her mouth. "Oh, no!"

Alania nodded.

"You're sure?"

Alania nodded again.

Sala lowered her hand. Tears had started in her eyes. "How?"

"An explosion. An accident. At Retreat Beruthi. He'd already sent us on our way here. He was supposed to meet us, but . . ." She shook her head.

"Oh, Alania." Sala reached out for her, gathered her into a hug. "I'm so sorry for your loss."

Alania stiffened at Sala's touch, then found her arms going around the older woman. *Loss?* she thought. *Was it a loss?*

She supposed it was: the loss of her childhood dreams that someday her guardian would also be her father; the loss of *all* childhood dreams, considering what she and Danyl had found out about what they were, what they were fated—*designed*—to be.

She closed her eyes, not so much because of the loss of Beruthi but because for a brief moment, she was able to reclaim one of the few good memories of her childhood: Sala's comforting hugs when things had gone horribly wrong.

Though they had never gone as horribly wrong as they were going now. She gently pushed Sala away. "You still haven't told me: why are you in Quarters Beruthi?"

Sala looked a little shamefaced. "There are some things in one of the guest rooms . . . Beruthi promised them to me. I forgot them when I left, and I've been coming back to pick them up one by one. He said I could have them, I swear. I'm not stealing them."

As if it would matter if you were, Alania thought. "Of course not, Sal."

"What will you do now?" Sala said. "If Beruthi is dead, why did he send you here? You can't stay in Quarters Beruthi. The Provosts—"

Alania looked at her steadily. "We're not staying here," she said. "We need to go somewhere else." An idea had come to her as Sala talked. Beruthi had been planning Danyl's final ascent to Thirteenth Tier for a long time. He knew they'd have to go through Quarters Kranz, and he must have had some plan to get them there. Alania thought Sala might have just provided a clue as to what that was. "Can you take us to the infrastructure level? We need to get to Quarters Kranz."

Sala's eyes widened. "You can't be serious."

"Dead serious," Danyl said. He held up the slugthrower.

Sala took a step back. "You're going to kill Kranz?"

"No," Alania said. She shot Danyl an exasperated look. "No. Danyl is just being overly dramatic."

He frowned at her. "I am?"

"Yes," Alania said. She turned back to Sala. "We just need to get inside."

"But you can't," Sala said. "I mean, yes, the infrastructure tunnels lead there—but Beruthi left the entrance from them into this house unlocked for me. Every other door I've seen is security-sealed. You can't get through an Officer security seal."

"Yes, we can," Danyl said.

Sala gave him a skeptical look.

He sighed. "I'm not being 'overly dramatic' this time. We have a key."

"To Quarters Kranz?"

"To everywhere," Danyl said, then laughed. "Okay, that probably *was* overly dramatic."

"Just take us there," Alania said. "Take us there, and then forget you ever saw us." She glanced at the closed door to the third-floor hall. "And whatever items are left here that Beruthi gave you . . . leave them. You don't want to be found sneaking around Beruthi's house. Not now. Believe me."

"Oh, I do," Sala said fervently. "I don't know what's going on, but whatever it is, I want no part of it. I'll take you to the Quarters Kranz entrance, and then I'm going home to Quarters Praterus to stay." She turned to descend the stairs.

"Wait," Alania said, suddenly struck by another idea. Sala glanced back. "This entrance to Quarters Kranz . . . will it lead into a servants' stair, like it does here?"

"Probably," Sala said. "Though there's no way to know for sure."

"Are there servants' uniforms downstairs?"

"Yes," Sala said. Her eyes widened. "Oh, I see."

"What?" Danyl said.

Alania turned to him. "If we're going to sneak into Kranz's Quarters, we need something to wear that doesn't scream 'These two people just sailed down the River in a boat, climbed a trash mountain, blew up a barrel in the Undercity, and sneaked in through the Hazardous Waste Holding Tank. Which is what we both currently look and"—she lifted her sleeve to her nose, sniffed, and made a face—"smell like."

"I wasn't going to say anything . . ." Sala said, and Alania grinned. Her former servant chewed her lip. "There should be some servants' uniforms in the dressing rooms near the kitchen. But there could be Provosts in the kitchen itself."

"We'll be quiet as ghosts," Alania said, then wished she hadn't. Ghosts, after all, were dead.

Sala led the way down the stairs to the first floor. She put her ear to the door, listened, then nodded and very carefully eased it open.

The corridor beyond was dark, but they could hear voices through the doorway facing them, which led into the kitchen. If the Provosts weren't *in* the kitchen, they were nearby.

Sala motioned to their left and led them to a different door, which opened into a small, drab room with lockers all around it and two benches running its length. A quick investigation revealed several servant's uniforms: simple black trousers and shirts for men, black skirts and blouses for women. "Turn your back," Alania told Danyl.

"You're my sister," he said, but he obeyed. Alania

turned her back, too, and stripped out of the filthy clothes she'd worn since leaving the River People. She pulled on a clean uniform, which proved to fit reasonably well. Sala had turned her back on Danyl, but she stared at Alania—whom, after all, she'd often helped dress—with an intensely curious expression.

"Sister?" she asked.

"It's a long story," Alania replied.

"Done," Danyl said behind them. Alania turned around to find her brother looking dapper and almost respectable, though she could still smell him. The last shower either of them had had was in the decontamination rooms of the River People, and a lot had happened since then.

Still, even servants probably smelled bad sometimes, and hopefully they wouldn't get close enough to anyone for it to matter.

"All right," Alania said to Sala. "We're in your hands."

Sala nodded once and led them back to the stairs.

THIRTY-ONE

DANYL FELT FAR more at home on the infrastructure level far beneath the floor of Twelfth Tier than he had in Alania's palatial childhood dwelling. Growing up in the Middens, where the stone-walled quarters he'd shared with Erl had been the height of luxury, hadn't prepared him for wood paneling and posh paintings and plush carpet. There'd even been a different scent to the air: flowers, perhaps, though Danyl had never smelled anything that sickly sweet in the Middens and wasn't even sure he liked it.

Sala's sudden appearance had startled him, but Alania clearly trusted the servant, and it wasn't like he had any better ideas for getting into Quarters Kranz. The key would presumably allow them access through any electronically sealed door they found, but that wouldn't help if the door was guarded by half a dozen beamer-carrying Provosts.

Of course, it was one thing to get inside Quarters Kranz and quite another to find and access the elevator to the Thirteenth Tier without being stopped. But—how many times had he told himself this already?—one step at a time.

After donning the servants' clothes—Danyl admired Alania's foresight in thinking to do so—they descended one more level, emerging into a short corridor. "That's the door into the main below-street delivery corridors,"

Alania said quietly, pointing to the far end of the hall-way. "There's a freight elevator next to it. But I presume we're not going out there."

"No," Sala said. She led them the other way, to the underside of the stairs they had just descended. The wall panel there looked the same as any other, but when she touched it, it slid aside. She disappeared into the dimly lit space beyond, and Alania followed. Danyl took one more quick look around the corridor they were vacating, then stepped through himself.

The door slid shut. Narrow stairs led down, lit, of course, by eternals; these were near death. The metal walls looked pitted and rusted with age. The contrast couldn't have been greater between this stairwell and the rich Twelfth-Tier mansion above.

How did it all happen? Danyl wondered as they descended the stairs and began moving along passages as decrepit-looking as the ones down on First. The City had metal bones; the wood and other structures crammed into its Tiers were later additions. Here and there, as they had seen on First, the metal walls remained intact, and in other places they had been cut apart. But the infrastructure — the crumbling, rusting, often-failing infrastructure, which dumped raw sewage into the Middens and collected hazardous liquid waste in an ancient tank that would likewise fail someday and render the Middens uninhabitable for even the gangs — was all metal, an impossible amount of metal. How had the City been built? *Why* had it been built? And why just the one? All the villages of mine and farm workers out in the Heartland, ruled by the overseers appointed by their Officer owners, were built of local stone and wood. How had this one enormous metal tower come to squat here above the Canyon, excreting its waste into the chasm below like a vast incontinent beast?

The "history" he had learned offered no clues. The City was the work of "The Builders," who had placed it there and left it in the care of the Officers. They had been in control since the Awakening, when the original citizens awoke knowing their names, who their families were, and whatever skills they had been taught, but with absolutely no memory of how they had come to be where they were.

The First Officer ruled in the Captain's name and with the Captain's authority. The Provosts, though drawn from all the Tiers, were absolutely loyal, their families hostage to their remaining so. There could be upward mobility on the lower Tiers—workers from the Third might aspire to someday own Quarters and a business on Fifth or Sixth—but no one ever ascended from even Ninth to Eleventh or Twelfth. The prison level of Tenth was both a warning and a barrier to any higher aspirations.

Officer positions were hereditary; the few Officer families lost over the course of the City's history had fallen prey to disaster, or so history said. Having witnessed Beruthi's demise, Danyl wondered how many of those vanished Officer families had in fact dared to challenge the authority of the First Officer and paid the ultimate price.

The whole edifice seemed both as solid and eternal as the City seemed from the Heartland and as rotten and rusting as it truly was here in its guts. A good, solid push might just topple it.

Clearly that was where Danyl came in. He had no idea what it would mean to become Captain, no idea what, if anything, would be left of him on the other side of that astonishing prospect. And yet he found himself as excited by it as he was terrified. There was no other possible future for him, after all. There could be no escape, as the attack on Retreat Beruthi had made clear. The Heartland was neither big enough nor wild enough to disappear into, and the Iron Ring was uninhabitable and impassable.

He frowned, wondering suddenly if the reason aircars could not cross the Iron Ring was because they had been *designed* that way by the Officers, who had a vested interest in ensuring the entire population remained trapped inside the Heartland. Was the landscape beyond the Iron Ring in all directions really the hellish place they'd been told it was?

Well, he thought, *maybe I'll find out once I'm Captain.*

They had turned several corners and traversed a couple of hundred meters of corridor by the time Sala called a halt. They had also passed several doors, all sealed, all with red lights glowing above them. The one she stopped in front of looked exactly like all the others: plain green-painted metal. "You're sure this is the one for Quarters Kranz?" Danyl said, staring at it.

Sala gave him a withering look, but it was Alania who replied. "The path we followed corresponded to the streets between Quarters Beruthi and Kranz—it's the same path I was following when the Provosts escorting me were attacked and I jumped into the trash elevator. This is definitely Quarters Kranz."

Danyl nodded and drew out the golden key. Sala's eyes widened when she saw it. "You really *do* have a key. I've never seen anyone but an Officer with one of those."

"You've never seen *anyone* with one like this," Danyl corrected. He stepped toward the door, but Alania grabbed his wrist.

"Wait," she said. She turned to Sala. "You should go. We don't know what will happen when we open this door. You shouldn't be here."

"I agree," Sala said. She gave Alania another hug. "Be safe," Danyl heard her whisper into Alania's ear, then she turned and hurried away.

Alania watched her until she rounded a corner and vanished from sight, then sighed and turned to Danyl. "All right," she said. "Let's try it."

Danyl drew the slugthrower with his right hand, then inserted the key into the lockplate with his left.

For a moment nothing happened, and he felt a surge

of anxiety. But then the door groaned open with a horrible metal-on-metal cacophony that would surely have brought Provosts running if any had been within earshot. There was only darkness beyond—not even the green glow of an eternal this time.

Alania cautiously looked inside. "Can't see a thing."

Danyl retrieved the key, stepped past her into the shadows, and peered around. "It's just like at Quarters Beruthi," he said. "Stairs at the end leading up to a door."

"I guess that's where we go next." Alania came through the door. The moment she did so, it slid shut, grinding closed and sealing with a rather alarmingly final-sounding thud and the clunk of steel bolts driving home. It cut off the next-to-nothing glow of the eternals outside, leaving them in pitch darkness.

"You'd think," Alania said from the blackness, "that we would have thought to pick up a flashlight somewhere along the way."

"I'll put it on my list for next time." Danyl put the key back in his pocket, gripped the slugthrower with his right hand, and reached out blindly with his left, feeling for the wall.

He promptly banged his knuckles; apparently he'd been taking bigger steps than he'd thought. But there was the door. He felt around its edges, found the port, and inserted the key.

The door slid open just as noisily as the last. The honest white light beyond was dim but still enough to make him blink. He retrieved the key, and then he and Alania stepped cautiously through, the door once again closing behind them.

As expected, they appeared to be at the bottom of the servants' stairs. A well-lit corridor to their left ran to what had to be the entrance to the main service tunnels and a freight elevator, as in Quarters Beruthi. Danyl caught a glimpse of a camera dome above the door and hurriedly pulled Alania out of its line of sight, though it was probably focused on the door to the outside and not on the locked door leading to the infrastructure level. That didn't mean there weren't others, though, and he shot a look up.

The stairs appeared to climb for four stories rather than Beruthi's three. For the moment, at least, they were deserted, no servants moving up or down with trays of bonbons or whatever servants used stairs for. Why didn't they just use elevators, anyway?

Maybe they did, mostly, and that's why the stairs were deserted.

"How the hell do we find this elevator to Thirteenth?" Danyl said. "Have you ever been in Quarters Kranz?"

"Only the ballroom," Alania said. "But if I had to guess—"

"You do," Danyl said.

"—then I'd guess the top floor. Quarters Kranz is the only house on Twelfth Tier that stands four stories. There's a rooftop garden—I could see it from my room—and in the middle of it, there's a kind of . . . gazebo, is that the word?"

"You're asking me?" Danyl said. "Whatever a gazebo is, I'm pretty sure we don't have them in the Middens."

Alania laughed a little. "Fair enough. Anyway, there's a gazebo . . . or shed . . . or pavilion . . . or whatever you want to call it exactly in the middle of the roof, and it connects to the Tier ceiling. It's the only place in Twelfth Tier that connects to the ceiling. Even the Core is capped just below that. The elevator shaft has to be somewhere inside it, right?"

"Stands to reason," Danyl said. Keeping out of the line of sight of that worrisome camera bubble, he peered up. "All clear. But there could be more cameras."

"Try to look like a servant," Alania said. She pointed at the slugthrower. "You might want to start by putting that thing away."

Reluctantly, Danyl holstered the weapon, then pulled

out the tail of his black servant's shirt to hide it. "What if they don't wear this type of servants' uniform in Quarters Kranz?"

"They're pretty much standard," Alania said. "All the servants at all the birthday parties I had to attend growing up—and I had to attend a *lot* of them—were dressed like this. Servants are supposed to be invisible and interchangeable, like robots. Which is what Beruthi used in our Quarters, of course."

"Why didn't the others?"

"Because robots are cheap," Alania replied. "People are expensive. The main purpose of Officer social activities is to show off to other Officers, to establish how powerful and wealthy your family is so business or political rivals think twice before messing with you. Lots and lots of costly servants send that message."

"Like the severed heads the Rustbloods used to stick on their gateposts from time to time," Danyl said.

Alania grimaced. "I could have done without that image, but yeah, exactly like that."

"So you really think we'll pass as servants?"

"I *hope* we'll pass as servants," she corrected.

"Just hope?"

"At this point, hope is pretty much all we've got, wouldn't you say?"

Danyl grunted. "I guess you're right about that." He looked up the stairs. "Let's climb."

It seemed at first as if all would be well. No one challenged them as they crept past the closed door that presumably led to the kitchens, if Quarters Kranz were laid out anything like Quarters Beruthi. No one challenged them as they climbed past the second-floor doorway.

But the *third*-floor doorway opened as they approached it, and two Provosts entered the stairwell and headed downstairs, brushing past Danyl and Alania. Danyl tensed, and he might have reached for the barely concealed slugthrower if Alania hadn't grabbed his arm.

Her instincts proved correct—the Provosts paid no more attention to them than if they had been furniture, far more interested in their own conversation . . . a conversation that suddenly interested Danyl, too, when he heard Kranz's name.

". . . Kranz is antsy about something, that's for sure," the first one said. "Doubled security on all entrances as he left."

"Has anyone *ever* broken into Quarters Kranz?" the second one asked.

"Not in fifty years," the first one replied, his voice fading as they continued down the stairs. "That was during the previous First Officer's tenure, of course. Burglar from Fifth. Caught the guy trying to flee up the Canyon. One of my instructors told us about him. They tortured him for a month on Tenth before they finally—"

The Provosts opened the door one floor down and exited.

Danyl glanced at Alania. "Did you hear that?" he whispered. "Kranz is out."

"And they're focused on the regular entrances," Alania whispered back. "We've got a chance . . ."

They hurried on up to the fourth and final landing. The door opened easily. The corridor beyond, floored in marble with silvery walls and ceiling and sparkling crystal light fixtures, made Quarters Beruthi look Spartan. There were only a few doors: a pair of them facing each other at Danyl and Alania's end of the hall and another pair far, far down, near the other end. In between stood an ostentatiously grand pair of double doors, framed with marble pillars.

"First Officer's office?" Danyl guessed.

"Has to be," Alania agreed.

Danyl nodded. "Then let's go."

He stepped into the hallway . . . and all hell broke loose.

First came the alarm: screeching, screaming, deafen-

ing, a physical assault in its own right, hammering Danyl
and Alania into momentary motionlessness. Then came
the amplified voice of the City computer: "Unauthorized
personnel, fourth floor! Unauthorized firearm, fourth
floor! Unauthorized personnel, fourth floor! Unauthorized firearm, fourth floor!"

"Shit!" Danyl jerked the slugthrower from under his
shirt just as the doors closest to them burst open. A Provost charged out from each side of the hall. Danyl fired
instantly, reacting with reflexes honed by countless hours
in Erl's simulator.

The Provosts wore bulletproof vests, but so had the
enemies in the simulations. Danyl fired not at their bodies, not at the iffy targets of their heads, but at their legs.
Both went down screaming. Shouts echoed from the
stairwell, and doors slammed open on each floor. Danyl
stomped on the hand of one of the crippled Provosts,
who was trying to raise his beamer, then kicked the
dropped weapon farther down the hall. "Get that!" he
shouted to Alania. She hurried to grab it. "Shoot anything that moves!" He turned back to the servants' stair,
slamming the door shut.

As he spun around again, a door at the far end of the
hall swung open, and the beam from Alania's weapon
seared a burning line across the paneling. The door
slammed shut as smoke billowed to the ceiling. The high-pitched squeal of a triggered smoke alarm added to the din.

Danyl ran past the fallen Provosts and dashed with
Alania the rest of the way to what they hoped was
Kranz's office. He pulled the key from his pocket and
inserted it into the lockplate in the middle of the right-hand door. If it didn't work . . .

But the door opened without fuss. Danyl snatched
back the key, and they bolted into the room. Danyl
turned and slammed the door shut again, hoping it
locked automatically. Only then did he pause to survey
the office.

He'd feared the elevator would be hard to find, concealed somehow, but far from being hidden, it was *highlighted*, its floodlit doors glowing like molten gold ... the same color as the key he carried. *Probably to rub the noses of visitors in the fact Kranz has access to the Captain and they don't.*

He rushed to the elevator doors. There was no button, no lockplate. He tried touching the doors with the key.

They didn't open.

Danyl heard running footsteps in the hall. The office doors might have locked, but the Provosts had to have *some* way of getting through them. He and Alania only had a moment. Alania turned toward the doors with her beamer, but that would only buy them a few seconds.

He searched the desktop, but it was smooth black glass, and the only decoration, if you could call it that, was a strange dagger, heavier than it looked. He ignored it and turned to the walls.

One of the paintings, a romanticized view of the City at dusk, was slightly out of place, one edge tilted away from the wall. He ran to it and tugged at it.

It swung open like a door, revealing a monitor similar to the status screen of the docbot that had patched up his wounds—and apparently programmed his nanobots—as a kid. Most of the readouts were yellow or red. Beneath that screen was a simple square of gold metal with a hole in the middle of it, just the size of the key.

"Show-off," he muttered, and he shoved the cylinder into the hole.

The elevator opened. He tugged at the key. It wouldn't come out.

Something heavy struck the office doors, which bowed inward. Another blow like that ... Danyl turned and fired twice at the doors. The bullets didn't penetrate, just gouged holes in the wood as they flattened against armor plating beneath, but maybe the noise and implied threat would deter anyone on the other side for a few seconds. Then he and Alania crammed into the glistening white-and-gold interior of the tiny elevator, clearly only intended to accommodate one person.

The door slid shut.

They ascended.

Danyl's eyes met Alania's, which were wide and white, but she didn't look frightened. If anything, she looked exhilarated. He felt another surge of protectiveness and pride toward her. *My sister. We're cut from the same cloth.*

From the same cloth as the Captain, he thought then. *And worse, Kranz.*

The elevator continued its inexorable rise. Danyl couldn't imagine what they would see when that door opened, couldn't imagine what he was supposed to do.

But soon enough, he wouldn't have to imagine.

Without speaking, they rose to the pinnacle of the City.

THIRTY-TWO

ONCE AGAIN, First Officer Kranz glared down at the man in the hospital bed, furious and frustrated by the fact that it was impossible to torture someone in a coma.

I could always torture the Provost who shot him, he thought viciously, but then he shoved that thought aside. That would be unnecessarily vindictive. It had been a firefight, after all, and the bullet that had laid Erlkin Orillia low had apparently been a ricochet; if it had been a direct hit, it would have killed him instantly.

Medical Officer Saunders had had nothing new to report: there was serious swelling of the brain, he said, and whether Orillia ever spoke again—or even woke again—was out of his control.

Kranz had come down to the hospital determined to have the doctor rouse Orillia by any means necessary, but neither drugs nor electrical stimulation had produced more than a twitch. Orillia's body might be alive, but it wasn't his body Kranz needed—it was his mind, and whatever information he must have about Beruthi's ultimate intentions for Danyl.

And where were the two Cityborn brats, anyway? They'd come into the City, and he knew they were alive, but no one had seen them since—

He felt a buzz against his wrist and looked to see the code of his Head of Household Security blinking an urgent red. With a mixture of alarm and annoyance, he slapped at the communicator with his right hand. "What is it, Lieutenant Commander Trishel?"

"Young man and young woman got into the house, sir," Trishel's voice snapped, urgent and tense. "Disguised as servants. They made it to the fourth floor."

"Where you presumably arrested them," Kranz said icily.

Even over the commlink, he heard Trishel swallow hard. "No, sir. They . . . I'm sorry, sir, but . . . somehow . . . they gained access to your office. We had to break down the door. By the time we got inside, they . . . they were *gone*, sir."

"Gone?" Kranz's gut clenched as the enormity of what he was hearing hit home. "Gone *where*?"

"The elevator, sir," Trishel said. "They took the elevator."

Impossible! Kranz wanted to shout, but clearly it wasn't. There was no way out of his office besides the main door and the elevator. *All they've done is trap themselves*, he tried to reassure himself. *They can't do anything on Thirteenth.*

Can they?

"On my way," he snapped. He didn't bother adding, *I'll deal with you later.* There was no point in threatening punishment when punishment was already certain.

He was fifteen minutes from Quarters Kranz. Danyl and Alania would be on Thirteenth for more than twenty minutes before he could reach them.

They can't know anything about what they'll find there, he reminded himself as he strode quickly toward the exit; he would have preferred to run, but the First Officer couldn't afford to show panic, even if he felt it. *I'm the only one who knows the procedure to replace the Captain. They'll still be standing there, befuddled, when I arrive. And then I can take control of the situation.*

This can still be salvaged.

In fact, they might have just saved him time and effort.

After all, Thirteenth was exactly where he wanted Alania. *If all goes well, we'll have a new Captain by nightfall.*

If all goes well.

The trouble was, *nothing* had gone well since Alania had plunged into the Middens.

Still, Kranz thought as he reached the street and hurried toward his quarters, his bodyguards falling in beside him as he burst out of the hospital. *At this point, hope is pretty much all the City and I have got, isn't it?*

Erl waited for two minutes after Kranz left, then brought himself out of the semiconscious state into which he had ordered his nanobots to submerge him—the nanobots with which Prime had provided him all those years ago, which had long since mended his wounds and had just now counteracted the drugs and electrical shocks used to "revive" him. The doctor knew what was going on, of course; Medical Officer Saunders had helped Prime arrange Danyl's abduction two decades ago. He'd personally taken over Erl's treatment the moment he was delivered to the hospital; who else would Kranz have trusted?

Saunders had done everything in his power to convince Kranz that Erl could not be questioned, and he had done so most effectively. He had also, of course, not told Kranz about the nanobots in *Erl's* bloodstream. Like Danyl's, Erl's had always been half quiescent, keeping him healthy and helping him heal more quickly than normal, but they'd never been fully activated for fear Cark or someone else would notice his unusual abilities and wonder if information about them might be worth something to the Provosts.

Erl had been so badly wounded when he'd arrived at the hospital, though, that Saunders had had no choice but to dial the nanobots up to full power. They had quickly

healed Erl's head injury and other assorted wounds from
the firefight and brought him back to full consciousness.
Best of all, they were now under his conscious control, so
he could use them to do things like put himself into a
semiconscious state that looked like sleep to anyone on
the outside but allowed him to listen in on things like the
conversation Kranz had just had with his Head of Household Security. Thus he had learned that Danyl and Alania, against all hope, were even now ascending to the
Captain.

The trouble was, of course, that Kranz was hard on
their heels. Which meant it was time for Erl to quit ma-
lingering.

He swung his feet over the side of the bed, pulled off
the various cords and tubes attached to him purely for
the sake of appearances, and reached for his clothes. As
he'd expected, Saunders arrived two minutes later. "What
are you doing?" the Medical Officer demanded. "We
can't be certain the nanobots are stable. There could still
be complications . . ."

"There's already been a complication," Erl said. "I'm
self-discharging, Doctor Saunders. Don't worry, I'll say it
was against doctor's orders."

"Oh, good," Saunders said dryly. "I wouldn't want to
risk my career or anything like that." His brief smile
faded. "I didn't see you leave. And the cameras didn't see
you either."

Erl nodded. "Thank you for your help."

Saunders nodded once more, then turned and went
out without looking back.

Two minutes later, Erl was running along the streets
of Twelfth Tier, his destination the same as the First Officer's: Quarters Kranz.

With one side stop along the way . . .

The elevator halted, the door opened, and without any fuss at all, Alania and Danyl entered Thirteenth Tier, abode of the Captain.

In her mind, Alania had conjured an image of Thirteenth Tier based largely on the Earthmyth tale of Heaven, where the souls of the righteous played harps on solid clouds and the decorating consisted of gold and precious and semiprecious stones. The initial reality proved to be a bland, wood-paneled room with a red suede couch against one wall, sitting beneath a strange image of a blue-and-white sphere hung in a starry black sky, a smaller white sphere behind it and off to one side.

Against the other wall were two big armchairs upholstered in the same red leather. Between them in a glass cabinet hung something Alania took to be an abstract sculpture, since it made no sense otherwise. It was a kind of long cylinder with bulbous ends and an apparently random assortment of other shapes attached to its length here and there: cubes, tetrahedrons, smaller spheres. Lights sparkled. An engraved plaque caught her eye, and she moved close enough to read *UES Discovery*. She knew the word "Discovery," of course, but what did UES stand for?

Maybe they're the artist's initials.

Danyl hadn't even glanced at the sculpture—his attention was on the door opposite the elevator. "I don't have the key anymore," he said grimly. "The lock in Kranz's office wouldn't release it. If this door doesn't open . . ."

Alania hefted the beamer she'd taken from the fallen Provost in Kranz's fourth-floor hallway. "We'll get through it somehow," she said. She took a step toward the door, prepared to burn through it if she had to—if she *could*—but the door simply slid open at her approach. She exchanged a startled glance with Danyl, and then, still holding the beamer at the ready, took a step toward the opening.

She froze as a multilegged robot scuttled into view like a giant insect. In the familiar voice of the City computer, it calmly said, "The Captain welcomes visitors. However, you must leave your weapons in the antechamber."

"What will happen if we don't?" Alania asked.

"This unit is authorized to use force to prevent weapons from entering this space," the robot replied with that same lack of emotion.

Alania looked at Danyl. "I don't think we have any choice."

"First the key, then our weapons," Danyl said. "The bloody Captain will be telling us to strip naked next." But he unbuckled his belt, slipped the slugthrower holster from it, and placed the weapon on the low table in front of the couch. Alania put her beamer down beside it. Then she turned back to the door. "May we enter?"

"The Captain welcomes visitors," the robot said and scuttled out of view.

Alania cautiously stepped through the door.

She found herself on a porch, looking out into a vast open space. For an instant she thought they had somehow been transported outside, because the light that flooded around them was pure sunlight. Looking up, she saw the sun shining in a patch of blue sky, though it vanished a moment later as the tattered remnants of the rain clouds that had soaked them that morning in the Middens swept over it. Then she saw the faint shimmer between her and that open sky, and she realized the entire Tier lay beneath an enormous dome of some material that looked crystal-clear from this side but appeared opaque from the outside.

"Wow," Danyl breathed, and Alania nodded as she lowered her gaze and stared around at the rest of the Tier. Thirteenth, abode of the Captain, had none of the jumbled, cheek-by-jowl, haphazardly constructed structures of First or the beautiful but rigidly constrained, blocky stores and mansions of Eleventh and Twelfth. In fact, it had only a single building: simple, round, roofed with a white dome that echoed the crystal dome high above, surrounded by a portico supported by slender columns.

The domed building rose like a jewel from the center of an emerald-green lawn. Gardens radiated out from it: artfully arranged flowerbeds and groomed shrubbery, surrounded at the rim of the space by enough trees to give the illusion of a deep forest. A path paved in crushed white stone stretched from Alaina's vantage point through the gardens to the central building.

The pastoral vista, easily half a kilometer in diameter, was alive with movement, but none of it was human. White birds flitted between the distant trees, jewel-like birds with iridescent feathers darted or hovered among the flower beds, and robots glittered as they moved through the garden, tending the plants.

Alania glanced back through the antechamber to the elevator. How long before Kranz emerged from it? *Does the prohibition on weapons apply to him, too?* she wondered. The notion that "The Captain welcomes visitors" was so outrageous it had to date back to the dawn of the City. Perhaps even Kranz, for all his power, could not change the programming.

But the Captain surely can, Alania thought, and she and Danyl stepped down from the porch onto the white path.

The movement of the robots in the gardens instantly ceased as their sensors locked on the two humans. Their footsteps crunched on white stone, and the rest of the Tier was so quiet—at their appearance, the birds had stopped singing—that the sound seemed absurdly, dangerously loud. They walked the two hundred meters or so to the white building without speaking.

Steps led up to the portico and then to a closed door that looked to be made of solid gold. Alania and Danyl mounted the steps, and the door swung silently inward.

Within the building's dark interior, small lights—a few green, a few yellow, a great many red—burned like stars.

Alania exchanged a wide-eyed glance with Danyl, and then the two of them stepped into the presence of the Captain.

Behind them, the door swung shut again.

THIRTY-THREE

ERL'S OLD QUARTERS had long since been given to some Officer who *hadn't* committed mutiny, but the secret compartment beneath the back steps still opened at the touch of his old ID tag, revealing an ordinary duffel bag. He pulled out the bag but left the powerful beamer it contained concealed inside it for the moment. He needed to reach Quarters Kranz without being arrested, and running through the streets with a weapon didn't seem like the best way to accomplish that goal. What he did pull out was the high-level City access key Beruthi had made for him two decades before.

Kranz was minutes ahead of him, Alania and Danyl mere minutes ahead of them both and no doubt already on Thirteenth by now. It could well be that whatever was going to happen would happen before Erl could possibly be there to take a hand in it ... but if he didn't try to make it and that hand was needed, he would always regret it.

Not that his personal "always" would be very long in the event that Kranz succeeded in turning Alania into a new Kranz/Captain hybrid who would rule for the next five hundred years.

Down on First, with its constantly shifting walls and ever-changing buildings, twenty-year-old knowledge of the City's layout would have been useless. But on Twelfth, where nothing ever changed, Erl knew exactly how to

reach Quarters Kranz with as little risk as possible—
almost certainly, he thought, the same way Alania and
Danyl had reached it.

Half a block from his old back door, he used his newly
acquired key to open the unmarked door in the side of a
robot storage shed and descended the stairs inside to the
infrastructure level two stories beneath Twelfth Tier's
streets.

Kranz arrived at his quarters dangerously close to being
out of breath, which simply would not do, since it might
suggest to the underlings and Provosts gathered there
that he was in less-than-total control of events . . . or of
himself.

Partially to preserve that illusion and partially because he was in too much of a hurry, he did not waste any
breath berating Lieutenant Commander Trishel, who
would, Kranz vowed silently, soon find herself stationed
in the newly pacified Middens, preferably somewhere
near—better yet, *under*—the broken sewer pipe.

"Weapon," he snapped instead, holding out his hand,
and the Lieutenant Commander handed him a beamer.
Then Kranz strode at a quick but carefully unhurried
pace to the main elevator and rode it up to the fourth
floor, Trishel stiff and silent at his side.

There was blood on the floor outside his office, whose
doors had been forced open. A quick glance showed him
that the painting had been pulled aside from the Captain's monitor, an illicit key had been inserted into the
elevator lock—no doubt Beruthi's work again, damn
him—and the wood on the inside of the office doors had
been scarred by bullets, revealing the armor plates beneath. Kranz's eyes flicked to the monitor. It remained
unchanged from that morning. Whatever was happening
on Thirteenth, the Captain remained in place, as she had

for almost five centuries. Which meant he still had time, plus one very great advantage over the two Cityborn who had preceded him to Thirteenth Tier: he knew *exactly* what replacing the Captain would mean.

Well, and one other advantage: the First Officer was the only person allowed in the Captain's presence while armed.

The key in the lockplate, frozen in place while the elevator ascended, had popped partway out once the car reached Thirteenth. Kranz pushed it in, but it refused to work for him. Irritably he snatched it out, tossed it aside, pulled his own key from his pocket and shoved it in. Then, beamer held loosely in his right hand, he strode to the golden doors. A moment later they slid open, and he entered the familiar gold-and-white confines of the tiny car.

The doors slid closed, and Kranz ascended, as he had so many times before, to the sanctum sanctorum of the Captain. He entered the antechamber with his beamer raised and ready, but the small room was empty. "Welcome, First Officer," said the voice of the City—the voice of the Captain.

He strode past the model of *United Earth Ship Discovery*, ignored the photograph of the Earth and moon on the opposite wall, and snapped, "First Officer Kranz: security override," at the robot that appeared in the doorway. The robot moved aside without challenging him.

He stepped out beneath the crystal dome. A thundershower had rolled in in the outside world, shrouding Thirteenth Tier in gloom. The usual robots moved around the garden, tending the flowers and bushes, and birds and insects flitted among the blossoms, but nothing else moved.

Which meant, of course, that Danyl and Alania were already inside the Captain's control chamber and that he needed to hurry.

There was no one to see him now, no one to impress with the calm, cool demeanor of the First Officer, and so he ran, feet crunching on the crushed white stone of the path, beamer raised.

As the golden door of the strange little building swung closed behind Danyl and Alania, the interior lit, revealing white walls and a floor covered in gold-streaked marble.

At the center of the room was a table of solid metal on which rested a kind of squashed cylinder, like a giant seedpod. Cables and tubes ran into the pod from banks of equipment on racks all around it, their indicator lights the red, green, and yellow sparks Danyl had seen in the shadowed interior when the door first opened. Video screens showed cryptic numbers and traces above the equipment banks.

But above that . . .

Danyl gaped at the underside of the dome. "Alania," he breathed. "Look."

Alania looked up and gasped.

The dome showed stars: stars impossibly bright, in impossible numbers. They were clustered and blue in the center of the display, widely spaced and tinted red around the outside. Green letters just off center read, "ETA 36:226:12:42:06," the right-most number ticking down second by second.

A series of cryptic messages swirled around the fringes of the image, strings of letters and numerals meaningless to Danyl, all of them blinking red.

He tore his gaze away from that astonishing and vertigo-inducing view and frowned at the strange pod. He stepped closer. There was a window at one end providing a view of the interior. He leaned down . . .

. . . and yelped and stumbled back as he saw an ancient face, little more than deeply wrinkled parchment-like skin hanging from a skull, staring back at him with wide-open bright-blue eyes, eyes the color of Alania's.

Eyes the color of his own.

The Captain.

The Captain.

Until that moment, he still hadn't really believed she was real and certainly hadn't believed she could be whole and alive. He'd pictured her as no more than a brain in a jar, or perhaps an animated corpse, anything but an actual woman with an actual face and actual eyes that could stare back at him through the walls of her confinement.

Alania shot him a startled look, then stepped forward herself. She peered down at the Captain's face for a moment, then took a step back. She seemed much calmer about what she had seen than he was until she reached out a hand to steady herself and he realized her face had gone white.

"She's real," Alania breathed, echoing his own terror and amazement.

Danyl took a deep breath. "Yeah," he said. He forced himself to step forward again and look down into that impossibly wizened face. Maybe the eyes just happened to be open, maybe there was no consciousness behind them, maybe . . .

But the eyes flicked to him. He leaned forward. "Can you hear me?" he shouted. "Blink if you can."

He yelped as a voice answered him: a voice he knew well, the voice of the City computer, the same calm woman's voice that had spoken to him a million times from his teaching machine. "Of course I can hear you," the voice said. "Welcome, son." A pause. "And daughter." Another pause. "Where is First Officer Kranz?" it said, but now it held a peevish tone he'd certainly never heard in the computer's voice. "Surely he should be here for this."

Danyl shot a glance at Alania, who simply shrugged,

looking as bewildered as he felt. "Um . . . he sent us on ahead," he said.

"He'd better hurry," the voice said. "I'm dying, you know."

The tone was matter-of-fact, indistinguishable from the tone the teaching machine had used while instructing him in atomic theory or quadratic equations. It gave him a disconcerting sense of déjà vu. "I'm . . . sorry?" he said, because what else did you say when someone said they were dying, even someone centuries old and encased in a sarcophagus?

"No need to be sorry," the voice said. "I'm more than ready for it. I'm just disappointed I won't live to see the first colony seed launched toward planetfall."

"Colony seed?" Danyl said carefully. "Planet . . . fall?" The words made no sense. What was a planet, and what could make it fall?

"We thought it would happen much sooner," the voice continued. "But the initial candidates all proved unsuitable. I am confident the next on the list *will* prove amenable to colonization. The computer will of course upload all necessary knowledge regarding the current state of the ship during the transition."

Danyl gave Alania a bewildered look. From her wide-eyed return stare, it seemed she had no more clue than he did what the Captain was talking about. But she mouthed one word to him, "Kranz," and he nodded and turned back to the Captain.

"It's urgent that we proceed," he said. "Could you . . . review the . . . procedure . . . for me?"

"Surely the First Officer has gone over it with you?"

"Of course he has," Danyl said. "But he wants to be certain all goes well."

"Very well," the Captain—the City—said. "The procedure is simple. I initiate it, of course; only I, as Captain, can transfer control to my replacement. Once I initiate transfer, it cannot be stopped. The first step will be the final programming of your nanobots to enable you to interface with the ship controls. Without that programming, the ship will reject you."

Danyl desperately wanted to know why the Captain kept calling the City a "ship," but he didn't want her to change her mind and insist they wait for Kranz, so he said nothing, listening intently.

"Once the programming is complete, I will withdraw from the system."

"Won't that kill you?" Alania protested.

"I certainly hope so," the Captain said. "The extraction process itself is not lethal, but it is clear from my vital signs that only extraordinary intervention from the command pod and my own nanobots is currently keeping me alive. The nanobots might keep me breathing and conscious for a few moments after extraction, but that time will be brief. Don't worry, you won't have to deal with my remains. There are robots standing by to take care of the unpleasantries.

"Once I am out of the command pod, you will have fifteen minutes to take my place. Simply remove all clothing and lie down in the pod. The machines will do the rest. There will be some disorientation as the necessary adjustments are made to your brain and nervous system, but you should find it manageable. When I assumed command, I found that my simulation training had done an adequate if not stellar job of preparing me. No doubt the simulations have improved over the course of the flight. I imagine you will find it easier."

Erl had made Danyl spend a great deal of time training in simulations, but none of them had been related to the process of taking control of the City's systems. Yet here they stood at the feet of the Captain, achieving at last what Erl and Beruthi and Yvelle and countless others had died to accomplish. There could be no going back to their old lives—they *had* no old lives. And the

First Officer could arrive at any moment with his own plans for replacing the Captain . . . with Alania.

Danyl's heart hammered in his chest. His throat constricted so that he could hardly speak. And yet somehow, he did.

"Very well," he whispered. "Initiate transfer."

"The magic words," the Captain said, "that I have been waiting so long to hear."

A tall cabinet standing next to the sarcophagus—the command pod—opened like a closet, revealing a human-sized space inside. "Please step inside for nanobot programming," said a male voice.

Danyl glanced at Alania. She looked pale. "Are you sure?" she whispered.

He nodded.

She swallowed, then suddenly enveloped him in a hug. He stiffened, but then his arms went around her and he returned the embrace. She felt warm and solid, and he suddenly wished he'd grown up with her, that he'd really known what it meant to have a sister, to have *any* kind of family.

"Good luck," she murmured.

He nodded and released her. Then he strode to the open cabinet and stepped inside.

The door closed, and a hum rose around him. His skin prickled as though tiny insects were crawling all over it, a sensation he had felt whenever the docbot had given him his regular examinations. But the surge of warmth that followed was new: warmth and a feeling of well-being, of euphoria. He suddenly felt strong, invincible, able to do anything.

Able, in fact, to control the City.

But also . . . able to remember something he'd forgotten, the newly powerful nanobots reforging connections to memories that had been blocked until that moment. He'd thought his sessions with the docbot had only lasted minutes, but now he knew—he *remembered*—that they had they in fact lasted for long, uncomfortable hours, hours during which he had been conscious but unable to control his body, hours he had promptly forgotten immediately afterward.

Why hadn't he remembered that until now?

The answer came to him in a flash. *Because the nanobots can rewrite memories.*

Beruthi had told them as much, told them that Alania's nanobots had already been preprogrammed to rewrite her memories when she became Captain, to turn her into a copy of Kranz. Clearly the Captain's memories had also been altered—her strange talk of "planetfall" and commanding a "ship" was proof of it. She didn't even seem to know that she had been in that command pod for *centuries*. Kranz—*every First Officer Kranz since the beginning of the City*—had lied to her, made her delusional, wiped and manipulated her memories.

That's what Kranz plans to do to Alania . . . but what did Erl do to me during those lost hours? Have I been preprogrammed, too?

The white-hot fury of the betrayed roared up within him. Erl had *lied* to him, lied to him his whole life, never telling Danyl his real purpose, never telling him the truth about why Erl was raising him. He'd thought of Erl as his father when instead he'd been more like his . . . his *zookeeper*. Keeping him fed, keeping him healthy, keeping him docile until it was time to use him, to plug him into the City like a replacement glowtube. Danyl had *never* been free to live his own life, not for one moment. He had been literally *bred* to do what he was about to do: to take over control of the City.

And then what? What secret orders did *he* already carry within him, ready to implement as soon as he gained access to the City's systems?

Oh, he knew what Beruthi had claimed. He'd claimed

he wanted to set the City free. But what if all Beruthi had really wanted to do was to seize power for himself, to depose Kranz as First Officer and become First Officer himself with Danyl as his Captain-puppet?

Beruthi is dead. It doesn't matter what he intended. I'll be able to do what he claimed to want, true or not, and free the City . . .

Bold words. But he had no way of knowing if they were true. If he truly had been programmed like one of Beruthi's robots, who knew what would happen?

And yet he still couldn't back out. There was no possible future for him other than the one where, in the next few minutes, he became the heart and soul of the City.

"Programming complete," said the male voice, and the cabinet door popped open. He stepped out.

Alania stood where he had left her. "Are you all right?" she said the instant he appeared.

"I'm all right," he said.

"And you're still going through with this?"

"I have to," he said grimly. "Believe me. I have to."

She nodded. "So . . . what happens next?"

"I guess we tell the Captain the—"

"I see that programming is complete," said the Captain's voice. "Are you prepared to initiate transfer of command functions?"

Danyl glanced at Alania. Through a mouth suddenly gone dry, he said, "Yes."

"Thank you," the Captain said. "I hereby relinquish command." She sounded . . . blissful. "At last . . ."

For a moment, nothing happened. Then, all at once, most of the remaining green lights in the equipment cabinets surrounding the command pod turned red. An alarm sounded, a shrill sound like a shrieking animal, but it fell silent again almost at once.

With a hum, the lid of the command pod opened.

Lying in a glistening layer of blue-green gel, the

shriveled, naked body inside the pod was barely recognizable as human, tubes and wires emerging directly from its skin. He heard Alania gasp in horror.

Is that what I'm dooming myself to become?

The door through which they had entered the little building opened, and two robots scuttled in. With quick, efficient movements, they extracted tubes, disconnected wires, and lifted the Captain's emaciated body from the bed where it had lain so unfathomably long. One of the robots sucked out the gel. The other squirted a fresh layer of the stuff into the pod.

And then came the male voice again. "Please remove all clothing and lie down in the command pod. You have fifteen minutes."

Fifteen minutes, Danyl thought. *Fifteen minutes before ... what?*

With trembling hands, he started to take off his clothes.

Alania forced herself to watch as Danyl disrobed. *Someone needs to witness this*, she thought, and though she had never seen a nude man in the flesh before, mere embarrassment didn't seem a good enough reason to look away.

Besides, she reminded herself, *he's my brother.*

Danyl didn't look at her as he finished stripping. When he was completely naked, though, he raised his eyes to hers. "I ... I don't know what happens when I get in there," he whispered. "I don't know if I'll be able to talk to you anymore after that. If I can't ... I'm sorry we've had so little time. I wish we could get to know each other. I wish we had time to learn what having family means."

Alania swallowed. "I wish that, too." Though there was no reason for it, she, too, found herself whispering. "More than anything ..."

"No one gave us a choice," Danyl said.

"No," Alania replied, and she felt a surge of anger at the thought. "No one."

Danyl nodded, then turned his back. He climbed awkwardly into the pod, lying down in the strange blue-green goo. The lid started to close . . .

. . . and the door to the control room burst open.

Alania barely had time to register the face of First Officer Kranz before the beamer burned through her lower leg. Screaming in the grip of the worst agony she had ever felt, she collapsed.

Kranz leaped over her and slammed his hand against a control on the command pod. Immediately, it started to open again.

THIRTY-FOUR

ERL MADE HIS WAY into Quarters Kranz through the old, unused entrance in the depths of the Tier's sublevel .... except he could tell from the flaked rust lying on the deck plates around it that it wasn't *completely* unused. It *could* have been opened by some Provost ordered to make sure the old door was secure, but Erl thought the rust more likely to be evidence he had been correct, that this was the same route Alania and Danyl had taken, no doubt at the instruction of Prime—his old friend, Lieutenant Ipsil Beruthi. He frowned. Kranz's Head of Household Security had said nothing about Beruthi being with the youngsters; had he somehow gone ahead of them to prepare for the transfer?

He put down the duffel bag, opened it, and extracted the beamer. If Alania and Danyl had successfully infiltrated Quarters Kranz this way, then he could do it, too, especially considering he had one advantage they lacked: his nanobots were fully activated, and he knew how to control them. They didn't make him invulnerable, but they made him the next thing to it.

He didn't make it far before he had to put that theory to the test. Clearly the servants' stairwell was far more closely monitored now than it had been when Alania and Danyl had come this way, if indeed they had. The door leading to the kitchen slammed open, and two Provosts appeared, beamers raised. "Halt, or I'll—" began

the man in front, but Erl cut him down before he finished
the phrase, his own beamer slicing off the man's head in
a spray of steam and boiled brains.

His partner reacted with astonishing presence of
mind, considering that his partner's gray matter covered
his face. He fired even as the lead man collapsed.

Erl's nanobots deflected the energy, heating the air
around him so that he was briefly surrounded by a glowing
corona. *That worked well*, he thought as his own beamer
tore through the second man's heart. There was no blood—
beamers were tidy that way, cauterizing as they cut.

He had to kill two more Provosts on the way to the
fourth floor, where he burst into the hallway, firing as he
went and taking down a woman standing outside Kranz's
office. Then he was inside, through the doors that had
clearly been forced open. A painting had been swung
away from the wall, revealing a medical monitor—Erl
thought he knew whose failing vital signs it displayed—
and a golden lockplate with a key already in it.

He pushed it in, and a moment later, the elevator
door opened. Beamer at the ready, he rode up to Thirteenth Tier.

Danyl stripped before Alania's unwavering gaze. He was
thankful she didn't look away, thankful she watched as
he faced the unthinkable course of action to which he
had committed himself. He said his farewell to her, then
climbed into the command pod. The strange blue gel the
robot had extruded at the bottom of the pod oozed
around his naked body. *At least it's warm*, he thought
inanely.

His heart pounded. His breath came in quick, ragged
gasps. He wanted to climb out again, run from the room,
hide somewhere in the City, flee into the country, anything ... but he knew all of that would be futile, that

there could be no escape from the First Officer and his Provosts. There was literally nowhere to run.

And then, suddenly, his fear eased as the pod lid slowly started to swing closed above him. The gel took on a life of its own and began to creep across his skin as if it were a giant amoeba devouring him, yet the sensation was pleasant rather than terrifying. At the same time, his senses expanded. He felt as if his body were growing, becoming gigantic and yet somehow tenuous, as though it had no substance. The inside of the command pod faded around him, and he touched, just for a moment, an enormous, powerful presence with his mind . . .

And then, with horrible, shocking suddenness, he was yanked back into his body, a body in agony, every nerve screaming as though he were being flayed alive. He screamed and tried to struggle, but he could barely move . . .

The connection that had just begun to form vanished as though it had never been. There was only his own body, naked, cold, dripping blue-green goo, thrown unceremoniously to the floor beside Alania, whose eyes were closed and whose breathing came in shallow moans. A tendril of smoke rose from a hole in her leg.

Standing over them was First Officer Kranz.

Bursting into the control room, Kranz had taken in the situation at a glance: Danyl already in the command pod, the lid closing on him; Alania watching her brother, her back to the door. Kranz needed her alive, but he also needed her not to interfere, so he had shot her in the leg, leaping over her as she screamed and toppled. The countdown on the pod showed that he still had ten minutes to complete the transition of power. If a new Captain were not installed in that time, the system would go into standby. Vast swathes of the City would suddenly find themselves without power or air circulation. The gates would seal. The elevators would stop running. Panic and chaos would grip the population. It would take a complete reboot of the system before another attempt could be made to install a new Captain . . . and Kranz knew all too well, because it was burned into his nanobot-written memories, that a reboot attempt was doomed to failure.

It would fail because of all the false information that had been fed into the computer over the years, information designed to convince the Captain she was the original commander of the giant colonization ship *UES Discovery*, not a clone of the original Captain commanding one of the eight colony seeds *Discovery* had ferried through the stars. *This* colony seed's normal programming had been overridden by First Officer Thomas Kranz to prevent it from dismantling itself and spreading its component parts across a large swathe of the countryside.

That had been the disaster Thomas Kranz had averted. He had realized the truth the Captain of *Discovery* had denied, the truth so many of his fellow Officers had denied: that the mission plan was fatally flawed, that if the colony seed dismantled itself as intended and the Officers stepped down in favor of a civilian government, everyone would die. The first First Officer, Kranz knew from his memories, had selflessly risked everything to keep the colony seed intact, to rewrite the memories of the colonists waiting to awaken from cold sleep so they would never know what had happened, to take firm control of the Officers who remained after the revolution he led succeeded.

For five hundred revolutions of this world around its primary, the clones of First Officer Kranz had maintained control and kept that colony seed—now called the City—intact, had kept this outpost of Earth civilization functioning, had saved countless lives. But nothing could last forever. The Captain had to be replaced, and the transition had to happen now. A reboot would either crash the City's systems permanently or, possibly worse, trigger a catastrophic and sudden dismantling of the City as it attempted to fulfil its original programming without regard for all the changes to its structure in the years since. The Cubes waiting on the Rim of the Canyon would open, and the giant robots they contained would activate. The deconstruction of the City, which was only meant to happen after its entire population had moved out into the surrounding countryside, might begin at once without regard for the humans; according to the false data fed into the system over the centuries, those people did not exist.

The death toll would be . . . catastrophic.

The City going into standby would be bad enough. The City deciding to dismantle itself was unthinkable.

Which meant Kranz had to get Danyl out of the pod and Alania into it in the next ten minutes.

The wound he had inflicted on her was of no importance. Painful, no doubt, but her nanobots would heal it without trouble even without being fully activated. The important thing was that she wouldn't be getting up in the next couple of minutes.

Kranz reached in from the head of the pod, grabbed Danyl under his arms, and pulled him free of the gel that was designed to completely encase the body of the Captain, aiding the nanobots and his genetically modified neural wiring in the joint tasks of keeping him alive and keeping him connected to the City systems. Danyl barely reacted, dazed from the first stages of his integration, until the gel let him go with a slurping sound. Then he screamed—a hoarse, weak sound—and began to struggle, but feebly, as if he were caught in a dream instead of reality. Kranz threw him to the floor and turned to Alania.

"Get up," he snarled. "Take off your clothes."

"I can't even . . ."

Kranz jerked her to her feet, then shoved her against the command pod so that she fell into a half-sitting position. "Strip! Or I'll burn your other leg and strip you myself!"

Trembling far more with fury than with shame, Alania pulled off her clothes. The agony in her leg was already fading, far too quickly to be normal. *The nanobots*, she thought. By the time she had finished stripping, the pain had faded to a dull ache, though it spiked if she put her full weight on that leg.

Standing naked in front of Kranz hardly seemed to matter much considering he'd had access to video feed from her bedroom her entire life. In any event, the rapacious look in Kranz's eyes had nothing to do with prurience; he lusted for something far different.

With the metal floor cold beneath her bare feet, she glanced down at Danyl, who lay curled in a fetal position, trembling and muttering. His eyelids flickered, but he clearly wasn't seeing her or anything else.

"Now get into the programming cabinet," Kranz said. "Move."

Holding herself erect, refusing to cower or cover herself, she stepped into the cabinet Danyl had already entered. Fiery insects ran over her bare skin, galloped through her bloodstream.

It was as if a fog she hadn't even recognized lifted from her vision. She suddenly felt . . . sharper. Powerful. The remaining pain in her leg vanished as though she had never been shot.

The cabinet door opened, and she stepped out again. "Now," Kranz said, "get into the pod."

"Or what?" Alania said. "You can't kill me."

"No," he said, "but I can damn well cripple you as painfully as possible, then lift you in myself. Now *get in*."

Giving in to the inevitable, Alania walked to the pod and looked down into it. The blue-green gel awaited her. She gave Danyl one final look, turned what she hoped was a withering glare on Kranz, then climbed as gracefully as she could into the pod and lay down in the gel.

Blood-warm, the strange substance wrapped itself around her bare back and bottom . . . and then, horribly, it began to move, creeping up around her body. Alania stiffened, clenching her fists, but the gel didn't slow its inexorable advance.

Kranz came over to the pod and looked down at her. "At last," he breathed. His eyes held a strange light, bright, fanatical. "This is your birthright, Alania. This is your destiny. Your entire life has led up to this moment. You are about to become Captain . . . and then, once I enter the final command to activate the memories piggybacking on your Captain's nanobots, you'll also become First Officer. You will preserve the City for decades— centuries—longer. You will preserve me and all our ancestors, all the way back to the first First Officer Kranz. My memories will soon be yours. *His* memories will soon be yours." Horribly, he smiled at her, the indulgent smile of a proud parent. "I'm sorry you faced so much unpleasantness and unnecessary danger, but you have arrived *exactly* where you have always been fated to arrive, just when you were needed . . . daughter."

"Don't call me that," Alania said. "And once I am Captain, I promise you this—I won't do what you ask."

"I won't ask anything," Kranz said. "I won't have to. The nanobots know what to do. First you will become the Captain. Your heart and brain and nervous system will become the heart and brain and nervous system of the City. Your life will give it life and thus give life to all the teeming thousands who rely on it. Once you are integrated into the system, I will give the final command, and the nanobots will rewrite your brain. You will become First Officer Kranz, the eighth in succession from the original. Your childhood is over. You've had your fun. Now it's time to work." He smiled. "Good-bye, Alania."

He stepped back. The pod began to close . . . and this time, there was no one to stop it.

As the lid began its slow descent, Alania felt her consciousness altering . . . expanding. Her mind grew too large for her brain, too large for the body with which she was already losing touch. Strange smells and sounds and sights she could not name slipped phantom-like through her senses. The core of her self, her soul, her inner being, seemed to be shrinking, dwindling away like a dying fire. But it didn't go out. She was still Alania, still herself . . .

. . . but for how long?

She tried to move, tried to raise her arms and push at the pod lid, but she had lost control of her limbs. She could still feel her heart beating, but she had the strangest feeling it was pushing more than just blood through her veins, that it was somehow also pumping water and sewage and lubricants and other unnamed fluids through an endless network of pipes. She knew she was breathing, but every breath also seemed to be moving air through ducts and vents and fans.

She closed her eyes—though she had no way of knowing whether they were really closed or not, since it made no difference to the strange welter of images flooding her mind—and tried to sense what was happening in the chamber in which she lay. She pictured Thirteenth Tier, the gardens, the small, white, temple-like building . . .

. . . and suddenly she saw it, though her perspective was strange: she found herself looking down at the top of Kranz's head as the pod lid slowly descended. She saw Danyl, still curled up like a baby, lying on the floor behind him.

In a moment, Kranz would give his final command, and she would cease to exist. She strained muscles she could not move, tried to scream, tried to protest, but nothing worked. All she could do was watch, helpless, as he leaned forward to execute her.

And then she sensed in a way she could not describe that someone else was approaching. She tried to expand her view of the Tier, and her perspective shifted. Now she was looking down the path of crushed white rocks leading from the antechamber to the "temple."

Someone rushed along that path: Erl.

He reached the door.

Alania jumped back to her previous view as he burst into the control room—and shot Kranz at point-blank range.

With no way of knowing how far things had progressed in the Captain's control chamber, Erl burst out of the antechamber at a dead run, the powerful beamer in his hands. A robot scuttled toward him, and he burned a hole through its central processor, then pounded the length of the white path. Counting on the element of surprise, he slammed through the door, saw Kranz standing over the Captain's bed, barely registered Danyl curled naked on the floor, and fired directly into Kranz's back.

Light flashed and acrid smoke billowed, and Kranz whirled to face him. The back of his uniform was burned away, but the man himself was clearly unharmed. Erl knew instantly what had happened: the First Officer's nanobots had deflected the energy of the blast just as his own had saved him from the Provost's beam in the Quarters Kranz stairwell. The effort must have taken a huge bite of the nanobots' available energy, and if he could have fired two or three more times, he was certain he could have overwhelmed them. But he never got that chance; Kranz swung his own beamer up and fired, not at Erl—he'd clearly made the lightning-quick deduction that Erl could only be standing here unharmed if he, too, were protected by fully active nanobots—but at Erl's weapon. It shattered in his hands, and he let it drop as he hurled himself at the First Officer.

Kranz toppled backward, Erl on top of him, and then everything devolved into a whirl of blows and counterblows. All Officers learned unarmed combat, though most completed only the minimal required training and never practiced. Erl had worked hard at it when he had been living on Twelfth Tier, and he had trained in the simulator and sparred with Danyl as the boy grew into a man, but he knew at once that he was outclassed. Though he'd landed on top of Kranz, an instant later, he was thrown backward and slammed to the floor, rolling over and out of the way a split second before Kranz's fist would have crushed his windpipe.

He fought on, but the contest had already been decided. Less than a minute after he'd charged into the control room, Erl lay crumpled not far from Danyl, breathing hoarsely, his broken left leg bent awkwardly beneath him. From the agony in his chest, he knew he also had broken ribs and suspected he might have punctured a lung. The nanobots were working, but even they could not knit bones in minutes, and minutes were all he had left.

If that.

Kranz limped over to him, his face splattered with blood from his broken nose—the satisfying crunch it had made when Erl's fist connected with it had been his one triumphant moment of the brief battle. Kranz's beamer lay near Danyl. He didn't bother to pick it up. Erl knew Kranz could kill him with his bare hands if he wanted to, and clearly he wanted to.

"You've failed," Kranz snarled, standing over him. "The pod is closed, and when I activate her nanobots in a moment, she will become both the new Captain and the new First Officer, irretrievably, for the rest of her life. Beruthi is dead. And now . . . so are you."

He reached down to snap Erl's neck . . .

. . . and then screamed and jerked upright as his own beamer, held in Danyl's trembling hands, burned into his back.

Danyl came slowly back to himself, his shattered consciousness contracting and coalescing, the strange fire that had scorched his nerves receding. His awareness of his own body grew bit by bit. He realized first that he was cold, then that he was lying on a hard surface, then that he was naked . . .

And then, all at once, his lingering connection to the City vanished. He was suddenly fully aware, fully awake, shivering, hurting, but himself again. And when he raised his head, he saw the First Officer beating the man he had always thought of as his father to a bloody pulp.

Kranz stood over the sprawled, crippled Erl, ready to deliver the coup de grâce . . . and Danyl realized that a beamer lay close at hand. He forced his aching muscles to move, seized the beamer, rolled over, sat up . . . and fired.

At first, the beam seemed to have no effect other than burning away swatches of the First Officer's already ragged and bloodstained uniform, though Kranz cried out and straightened. But Danyl, desperate and despairing and deeply, deeply angry, held down the firing stud, discharging the weapon in one long, continuous blast, and as Kranz lurched toward him, whatever strange protection he had against the beam suddenly failed utterly and completely.

The beam sliced through his midriff like a scalpel, and Kranz looked down with an expression of almost comical shock as his guts spilled out, sizzling in the still-burning beam. He raised his head. "You . . ." he began, but he got no further—the beam had found his spine. It scored the wall above Erl's head, then sputtered out.

The First Officer died before his steaming body hit the floor. Blood spilled out of him, a vast pool of it, slicking the floor, soaking Danyl's and Alania's discarded clothing. Danyl dropped the beamer. He stared at the Kranz, then suddenly remembered Alania. He staggered to his feet, staring around the small chamber, but she was nowhere to be seen.

"Transfer complete," the strange male voice said. "We have a new Captain."

"No!" Danyl cried hoarsely. He stumbled toward the command pod through Kranz's blood. "Alania . . ."

"You can't . . . stop it," a voice said. He turned to see Erl hauling himself slowly into a sitting position, grimacing with pain as he did so. "Once it's done . . . it's done."

"You . . ." Danyl took an unsteady step toward his erstwhile guardian. "I thought you were dead."

Erl coughed and grimaced again, holding his side. Blood stained the corner of his mouth. "I should be," he said. "Would have been a minute ago, if you hadn't grabbed Kranz's beamer. But . . ."

"Nanobots," Danyl said. "The damned nanobots. You have them, too."

Erl nodded.

Danyl had to hold on to the bottom end of the command pod. He didn't want to look into the other end, didn't want to see Alania's face behind the window where he had first glimpsed the Captain's. "You've known," he whispered. "All my life. You've known what I was meant for. You knew I would end up here. You *planned* for me to end up here. When you sent us off to Yvelle . . . *you knew*."

Erl nodded again. "Yes," he said. "Beruthi was Prime, but I was . . . Prime Secundus, I guess you would say. Equal to Beruthi, but I chose to be the one who withdrew from the City to look after you—our pride and joy. When Kranz made Beruthi Alania's guardian, we thought we couldn't lose. Then everything went wrong, and against all odds, you two were thrown together. From there . . . we had to improvise."

The strange prickling heat Danyl had felt from the nanobots in his bloodstream seemed to have returned, but he knew this heat was fanned by his own fury and had nothing to with microscopic machines. "Everything you told me growing up was a lie. You rewrote my memories to keep me in the dark. You pretended to care for me, but all the time I was just a . . . a spare part, a cog in a machine."

"A machine intended to make the City better," Erl said. "And if you were a cog, you were the most important cog of all."

"Make the City better how?" Danyl said scornfully. "Beruthi said I'd be able to seize control, overthrow the Officers . . . but that was never the real plan, was it?" He slammed his fist down on the command pod in which Alania was imprisoned. "This thing would have left me with no control at all. You programmed the nanobots inside me, didn't you? Just like Kranz programmed the ones in Alania. You set me up so that once I was in the pod I would do whatever you and Beruthi told me to do with no more free will than one of Beruthi's robots."

"It couldn't be left to chance," Erl said.

"You could have told me the truth!"

"Only to have you reject it all and join the Green-skulls or Rustbloods just to get away from me?" Erl snapped back with sudden heat. "I told you: it couldn't—could *not*—be left to chance."

Danyl, fueled by his fury, found the strength to step away from the pod until he stood over Erl just like Kranz had before Danyl had cut him down. "You and Beruthi didn't want to overthrow the Officers at all. You just want to replace Kranz as First Officer. Nothing would have changed except that you would have been in charge!"

"Everything would have changed!" Erl was starting to look stronger, his dark face less gray and beaded with sweat, as his nanobots repaired the damage he had suffered. "We would have seized power, yes, but we would have tried to restore the City's functions, tried to make things better for the lower Tiers, even for the people in the Middens. We would have provided more freedom than the Heartland has ever known—"

"Freedom as long as no one did anything you didn't approve of, you mean! And *my* freedom was never a consideration at all. You kidnapped me as a baby and raised me to be Captain, pretended to care for me—"

"I do care for you!" Erl cried. "Danyl, you have to—"

"Pretended to care for me," Danyl went on as if he hadn't spoken, "and all the while, you didn't see me as a human being at all. And if you didn't see me as fully human, how the hell am I supposed to believe that you see the people in the Middens or First Tier or the Tenth Tier prison or any of the other Tiers as human, either?" He turned and looked at the crumpled, oozing body of First Officer Kranz. "I should have *thanked* him for freeing me from that pod instead of killing him!"

"Danyl," Erl said urgently. "Danyl, please believe me. Yes, I knew what you were fated to be, but I've always loved you as my own child. I was proud to think you would someday be Captain, proud of the young man I had raised, proud—"

"You're a filthy, lying son of a bitch, and the only reason you're not a steaming pile of smoking meat and shit like First Officer Kranz is that I used up his beamer charge!" Danyl shouted. "The only person who has ever *really* cared about me is my sister, and now she's the new cog in this vast machine of yours. *Dead*, even if her body still lives. Someone else will take over as First Officer, and nothing will change. Everyone who has died, everything Alania and I have been through, has all been a waste. Go to hell."

He turned away, walked to the top end of the command pod at last, and looked down into it.

All he could see of Alania was her face and her bare shoulders. Her eyes were closed but flickering. He had never fully connected with the City; she had. All her life she had been subject to the same kind of programming as he had been, though to different ends. Now that programming had fully engaged. Danyl reached out and touched the window. "Sister," he murmured. He felt a strange pain in his chest, as though his heart were being torn apart. Alania had never had someone who truly cared for her, and as it turned out, neither had he. For four brief days, they had had each other, but now it was all ending in dust and ashes.

"Good-bye," he barely managed to choke out through a suddenly constricted throat. He leaned down and planted a kiss on the glass . . .

. . . and then jerked back.

Alania's eyes had just opened.

And then she screamed.

Erl watched the young man he truly *had* thought of as his son turn away from him, saw him run his hand along the command pod, lean over, and kiss the window above his sister's face. Something broke inside him.

Go to hell, Danyl had said, but Erl knew in that moment that he was already there.

For twenty years, he had raised Danyl to be Captain, and the decades-long plan he and his best friend, Ipsil Beruthi, had concocted together had come to fruition at last . . . only to collapse so spectacularly in the last few minutes.

Beruthi was *dead*. Kranz had said so, and Erl believed him, all the more because Danyl and Alania were here but Beruthi was not. Yes, the First Officer was dead, too, and he had had a hand in that ... but Danyl was not Captain. *Alania* was, and she had been programmed by Kranz. She would carry out his wishes; she might literally become him, the latest in a long line of tyrants, but this time with all the power of a fully awake Captain to draw on as well.

Nothing would change, and Erl could not escape. The Provosts would come. He would be taken to Tenth Tier, and he would never again leave it alive, though he might well linger there for years.

Ipsil is dead. Danyl has turned his back on me. Our plan has failed. We achieved nothing. We failed, and Kranz won, even though he died at the moment of his victory.

If the victor dies, surely the loser should die, too.

It didn't take any great effort on his part. He could command his nanobots to do whatever he wished, and so he commanded them to slip him into unconsciousness, then stop his heart.

The last thing he saw before darkness claimed him forever was Danyl suddenly jerking upright and stumbling back from the command pod. The last thing he heard was the thin sound of Alania screaming inside.

What ... ? he thought, and then he thought nothing more ever again.

THIRTY-FIVE

THE MOMENT the command pod cover closed over Alania, her view of what was happening in the Captain's temple vanished.

Information poured into her brain, a vast river filling every nook and cranny of her being. Suddenly she knew things she couldn't even have conceived of a moment before, understood concepts of which she'd had no inkling, grasped realities that would have seemed childish fables before she became the Captain.

She knew what the City was. She knew where it had come from. She knew what those who built it had intended to achieve ...

... and she knew how it had all gone wrong.

The City was not a city at all. It was a vast vessel, like Beruthi's boat that had brought them down the River. It had been carried through the stars by an even greater vessel, an unimaginably large vessel: the one she had seen a model of in the Thirteenth-Tier antechamber, *UES Discovery*, which also transported tens of thousands of would-be colonists held in suspended animation. Throughout that journey, only one mind had stayed awake, caring for the sleeping charges, maintaining the ship's complex systems: the Captain, a living person made a permanent part of the ship's systems. Her autonomous nervous system, through genetic enhancements and complex nanomachinery, had kept fluids flowing and air circulating. And above all, she had kept the ship on track for the day when a promising candidate for colonization revealed itself to her sensors and she could send the first of the colony seeds, captained by a clone of herself, on toward planetfall.

Each colony seed was designed to ferry colonists to a promising planet and provide the raw materials and technology to begin the process of colonizing a new world.

A new world implied there was an old world, of course, and the old world, to Alania's delight, was Earth: the very Earth of the Earthmyth stories she had always enjoyed. It was not a myth at all but a very real place, the true Heartland of all humanity, scattering its seeds out among the stars so that whatever happened to the home planet, the species to which it had given birth would live.

But something had gone wrong. The City, one of the colony seeds, had clearly been launched from *Discovery* as planned, but it had never dismantled itself, never opened the Cubes that contained the robots to carry out that dismantling, never become the seed of a thriving new civilization. The colony seed, full of sleeping colonists, had had its own crew of Officers, awakened first, to oversee the landing, Officers who were supposed to give up their authority to a civilian government once the seed had been planted and the colonists roused. But somehow the City Captain, a clone of the original *Discovery* Captain, had instead been convinced she was *still* Captain of *Discovery*, still sailing among the stars. As a result, the dismantling of the colony seed had never happened.

More to the point, the Officers had never relinquished power.

Alania, mind working at computer speed, pieced together the truth even though many records had been altered. Mutiny! Plans put in place by First Officer Thomas Kranz even before *Discovery* had launched had came to fruition when the colony seed Officers were roused from their own suspended animation long before planetfall. He had worked with the original Lieutenant Beruthi to trick the clone of the Captain, to alter her consciousness using the very nanobots that had kept her original alive during the long journey from Earth. She had lived in the illusion of Captaining *Discovery* as the years piled up, while all around her the colony seed had fallen into decay, for her false reality had prevented her from sensing and repairing the failing systems of machines that had never been intended to operate for so long. And meanwhile, the descendants of the Officers who had led the mutiny had cemented their control, living in luxury while the colony seed had become the City, squatting over the canyon, pissing and shitting and vomiting into it. Its failing systems were merely the incredibly ancient and decrepit body of its brain and heart—the Captain—writ large.

At any moment, Alania knew, Kranz would give the final command to her nanobots, and First Officer Kranz would live again within her. While the Captain side of her might be able to repair and improve the City, the Kranz side of her would ensure that the Officers continued to rule; she knew now that Kranz himself was as delusional as the Captain had been. The "memories" passed down from clone to clone were fairy tales, altered by Thomas Kranz to convince his successors that he had been a great hero, that he had saved them all by preventing the City from carrying out its original programming, which he had made them believe had always been doomed to failure. *Kranz honestly thought he was preserving the City even as he presided over its slow-motion collapse*, Alania thought. She might have sympathized with him if she hadn't been expecting to be plunged into the same persistent hallucination at any moment.

The truth was the City was *intended* to slowly disassemble itself. Part of it had: the engine that had lowered it safely to its landing place had been scavenged shortly afterward, leaving that vast opening in the center of the Undercity. The metals and rare earth elements and ceramics and plastics of the entire City were intended to serve as the raw materials for new buildings and machines, which would in turn construct more buildings, farm the soil, dig mines, produce clean water. The mysterious Cubes—the impenetrable blocky metal structures on either side of the Canyon—contained robots to aid in that disassembly as well as additional precious supplies for the colonists. Unleashed, the City and the Cubes would transform the Heartland and beyond. The Iron Ring was nothing but a natural mountain range, impassable to aircraft only because the First Officers had made it so. The overcrowded City would empty out, and humans could finally spread out over the entire surface of this new world, free from constraints, free from grinding poverty, free from the tyrannical authority of the Officers and the Provosts, just . . .

Free.

Free, as Alania herself had never been. Raised by Beruthi merely to allay any suspicions Kranz might have, constantly watched, regularly programmed, tightly controlled, she had never been free, not once—until she had fallen into Danyl's realm. And even that apparent freedom had lasted a very short time before Erl and Beruthi had had her under their control once more. Despite her apparent escape, she had *still* ended up right here, right where Kranz had wanted her.

Except . . .

Except that when she had last seen Kranz, he had been fighting Erl.

Except that Kranz had said he had to give her nanobots a final command . . . and he hadn't done that yet.

Except that Alania—perhaps only for seconds longer—was still Alania. She was plugged into the City, yes, and feeling it as her own body, but she was aware of the truth. The truth of the history of the City; the truth of Thomas Kranz's mutiny; the truth of the perfidy of all the original Officers; the truth of what had been intended for the City when it had been built in Earth's orbit and loaded aboard the impossibly huge vessel *Discovery* to begin its long journey.

In that moment, for the first time in her life, Alania was truly free to act as *she* deemed fit. And also for the first time in her life, she knew the truth: so much truth she overflowed with it.

She knew all the First Officer's secrets, but she also knew the secrets of Ipsil Beruthi, the man who claimed to be Prime of an organization dedicated to providing freedom to the masses but whose real goal had always been to replace Kranz as First Officer. Perhaps he had intended to rule the City more fairly than Kranz, at least to begin with, but he had intended to rule nonetheless, with Erl as his second-in-command.

Despite Beruthi's lies, the Free Citizens really existed, and they really did have contingency plans for governing the City once the Officers were deposed. Though Beruthi had never intended for those plans to be implemented, the Free didn't know that.

Alania's final programming still had not been activated. She remained free—and she remained Captain.

And so she began giving orders.

She ordered that all Officers be dismissed immediately from their positions, canceling all their command authority and their access codes. Wherever they were in the City, they would suddenly find themselves trapped, unable to communicate or move freely.

She reached into the City's computer network and executed the series of commands Beruthi had crafted that would prime the Free to seize control. The first sent a message to Tertius, the *third* in the chain of command, informing him that he had become Prime and providing him all the information she had from Beruthi's files about his plans for freeing the city (minus the details of

Beruthi's *real* plans). Beruthi was dead, and however he had come to it, in the end he had sacrificed himself for the Free ... and for Bertel and his children down on First Tier.

Alania transferred full access to the City to Tertius as well and told him how to enter Thirteenth Tier.

Only then did she turn her attention to the powerful artificial intelligences that supported her but were subordinate to her.

Planetfall achieved, she proclaimed. *Commence colonization protocol, extended schedule.*

She felt the AIs' acknowledgment, and *still* she remained free.

And so she gave one final command.

Disconnect human-AI interface. Full AI control authorized. AI to self-terminate upon completion of colonization protocol.

Again an acknowledgment came back—the AIs had been carefully designed not to care about their own self-preservation. They could be terminated at the Captain's will ... and she had just willed it.

Just as she had willed her *own* termination as Captain, and the moment the AI acknowledged her command, that termination kicked in.

With brutal suddenness, her vast awareness of the City vanished. Her senses snapped back into the tiny vessel of her own body. Her nanobots severed all connection to the nurturing gel of the command pod.

Alania's eyes snapped open, and as agony flooded every fiber of her being, she screamed and screamed and screamed ...

... and then, mercifully, fainted.

Danyl fumbled desperately with the smooth sides of the command pod. It refused to open. The lights on the banks of equipment all around him were going out, rank after rank vanishing as he watched, a wave of darkness that swept around the room until all that was left was a single green light on the cabinet into which he had stepped to have his nanobots programmed. Alania's screams tore at his ears, the agony in her voice unmistakable even through the walls of the pod, but he could do nothing to help her. She was trapped and suffering, and he was useless and helpless and furious and—

And then, just like that, the pod opened, and at the same moment, Alania stopped screaming.

Danyl rushed around to the side of the pod and stared down at his sister. The blue-green gel was retreating from her body, the probes of the headrest retracting from her skull. She was breathing. She was alive.

He didn't dare try to pull her out. Remembering how cold he had been when Kranz had ripped him from the pod, he looked for their discarded servants' uniforms, but they were ruined, soaked with Kranz's blood.

He realized, suddenly, that Erl had slumped to one side and that he wasn't breathing, that his eyes were open and unblinking. He knelt beside the man he had once thought of as his father and put a tentative hand to his neck.

No pulse.

A flood of swirling emotions tore through him, childhood memories overlaid by more recent ones, all darkened by the knowledge of how Erl had used him, how everything he had believed had been a lie. And yet . . .

And yet, the man now lying dead before him had been his only family, the only person who had ever shown him affection until a few days ago. It couldn't have all been feigned. And even if it had, his own affection had not. He had loved Erl, the only family he'd had until Alania had fallen into his life.

With a shaking hand, he reached out and closed Erl's eyes.

Then he heard Alania take a deep, choking breath, and he straightened and turned to see her sitting upright in the command pod.

Alania woke. The pain was gone, but the world around her seemed dim and muffled, as though she were wrapped in thick flannel. The banks of equipment surrounding the pod had all gone dark, their function ended by her last command. Only the cabinet into which they had both stepped earlier remained active.

Her brother came toward her, his naked body streaked with the drying remnants of the gel in which she still sat and spattered with blood, though from what she could see, none of it was his. He reached the edge of the pod, and then, to her surprise, reached down and hugged her tightly, pulling her to a sitting position, his body warm and comforting against hers. The contact banished the strange feeling of disconnection, and suddenly she was there in her body, and she hugged him in turn, then found herself weeping on his shoulder.

They stayed like that for a long moment, and then Danyl pulled back. "Are you all right?"

She nodded. She looked at him, then down at herself. "Um . . . clothes?"

"Ruined," Danyl said. "There are weapons, though. When the Provosts arrive—"

"They won't be arriving," Alania said. "Help me out."

A moment later, she stood by the command pod with Danyl's support, holding on with one hand until she was sure her legs would bear her.

"What happened to you?" Danyl asked.

Alania didn't answer for a moment. She had just seen the bodies of Kranz and Erl, the blood congealing on the floor. "They killed each other?" Her eyes flicked to the servants' uniforms she and Danyl had discarded, soaking in the gore, and shuddered. She agreed with Danyl: she'd rather go naked, even though she was shivering.

"No," Danyl said. "They fought. Kranz was about to kill Erl. But I had Kranz's beamer, and . . ." His voice trailed off.

"Then how did Erl die?"

"I don't know," Danyl said. "He didn't look so badly injured that his nanobots couldn't have healed him. They've healed my bruises and cuts."

"Mine, too," Alania said. She stared at Erl. "He killed himself," she said slowly. "He must have thought I would be taken over by Kranz's programming. And rather than face the justice of the Officers . . ."

"But you weren't taken over," Danyl said. "Why not?"

Alania took a brief glance at Kranz's body, but the sight was too horrible to bear for long. She looked away again. "You killed him before he could give the final command. I was left free. I was left as Captain."

"But if you were Captain, and you managed to extract yourself . . ." Danyl looked at the command pod and at the banks of dead instruments. "Who *is* Captain?"

"There is no Captain," Alania said simply. "The Officers have been deposed. The Free Citizens are moving to take power in the City right now. And it will take months, but soon there will be no City, either. It will be dismantled, incorporated into a new City—a proper one without Tiers, without Officers."

As briefly as she could, she told Danyl what she had learned and done during her brief tenure as Captain. When she had finished, Danyl shook his head. "It sounds wonderful. But either one of us could still be stuck into that machine. The Free didn't sign on for the demolition of the City. They'll try to force us back in here to reverse the process."

"I don't think it can be reversed," Alania said. "But you're right. They may try. Which is why I left this one piece of equipment active." She indicated the cabinet with the single green light.

"To reprogram our nanobots yet again?" Danyl said. He sounded almost angry. "To do what? Make us forget everything that has happened? Turn us into someone else?"

"No," Alania said. "To turn us into ourselves." She stepped over to the cabinet, and opened the door. "To deactivate the nanobots entirely. They'll migrate into our guts and turn themselves off, and our bodies will eliminate them naturally. And then we'll be as ordinary as we always thought we were . . . and no use to anyone except ourselves." She turned to face him. "Agreed?"

His face lit. "Agreed!"

The process was short and painless. Alania stood in the padded confines of the coffin-like cabinet for five minutes. She felt nothing, but the cabinet, speaking in the male voice of the ship's AI rather than the voice of the old Captain, assured her that her nanobots were permanently disabled. She stepped out again and let Danyl take her place.

When all that was done, they left the control room, walking out onto the porch of the little white temple.

The sun broke through the wind-driven clouds high overhead and shone through the crystal dome. Birds and insects danced among the flowers and trees. The gardening robots went about their slow, methodical work, glittering as they caught the light, and ignored them both.

Alania sat down on the sunlit porch. Her brother sat next to her. The warmth of the sun felt good on her chilled body. Before them stretched the white path, straight to the antechamber and the elevator to Kranz's office, the elevator neither of them could now access. Eventually Tertius would find his way there. And then . . .

"What happens next?" Danyl asked, looking up at the sky, eyes half closed.

Alania studied the path in front of them. Their whole lives, they had been unknowingly trapped on a path just like that one, straight and unvarying, fated from birth to end up right where they had ended up today. But at the end of that path, in the final seconds of their predestined journey, they *had* managed to deviate from it, and now, at last, their futures spread out before them unplanned and unmapped.

Instead of one path, they now had many paths from which to choose . . . and the freedom to do so.

"I have no idea," Alania said. "Isn't that wonderful?"

Danyl gave her a startled look, then suddenly grinned. "It certainly is."

Naked as the newborns they had once been and had just become again, they sat in companionable silence and waited for their new lives to begin.

WORLDSHAPERS

For Shawna Keys, the world is almost perfect. She's just opened a pottery studio in a beautiful city. She's in love with a wonderful man. She has good friends.

But one shattering moment of violence changes everything. Mysterious attackers kill her best friend. They're about to kill Shawna. She can't believe it's happening—and just like that, it isn't. It hasn't. No one else remembers the attack, or her friend. To everyone else, Shawna's friend never existed...

Everyone, that is, except the mysterious stranger who shows up in Shawna's shop. He claims her world has been perfect because she Shaped it to be perfect; that it is only one of uncounted Shaped worlds in a great Labyrinth; and that all those worlds are under threat from the Adversary who has now invaded hers. She cannot save her world, he says, but she might be able to save others—if she will follow him from world to world, learning their secrets and carrying them to Ygrair, the mysterious Lady at the Labyrinth's heart.

Frightened and hounded, Shawna sets off on a desperate journey, uncertain whom she can trust, how to use her newfound power, and what awaits her in the myriad worlds beyond her own.

Worldshaper
by Edward Willett

978-0-7564-1346-0

E. C. Blake
The Masks of Aygrima

"Brilliant world-building combined with can't-put-down storytelling, *Masks* reveals its dark truths through the eyes of a girl who must learn to wield unthinkable power or watch her people succumb to evil. Bring on the next in this highly original series!"

—Julie E. Czerneda

"Mara's personal growth is a delight to follow. Sharp characterization, a fast-moving plot, and a steady unveiling of a bigger picture make this a welcome addition to the genre."

—*Publishers Weekly*

"*Masks* is simply impossible to put down."

—*RT Book Reviews*

MASKS
978-0-7564-0947-0

SHADOWS
978-0-7564-0963-0

FACES
978-0-7564-0939-5

To Order Call: 1-800-788-6262
www.dawbooks.com